Zara Cox writes con
She lives in the Gard
with her hubby and tv
travel. In 2017 she m
one bucket list destin
actively pleading with her husband to live there! She
loves to hear from her readers; you can get in touch
with her via Twitter (@zcoxbooks), on Instagram
(zaracoxwriter) or Facebook (zaracoxwriter).

New York Times and *USA TODAY* bestselling author
Cathryn Fox is wife, mom, sister, daughter, aunt
and friend. She loves dogs, sunny weather, anything
chocolate—she never says no to a brownie—pizza
and red wine. Cathryn lives in beautiful Nova Scotia
with her husband, who is convinced he can turn her
into a mixed martial arts fan. When not writing,
Cathryn can be found Skyping with her son, who
lives in Seattle—could he have moved *any* farther
away?—shopping with her daughter in the city,
watching a big action flick with her husband, or
hanging out and laughing with friends.

If you liked
Enemies with Benefits and *Exposed*
why not try

The Pleasure Contract by Caitlin Crews
Bring the Heat by Margot Radcliffe

And meet the rest of Zara Cox's
The Mortimers: Wealthy & Wicked in

Worth the Risk
Pleasure Payback
Her Every Fantasy
Driving Him Wild

Also by Cathryn Fox

On His Knees
On Her Terms
Under His Touch
Under His Obsession

Dirty Rich Boys

Corrupted
Devoured

Discover more at millsandboon.co.uk

ENEMIES WITH BENEFITS

ZARA COX

EXPOSED

CATHRYN FOX

MILLS & BOON

First Published in Great Britain 2021
by Mills & Boon, an imprint of HarperCollins*Publishers*
1 London Bridge Street, London, SE1 9GF

Enemies with Benefits © 2021 Zara Cox

Exposed © 2021 Cathryn Fox

ISBN: 978-0-263-29794-2

MIX
Paper from
responsible sources
FSC
www.fsc.org   FSC™ C007454

ENEMIES WITH BENEFITS

ZARA COX

MILLS & BOON

To authors everywhere who have to deal with a 'birthing-a-pineapple' book every once in a while.

I took one for the team with this book.

You're welcome.

CHAPTER ONE

'I CAN TRUST you to behave yourself, can't I?'

Shit.

I dragged my gaze from the statuesque brunette weaving her way through the one-hundred-plus guests sipping vintage champagne on a chilly autumn evening. The five heating towers positioned around the terrace and immediate lamplit grounds of the Surrey mansion were doing their damnedest to warm up the abysmal temperature and failing, but I, for one, didn't need their help.

My body had heated up the moment I spotted Wren Bingham, wearing a clingy jumpsuit that lovingly followed every curve of her spectacular body. Fringed, shoulder-length jet-black hair brushed the frilly-looking scarf wrapped around her shoulders. Stilettos on her feet and a diamond bracelet circling her wrist completed her outfit. Her guests wore double and triple layers but she was obviously nowhere near cold, either.

I didn't mind one bit because she looked fuckable in the extreme—

'Jasper?'

I reeled myself in at Aunt Flo's sharper tone. An apologetic glance her way showed pursed lips and a disapproving glint in her eye. I was usually more circumspect but being in the same vicinity as Wren Bingham always scuppered my concentration.

I cleared my throat. 'Of course I'll behave. Scouts' honour.' The woman who'd been more of a mother to me than my own living parent snorted her disbelief.

'As if they'd have let you anywhere near a Scouts camp. You'd have scandalised them all within an hour.'

I grinned at her no-nonsense reply because her tone was couched in familiar, reassuring warmth. Warmth I let wash over me to disperse the soul-shrivelling chill that came from thinking about my birth mother, which inevitably led to thoughts about my father. Specifically, their arctic wind of rejection, far more brutal than any winter I'd experienced since their desertion. No, tonight most definitely wasn't the time to dwell on that noxious period of my childhood and how it'd ruined not just me but my siblings, too.

Tonight was about bringing recalcitrant business partners to heel. Mostly…

After another search failed to reveal my elusive prey, I focused once more on Wren, that compulsion since Aunt Flo and I had walked through the impressive double doors of the Bingham mansion in Esher forty-five minutes ago pulling at me.

So far I hadn't spotted Wren's brother, Perry Bingham, my primary reason for being here. Sure, I'd nodded and reassured my favourite aunt that accompanying her to this soirée was my pleasure and the right Mortimer thing to do. Also because, on some weird rota only Aunt Flo was privy to, it was apparently my turn to escort her to another social function. What I'd failed to mention was that I was on the hunt for Perry Bingham, CEO of Bingham Industries, who had stopped answering my calls for nearly two weeks, thereby threatening to throw one serious spanner into my latest project.

With my patience wearing thin, I'd grasped the opportunity to track him down at his family estate. Except it looked as if he was a no-show here, too.

But Wren was here, and I intended to drill his sister about his whereabouts. My choice of words brought an inner smirk I wisely kept off my face as I downed my whisky and turned to my aunt.

'Can I get you another drink?' I indicated her half-empty glass of sherry.

Several waitstaff circulated with trays of drinks but I didn't plan to grab one from them. Not when Wren stood next to the bar, chatting with two of her guests. As I watched, she threw her head back in laughter, her smooth, swanlike neck thrown into perfect relief.

Immediately, I imagined my lips there, beneath

her jawline, tasting her silky skin, then lower, tonguing her pulse. Would she cry out in delight or moan with pleasure?

'We both know that's an excuse to get away from me. Go on, then. Just don't do anything we'd both be ashamed of come morning, would you? I could do without a Mortimer tabloid scandal before Christmas,' Aunt Flo said.

Brushing a kiss on a well-preserved cheek, I muttered, 'You've taught me the importance of not making promises I can't keep. Don't make me start now.'

She rolled her eyes but her smile deepened.

I grinned again as I made a beeline for the bar, and I wasn't one little bit ashamed to admit that I was hard as stone.

I made sure to wipe the smile off my face, my eyes settling in the middle distance to prevent business acquaintances engaging me in conversation. A few feet from Wren, I paused to ponder why this woman, amongst so many others, had fired me up ever since she'd crossed my path five years ago.

Perhaps it was discovering that, far from being a superficial heiress and supermodel flitting around the globe between the ages of nineteen and twenty-three, she'd attained a master's degree in business while slaying the runways of the fashion capitals of the world. More besides, she'd graduated top of her class and was, at twenty-eight, now on course to become one of the youngest power executives in the city. Or perhaps it was some twisted attraction born from our family being embroiled in a generations-old feud, which dictated we should hate each other on sight like some pathetic Roman tragedy.

Whatever. All I knew was that Wren had intrigued me with increasing intensity over the past few years.

Intense empire-building in order to establish my role in my family's company as President of New Developments in Europe, Africa and the Middle East, and perhaps even the arrogant belief that our chemistry was a passing whim and wasn't worth turning my family upside down for, had so far kept me from pursuing Wren, but each encounter only deepened whatever this phenomenal chemistry was that stopped me from seeing any other woman but her whenever we were in each other's orbit.

Lately, I'd accepted that it simply wasn't going to go away by itself, as I'd assumed. Not until I did something about it.

I realised my motionless state was drawing curious attention from nearby guests, not to mention Aunt Flo's disapproving glare from across the terrace.

Discarding my glass, I stepped beside Wren. 'Good evening, Wren. You look incredible.' I said, my voice pitched low.

She tried not to stiffen, but didn't quite succeed, nor could she disguise the flare of awareness in her vivid green eyes when she turned to me. She didn't reply immediately, instead she scrambled for the jaded expression that had been her trademark in her modelling days.

I stifled the urge to tell her not to bother. Witnessing a demonstration of her fiery passion and stiletto-sharp business acumen five years ago across a boardroom table for an unforgettable fifteen minutes had etched a different Wren Bingham in my mind from the façade she wore for the public.

'Jasper Mortimer.'

The way she said my name, striving to be curt when different textures sizzled beneath, ramped up my temperature. I wanted her attempting to say my name just like that while she was tied to my bed with silken restraints, naked and wet.

'I don't recall seeing your name on the guest list.'

Pausing just as long as she did before answering, I snagged a glass of champagne from the bar. 'Because it wasn't there. I'm privileged to be my aunt's plus one. What I haven't had the privilege of is being acknowledged by the hostess since my arrival. I'm feeling sorely neglected.'

She tried to look through me, as if that would stop the arc of electricity zapping between us. As if she hadn't performed a quick once-over of my body as I got my drink. I planted myself in her line of vision until she had no choice but to focus on me, her nostrils flaring slightly as her green eyes—alluringly wide and sparkling with an interest she was trying to hide—connected with mine.

I barely heard her guests murmur their excuses and drift away, leaving us in a tight little cocoon.

'Perhaps I would've already greeted you, if you hadn't arrived half an hour late.'

I curbed a smile, inordinately pleased she'd noticed my arrival. 'I'm willing to make amends by doubling my donation to tonight's cause.'

One elegantly shaped eyebrow arched. 'Name it.'

I frowned. 'Name what?'

'The beneficiary of tonight's cause. What's this mixer in aid of?' she challenged.

Crap. I'd tuned Aunt Flo out when she'd mentioned it in the car, my frustrated attention on the echo of the ringing phone Perry was—yet again— refusing to answer. 'Something to do with pandas in Indonesia?' I hazarded.

Sparks gathered in her eyes. 'Why am I not surprised you don't know?'

Heat surged through me. 'That suggests a curious level of personal knowledge. Have you been attempting to get to know me behind my back, Wren?'

She gave the smallest gasp, then tried that bored look again. 'I've no idea what you're talking about. I can't help it if others feel the need to gossip about you Mortimers.'

'Oh, yeah? What else do they say about me? What else has that brilliant brain of yours retained?'

Her nose wrinkled in distaste. 'Nothing worth repeating.'

Unable to resist, I stepped closer. 'Are you sure?

I'm happy to hear you out, set a few things straight if you get anything wrong.'

She didn't reply. After an age of trying to decipher which I liked more on her skin—the scent of bergamot or the underlying allure of crushed lilies—I looked up to catch her gaze on my mouth.

Hell yes, that insane chemistry was still very much alive and well—and sizzling, as usual.

'Stop that,' she said in a tight undertone.

I raised my glass, took a lazy sip before answering. 'Stop what?'

'That extremely unsubtle way you're looking at me,' she hissed in a ferocious whisper, then glanced around. Thankfully, the music was loud enough for her words to reach my ears only. 'The way you look at me every time we meet.'

I laughed under my breath. 'And how do I look at you, Wren?'

'You might lure some women with those come-fuck-me eyes but I'm not one of them so stop wasting your time.'

My laughter was a little louder, genuine amusement reminding me how long it'd been since I'd enjoyed the thrill of a chase outside the boardroom. 'Come-fuck-me eyes? Really?' I didn't bother to keep my voice down.

Several people stared but I watched Wren, keenly interested in her next move.

She flashed the patently false smile she'd been doling out all evening but I caught the strain beneath the thousand-watt beam. Taking in the rest of her, I sensed tension in her lithe frame, in the fingers that clutched her glass a little too firmly. For reasons I suspected went beyond our conversation, Wren was wound extremely tight tonight.

And I was curiously concerned about it. 'Is everything okay?'

'Of course. Why shouldn't it be?'

I shrugged. 'You seem a little…stressed.'

Her chin notched upward. 'You don't know me well enough to make that assessment.'

'Ah, but I've attended enough of these shindigs to see when the hostess is fretting about the vegan-to-carnivore ratio of her canapés, and when it's something more. This is something more.'

Her delicate throat moved in a nervous swallow, but her gaze remained bold and direct, swirling with a deep, passionate undercurrent I craved to drown in. 'Even *if* it's the latter, it's none of your business. Now, if you'll excuse me—'

'Where's Perry?'

She froze mid-brush-off, her eyes widening fractionally. 'What?'

No, she wasn't as carefree as she pretended.

The rumours that Bingham's was in trouble had been circulating for a few years now. The veracity of those rumours was partly why I'd initially been reticent about joining forces with them. But, hell, call me a sucker… I'd always had a thing for the underdog.

Maybe it was a hangover from my daddy issues.

Or a tool I used to my advantage when idiots under-estimate me. Either way, my instincts hadn't failed me thus far.

There were certain family and board members who considered me, at thirty-one, too young for the position I was in, notwithstanding the fact that my older brother, Damian, and my cousin Gideon had been wildly successful in their newly minted co-CEO positions of the entire Mortimer Group despite being only a few years older. Or that my cousin Bryce was acing his similar position as President of New Developments in Asia and Australia. Even my sister, Gemma, and my cousin Graciela, who'd both resisted joining the board until recently, were excelling in their chosen areas of expertise.

I was damned if I'd let Perry Bingham's antics prove them right. Especially after going against all my business instincts and signing him onto my deal.

'There's nothing wrong with your hearing, Wren. Where's your brother?' I steeled my voice because, however much I enjoyed this erotic dance with her, Perry was at risk of tanking everything I'd worked for during the last eighteen months.

Several expressions filtered through her eyes—alarm, worry, irritation, mild disappointment. She finally settled on indignation. 'Is that why you came?'

'I told you, I accompanied Aunt Flo—'

'A ruse to hunt down my brother,' she interjected.

'That implies awareness that he's hiding. Is he?'

A look flickered across her face, gone too quickly

but revealing enough to intensify the unease knotting my belly. 'Tell me where he is, Wren,' I pressed. 'He's been avoiding my calls for almost two weeks and it's getting really old.'

'I'm afraid you'll have to do your own hunting. I'm not Perry's keeper.' Her tense reply gave her away. As did the minuscule tremble in the fingers that held her glass. Both intrigued and disturbed me but before I could push for more, she added, 'You've monopolised me quite enough. Enjoy the rest of your evening, Jasper.'

Just for the hell of it, and because something wild and reckless yearned for another demonstration that she wasn't immune to me, I brushed my fingertips down her arm. 'This isn't over.'

She attempted to cover her tiny shiver of awareness with a wide sultry smile that diverted my attention to her luscious lips. 'How can something be over when it didn't start in the first place?'

With that, she sailed away, her hips swaying in that unique way that'd held male and female gazes rapt during her modelling days. Since then, Wren had gained even more confidence in her womanhood, and left a swathe of admirers slack-jawed in her wake. I wracked my brain, trying to recall if she had a current boyfriend. The gut-tightening rejection at the idea of her being attached made me grimace into my champagne.

Until my gaze fell on the woman who placed herself directly in Wren's path before manoeuvring her away from the nearest guest.

Agnes Bingham—Wren's mother and powerhouse socialite in her own right.

The tall, slim woman was what Wren would look like in thirty years. Except where Agnes's beauty was classically cool, Wren was vibrant, passionate, even though she seemed hell-bent on suppressing it.

Why?

None of your business.

But I wanted to make it my business. I wanted Wren in my bed and damn all the consequences to hell. And more and more I suspected I wouldn't get over this fever in my blood until I'd had her.

Tension of a different kind raced up my spine when mother and daughter glanced my way. The touch of rebellion in Wren's gaze made me raise my glass in a mocking toast, even while I observed the animosity emanating from Agnes Bingham.

Bloody hell.

Family feuds, Perry Bingham going AWOL and now Agnes Bingham. Three stumbling blocks in my intent to have Wren. But despite the damning words my father had taken pleasure in decimating me with as a child, I wasn't afraid of a challenge.

All the same, my gut twisted as I made my way back to my aunt, the thought of broaching the subject of my father making my stomach curdle.

'Everything okay?' Aunt Flo asked, after smiling an excuse to the guest she'd been chatting to.

ZARA COX   19

I let her fondness wash over me for a moment before I pulled myself together. Wishing her warm concern came from a different female voice had been fruitless when I was a child. It was even more foolish now. The woman who'd given birth to me wasn't interested in taking up her maternal role. Not for her first or second born, and certainly not for me, her third child. My arrival had spelled the end to her obligation and she couldn't get away fast enough. Years of hoping, of saving my allowance in a childish hope of enticing her financially had been laughed off. I was no longer ten years old, fighting to stop myself from crying as Damian advised me to give up my foolish hoping.

'George Bingham. I need to know the full story,' I said to Aunt Flo, my low voice brisker than she deserved.

'What's brought this on? You've never wanted to know before,' she said after eyeing me in frowning silence.

I shrugged, moving her away to the more private edge of the terrace. 'I've never cared enough about the finer details. Now I do because whatever happened all those years ago is endangering an important deal and I've just about had it.'

'Dear boy, money isn't—'

My bitter laugh stopped her. 'Do me a favour, please, and don't finish that sentence, Aunt Flo. We both know money is definitely everything to any red-blooded Mortimer.'

She harrumphed. 'Well, I don't agree but, since you seem to have a bee in your bonnet about it, I'll let it go. To answer your question, it was your father's last deal before he and your mother stepped away from the company, and the family. He and George Bingham were supposed to go fifty-fifty but George messed up somehow and could only come up with a fraction of the investment by the deadline date. There was a clause in their agreement that it was fifty-fifty or nothing and that loophole gave your father the right to cut him out regardless of how much money he'd pumped into the deal up to then. He didn't take it well. He wasted money he didn't have trying to sue your father. But Hugh was a brilliant, if some-what ruthless, businessman.'

There was no *somewhat* about it. I'd come across some of his deals while my father had actively worked in the family firm. His cut-throat antics were legendary. If you liked blood and gore with your ne-gotiations.

A memory shot through my head. 'Was closing that Bingham deal part of my father's walking-away package?' I asked.

Aunt Flo sighed. 'Yes, it was. Back then, every deal closed by a member of the board came with a ten-per-cent profit bonus. Cutting out Bingham and making it an exclusive Mortimer deal meant Hugh received a bigger bonus. About two hundred million.'

And he was probably in such a hurry to walk

away from his family that he'd been unflinchingly ruthless. 'I see.'

'What's going on, Jasper?' Aunt Flo asked curiously.

The cocktail of bitterness, anger and arousal swirled faster inside me as I looked over her shoulder to find Wren watching me. 'It's just business.'

'No, it's not. You're not cut-throat like your father. But you're just as dogged. I had my reservations when I heard about your deal with Perry, considering his problems,' she murmured. 'But knowing you, you'll move mountains to make it work.'

'Forgive me if I don't welcome the comparison to Hugh,' I rasped.

Her eyes clouded with momentary sadness. 'His blood may run through your veins but you're your own man where it counts, Jasper. Whatever you're getting involved in, just…protect your heart. I don't want to see you hurt again.'

Another harsh laugh bubbled up, but I swallowed it down. And just about managed to stop myself from telling her that, while I'd struck a deal with Perry Bingham in a moment of madness, perhaps even a sting of conscience and despite Perry's rumoured drinking problem, somewhere in the mix was the reasoning that it would put me in a good position to strike a better deal with Wren in the near future. Business-wise and in other ways, too.

'You have that gleam in your eye, Jasper. Am I

wasting my breath by telling you to be a dear and spare my nerves?' Aunt Flo asked.

I couldn't promise that. Hell, I *knew* there would be plenty more fireworks between Wren and me in the future. 'I can promise dinner at The Dorchester as soon as my schedule lets up a little. I know how much you like their new chef. We can check out the competition in the process.'

She smiled. 'Cecil is a culinary genius. And very easy on the eyes. I'll hold you to that promise,' she said, just before another acquaintance snagged her attention.

Briefly alone, I tried to suppress the tangled emotions churning through me.

I don't want to see you hurt again.

As much as I wanted to put my parents out of my mind for ever, to rub them from my existence as much as they'd rubbed me from theirs, the ten-year-old boy's anguish from relentless rejection, which I'd never been quite successful in smothering, wouldn't let me. But it was a good reminder not to count on anyone but myself. Not to let frivolous emotion get in the way of business.

I wanted this deal with Bingham because it was sound and profitable.

I also wanted to fuck Wren Bingham, once she got over the pesky family-feud thing. The two were mutually exclusive enough not to cause me to lose any sleep.

Which was why when Wren hurried away from

her mother, her shoulders tight with barely-harnessed emotions, I followed.

She was heading towards the far end of the grounds, her heels sinking soundlessly into the grass. She didn't hear me until I was six feet from her.

'Wren?'

Her head whipped around. 'Are you following me?' she asked sharply. But then she trembled. A tiny reaction, but, coupled with the slight wobble of her mouth, it hastened my steps, the peculiar punch in my chest unsettling me.

'What's wrong?'

'Other than the fact that you're stalking me now?'

'Hardly. You just seem—'

'There's nothing wrong. Just leave me alone, please?'

I looked beyond her to the high hedges of what looked like an elaborate garden. 'If everything's fine, why are you running away from your own party?'

'I'm not running away. And it's not my party—' She caught herself and snatched in a deep breath. 'Why the hell am I explaining myself to you?'

'Because sometimes it helps to vent.' Not that it'd done me much good. Ever. All my good intentions had ended in disaster, the repercussions of which I still lived with. But this wasn't the time or place to examine old scars. 'Or so I've heard, anyway.'

'Do you go around dishing out inexperienced advice?'

I shook my head, unwilling to drag my far from

delightful childhood into this moment. 'We're not talking about me.'

'You're right, we're not. In fact, I'm going to pretend you're not here at all. Feel free to make that a reality,' she suggested, right before she turned on her heel and marched away from me.

And since I was far too intrigued to heed her brush-off… I followed.

If she gave even a hint of needing comfort, I'd offer her a shoulder, and other parts of my body, to cry on.

Bloody hell. I cringed at my own crassness. Then shrugged it off. *I am who I am.* And that person wanted Wren Bingham any way he could get her. Besides that, though, I was here on Mortimer business. Technically.

She ignored me until she reached a bricked pathway. Then she turned and stared at me for several seconds without speaking. For a moment, a deep yearning flitted over her face, then her expression blanked. 'You're really not going to leave me alone, are you?' she murmured.

'Not until you tell me what's wrong.' Before she could reply, I jerked my chin at the hedge. 'What's behind there?'

Her eyes narrowed, her fingers twitching against her thighs. 'Nothing interesting. Just the garden. A pool. Gazebo. The usual.'

She was lying. Or at least holding something back. 'What else?'

'Why do you want to know?' she demanded, then flinched as someone laughed loudly nearby.

'You look like you need a breather. What's out there?'

'A maze,' she confessed with reluctance. 'I go there sometimes…to think.'

Before my brain could growl its warning that this was a bad idea, I stepped closer. 'Show me.'

She tensed. 'Excuse me?'

'I'd like to see this maze. A quick tour. Then, if you still insist, I'll leave.'

Something flickered in her eyes, undercurrents of lust zinging between us. Her gaze dropped to my lips and I almost wanted to crow in triumph. 'Fine. Let's go.'

She wrapped her scarf tighter around her neck and I stopped myself from mourning the loss of the sight of her satiny skin.

Even in the cold, my libido was racing feverishly. I cleared my throat. 'So, what was that with your mother?'

Stubborn fire lit her eyes. 'I'll allow you to stay on condition we don't talk about my mother. Or any member of my family.'

I didn't protest her condition. Families like mine were complicated and she didn't need to vocalise her feelings towards hers for me to get it. Why that little commonality turned me on, I refused to contemplate.

In silence we walked along a dark red-bricked pavement until we reached a tall iron gate set into a walled-off section of the garden. Pushing it open, we followed the path until we reached a tall hedge the size of a barn door that remained full and thick despite the low temperatures. Wren's hand disappeared between the leaves and a section of the hedge sprang open.

With another glance at me, she stepped inside. I followed and stepped onto two diverging paths. She took the left one, her footsteps barely making a sound on the grass as we walked between tall hedgerows. Further chunks had been cut out intermittently and lower hedges transformed into shapes of animals, with a large space transformed into a picnic area with benches and seats.

We went deeper into the maze, her head bent forward as if weighed down by her emotions. I wanted to reach out and cup my hand over her nape, test the suppleness of her skin, feel that electricity between us. Instead, I shoved my hands into my pockets, willed the urge to pass. Jumping her right now would be the wrong move.

Eventually her steps slowed. 'We're almost at the centre,' she said, her voice low, as if she didn't want to speak.

'How big is this place?'

She shrugged. 'Big enough when you're a child seeking adventure. Not big enough when you're a teenager, attempting to flee from your demons.'

I wanted to ask about her demons but her pursed lips suggested she already regretted her revealing statement. I tried a different tack, hoping to take her mind off whatever was bothering her. 'Tell me one good memory you have of your maze.'

She didn't speak for several seconds, and I watched as she trailed her fingers over the tall green foliage. 'That's easy. I had my first kiss in here.'

Envy knotted my stomach. 'It was that good?'

She shook her head. 'It was that bad. It's what happened afterwards that makes it a good memory.'

'Tell me more,' I said, intrigued by the barely there but infinitely more genuine smile tugging up the corners of her full lips.

'I told Winslow Parker I didn't want to be kissed.' She shrugged. 'Call me shallow but I didn't want my first kiss to be from a boy named Winslow with a wet nose and clammy hands. He went ahead and stole a kiss anyway. So I blocked the exit to the maze and left him to freeze his arse off for three hours. When I came back to rescue him, he was crying.'

My lips twitched, a wicked part of me enjoying hearing that her first kiss had been less than memorable. 'So you enjoy making boys cry?'

We reached a dead end and she turned to face me. 'If they deserve it? Absolutely.'

A compulsion I didn't want to fight pulled me closer until I towered over her. Until she had to raise her head to meet my gaze. Despite the darkness around us, every inch of her stunning face and graceful neck was exposed to my keen gaze. 'What else do you enjoy making boys do?'

'I'm not nine years old any more. I'm a grown woman and I prefer grown men to boys now,' she murmured, her gaze fixed boldly on mine. A shiver caught her a second later and I drew closer, locking my fingers in the trellised hedge, caging her in.

'And what do you want this grown man to do for you?' I asked, aware my voice was gruff with the lustful urges running rampant through my bloodstream.

She stared at me for a minute, then cast her gaze around her, looking a little lost for a minute. 'Is it bad to say I don't want to be here? That if I could leave right now, get on a plane and go far away, I would?'

'Because of your mother?'

Her eyes darkened and she didn't repudiate me for ignoring her condition. 'Amongst other things.'

I got it. A long time ago, I'd accepted that it was better my parents lived in another country. Out of sight…out of mind…out of heartache… 'There's absolutely nothing wrong with wishing to be elsewhere.'

'But I can't, can I?'

I didn't answer because there was no right answer to that. I was born into a family where bullshit and dysfunction were the norm but where conversely fierce loyalty and absolute dedication to duty were the cornerstones that held most of us together. I suspected the Binghams were the same.

'Tell me what you want, Wren,' I said instead.

I watched a hot, determined look slowly fill her eyes. She shivered again and my gaze dropped to where her nipples had turned into twin points of succulent torture. Whether her body's reaction was from the cold or the arousal gathering heat in her eyes, I wasn't completely sure. Still, I shrugged off my jacket, draped it over her shoulders, wrapped my hands around her trim waist.

And waited.

Slowly, she slicked her tongue over her bottom lip. I bit back a groan as blood gleefully rushed south.

'Distract me,' she said, a mixture of challenge and pleading in the low, thick words that hardened my rousing cock. 'I don't want to go back to the party. I don't want to make stupid small talk. So just… make me stop thinking about all the crap I have to deal with now that…' She stopped and took a shaky breath.

Despite the flames licking through my veins, I hesitated. 'Are you sure?'

Her gaze grew defiant. 'Are you a boy or a man, Jasper Mortimer?'

I gave a low laugh. 'You don't want to ask me that, even as a challenge.'

'Why not? Will you punish me?' Her voice was breathless, edged with sexual anticipation.

My cock leapt to full attention. Jesus. 'Is that what you really want, Wren? For me to turn you around against this hedge and spank your tight little rump red for daring to question my manhood?'

Her eyes darkened, her mouth parting on a hot little pant. When her hips jerked forward a fraction, I yanked her the rest of the way, until our groins connected. Until she felt the hard, eager rod of my cock against her soft belly.

Hunger exploded over her face, her hands rising to grip my neck. 'Do your worst,' she invited with bite.

I fused my mouth to hers in a rough, carnal kiss powered by every single filthy fantasy I'd had about this woman. And there were hundreds. Thousands.

She opened for me immediately, her tongue gliding against mine in an erotic caress that weakened my knees. I tasted it, sucked on it, bit the tip and felt her shudder. Deepening the kiss, I trailed my hands up her flat belly and midriff to cup her soft, heavy breasts. Another moan escaped her, crushed between our lips as the kiss grew even more frantic.

She tasted intoxicating. Like the shot of adrenaline that brought every sense into vivid focus. I brushed my thumbs over the hard peaks of her nipples, then, giving into the wild clamouring, I nudged her zip halfway down her belly and pushed aside her bra. Before her gasp was fully formed, I swooped down and drew the exposed tip into my mouth. I suckled long and deep, then flicked my tongue rapidly over her burning flesh.

Her fingers bit into my nape. 'God…yes!'

Frantically, I freed the other breast, caught the tip between my fingers and teased. Her fingers gripped my nape, her breathing erratic as she held me to her breasts. After delivering equal amounts of attention to each, I pulled back, again wracked with the need to see her face.

She looked even more spectacular than before. Defiant. Aroused. Wanton.

'You're so fucking gorgeous,' I groaned.

An impatient sound escaped her, intensifying the heat in my veins. Dragging my hands from her breasts, I cupped her bottom, using the firm globes to pull her harder into my erection. She rewarded me by grinding her pelvis against my length, drawing needy sounds from both of us.

'I really, *really* want to fuck you, Wren,' I confessed, my voice a hot mess. 'I've wanted you since you stepped into my boardroom five years ago.'

She gave a cheeky little laugh, her eyes lighting up for the first time tonight. 'You mean when I turned down your internship offer?'

My fingers tightened on her bottom. 'I'll freely admit, I'm still a little salty about that.'

Her smile widened. 'Poor Jasper. Not used to hearing no?'

I smiled in return. 'I'm only sore at losing when what I want goes to a less worthy competitor. We both know why you turned me down.'

She licked her lips, her eyes lingering hungrily on mine. 'Pray, enlighten me.'

I wasn't going to ruin the moment by mentioning our family feud. 'Because neither of us likes to mix business with pleasure,' I said instead, running my thumb over her lower lip. Immediately her teeth nipped at my flesh, drawing a deep groan.

'I'm not going to confirm or deny that assertion.'

'Have it your way. I still want you. Badly.'

Eyes wild with defiance, she nodded eagerly, sucking my thumb into her mouth for a few seconds before she released me. 'Yes. *Now*.'

I planted a long kiss on her mouth as I lowered her zip. Only to groan when shocking reality hit me. For ten long seconds I remained paralysed. 'Shit.'

'What?' Her voice was beautifully slurred, her gaze hazy with arousal as she stared up at me. I wanted more of that look. Wanted to watch her shatter completely. Wanted to feel her pussy grip my cock as waves of ecstasy rolled over her.

'I don't have a condom,' I confessed through gritted teeth.

She stared at me blankly for a few seconds before disappointment drenched her beautiful face. 'Oh.'

I clenched my jaw tighter, unwilling to let go of this unique moment. 'Are you on the Pill?' I asked with more than a little hope. It wasn't my usual practice. I liked to be in complete control of my sexual fate. But just this once I prayed for a *yes*.

'No,' she replied, pained resignation in her voice.

'There are other ways, Wren.' I pulled her closer, trailed my lips over her jaw until I reached her ear. 'Let me make you come with my mouth. I want to taste you on my tongue. Lick you dry. You want to be transported? I can't do it with my cock but I can give you a little relief. Don't you want that?'

For a moment, she wavered, on the verge of calling quits on this madness. Selfishly, I didn't want to let her.

'I will eat you out for as long as you want me to. Think about how much I'll suffer while you do. You get to ride my face while you torture the hell out of me,' I invited.

Her fingers clenched harder into my skin. 'Yes,' she responded breathlessly. 'Please. Yes.'

Satisfied that I had her back in the moment with me, I caught the soft fabric of her jumpsuit between my fingers, careful not to wrinkle the material. Normally I wouldn't care but she had to return to a party filled with gossip-hungry guests and a mother she was clearly locked in tense disagreement with. I didn't want to draw any more attention to what we'd been doing than necessary.

I trailed my lips back to hers and kissed her hard before releasing her. 'Take this thing off for me,' I instructed.

Soft hands drifted down my forearms and wrists and covered mine for a second before she complied. I stepped back, eager for a snapshot of her leaning against her favourite hedge, undressing for me.

When she stepped out of the jumpsuit, I re-draped my jacket over her shoulders to keep her warm.

Call me primitive but the sight of her in my clothing threatened to undo me. With her hair loose and straight and falling around her face, her upper body almost lost in my coat and her lower half almost exposed to the elements, she was breathtaking. Her legs alone were worth an extra minute of worship. But it was cold, and we couldn't stay out here for ever.

With more than a throb of regret, I stepped forward and trailed the backs of my hands up her inner thighs. She gave a soft gasp and quivered. My gaze raced up from her thighs to her face, unwilling to lose a second of her reaction. Her lips were parted, her eyes hooded but not shut. She watched my hand draw closer to where her pussy was hidden behind a layer of sexy black lace.

'Open your legs wider.'

Her gaze rose and caught on mine for a second before she obeyed, widening her stance until I could fit my closed fist at the juncture of her thighs. Slowly I dragged my knuckle lightly against her flesh; from where she was hot and sodden to the swollen nub pushing against the fabric.

She gasped again, thicker, louder, her breath a puff of vapour in the air between us. I repeated the action. She caught her lips between her teeth and moaned.

'You like that?'

She gave a jerky nod, her gaze once again dropping to follow my hand. On the next turn her hips rolled, her body chasing the exquisite sensation. I felt her grow hotter, wetter with need.

'More,' she moaned on the next pass.

'Look at me, Wren.'

Her gaze rose. Defiant fire and deep arousal. God, what a combination. I cupped her chin to hold her gaze, then I slipped my fingers beneath her panty line.

A wet, decadent sound wrapped itself around her gasp as I inserted two fingers inside her. She was hot. And wet. And so damned tight. For the first time in my life I wondered how it would feel to fuck a woman bareback. To replace my fingers with my cock and experience that snug channel sucking me in.

Her hips moved and she gave a greedy little moan. Slowly, I withdrew and pushed back inside her. Her mouth dropped open and her eyes glazed.

'You're gorgeous when you're lost in pleasure. Do you want more, Wren?'

Without replying, she shifted her stance wider, wrapped her hand around my wrist and directed my movements, pressing my fingers inside her.

'I'll take that as a yes?'

Despite the rampant arousal coursing through her, her eyes flashed at me, reminding me that beyond this temporary haven of her maze our families detested each other. That she was using me simply because I was here. That any man who happened to be in her vicinity at the right time would probably have done?

No. Every cell in my body rejected that idea.

'Either you're too turned on to speak or you're

attempting to make this a party for one.' I resisted her when she attempted to hasten my movements. I slowed down, then pressed my thumb against her engorged clit. She shuddered hard, and a hoarse cry broke from her lips. 'Which one is it, Wren?'

'I… I…'

I moved my thumb again and another cry ripped free. 'Do you want me to make you come, baby?'

She hesitated for a mutinous second. Then nodded frantically. *'Yes,'* she hissed.

'Then I want to hear exactly how you want it. And I want you to say my name when you do.' I hoped she wasn't dating anyone, but hell if I was going to be a replacement for some absent arsehole.

I circled my thumb and her head jerked back, pushing into the hedge. 'I want it deeper, Jasper. Faster.'

I smiled in unashamed triumph and increased the tempo. Immediately, she got even wetter…

Bloody hell. Any more and she would blow the top of my head clean off. Or more likely make me blow my load in my pants like a damned schoolboy. But I couldn't stop fucking her with my fingers any more than I could stop breathing. The sounds she was making from both sets of her lips were driving me insane.

'Slide two fingers into your mouth for me, baby. Make them nice and wet.'

Her eyes widened but she obeyed my instruction. The sight of her sliding her digits slowly into her mouth was almost too much to bear. Unable to resist, I swooped down and added my tongue to the play, licking her fingers as she withdrew them. Her pussy clenched around my fingers, a sign that she'd enjoyed that little action. I filed it at the back of my mind for next time as she rested her wet fingers against her lips.

'I have a few ideas of what you can do with those fingers. But I'd love to see you play with your gorgeous nipples.'

Her breath caught then released, and her fingers dropped to one exposed, beaded nipple. Slowly, she circled the bud, gasping as sensation piled high. Then she transferred her attention to the other peak, her breath coming faster as she pleasured herself.

Her pussy began to tighten around my fingers, making pushing inside her both a sizzling thrill and a torture. She wetted two more fingers, then, with both hands, tugged and tortured her nipples as I pumped inside her.

In under a minute, she started to unravel. And it was the most stunning thing I'd ever seen.

'Don't stop. Please… I'm close. So close…' Her hips jerked as she chased her bliss. With a sharp cry, she started to come.

Driven by lust, I dropped to my knees and replaced my thumb with my mouth. Gripping her thighs to hold her open, I sucked her clit hard and long.

A keening cry surged up her throat, the sound

tormenting me as I groaned and sucked her harder. Rolling convulsions slammed into her, fresh wetness dripping over my lips.

'Jasper!'

Frantic fingers gripped my hair and her whole body shook wildly. I cupped her bottom to hold her steady as her knees weakened and her body sagged. I wanted to eat her pussy for ever, but her frantic whimpers turned a little urgent.

The kind that suggested reality was returning.

I stayed an extra minute, licked her clean with gentle laps of my tongue as her trembling quieted and the hold in my hair loosened. And just for the hell of it and because she was too addictive to resist, I shoved my fingers inside her one last time as I kissed my way up her body to her mouth. Our lips fused and our tongues tangled for another minute while I committed her taste to memory before removing my fingers from her.

Still watching her, I brought my hands to my mouth and licked the last of her taste off. When I was done, I readjusted her knickers and helped her redress.

Silence throbbed between us as she furiously avoided my gaze. I suppressed a sigh and shoved my fists into my pocket to stop myself from reaching for her.

'Are you okay?'

She stared at me for a handful of seconds before

she nodded. 'Yes.' Another several seconds drifted by. Then, 'Thank you.'

'My pleasure,' I replied, my voice more than a little gruff.

Her gaze dropped tellingly to the raging hard-on tenting my trousers. I laughed around the agony of my erection. 'Believe it or not, watching you come was a pleasure. Maybe we can—'

The words dried in my throat as her expression altered. Within a blink of an eye she was no longer the sated siren at one with the foliage around her.

She was a cool and collected princess, dispensing rejection. 'This was a one-time thing. Gratefully received but something I intend to forget at the earliest opportunity.'

Disappointment—and, yes, blistering anger because I'd hoped this could be the start of…something— unravelled through me. 'You think I'm that forgettable, sweetheart?' I asked, modulating my voice to that deceptive pitch that always confused my opponents. They weren't sure whether I was pissed off or indulging whatever mood they were in.

Fleeting uncertainty chased across her face before she marshalled it.

'I do.' She handed back my jacket, her lips once again curved in that fake, dismissive smile. 'Because it's already in the past,' she said.

'Like hell it is. We're going to fuck, Wren. I'm going to make you come many, many more times. It's simply a matter of when.'

I gave her props for attempting to fight her excitement. She fussed with her hair, rearranged her scarf and tugged her zip another fraction upwards. And when she achieved that facade of outrage, I allowed it. I intended to disprove it at the very next opportunity.

'I allowed a moment of temporary madness, Jasper. Don't hold your breath that it'll happen again.'

She started to walk away. I shrugged on my jacket and followed. 'Wren.'

She paused without turning.

I stepped around to face her. 'I still want to know where your brother is. This time I'm not taking no for an answer.'

The eyes she lifted to mine were haunted, filled with the tension I'd sensed in her all evening. For a handful of seconds, she pressed her lips together. Then her gaze shifted away from mine. 'I don't know.'

Instinct suggested she wasn't lying. 'When was the last time you heard from him?'

A shaft of pain crossed her flawless features. 'My mother spoke to him a week ago.'

Her mother. Not her. Was that the reason for the tension between them?

'I need to reach him, Wren.'

Her face tightened. 'Is that why you followed me here? To pump me for information?'

I bit back my irritation. 'We both know what just happened has been a long time coming, pun intended. Don't demean it.'

Her eyes flickered and I could've sworn she blushed. Slightly mollified, I trailed my knuckles over her warm cheek. 'Doesn't change the fact that I still need to hear from Perry, though.' I dropped my hand. 'When you do get in touch with him, tell him it's in his interest to contact me, asap.' Knowing I needed to leave before I gave in to the urge to re-enact that heady episode again, I stepped away.

'That sounds like a threat,' she challenged.

I turned back to the woman I intended to have, again and again, in the very near future, and smiled. 'You can see it as such if you want. It's a simple statement that says I'm done playing games. He's fucking around with something important to me. Sooner or later, he's going to have to answer to me. How much mercy I show him is entirely up to him.'

CHAPTER TWO

THE FILES ON the desk in front of me had increased three-fold in the last three weeks. Each one was flagged with a red Post-it note that indicated it required urgent attention.

Except three weeks ago, I'd been in *front* of the desk and Perry behind it. My brother had been the CEO with the full backing of the board of directors at Bingham Industries. Whereas I'd had to fight my way into an *acting* CEO position, even after Perry finally resurfaced a few days ago and accepted that he needed help.

Unfortunately, it'd been too late to stop the tabloids from splashing his alcohol-fuelled downward spiral on the front pages, plunging the company into a stock-market nightmare and me into a fight to protect my own family firm from ruin.

Bitterness soured my mouth as I inched my chair closer to the desk. I'd been here for fifteen minutes and was yet to reach for the first file.

I couldn't. Not because I was scared. Far from it.

I couldn't reach for it because everything in this office reeked of my father. With strong undertones of Perry, the son and heir he'd treasured above everyone else. Including me.

Both hard, intransigent men with firm, ingrained views about a woman's place. Perry had tried to disguise his beneath brotherly concern, but that conceit had been there, inherited from the man he'd looked up to. A man who'd taken reckless risks with the Bingham name and died bitter and broken when those risks had shattered his family.

With hands I refused to let shake, I reached for the phone. My PA answered on the first ring. 'Alana, can you find me a replacement desk asap? Ideally today?'

'I…yes, of course. Right away, Miss Bingham. What do you want done with the old one?'

'Have it couriered to the house in Esher. They can put it in my father's study.'

I set the phone down, took a deep cleansing breath. My position as Acting CEO might well be temporary if I lost my fight against the Big Boys Establishment that were my uncles and cousins. But I intended to do things my way for however long I was here.

And before my stint ends, I'll show them…

That silent vow echoing through me, I picked up the first five files, rose and moved to the chesterfield sofa situated beneath the window. Everything in the office was stuffy and old-school but the chair and coffee table would have to do as a working area until the new desk arrived.

Setting the files down beside me, I opened the first one. Then immediately shut it when the name on the letterhead jumped up at me.

The Mortimer Group

My breath rattled around in my chest, echoing the sensations in my body. Mainly of the hot and bothered kind. Mainly between my legs. All because of Jasper Mortimer and what I'd let happen in the maze a week ago.

I'm done playing games.

The words might have been aimed at my elusive brother, but they resonated deep within me. Probably because Jasper and I had been playing a game for the better part of five years, ever since I walked into the boardroom at the internship fair and first experienced his dynamic magnetism. Heat flared up my body and I fought a squirm as total recall plunged me into that lustful state that never failed to materialise whenever I thought of him.

That searing, dangerous attraction had partly fuelled my decision to decline his internship offer. That and my family's abiding hatred for everything attached to the Mortimer name.

I tossed the file away. I wasn't ready to deal with him. Or the Mortimer Group. Nor did I want to think of how hard he'd made me come. How wanton he'd made me feel.

How much I'd craved a repeat performance ever since...

That madness in the maze was a shameful episode I'd intended to put out of my mind. If only it'd been that simple—

I jumped when the second office phone, positioned conveniently on the coffee table, rang. I didn't want to picture my brother in this chair, drinking himself into a stupor when he should've been safeguarding our family. Unfortunately, so far all evidence pointed that way.

To stop thoughts of the brother I'd never really got on well with, despite my desire to, I snatched up the phone. 'Hello?' I said, then grimaced at the lack of professionalism. Must do better in future.

'Congratulations on your official instatement as Acting CEO.' The deep voice of the last person I wanted to talk to filtered through the handset.

Shock rippled through my body. 'How do you know about that?' The board meeting had only ended at ten. It was barely noon. 'And how did you get my direct number?'

'I have my ways,' Jasper Mortimer said.

'You mean you have a spy in my company,' I deducted.

He chuckled, a rich, indulgent sound that threw me back to the maze. To his very male groans of sat-

isfaction as I lost my mind. 'Let's not start our relationship with accusations.'

'We don't have a relationship.'

'Yet,' he countered smoothly.

'We never will. I suggest you accept that now.'

'Thanks for the suggestion. But how are we going
to work together on this Morocco project if we don't
have even a basic rapport?'

My gaze flitted to the file I'd flung away. Something inside me shook. 'Why are you calling me?'

'To set up a meeting. The sooner the better.' The
lazy indulgence had left his voice to be replaced by
a crisp, uncompromising tone. 'Now that you're of-
ficially the head of Bingham's, we need to get this
deal back on track.'

The ambitious deal that had, by all accounts,
driven Perry over the edge. The thought hardened
my resolve. 'No.'

'Excuse me?'

'You heard me. The official Bingham position is
that we won't be going ahead with the Morocco deal.
You'll receive our official statement shortly.' I hung
up before he could reply. Then stared at the silent
phone, my heart banging against my ribs.

After five minutes without it ringing, my stomach started churning.

Had I been too reckless? The board I'd battled
to win over—the same board who'd expressed their
wish to remain leaderless until Perry returned from
his six-month rehab stint in Arizona—would love

to be proven right that I wasn't suitable for this position. Had I, with my very first act as CEO, played
right into their hands? Tentatively, I reached out towards the phone. To do what? Admit to Jasper that
I'd been too rash? Give him an opening to gloat? I
snatched my hand back.

He'd waited for a week. He could wait another
day.

Resolute, I opened the second file, putting
thoughts of Jasper, his masterful fingers and wicked,
orgasm-giving tongue out of my mind.

By five p.m. I'd resolved a third of the issues contained within the various files, and unfortunately
received even further insight into Perry's true state
of decline— they'd been drastically neglected for
months.

My chest tightened the more my thoughts dwelled
on my brother. According to the family doctor who'd
examined him, he'd been dangerously close to alcohol poisoning, a fact my mother had actively denied
even though it'd been an open secret that Perry—
like most Bingham men—had harboured a drinking
problem for years.

And just like my father, Perry had refused to
admit he even had a problem. The board had turned
a blind eye to his addiction since he'd managed to
keep Bingham Industries above the red line since
stepping into Father's shoes seven years ago.

My heart ached as I mourned our deteriorated
relationship. Our interaction on the occasions we'd

been forced to socialise had been stilted to the point where we'd been relieved to be largely out of each other's orbit for the last three years. Still, his chilled silence when I'd accepted a junior marketing position at another firm had hurt.

Ultimately, he'd been as dismissive of my ambitions as my father had been; he'd fully supported my mother's and aunts' view that I should marry into some wealthy investment family, with guaranteed connections and endless resources, instead of striving to make my own way in the world.

Tears prickled my eyes and I blinked them away.

The bottom line was, Perry was getting the help he needed and I was in charge of steering Bingham's away from bankruptcy.

Frankly, I was surprised the corporate sharks hadn't started circling already.

My gaze dropped to the royal-blue Bingham's logo on the file I held. Once a powerhouse in its field, my family's logistics and hospitality supply reputation had dropped several rungs in the last decade, forcing us to make poorer business choices that'd led to an even steeper decline.

Was that why Perry had joined forces with Jasper Mortimer? Because while Bingham's had faced significant fiscal woes, the Mortimer Group had grown exponentially, expanding its initial construction arm into several other industries at a breakneck rate that I'd watched with secret awe and, admittedly, a little resentment. How could I not, when a part of me wondered if some of that fortune had been achieved at the cost of my family's decline?

I tossed the file away, irritated with myself for my unhelpful thoughts. Whatever the reason for my family's current situation, nothing would be achieved by dwelling on the past. And especially not thinking of the incident in the maze!

My intercom sounded and I pressed the button with guilty relief. 'Yes?'

'I have a message from a Mr Jasper Mortimer for you.'

My pulse leapt. 'Is he on the phone?'

'No, he just wanted me to tell you he'll call again at six. And that you should make sure you're all read up on the project.' The hint of nerves in Alana's voice made me wonder what else he'd said. And why a sensation a lot like disappointment twisted in my stomach that he hadn't asked to speak to me.

'Thanks, Alana. I'll see you tomorrow.'

I hung up, cursing the untrammelled excitement fizzing through me, then my complete inability to slow my heart's crazy racing as the clock approached six.

Wren picked up on the first ring, and even before she spoke my pulse had rocketed to ridiculous levels. Then came her incredible voice.

'I'd appreciate it if you didn't disturb my assistant with unnecessary messages or me with ultimatums.'

'You made going through her necessary by hanging up on me earlier. I simply used her to let you know we'd be skipping the foreplay this time and getting straight to business. Unless, you specifically want the foreplay?'

'I don't want anything from you, Jasper,' she said briskly.

'Are you absolutely sure?'

'Yes, I'm unique like that, you see.'

I laughed a touch incredulously under my breath. 'You think I don't know that? Believe me, Wren, I do.'

I could've sworn I heard her breath catch, but her voice was curt when she replied, 'Trust a man like you to make allusions.'

I laughed harder, knowing it would irk her more. Cool, calm and collected Wren was intriguing, but I'd discovered I preferred the fiery, passionate woman in the maze who'd lost control, if only for a brief time. 'A man like me? And here I thought, like you, that I was one of a kind…'

'Sadly, you're not as rare a specimen as you think you are.'

I gave a dramatic sigh. 'That just makes me want to prove you wrong.'

'You can't. You won't be able to.'

I gripped the phone tighter, felt myself drawn in deeper into the compulsion I couldn't fight. 'Why not? Because every guy you've been with has made you come as hard as I did in that maze?'

'Seeking validity of your male prowess? How predictable. You disappoint me, Jasper,' she said, her voice a touch huskier.

Despite the curious throb in my chest, I smiled. 'I'm wholly satisfied with my strengths, thanks.' *But you weren't always, were you?* I pushed away the taunting voice. 'As for seeking validity, the end result in that maze is all the validity I need where you're concerned.'

'Can we get off that subject, please?' she whispered fiercely. 'I don't have time for personal conversation.'

'Do you despise me as much as you pretend to, or is this you simply toeing the family line?' I taunted, a sudden restlessness prowling inside me.

She inhaled sharply. 'You'll never get the chance to find out. Goodbye, Mr Mortimer.'

'Before you dramatically hang up on me again, let me remind you that your continued failure to engage with me only brings Bingham's closer to being in breach of contract.'

'I've read the file. Nothing in there remotely suggests a breach,' she said tightly, and I got the feeling I'd upset her by that family comment.

Bloody hell.

I tried to get my head back into business mode. 'May I suggest that you read the paperwork again. Carefully.'

Silence greeted me and I imagined her bristling, those eyes flashing with low-burning anger. I wondered what she'd look like in full blaze. God, it'd be glorious.

'I graduated university at the top of my class. You know this because you came sniffing around, trying to headhunt me, remember?'

'I remember you turning me down flat and accepting an internship at a much more inferior company.' That still grated, but it'd been the first inkling for me that, all these decades later, the Binghams were still as bitter about the fallout between our families. Now I knew the depths of my father's ruthlessness, I wasn't surprised. 'Do you regret that decision?'

'Not for a single moment. So I can only conclude you're trying to insult me by insinuating I would've missed something as crucial as a break clause in a contract.'

I took a beat to formulate my reply because this was where it got tricky. Saying anything negative against Perry might backfire. And as much as I liked tussling with Wren, the project I'd worked my arse off for needed to be kept on track. 'No offence intended. But the clause is there, I assure you. I can courier over a copy if you'd like?'

'Now you're implying I'm sloppy with paperwork. And blind, too?'

'You seem hell-bent on taking offence no matter what I say. A meeting will resolve this quickly enough, don't you think? Even if it's so you can put me in my place?'

'Inviting me to prove you wrong won't work, either. I don't need my ego stroked.'

It was time to pull out the big guns. 'I suggest you make time in your schedule. I'm not losing this deal because of some chip you've got on your shoulder. I expect to see you in my office tomorrow.'

'Or what?'

'Or I'll have no choice but to make good on my promise. You're already mired in unwanted publicity. Divorcing yourself from this deal at this late stage is going to bring nothing but unwanted attention to Bingham's.'

'Are you threatening me?'

'I'm laying out the course of action I'll be forced to take if you remain intransigent. The ball is in your court, sweetheart.'

She hung up.

Despite the two-nil score against me, I wasn't overly disgruntled. She hadn't earned her position by being dismissive of a potential lawsuit. Not that it'd come to that. For starters, I wasn't champing at the bit to become *the* Mortimer incapable of closing my division's biggest deal yet. The labels my father had callously and frequently branded into my skin were enough.

No, I was willing to bet my very treasured vintage Aston Martin that Wren would make contact. And if not…

I smiled grimly to myself as I swivelled in my chair to enjoy my multimillion-pound view…

If not, I'd take delight in becoming a very significant pain in her delectable backside.

The break clause wasn't in the contract.

Jasper's insinuation that I'd missed something had spurred a wild need to prove him wrong. After a two-hour search, I'd given up and headed home. Nothing in the electronic or paper files showed Perry had agreed to an early break clause. Sure, there were several clauses—all dishearteningly skewed in favour of the Mortimer Group—peppered within the contract but nothing that stated what would happen if Perry changed his mind about proceeding with the Morocco deal. Because he hadn't planned on it? Like my father, had he gone into this with unshakeable hubris, only to fall?

My heart twisted in dull pain and a little shame for assuming his culpability. He wasn't here to defend himself. And for all I knew, Jasper had twisted his arm into agreeing to this deal. The man was clever enough.

And not just with his words.

My heart skipped a beat and shame deepened, but for a completely different reason. Our heated verbal exchange had sparked something to life inside me. Something that, hours later, made me feel restless. *Needy.* I'd been spoiling for an argument. Then ended up spoiling for something totally different. Something to ease the ache between my thighs.

Like his mouth. His fingers.

His cock.

I pressed my fingers into my eyes, hoping to erase the image of him looking far too handsome for my sanity at the party. But the images simply reeled…of him caging me against the maze hedge. Of him on his knees, enthusiastically bringing me to an insane climax. Hell, even watching him suffer with that incredible hard-on had turned me on. God, what the hell was wrong with me?

You need to get laid.

I dropped my hands in frustration. If only it were that simple. Despite my short, rebellious modelling stint, I was a Bingham, cognisant of my ever-increasing family responsibility. The tabloids would love nothing better than to splash the front pages with details of whatever brief hook-up I indulged in for the sake of getting my rocks off. Especially now I was Acting CEO of a once multimillion-pound company now on the brink of collapse.

While my last two relationships hadn't worked due to lack of chemistry, behind it was the same resentment that had led me into modelling at nineteen. Resentment and rebellion stemming from my mother's attempt to orchestrate those relationships.

Unable to control either my father or Perry, she'd turned her attention to me the moment I reached puberty. Attention I'd mistakenly believed was affection I'd sorely missed in my childhood years when I'd needed her most. Discovering that she was simply using me to while away her time until her husband or son needed her, whereupon she set me back on my isolation shelf, had hurt long before I'd reached maturity. Of course, it didn't stop the foolish hope that sprang inside me whenever she turned her attention on me.

Not until lately. Not until her indifference—identical to Perry's—to my announcement that I'd accepted a marketing position at a different company had forced me to accept that true affection or acknowledgement from her would never happen. I was merely an ornament to be displayed when it suited her.

More fool me…

Exhaling through another tide of hurt, I padded over to the window, while parsing Jasper's parting words. He wanted Bingham's to hold up their end of the deal, agree to a three-year plan to supply the hospitality infrastructure for the four luxury hotels and casinos he was building in Morocco.

On the surface, it sounded like a deal made in heaven, but the reality was that Bingham's would be operating at an eighty per cent loss for the first year with possible gains coming only in the second and third years. Perry had tried to push for a five-year contract. Jasper had refused. Because like a typical Mortimer, he wanted to keep the initial financial gains for himself.

Well, I wasn't going to let the past repeat itself. The maze incident and our phone call tonight had proven two things: this insane attraction between us that made me want to tear off his clothes when he was within touching distance was untenable, and working with Jasper would be a nightmare.

The man was too full of himself. And I was woman enough to recognise that not all battles needed to be fought. Besides, I had several ideas of how to put the resources Perry had earmarked for the Mortimer deal to better use.

Striding over to my phone, I checked my schedule for the next day, then slotted a half-hour to deal with Jasper. It wouldn't take more than that to send the message home.

And if my belly somersaulted and my pulse raced at the thought of tangling with him again…it was only because I looked forward to emerging the victor.

Nothing else.

I strode through the doors of Mortimer Tower after business hours the next day, power-suited and determined not to be impressed with my surroundings. The reminder that all of this had been built by cutthroat Mortimers helped me focus as I entered the executive lift that serviced the upper floors where Jasper's office was located.

A part of me regretted leaving this meeting until last thing on Friday. If I'd tackled it first thing this morning, I'd already be free of this disquieting… *thrumming* in my veins. My brain wouldn't keep flashing scenarios of what could happen when I saw him again. I wouldn't have wasted precious stretches of time replaying his promise that *'We're going to fuck, Wren'* and *'I'm going to make you come many, many more times'*.

I sure as hell wouldn't be riding the empty lift with trembling hands and panties slightly damp from that memory of him going down on me in my family maze.

Enough, already...

The self-admonition worked for the thirty seconds it took for the lift to spit me out into the pristine, ultra-sleek reception area. The whole building had been redecorated recently at huge expense by Bryce Mortimer, the award-winning architect in the Mortimer clan. I might have ignored the impressive atrium downstairs, but I couldn't avoid the burst of bold colours softening the sharply angled steel and dark grey surfaces.

A smartly dressed receptionist smiled as I sucked in a breath and approached her.

'Hi, I have a meeting with Jasper Mortimer. He's expecting me.' Half true. Jasper might have summoned me here today but I hadn't bothered to inform him when I would be making my appearance.

Her smile slipped. 'Is he? Only, he went into a meeting ten minutes ago.'

'We didn't agree on a specific time. Just show me to his office. I'll wait.'

'Of course, Miss Bingham. Right this way.'

The greys were more pronounced than the steel in Jasper's office and the colours came from art rather than flower arrangements, but the effect was the same—sleekly professional, contemporary and elegant. But what made the space different was his lingering scent in the air, coupled with the aura of power I couldn't dismiss as I stared at the immense dark-wood desk and black high-backed chair, and I couldn't help the shiver that coursed down my spine. A throat cleared beside me. Composing myself, I glanced at the receptionist. 'Thank you.'

'Can I get you anything?'

I started to refuse, then changed my mind. 'Coffee with cream, no sugar. Thank you.'

She nodded and glided away. I returned my gaze to my surroundings, noting the absence of files or paperwork. Either Jasper was naturally meticulous in maintaining a paper-free environment or he'd anticipated my arrival. My instinct suggested the latter, eroding a layer of that upper hand I'd hoped to gain by my unexpected arrival.

After the receptionist served my coffee and left, I sat on the wide grey velvet sofa facing the spectacular view of the Thames and attempted to immerse myself in Bingham business. I wasn't sure where the notion of how to handle Jasper came from. All I knew was that it happened somewhere between sipping the excellent java brew—purportedly supplied to every Mortimer establishment by Graciela Mortimer—and when the door suddenly sprang open to reveal Jasper Mortimer in all his breathtaking glory.

Perhaps I sensed the moment I saw his face that

walking away wasn't going to be as easy as I'd convinced myself. Here, in this space, in his *domain*, I realised my first mistake—we should've met on neutral ground.

Because the man striding towards me teemed with quietly ferocious purpose. And yes, regardless of how late it was, he'd *known* I would come. 'Sorry for the wait. I couldn't get out of the meeting as quickly as I wanted. Do you mind?' He pointed to the coffee on the tray.

I shook my head. 'Go ahead.'

He poured himself a cup, added a dash of cream, and took a seat next to me.

Immediately, his dark woodsy smell engulfed me. The strong, visceral urge to breathe him in made me lift my own cup, hoping the coffee smell would dilute the potency of his scent.

That particular quest became redundant because my gaze was on a mission of its own. It took in the strong fingers lifting the cup to his lips for a large gulp, then followed the lines of his throat as he swallowed. The play of his powerful thighs as he crossed his legs and set the cup and saucer on his knee.

'First things first, did you come across the clause we talked about?'

His assumption that I'd gone looking set my teeth on edge. But I answered anyway. 'No, I didn't. We must be looking at different documents because there's nothing in my copy of the contract to support what you're saying.'

Jasper's hazel gaze narrowed on me for a tight, long stretch. Then he set his cup down, rose and crossed to his desk. When he returned with a sleek laptop, my heart lurched, then dropped to my toes as he fired up the machine. A few taps and he turned the screen to face me.

'Perry signed this document down the corridor in my conference room three months ago. It was duly witnessed, and I couriered him a copy for his records. The break clause in question is on page forty-seven.'

With not quite steady hands, I placed my cup on the coffee table and took the laptop. I wanted to blurt out that the presence of the break clause didn't change anything. But I couldn't delude myself. Break clauses were notoriously costly and I suspected Bingham would end up shouldering the burden if I didn't play my cards right.

That outlandish idea that struck me five minutes ago returned, more forcefully, as I read the document. It looked similar to my copy except for the crucial page missing from mine.

'Why is this one different from mine?'

Jasper didn't answer immediately. He drained his coffee before glancing my way. 'Negotiations with your brother weren't…smooth. He insisted on renegotiating several contracts before things were finalised.'

Given Perry's debilitated state, I wasn't surprised. But a question had been gnawing at me since I became aware of this deal. 'Why Bingham's? There are literally thousands of companies out there you could've partnered with. Why us?'

His lips firmed. 'You mean considering our family history?'

He wasn't beating about the bush. I didn't see why I should. 'Yes.'

'Would you believe me if I said that ultimately didn't factor into my decision?'

Who was he kidding? 'No, I wouldn't.'

He sighed. 'Didn't think so. Wren, if you're asking then I'm going to presume Perry didn't tell you.'

'Tell me what?'

Hazel eyes locked on to mine, pinned me in place. 'That he begged me for this deal. He pretty much stalked me for the better part of three months before I even agreed to meet with him. I was all set to go with someone else.'

A flush of shame crept up from my belly and soon engulfed my whole body. I'd seen the books. We were in a precarious financial position. But we weren't crawling-on-our-bellies desperate. Yet. Not enough for Perry to beg for scraps from our sworn enemy. 'I'm not sure why he did that—'

'Aren't you?' Jasper's expression was entirely cynical.

Pride swarmed through me. 'No, we're not destitute. I'm not going to lower myself to prove it to you. You'll have to take my word for it.'

He frowned. 'No need to be so defensive. I'm

simply relating things as they happened. For whatever reason your brother wanted this deal to happen.'

'Then why did he drag his feet?'

Jasper's lips twisted. 'At least you're admitting he did.'

I handed him back his laptop. 'Clearly he wasn't satisfied with something. I've looked at the projections. We supply you with everything from gambling tables and staff to tea towels and garden fertiliser but see very little profit for twelve months? Why the hell should I come on board with something like that?'

His gaze hardened and I caught a glimpse of Hugh Mortimer, the adversary my father had faced—and lost to—decades ago. Was Jasper his father's son in every sense of the word? Whatever. I didn't intend to stick around to find out.

'Because he signed on the dotted line. It's too late to back out now. This project has been delayed by months already. I won't let it suffer another setback,' he said grimly.

I rose from the sofa, gathered my tablet and briefcase as calmly as I could, despite the roiling in my stomach. I'd seen the books. Our company was haemorrhaging money, yes, but we still had substantial assets to hold back the dam for a while. 'I'll look over your papers and get back to you.'

He rose to join me. Despite my above average height, he towered over me, made me feel small and delicate in a way very few people could. And...I didn't exactly hate that feeling. Which was totally absurd. I turned away as he glanced at his watch.

'Let me take you out to dinner. We can discuss this over—'

'No, thanks. I only eat with people I trust.'

His eyes darkened. 'Ouch,' he drawled without a hint of the purported affront. 'You really are determined to make this adversarial, aren't you?'

For some reason, the softly voiced accusation niggled, striking me with a wild urge to apologise. *Stay strong.* 'I'm just looking out for my family's best interests.'

That brought a wry, twisted smile to his lips. 'Can't say I blame you, but I'm really not the enemy here, Wren.'

God, the way he said my name—that name I'd hated for so long—somehow sounded pleasant on his lips. 'If you're not the enemy, then agree to end this amicably,' I replied.

His smile turned edgy, delivering another glimpse of the true man beneath the suave exterior. 'I haven't made it this far by being sentimental over business, Wren. I'm a little disappointed you would play that card. Your brother signed an agreement. I expect you to honour it. Starting on Monday, you'll devote the required time and energy into progressing this deal.'

'Or what?' I dared, even though my stomach dipped wildly. There was something raw and primal in that command, something that incredulously turned my blood hotter, my skin more sensitive. With a compulsion I couldn't deny, my gaze dropped to his lips. Mine tingled, a need to taste him almost overpowering me. It was enough to make me take a step back. But I wasn't totally out of his reach. So when he raised his hand and slowly extended it towards my face, there was absolutely no reason not to take another step away. Out of the path of temptation. Except I didn't.

His knuckles brushed my cheek, slowly caressing down to my jaw. Electricity charged up my thighs, making me bite back a gasp. Why the hell was I getting so wet? *Dear God...*

'You say you're looking out for your family? Then what was that in that maze last week? Was it a touch of much-needed self-indulgence? One you wouldn't be averse to repeating?'

'I...no.'

'Try that once more, with feeling. But before you do, remember my promise. I intend to fuck you, Wren. Very hard and very thoroughly. In every position you desire.'

My clit throbbed and fresh flames shot through me at the thick drawled words. Suddenly, I was very aware of the sofa nearby. That all I had to do was say the word and I'd have him.

But then what? He would be just another temporary act of rebellion that could go nowhere when I should be concentrating on dragging my family's company out of the quagmire. Perry was in rehab. The last thing I should be doing was adding flames to a roaring scandal-hungry fire by embarking on a tryst with the enemy.

'Business,' I insisted, even as a thick coil of regret unravelled inside me, reminding me of how many times I'd denied myself for the sake of family. 'I'm here to discuss business. Nothing else.'

That overconfident smile returned, turning his far too gorgeous face even more spectacular as his hand dropped. 'Good. Then do the right thing. Or you'll leave me no choice but to fight your hot little fire with flames of my own,' he answered, a growl of anticipation in his voice that hastened my heartbeat.

'You don't want to go to war with me, Jasper.'

'To get this deal done, I'll take you however I can get you, sweetheart.'

Much too late, I took that vital step back. Then another. 'Goodnight, Jasper.'

'Would you like me to walk you out?' he asked, right after his hooded gaze circumvented my body, leaving me even hotter than before.

'I can manage on my own, thanks,' I replied, aware my voice was a little hoarse when I needed it snippy.

'Okay. I'll see you on Monday for the phase two meeting at nine a.m. Don't be late.'

I turned and walked away without answering. In the lift, I sagged against one wall, a traitorous little tremble seizing my body as snippets of the conversation scrolled across my brain. Nothing had gone as I'd smugly predicted. If the agreement he'd shown me was valid—and I didn't see why it would be fabricated—it meant Perry had agreed to a deal that would be impossible to walk away from without seriously crippling Bingham's. So why had he signed it? And why had he left it out of the file?

My phone pinged as the lift reached the ground floor. I stared at the text, my heartbeat hammering as I saw the familiar-looking number. Jasper.

I've emailed you a copy of the agreement for your records.

I checked my email and, sure enough, the agreement was in my inbox. I tapped out a reply as I walked through his stunning atrium, once again determined not to admire its grandeur.

Email received. Thanks.

I discovered other hidden bombshells once I was back home in my maisonette in Fulham, showered and dressed in my favourite pyjama shorts set. The glass of red wine was forgotten in my hand as I read and reread the agreement, tiny waves of shock building into a tsunami as I absorbed just what Perry had committed Bingham's to.

Besides the supply agreement, which would eat heavily into our cash reserves, Perry had agreed to being on hand, day or night, to troubleshoot any problems that arose either in London or on sites in

Morocco for a minimum of twenty hours per week. To 'help' with that particular clause, Jasper had offered the use of his empty office in London or a suite in the Morocco hotel.

Even before I'd taken up the mantle at Bingham's I was working long hours. Hard work had earned me a fast track from junior to senior executive in my last firm. Adding a few more hours to my workday didn't faze me. What disturbed me was the thought of being that close to Jasper. Because when he'd touched me tonight, every cell in my body had roared to life in a way that shocked me.

I downed the rest of the wine, set the glass down and reclined on my sofa. I had the rest of the weekend to figure a way out of this.

For Perry's sake. For my family's sake, I couldn't fail.

Eyes closed, I tried to work out how to best the man with the wicked tongue and clever fingers.

I'll take you however I can get you...

Why did those words make me so hot? Why the hell couldn't I get his voice out of my head?

I'll take you...

I was flushed and panting as my hand crept down my belly. I bit my lip, hating myself a little for succumbing to the lust trickling through my blood. My nipples beaded as sensation unfurled in my pelvis, heating my pussy and engorging my clit. Uncustomary anticipation fired me up, my fingers tingling as

I spread my legs and slipped my fingers beneath the waistband of my pyjama shorts.

A hot little gasp left my lips when I touched myself, shivering when I noticed how wet and slippery I was.

I'll take you...

Need and lust built. My fingers worked my clit in desperate circles, the realisation that, for once, I didn't need the assistance of my trusted vibrator, ramping up my desire. Working my clit with my thumb, I slipped my middle finger inside my wet heat, finger-fucking myself while I imagined thicker fingers filling me. Or a cock... Jasper Mortimer's cock.

Inside me.

Pounding me.

Making me scream.

My orgasm curled through me, arching my back off the sofa as liquid bliss drowned me from head to toe.

It was as I came down from that intense high, my heartbeat roaring in my ears, that a line from the agreement suddenly flashed across my mind.

I jackknifed off the sofa, almost knocking over the wine glass as I reached for the laptop. And there, on page fifty-one, was my answer, my saviour, in black and white.

I read and reread it for good measure.

The Mortimer Group has the right to terminate this agreement, with due notice, in the

case of non-performance by Bingham Indus-
tries. This includes, but is not limited to, con-
tinued disruption of services...

I smiled.
For now, Jasper Mortimer had the power. I was
going to take it from him by simply doing...nothing.
Even while I blew his mind *out* of the boardroom.

CHAPTER THREE

WREN WAS FORTY-FIVE minutes late. Irritated, I hit my intercom button again.

'Yes, sir?' my PA answered.

'Try her mobile again. If she doesn't answer, call her office. I want to know where she is,' I growled.

'Of course.'

Why I expected Trish to succeed when my own numerous calls had gone straight to voicemail was a mystery but it beat just sitting around fuming because Wren was a no-show. I'd hoped providing her with the valid copy of the agreement would make her see sense but, clearly, I'd overestimated her.

Jaw gritted, I acknowledged that my disappointment in her was more acute than it'd ever been with her brother. Yes, I loved a challenge and I'd known getting involved with Bingham's, all things considered, would be difficult, but I'd convinced myself I could handle it.

Handle *her*.

When the hell was I going to learn my lesson?

Bitterness rose up to fuse with my annoyance. I tamped down both emotions. I wasn't dealing with my father's scathing remarks, disparaging me about wanting peace when we Mortimers were a proudly bloodthirsty lot.

I was dealing with an intelligent, if extremely stubborn, woman. I needed another way to deal with her.

Immediately my mind flew back to the maze, as it had been doing increasingly over the past week or so, but especially since Friday night. It'd taken every ounce of willpower not to kiss her in my office. But I'd needed to prove to her that I wasn't driven by my desire.

Succumbing to the urge to keep touching her, to kiss those luscious lips, would only convince her I was driven by base instincts. Yet I couldn't deny that she only needed to flash those green eyes to trigger a fever in my blood.

I laughed under my breath. I'd had my share of women, some more beautiful than Wren. This rare phenomenon where she was concerned was inexplicable. Why the hell did she trigger this strong reaction in me?

I shook my head, growing more annoyed when I clocked that I'd wasted almost an hour waiting for her. About to open one of the many files that needed my attention, I paused when my intercom buzzed.

'Yes?' I responded, a little too eagerly.

'I'm sorry, Mr Mortimer, I couldn't reach her. Her secretary says she's in a meeting.'

'I know. She's *supposed* to be in a meeting, here, with me.' Aware that I was snapping at my PA, I throttled down my emotions. Christ, she drove me crazy. 'Thanks, Trish.' I collapsed in my seat, forcing calm into my bones.

I'd always been a strategist. A planner. Favouring dialogue over conflict. But I was a Mortimer, as my father had taken delight in reminding me every time I'd displayed what he'd termed my *weakness*. Did Wren really want war with a Mortimer?

Especially when Bingham's, according to trusted sources, was one ill-judged deal away from complete collapse? She couldn't afford to take me on in a corporate battlefield. So why the hell was she trying? Perry had been equally hard-headed but evidently his intransigence had been mostly fuelled by alcohol. Wren was simply stubborn.

And loyal. Perhaps blindly so, but loyal.

It was a stark reminder that my family was acutely different. Mortimers—my father especially—didn't do blind loyalty and, as he'd proven with his callous desertion, wouldn't fight to the death for anyone else but himself.

But wasn't that what had made us who we were today? Successful. Feared. A global powerhouse with immeasurable clout. Sure, we wouldn't win any Family of the Year prizes but there was a lot to be proud of. I wasn't going to let a woman with brains, beauty and fireworks in her green eyes convince me otherwise—

As if I'd conjured her up by my imagination, my door opened and there she stood.

My annoyance didn't recede as I stared at her, but several new sensations crowded in. First, the jolt of electricity just the sight of her rammed through my body. I attempted to control it by taking another deep breath. And failed.

The second was utter shock as I took in the state of her.

She looked as if she'd stumbled in from a night of hard partying. And even harder fucking. Her hair was dishevelled as if some lucky bastard had won the privilege of running his fingers repeatedly through it. Her lips were faintly bruised and smeared as if someone had eaten off her lipstick. Then came her smudged make-up. Dark jealousy spiralled through me as my gaze dropped lower and my gut tightened against the inevitable hard-on heading my way as I took in the rest of her.

Holy hell, she was wearing a trench coat. Not necessarily a fashion *faux pas* considering the time of year, but it was tightly belted at the waist in that highly suggestive *sexual* way that screamed she was wearing very little or nothing at all underneath. Fire lit through my groin as she took a step towards me and justified my suspicions by flashing a bare leg.

Jesus, she wouldn't. Would she?

'Good morning, Jasper.' Whether that husky greeting was deliberately exaggerated or the result of long hours of screaming in ecstasy wasn't something I particularly wanted to dwell on. Either way, it threw another gallon of flammable fuel on my libido. I clenched my gut as I grew even harder.

'You're late,' I bit out, watching her strut across my office in sky-high heels.

With each step, I caught a glimpse of her leg, and nothing else. My nape heated and I desperately scrounged around for every scrap of willpower not to drag my fingers over my jaw and stop myself from salivating like a pathetic dog. I tried to remain pissed off, but my mind fixated on one thing.

Was Wren Bingham totally naked under that coat?

She reached my desk, laid her hands flat on it, and leaned towards me. I kept my eyes on hers, determined not to be drawn into whatever game she was playing.

'Am I? You said the meeting was at ten. It's now…' she paused, glanced around the office before reaching into her pocket for her phone '…nine fifty-nine. Oh, look, I'm a whole minute early.' She waved her phone at me and I caught a glimpse of her home screen.

It featured a picture of her, head thrown back, laughing into the camera. The image only showed her from bare shoulders up but it was again suggestive that she was naked. Arousal attacked my body, leaving me with a serious urge to fidget. I steepled my fingers on my belly, thankful my suit jacket and desk hid my compromised state from her.

'I told you the meeting was at nine o'clock. I've had to put off the Moroccan team twice already.'

'Heavens! In that case I can only apologise. There must have been some sort of mix-up.' She slipped the phone back into her pocket, the movements exaggerated enough to make her coat gape wide. I saw the curve of her breast and swallowed hard.

'What the fuck are you doing?' I bit out.

Her eyes widened. 'I don't know what you mean, Jasper.'

'Do you attend all your meetings dressed like that?'

'You don't like what I'm wearing?'

I gritted my teeth, knowing I was getting close to the danger zone. 'We abide by a dress code here.'

Her smile. 'Ah, but then I don't work for you, do I, Jasper?' she asked softly, but there was a hard glint in her eye, a stubborn flame flaring to life.

Before I could answer, my phone rang. I allowed myself a small smile as I met her gaze. 'You're right. You don't work for me. But we're working together and I expect professionalism, like being on time. I'll let it slide just this once.' I reached for my phone. 'Yes?' My PA relayed the information I wanted to hear, and I hung up. 'Are you ready?'

She tensed. 'Ready for what?'

'I told you I rescheduled the videoconference. The Morocco team is waiting for us in the conference room. Since you made the effort to come all this way despite being late, I'm assuming you'll join me?'

I watched her jaw drop, her whole act vanishing for a second before she composed herself. 'Of course, lead the way. I hope they're just as accommodating as you about my tardiness,' she said, her voice saccharine sweet.

I managed to stop my teeth gritting as I rose, buttoned my jacket and rounded the desk. The last thing I wanted to do was to walk her through my open-plan office floor dressed as she was. Call me a chauvinist but having every guy out there wondering what she was wearing under that coat made my blood boil.

But…business was business. And I wasn't about to let this deal fall apart over yet another hurdle.

I stepped out of my office, keenly aware that she was following, those sky-high heels perfectly displaying her spectacular endless legs with every step. Of course, as I'd feared, seemingly every male in the vicinity suddenly needed to be in the hallway leading to the conference room right at that moment.

Avid eyes gravitated to Wren, her sexily dishevelled state triggering more than one male fantasy. I hurried into the conference room, barely stopping myself from snarling at my own employees as I shut the door behind us.

Strolling to the head of the table, I grabbed the remote and flicked it on. The four women and three men who made up the Moroccan executive team stared back at us. Then, one by one, they switched their attention to Wren. Eyes widened, and wild speculation flickered across their faces.

I cleared my throat, rearranging what I suspected was a scowl into professional neutrality. 'Ladies and gentlemen, my apologies again for the delay. Let me introduce you to Wren Bingham. As of today, she'll be taking over Bingham Industries' side of the project.' I glanced at Wren, who'd taken the seat across from me.

She was staring at the screen with a sultry, faintly challenging smile. As I watched, she swivelled her seat towards the screen, dragging one hand slowly through her long hair before flicking it over one shoulder. With her other hand she waved at the team. 'Hi, it's lovely to meet you all,' she murmured, right before she crossed her mile-long legs.

I didn't need to be on her side of the table to know she was flashing more than a hint of thigh. The expressions on the screen—especially the male ones—telegraphed her effect on them, plain as day. Silence reigned in the room as their gazes flicked between Wren and me.

Bloody hell.

'Wren?' I prompted, aware of the bite in my voice.

She slanted green eyes at me and blinked slowly. 'Yes, Jasper?'

'Are you going to give the Bingham briefing? The team is pretty much on page as to where the Mortimer side of things stand. They need you to confirm the various timetables for delivery of phase two. You did get up to speed on where we are, didn't you?'

Her eyes flashed irritation at me but she main-tained her bored expression. 'Oh… Right. Phase two…' She didn't say anything else, just continued to stare at me with those eyes.

'Yep. Phase two. Don't keep us in suspense,' I taunted, ignoring the stares from the screen as our intrigued audience watched our silent battle, suddenly enjoying this tussle with her.

She shrugged, indicating she was going to do just as she pleased. That she was going to enjoy watching me twist in the wind.

After another stretch of mutinous silence, I swivelled my chair towards the screen. 'My apologies, but I didn't quite make a full introduction, did I? I should have mentioned that Wren has a master's degree in Business from Oxford University.'

I felt her gaze sharpen on me. 'She was recently featured in Business Tomorrow's Young CEOs Under Thirty. She's too modest to tell you herself, but she graduated at the top of her class and, according to one of her professors, she has one of the most brilliant business minds of her generation.'

'Stop it,' she hissed under her breath for my ears only.

I ignored her. She wasn't going to win this game. 'I tried to poach her even before she'd finished university but, alas, I lost her to another company. So I guess you can imagine how stoked I am to finally have her on board?' I flicked a mocking smile her way before returning my gaze to the team. 'The reason she doesn't have any files with her this morning is because she doesn't really need them. All the facts and figures she requires are right up there in that exceptional brain of hers. On top of her many accomplishments, she also possesses a photographic memory. I haven't seen it in action myself but I'm dying to. Wren?' I prompted again, finally focusing on her, the gauntlet writhing on the table between us.

Hellfire erupted from her gaze as her hands balled into fists.

I smiled inside, satisfaction eroding my irritation. She'd meant to test me by pretending lack of interest, boredom, even apathy. But the one thing Wren Bingham couldn't do was let our audience walk away with the impression that she was dumb. I suspected, like me, she'd fought too hard for her accomplishments and her true place in her family to let herself be so easily dismissed.

When she swallowed, surreptitiously pulled the lapels of her coat together and slowly uncrossed her legs, I allowed myself an inner fist pump.

Uncurling her hands, she glanced at the screen. 'What do you need to know about phase two?' she asked, the sexy seduction in her voice gone.

At my nod, the team launched into their questions. As I'd suspected, Wren knew the project inside and out. She answered every query concisely, offering alternatives when needed without once requesting information from me or consulting the electronic documents I'd emailed her yesterday.

When the meeting ended and the screen went

blank forty minutes later, she surged to her feet. 'You think you're very clever, don't you?' she snapped.

I reclined in my seat, taunting her with a smile. 'Don't throw a hissy fit just because your little game backfired on you, sweetheart,' I drawled.

Luscious lips pressed together as she raked her fingers through her hair, immediately making my imagination run wild about the array of sexual things I could do with every strand of that hair. 'This isn't going to work.'

I waved a hand at the screen. 'You just proved otherwise. It'll work even better if only you'd stop playing these silly games.'

Her eyes flashed. 'What makes you think I won't just let you list my accomplishments then show you up anyway next time?'

I shrugged. 'I don't. But I can guarantee that I'll keep coming up with different ways to ensure that you don't get away with whatever you have up your sleeve.'

She threw up her hands in exasperation, the closest I'd come to seeing her lose her cool. 'Why don't you do us both a favour and just end this?'

I exhaled slowly. 'I don't get it. Going ahead with this deal will benefit both of us.'

She performed a perfect pirouette and headed for the door. 'Keep telling yourself that,' she threw over her shoulder. 'In the meantime, I'm going to make it my business to make sure that you regret this.' She reached for the door handle. Started to turn it.

Everything inside me clenched tight. 'Wren.'

Fingers frozen, she glared at me over her shoulder.

'Please tell me you're not naked under that coat.'

That slow, cock-stroking smile returned, deadlier than before. 'I'm not naked under this coat, Jasper,' she echoed with a siren voice that transmitted straight to my groin. Then to taunt me further, her fingers dropped to toy with the loops of the belt. 'Would you like me to show you?'

Lust rushed through my blood, making me steel hard in moments. But I remained silent, swallowing down the *yes* that clawed at my throat. Without shifting her gaze from mine, she tugged on the belt. Her coat loosened and gaped. From where I sat, I couldn't see, but anyone who chose to enter in that moment would.

My stomach knotted and I lost the ability to breathe. 'Fucking hell,' I muttered under my breath.

'What was that?' she asked with false, wide-eyed innocence.

'I said keep that damn door closed, Wren.'

'Ah, I could've sworn you said something else.'

'Jesus, what are you doing?' I rasped, forgetting that I was meant to keep my cool.

'I'm going back to my office. I'm assuming we're done here?' she asked, one shapely eyebrow quirked.

My gaze dropped down the coat, fighting the urge to stand, rush over to her to see for myself what she was baring to the door. 'You know what I'm asking.

What are you doing with all that?' I jerked my chin at her attire.

Her smile deepened. 'Why, nothing. Not yet, anyway.'

Her hand dropped from the door. My throat clogged with tension as she slowly retied the belt, cinching it even tighter so her trim waist was fully displayed. My fingers itched with the need to capture that waist. I bunched them to stop myself from acting on the feelings rampaging through me.

'I need you back here tomorrow to discuss the casino outfitting.'

'I have a full day tomorrow.'

'Then we'll meet after you're done,' I countered, and watched her nostrils flare.

'I work pretty long hours. Are you sure you want to wait up for me? I wouldn't want to disturb your beauty sleep.'

'Thanks for your concern, but my beauty won't suffer too badly from a few extra hours of work. And, Wren?'

She cocked an eyebrow at me.

'Don't make me come after you. My patience won't hold out for ever.'

One corner of her lips lifted and she all but vibrated with the *Bring it on* she didn't utter.

I sighed under my breath. This game wasn't over, regardless of my daring her into displaying her intelligence just now. I watched as she opened the door and threw me one last look over her shoulder.

'Until next time, Jasper.'

I collapsed into my seat the moment she left, dragging my fingers through my hair as the rush of adrenaline drained from my body.

Maybe she had a point, damn it. Maybe the Mortimers should avoid the Binghams at all costs. Because even this small taster of what I suspected she had in store for me would wreck my concentration for the rest of the day.

Of course it will. Because you're just that weak, aren't you? Are you going to shy away from another fight, give in that easily? Debate *your way through another fight with an opponent? Maybe you should change your name, then. Because that is certainly not the Mortimer way.*

Arousal receded as my father's pitiless, unwanted voice echoed in my head. My jaw clenched as I fought a different kind of discomfort. But those disparaging words, branded into my soul from childhood, continued to echo through me, followed by bitterness for how long I'd let it rule every corner of my life.

But I'd done something about it…eventually. I'd taken control.

By letting Perry Bingham convince me to allow him to sign on to my deal? Knowing deep down it would probably piss my father off when I proved the generations-long feud meant nothing to me?

I shrugged the suggestion away. Regardless of the reason behind it, I was going to see this thing through. This project was my baby, the biggest deal I'd ever negotiated. I wasn't about to let it fall to pieces now.

Because Hugh Mortimer was still alive and well. Regardless of the fact that he'd removed himself from the immediate sphere of the clan, I knew he kept an eye on what happened within the company. And the last thing I was about to do was to prove him right. Even if I had to fight and wrestle Wren and her whole family under my control, I would bring this deal home.

Just to prove my father wrong about me.

Again.

CHAPTER FOUR

'WHAT KIND OF time do you call this?' I growled at the woman who stood in my doorway, thankfully wearing more clothes than yesterday. That moment of gratitude was fleeting though. On account of her succeeding where I was sure she'd fail at annoying me even more.

She sashayed into my office, looking stunningly immaculate, despite the very late hour, tossed her stylish briefcase on the sofa and shrugged. 'I'm pretty sure I warned you.'

'Working late is one thing. Turning up for a meeting at almost midnight is just taking the piss. How did you get here, anyway?'

'I took a cab. Why, were you worried about my safety?' she asked, one hand braced on her lean, curvy hip as she stopped in front of my desk.

Damn it, yes, I'd been worried. And increasingly vexed about it. I'd succumbed and called her office an hour ago, only to be blocked by her security who rightly wouldn't give out details of their boss's whereabouts. Not knowing whether she was going to turn up or not had kept me rooted in my office, tackling work that could easily have waited till tomorrow with dwindling concentration.

I shook my head as I stalked over to my liquor cabinet, poured myself a stiff Scotch. I toyed with being inhospitable for a few seconds before fixing her the mineral water with lime I'd seen her drinking at her party.

I offered the drink, daring her with my eyes to refuse. She glanced at the glass, a hint of surprise lighting her eyes before, frowning, she accepted it.

'I reread the contract today. The break clause might be skewed in your favour, but you realise I can simply do nothing for six months and watch you crash and burn?'

I tensed at her opening salvo. 'You'd really do that and lose close to half a billion pounds in profits?'

She hesitated for the tiniest revealing moment. 'Yes.'

'Are you sure? Don't you want to run that by your board first?'

Her chin went up and she boldly met my gaze. 'The board will stand behind any decision I make. Perry already had their backing to get out of this deal.'

Shit. That was news to me. 'After going to all that trouble of begging me for the partnership?'

Her lashes swept down and stayed down for a long

time. 'His reasons are none of your business. Same goes for mine.'

'Wrong, sweetheart. They are exactly my business, since we're effectively joined at the hip.'

She shook her head. 'You left him no choice. Not after you bought out the previous company Perry was supposed to partner with.'

I frowned. 'What are you talking about?'

'The Morocco deal. Isn't it true you only intended to go with two hotels?'

'That was the initial plan, yes. But—'

'But then you got greedy and bought up four more adjoining sites? Just because you could?'

'It wasn't a matter of greed, it was a matter of good business. And yes, because I damned well could. I'm failing to see what your point is here, Wren.'

'My point is, Perry came to you only after you became the new owner of the contract he was trying to secure. He didn't want to, but he'd been working on that deal long before you came on board. He…he was forced to come to you.'

My fingers tightened around my glass. 'Unless your family derives some macabre pleasure from hanging on to this shit even after twenty years, he could've walked away. Why didn't he?'

Her gaze rose and I caught a shaft of pain in her eyes. 'Perry hates losing. And some wounds run deep.'

Frustration bit through me. 'What about you? I'm not asking for a family reunion or even a suggestion that we bury the hatchet. All I'm asking for is a business deal where we both stand to profit for a very long time.'

Her lips twisted. 'Money isn't everything.'

I snorted. 'Then what are you doing in that office half a mile away? Running a charity?'

'I meant money isn't everything, *every time*.'

'Maybe not. But is that a strong enough reason to risk everything? For God's sake, who I am shouldn't matter in the grand scheme of things.'

'To my family, it does.'

I approached her until we were a foot apart.

She stayed her ground and that defiant stance made me instantly hard. Surprise, surprise. I leaned forward until her alluring perfume tortured me mercilessly. Until my thoughts began to fracture under the weight of the need to pull her close. Kiss her. Vent my frustration on anywhere she'd let me touch.

Starting with the silky skin of her neck. I'd work my way down, ridding her of that pristine cream shirt, which clung to her body. My gaze dropped to her chest, saw the faintest outline of her nipples. Sweet heaven, what I'd give to suck on those succulent nubs.

My eager mind strayed deeper into erotic realms.

I'd take off every single item of clothing except those red-soled heels, bend her over my desk and ram myself so deep inside her that we'd both see stars. Unlike last time, I had a condom nearby this time. Several, in fact. I'd taken to carrying the things with me wherever I went now. In case Wren Bing-ham happened to be there and begged me with her alluring mouth and eyes to service her as she had that night in the maze.

I leaned closer. She twitched and shuddered as my mouth brushed her earlobe. I wanted to catch the delicate flesh between my teeth, hear that control-destroying gasp she gave when she was caught in pleasure, but I restrained myself. Barely. 'Then they need to get over themselves, and fast. Because I'm not letting this one go. Now, shall we get on with this meeting? My casino isn't going to fit itself and, I promise, the longer you make me wait, the less reasonable I'll get about accommo-dating your behaviour.'

She froze, then jerked back a step. Whatever she read in my eyes made hers widen before it nar-rowed. 'This is your last chance, Jasper,' she said, her voice throbbing with an emotion I didn't want to examine.

'No.'

She stared at me for an age, then nodded. 'Fine. Let's discuss the casino.'

An hour later, I watched her walk out ahead of me—because I wasn't letting her catch a cab home at one o'clock in the morning, despite her protests—her sexy arse and endless legs an erotic sight that made my mouth water.

Just like last time, she'd come fully prepared. I had a set of approved timetables and proposed delivery of top-of-the-line gaming equipment in my briefcase, ready to green light in the morning.

I was buzzing with quiet excitement at her sheer proficiency while she'd grown increasingly despondent as the meeting had progressed. It was clear she wasn't happy about my insistence on our partnership continuing.

She reached the lift and shot me a look filled with venom. And despite a low warning hum at the back of my head suggesting that it wasn't too late to ditch Bingham's, I found myself smiling as I stepped into the lift with her.

I wasn't smiling two weeks later when I slammed my phone down after another failed call to the number that had risen to the top of my speed-dial list.

She didn't answer.

It was time to pull out the big guns.

I typed out a quick text.

I'm calling you in one minute. I suggest you pick up or the next call will be from my lawyers. Trust me, you don't want that.

The speech bubble that said she was answering rippled for several seconds—while I held my stupid breath—before it died. Exactly one minute later, I dialled her number.

'Hello?'

'What the fuck do you think you're doing, Wren?'

'Good afternoon to you, too, Jasper. How's your day going?'

'You know damn well how it's going. You went behind my back and cancelled our meeting with the advertising team. Yesterday you didn't bother to show up for the VIP guest hospitality meeting. The day before that—'

'If you're going to list everything I've done or not done in the last two weeks, do you mind if I pour myself a drink? I have a feeling I'll be thirsty by the time you're finished.'

'This is absurd. You're costing us both a lot of money.'

'Nothing earth-shattering I can't recoup eventually.'

'At the risk of sounding egotistical, I can withstand the losses way longer than you can. Have you thought about that?'

She hesitated for a split second. 'Maybe. But just as you've done your research on me, I've done mine on you. You have a board to answer to. And I dare say not everyone is thrilled about you hanging on to this deal when cutting me loose makes better sense. What do you tell them when they ask, Jasper? That you're holding on, on the off chance you'll get to fuck me as part of the deal?'

My stomach muscles knotted. I wasn't going to deny it. But it wasn't my *entire* reason. 'They trust my judgement, which is more than I'm guessing you can say for your own board.'

'Clearly you don't know as much as you think you do.'

'Enlighten me, then.'

'For starters? My board approved the list of willing partners who have indicated they'd be happy to buy out Bingham Industries' interest in this deal and they know you're refusing to entertain that idea on the basis that you're being a pig-headed—'

'Watch it, Wren. I won't be spoken to like that.'

To her credit, she didn't offer a scathing comeback.

'Has it occurred to you that prolonging this battle leaves you progressively exposed, not to mention in danger of ruining your personal reputation?' I asked.

'What are you talking about?' she replied, her voice tight.

'It's no secret that Bingham's is facing financial issues. Have you wondered why the corporate sharks haven't started circling yet?'

'Because we're not as weak as you think.'

'Bullshit. It's because of your association with the Mortimer Group. For now anyone with a lick of corporate sense knows not to mess with you because you've partnered with me. That protection erodes the second you give the impression we're not on the same page on this.'

'It's not an impression.'

I pinched the bridge of my nose and exhaled loudly. 'Christ, Wren, you're an intelligent woman. Don't let emotion cloud your judgement. I'm reaching the point where I won't feel inclined to keep the wolves from storming your door.'

'I beg your pardon?' she said sharply.

'Frankly, I'd rather have you begging for something else. But more on that in a while. For now, I want you to think hard about what you're doing.'

'I may be wrong, but I swear you just called yourself my saviour.'

'Take the advice or don't. And just so we're clear, the meeting has been rescheduled for tomorrow morning. If you're not in my office at eight a.m., I'll start playing dirty, too.'

I hung up before I lost it. Or let that sexy voice of hers wreak even more havoc on my self-control.

For the third time, I picked up the phone, this time to my assistant. 'Trish, reschedule the meeting with the advertising team for eight a.m. tomorrow and tell them Miss Bingham will attend. Then send her an email to say I want the boutique contracts I sent her last week reviewed and couriered over by close of business today.'

'Right away, Mr Mortimer.'

I replaced the handset and sat back, the throb of anticipation firing higher.

At five past five it'd turned to irritation. By five-thirty, I was pacing my office, my jaw locked in burning annoyance.

Striding to my desk, I hit the number for my assistant. 'Anything?'

'No, sir.'

'The courier is still there?'

'Yes, sir, he's still waiting at the Bingham Industries reception. Should I tell him to leave?'

'No. He stays there until I say otherwise.'

'Okay. Um… Mr Mortimer?'

I paused. 'Yes?'

'Don't forget you have the Art Foundation's Annual Gala at seven-thirty.'

I smothered a curse. I'd forgotten about my next social obligation while indulging in games with Wren. Thankfully, I'd prepared my speech weeks ago. 'Thanks for the reminder.'

'You're welcome. I've sent your new tux up to the penthouse and arranged for the car to be downstairs at seven.'

About to hang up, I tossed in one last question. 'How many more to go until gala season is over?' I asked, praying she'd say this was the last one.

'Another two, and your cousin Graciela sent an email today about the next Mortimer Quarterly launch party.'

'Thanks.'

After hanging up, I took several deep breaths. I was in danger of letting Wren unbalance me. As patron of several art foundations, I had a duty to attend this event. That it'd slipped my mind so completely made me grimace. The grimace intensified when I realised I'd been all set to track Wren down wherever she'd disappeared to instead of tackling the other time-sensitive deals I had piled up on my desk.

She was becoming an obsession.

Becoming?

I smothered the mocking inner voice and resisted the urge to call Trish again and find out whether the contract was on its way back to me. Instead I picked up a random file.

The knock on the door interrupted my focus an hour later. My pulse leapt but it was only Trish poking her head through the door. 'It's six-thirty, sir. And before you ask, no, the courier is still at Bingham's.'

My lips flattened. 'Tell him to leave. I'll deal with Miss Bingham myself.'

Several ways of dealing with her reeled through my head, all of which were most definitely NSFW.

Three hours later, the speeches were done, I'd handed over a very fat cheque and worked the room twice to ensure all present and future donors were appropriately satisfied with my attention.

Then I called the number I'd been hoping not to use any time soon. It was answered on the first ring. 'I need an address,' I said.

'Of course, sir,' my head of security answered.

Twenty minutes later, I leaned on the doorbell of the ground-floor maisonette in Fulham. Enough lights blazed within to make me comfortable she was home. Still, she kept me cooling my heels for a couple of minutes, during which time I wondered whether she was alone. What I'd interrupted.

'Who is it?' she said, her sexy voice coming through the solid wood.

'You know who it is. I just saw you looking through the security glass. At least you're not reckless about your safety.'

'It's almost midnight, Jasper,' she replied after a short pause.

The possibility that I'd caught her off guard pleased me. Which went to show how pathetic I was in gaining this tiny upper hand. 'Isn't that your favourite time of day to talk business? I'm merely obliging you. Open the door, Wren.'

'What could we possibly have to discuss that can't wait?'

Her sheer gumption drew an incredulous laugh from me. I dragged my fingers through my hair. 'I'm going to throw some names at you. Let me know if you're interested in discussing them. Palmer Jones Plc. Winlake Hotel. Morpheus Tech—'

She yanked the door open, her eyes wide with alarm. 'What did you do?'

'Do I have your attention now?'

Her jaw clenched and alarm morphed into a scowl.

'Invite me in, Wren,' I suggested softly.

Her fingers tightened on the door for a few stubborn seconds before she nudged it open.

I entered, walking down polished floorboards and Venetian wallpapered walls into a large sitting room decorated in white with splashes of warm, earthy colours. Exotic artwork featured majorly and I fought the urge to ask about her taste in art. This wasn't a social call.

'I said what did you do?' she repeated.

I turned to face her, noting for the first time what she was wearing. Her black satin, lace-edged top—clearly a nightie set designed to drive men insane—clung to her full breasts. The shorts skimmed her upper thighs, and even in the lamplight I saw enough bare skin to ramp my arousal through the roof. I dragged my gaze up past her face to the hair piled haphazardly atop her head. So far, I'd only seen it down, but she looked even more delectable in that slightly dishevelled, ready-for-bed state.

I tried to reel myself in. What the hell did she just ask me? Oh, yeah… 'So far? Nothing. But I know they're three of your top five clients.'

Her green eyes snapped with fire. 'So what? You've proved you have a spy in my office. Bravo, Jasper. And what exactly are you accusing me of? I sent your boutique contracts back an hour ago. Did you check your email before you came storming over here?'

'Yes, I did. And while I'll forgive the odd typo or two, which wasn't in my version, what the hell do you think you're playing at, allowing your sub-contractors the option to trigger an extended delivery clause?'

She shrugged. 'What can I say? I'm a generous boss. And that option was in exceptional circumstances only.'

'Which every single one of them will take advantage of! Here's a free tip, since you haven't been CEO for long—soft-balling your contracts like that is a sure-fire route to driving Bingham's out of business. Hell, even Perry knew that.' I mentally kicked myself the moment her brother's name fell from my lips.

She sucked in a quick breath and her lips flattened. 'Don't you dare say his name.'

I exhaled slowly. 'I'm done fucking around with you, Wren. This nonsense stops now or, come tomorrow morning, I'm going after your top five clients. You don't need me to tell you that I have enough personal resources to scupper every deal of yours, or, at the very least, stall it as much as you're trying to stall mine.'

Her fists balled. 'Get the hell out of my flat, Jasper.' The words were low but pithy, her eyes burning with anger and pain.

'I will, as soon as you give me your word that these shenanigans are over.'

Her chin went up. 'Agree to a five-year deal instead of three and I'll think about it.'

I considered it for half a second. 'No. As much as you won't like to hear it, it's for your own good as much as mine.'

'How utterly condescending of you,' she tossed back at me.

I didn't realise I'd been walking towards her until I caught the scent of her shampoo. Until I saw the tiny gold flecks in her eyes reflecting the lamplight.

Her head was tilted up and I couldn't help visually devouring the creamy smoothness of her skin.

'I may not deem it good business sense to renegotiate now but I won't deny you the option of doing so at a later date.'

She rolled her eyes. 'Please, stop trying to wrangle yourself into those sheep's clothes when we both know you and your family are wolves.'

Dear God, but she tested me. 'You know something? I regret not giving you that spanking you begged me for that day in the maze.'

She sucked in a quick, betraying breath. I enjoyed watching her nonplussed expression before her features closed. 'Your memory must be faulty. I never begged you for anything.'

'Not with your mouth. But we both know what you wanted that day.'

Her nostrils fluttered delicately, her eyes growing that shade of moss green that betrayed her. 'You have a vivid, and very flawed, imagination, Jasper.'

'I agree with the vivid part. I'm very happy to demonstrate just how flawed you think my memory is. Right now if you want.' I gestured at the wide sofa behind her and for the tiniest moment heat flared in her eyes.

'I don't want, thank you. Not that. Not any of this.' There was a desperate note in her voice. 'When are you going to accept it and end this?'

End our association? Watch her retreat behind that glass building half a mile away from my office that might as well have been a continent away for all the access I'd have to her? Not if I could bloody well help it. 'You know the terms of the deal as well as I do. So far I have zero incentive to give you what you want. Until such time as that changes...' I shrugged '... I want you to accept that and work with me.'

'I won't. And you'll be wise not to push me.'

'Or what?' I challenged.

'Remember those accolades you generously listed for the benefit of your Moroccan team? It's only a matter of time before I succeed.'

And as absurd as the feeling was, a part of me relished that fight with her. Glancing down at her, I drawled, 'It turns you on to fight with me, doesn't it?'

She snorted. 'Now you're just being plain ridiculous.' But her words lacked the punch of conviction.

'Am I?' I murmured. 'Then why are your nipples hard? Why's your skin flushed? I bet you'd be too proud to admit you're hot and wet right now.'

Her nostrils flared. 'Haven't you learned the futility in attempting reverse psychology with me by now?'

I smiled, enjoying myself for the first time today. 'I don't hear a denial, sweetheart.'

'Don't call me that,' she admonished. 'I'm not your sweet anything.'

'You're right. You're like a stiff shot of Scotch whisky, raging and burning all the way down. Problem is, one taste just triggers a need for another. And another...'

She stiffened. 'I wouldn't know. I don't drink.'

The tastelessness of my analogy hit home a second too late. 'Hell. I'm sorry. That wasn't meant—'

'You're still here, Jasper. Why?'

'Because your nipples are still hard. You're breathless and I know it's not because you're offended. Or annoyed with me. You want another taste, too, don't you, Wren?'

She opened her mouth, but I placed a finger on her lips. 'You can take the high road if you want, but I'm not ashamed to admit that I'm dying to kiss you. Can I?'

One perfectly sculpted eyebrow arched, and, God, even that was beyond sexy. 'You didn't bother to ask last time. Why ask now?'

'Last time was…different. Yet you did invite me to do my worst, as you put it. You needed me to take control. You wanted the fastest route out of your head and I provided it.'

She continued to glare at me. 'You think this makes you some kind of noble knight or something?'

I shrugged. 'Or something. So can I kiss you, Wren? Or do you want me to take the decision out of your hands again, give you the chance to tell me off later and claim it was all a mistake?'

The faintest flush of guilt stained her cheeks. 'You think you know me?'

'Not well enough. Not as much as I'd like. But we'll get around to that soon enough. For now…' I inched closer until mere millimetres separated our lips, until her sweet breath washed over my top lip.

Until I craved her so badly it was a physical pain not to just let the lust lashing us take over. But she was right. I wanted her to see me in a better light. Wanted her to want me without the speed bumps of our corporate skirmishes in the way.

Just when I started to give up hope, her beautiful eyes locked on mine. Still challenging. Still vexed. But also aroused. Interested. Hell, even craving.

Her gaze dropped to my mouth. And she swallowed hard. 'For now…you have one minute. Then I'm throwing you out.'

The words were barely out of her mouth before I was on her, intent on not missing a single second. Memories of kissing and touching her in the maze had haunted me for weeks and *finally* I was reliving them. My fingers in her hair held her steady as I stroked her tongue with mine. Yeah, I was a little forceful, but, hell, she'd driven me steadily insane and I wasn't in the mood to play gentleman.

She squirmed, fighting an internal battle, then, with an impatient moan, she gripped my shoulders. She rose on tiptoe, her movements increasingly demanding as she pressed her body against mine and opened wider for me.

Yes! I grabbed one hip, pressed her against me as I walked us back towards her sofa. Seconds later, she was on her back and I was on top of her, devouring her for all I was worth.

Sweet Jesus, she tasted even more sublime. Just as brazen with her needs as in the maze, she spread her thighs, accommodating me as I palmed one breast and toyed with her nipple. Her hips undulating, seeking the iron rod of my cock. We met, strained and groaned at the exquisite intensity of it. In slow, torturous rhythm, we writhed against one another, while the kiss turned hotter, wetter, simulating everything I wanted to do to her, and vice versa.

But through it all, I was keenly aware of the seconds ticking down, aware she could kick me out at any moment.

So I chose to play dirty.

On the next roll of her hips, I pressed hard against her, holding my cock tight against her satin-covered pussy, urging her to feel what I could do for her. What we could do to each other.

I bit back a smile when an involuntary spasm shuddered through her body. 'Let's renegotiate,' I rasped against her lips. 'One minute isn't going to cut it.'

She laughed a little unkindly, even while her fingers dug painfully into my biceps to hold me in place. Why did I love that she wasn't afraid to show me her fire? 'Poor Jasper.'

I growled. 'Give me ten minutes.' It was nowhere near enough for what I craved to do but it was a starting point.

She raised her head a fraction and bit my lower lip, making me shudder. 'No.'

'Christ, Wren. You're a ballbreaker, you know that?'

She stiffened slightly but didn't pull back. 'Five,' she countered after another round of furious kissing.

I yanked down one strap of her nightie top as she eagerly unbuttoned my shirt. Her fingers delved down to caress my chest and abs as I swooped onto one eager nipple. She hissed her appreciation and I feasted, groaning at her silken skin, the mouth-watering taste of her. Her back arched, offering more of herself.

'God, you're beautiful,' I rasped. 'Maddening but breathtaking.'

Against my temple, I felt her faint smile as she raked demanding fingers through my hair. Then, taking my head between her hands, she redirected me to her neglected breast. I teased, tortured and suckled until she was a glorious rose-pink. Only then did I trail one hand down, beneath the elastic of her shorts.

The brazen discovery nearly blew my head clean off. 'You answer your front door not wearing panties, sweetheart?'

'My home, my rules.'

I smiled, deciding to enjoy this particular gift before it was taken away. Spearing her with my gaze, I slid my hand lower, down over that silken strip of hair until I encountered hot, slippery flesh.

'God,' I muttered, a red haze passing over my vision. 'You're so wet.'

Expecting a smart retort, I watched as she sucked in a slow breath, her eyes not leaving mine as she chased my touch. 'Yes, I am. And your five minutes are almost up,' she said a little unsteadily.

'I'm aware, sweetheart.' I pressed my middle finger inside her and her hips jerked, her inner muscles clinging as she whimpered. 'Thing is, do I use that time for you or shall I be selfish and use it all for me?'

Her eyes widened a touch but she remained still, her hands gripping me tight. I was sure she wasn't aware of how her nails dug into me, and I bit back another smile.

Who the hell was I bluffing? I was going to use this for her. When I got around to fucking Wren, I intended to be inside her longer than whatever seconds I had left in this ridiculous game.

Bending low, I flicked my tongue over one ripe nipple as I speared her with my fingers. Her head started to roll, those insane sounds erupting from her throat again. I squeezed my eyes shut to regain some control.

But soon, much too soon, I was at that point of ravening lust, where my mind threatened to cease to function. She did this to me. Every single time. Even before we'd ever had a proper conversation, she'd pulled at me on some level. First with her brilliant mind and now, with her glorious body. The way it softened and moulded beneath my hands, the way she fought the groan tearing through her before finally letting it free to vibrate its feminine power through her body. The way those hips rolled so perfectly into mine.

Every. Single. Time.

But…hold on a sec. How long was I going to keep buckling? Sure, I might have started this, hell, *begged* for this, but she'd ended up dictating the terms anyway.

Because you're weak…

I gritted my teeth against Hugh Mortimer's damning words. Against the growing din of the clock counting down while I was getting lost in my own head. Against the even dirtier game I suspected I had to play if I was going to win this thing. Win her around.

Slowly, I raised my head. 'Wren.'

She ignored me, nibbling on my jaw before sinking her white teeth into my throat. I jerked back before I lost complete control.

'Wren. Stop.'

CHAPTER FIVE

I'VE ALWAYS HATED my name, ever since Perry let slip when I was nine that my father had given it to me as a cruel joke. George Bingham had possessed a rather dark sense of humour. Humour he'd often directed towards me in the rare times I was allowed in his vicinity.

He'd chosen a name with no softness to it, apparently, because he didn't want a soft child. Particularly, he hadn't wanted a daughter. So in his bitter humour and disappointment, he'd named me Wren. Nondescript. Forgettable. All hard angles and far too close to *wrench* for my liking. At school I'd been teased about it. *Wren the Wraith* because of my thinness, my paleness and my height. Coupled with the oppressive cloaks we'd been required to wear at my equally oppressive Hampshire boarding school, the name had fitted all too well.

But now, hearing it groaned from the depths of Jasper's arousal, it sounded…different. Not ordinary. Definitely lusty. Erotic and potent. A name uttered as if he couldn't help himself. As if he had to say it…or die.

Even as I dismissed my thoughts as a stupid flight of fancy, I leaned into him, silently pleading for him to groan it again, to fan the flames of my own arousal to that mindless place he'd taken me that chilly evening in my family's maze.

No, not back to that place.

I wanted a new place. One I could claim wholly for myself, without the spectre of my judgemental family looming over me.

As much as I hadn't wanted to let him into my personal space, now that I had him here, it wasn't so bad. My sofa would be a good starting point. Maybe eventually my bed…if we could drag ourselves there—

Except…he was already pulling away.

Far too quickly, painful reality rushed back in. Dear God, I was literally cavorting with the enemy. And even worse, he was about to leave me hanging moments away from another mind-shambling orgasm. Dazed and more than a little confused, I glanced down at myself, sprawled out with my breasts on display and my shorts pulled up tight enough to frame my crotch, highlighting the need coursing through me.

Somehow my fingers were caught in his and even though he'd rejected me, he still held on to me. Which made my exposed state even more humiliating.

I yanked myself out of his hold, face flaming as I pulled up the straps of my top until my shamefully erect nipples were covered. Jasper was still wedged between my thighs and despite his withdrawal, the outline of his erection pressed behind his fly. The sight of it reminded me of what I'd been grinding up against moments ago. His glorious thickness, the very masculine way he rolled his hips. The promise of how he would feel deep inside me…

Hunger and frustration threatened to overshadow my humiliation. But the very thought that I was considering, even for a millisecond, talking him into finishing what he'd started forced me to locate my elusive outrage.

'Can you get off me, please?'

His lips firmed. 'Wren, we need to—'

'Now, please,' I interjected, infusing my voice with necessary ice.

For several seconds, his hazel eyes narrowed, eyes that seemed to see beneath my skin, examining me intently before, thankfully, he rose from the sofa.

He crossed to the window and stared out onto the street. Whether to give me time to compose myself or because he needed a minute himself, I didn't question as I jumped up. I yanked my passion-tousled hair out of the band securing it, letting the strands fall around my shoulders and partly obscure my face in the vain hope of a shield. I contemplated going to retrieve my dressing gown out of my room and decided against the revealing move. The last thing I wanted was to lose further ground to Jasper Mortimer.

I sucked in a deep breath, exhaling slowly as he turned to face me. His stark hunger was throttled back and the eyes that stared at me held only iron resolution.

'Believe it or not, that wasn't how I wanted this to go,' he rasped.

Something fairly substantial lurched with disappointment inside me. 'And by this you mean what exactly? Storming into my flat or that half-baked seduction on my sofa?'

For some reason, my snippiness amused him. I hated myself a little for liking his smile. 'I didn't storm in and I may have stopped short of the full five minutes but there was nothing half-baked about it, sweetheart.'

Again, something lurched. It was the *sweetheart* I'd outwardly objected to but secretly didn't...hate. While I wasn't about to examine why, I knew it had something to do with the lack of softness and warmth in my life, both in childhood and now. And yes, I feared for my own gullibility at being taken in by a common term of endearment.

I crossed my arms over my chest, stingingly aware my erogenous zones were still on fire and one particular area was announcing it to the world.

'Whatever. You're going to use those extra minutes to leave, aren't you?' I said, striving for boredom.

This time his whole face hardened. 'Not until we've cleared up a few important things.'

'And what would those be?'

'You'll find out in the morning. In the meantime, fix the contract. Bring it with you tomorrow.'

I chose a silent glare as my answer.

He crossed the room to where I stood, gazed down at me long and contemplatively enough to make me tense against the urge to fidget.

'We both know you're better than this, Wren,' he murmured. 'There's absolutely no shame in proving me right. And who knows? You might get a nice surprise when you turn up tomorrow.'

When…not *if.* His confidence would've been insulting had I not spent the last two weeks and most of today confirming what I knew in my gut but hadn't been ready to admit.

I held my breath as he raised his hand, trailed his finger from my jaw to the lower lip that still tingled with the need to repeat that kiss. His eyes burned hot and heavy into mine for another moment before, gritting his teeth, he walked out of my living room.

A moment later, I heard the door close behind him. A breath shuddered out of me. I didn't exactly call it relief because that knot of hunger was still lodged in my belly, intent on reminding me how long it'd been since I'd had good sex. Or any kind of sex, for that matter.

It was only when I realised I was listening out for the sounds of his car leaving my quiet street that I sank onto the sofa. Head buried in my hands, I tried to breathe through confusion and need. Through all the reasons I'd allowed Jasper into my personal sanctuary. I wasn't melodramatic enough to fear that I'd never sit on my sofa without imagining him there wreaking sweet havoc on my body, but I suspected the experience wouldn't be easily dismissed.

Growling with impatience and frustration, I jumped up again, resolutely keeping my gaze averted from the wide expanse of the sofa as I left the room. Half an hour later, I conceded that I wouldn't get to sleep without expelling the sexual energy coursing through my blood.

As I reached for my vibrator, I cursed Jasper Mortimer loudly and succinctly. Then ruthlessly used his image to find a quick, semi-satisfactory but thankfully mind-numbing release.

I stepped out of the cab and paused on the pavement, tilting my head up to stare at the majesty that was Mortimer Towers. During my previous visits I'd used the barrier of righteous indignation to ignore its grandeur and, while I couldn't predict what would happen in the next hour, I instinctively felt today was…different. That it wouldn't be so bad to admit the masterpiece building that had won a clutch of accolades was worthy of them.

Or perhaps it was because I'd accepted on some level that the man I was dealing with was a lot more powerful than I'd given him credit for, and that power could irreversibly impact Bingham's.

Certainly, my visit to my company's archive department yesterday had uncovered the worst of my fears. Perry had been playing fast and loose with several contracts and had 'misplaced' important documents that could have severe repercussions on our business relationships.

That shocking discovery was the reason I'd buried myself in the basement of Bingham's till late last night. I was still staggered by how much Perry had been allowed to get away with by the board.

But truly, when it came right down to it, I wasn't surprised. The board was made up of the extended Bingham relatives and cronies who'd trusted Perry simply because he was male, and a Bingham. There'd been little to zero oversight and no one had dared to question his way of doing business. Just as long as he'd managed to keep the company just above the red and they collected their fat bonuses come Christmas.

Which reminded me…no Christmas bonuses this year.

I sucked in a deep breath, lowering my gaze to the glass doors that led into Jasper's domain. After a restless night that my vibrator had done very little to cure, I'd given up on sleep at five o'clock. The boutique contract was fixed and an email sent to the subcontractors apologising and withdrawing the clause I'd inserted in the last-chance hope that it would frustrate Jasper into releasing me from the contract.

We both know you're better than this...

Perhaps more than anything else that had happened in my flat last night, those words had made the most impact. Because Jasper was right.

Despite my attempts to aggravate him into dropping this deal, a significant part of me had cringed at the depths I was sinking to; the mockery I was making of my own hard-won achievements.

I hadn't quite decided what the new course of action in fighting him would be but I most certainly wasn't going to lie down and let him walk all over me.

Heat caressed my neck and flowed up into my face at the sexual connotation of my thoughts. I'd been more than prepared for him to do exactly that on my sofa last night. Firming my lips, I attempted to push the memory out of my head as I strode towards the lift.

His receptionist greeted me when I stepped out on his floor.

'Good morning, Miss Bingham. Mr Mortimer is waiting for you in conference room six. He says you're to go straight through.'

I told myself my escalating heartbeat was because I was irritated that he'd assumed I would turn up this morning. Not because I wanted to see him again. Not because the smell of his aftershave on my skin and the rasp of his stubble burn on my inner thighs had made me groan into my pillow more than once last night.

And most definitely not because he knew that two of the three company names he'd thrown at me last night were threatening to pull out of their deals with us.

Struggling to empty my mind of the challenges that awaited me back at Bingham Industries, I took a few calming breaths. I'd need optimal mental dexterity to survive this meeting with Jasper.

Running a hand over my stylish skirt suit, I strode down the wide hallway, pinning a cool, professional smile on my face as I passed his executives. I was absolutely not going to wonder how many of them had seen my trench-coat-and-promiscuous-heels performance. I'd been forced into a corner, and doing something was better than doing nothing and letting Jasper win.

What if it was all for nothing?

I mentally shrugged, gritting my teeth when I noticed that conference room six was the last one down a long hallway. Had Jasper orchestrated this walk of shame so his employees would see me? Was he that petty?

A flash of anger whipped through me, threatening to wipe away my smile. I fought to keep it in place as I pushed the door open.

He stood at a long cabinet that bordered the far wall, helping himself to a cup of the same java blend his secretary had offered me that first visit.

As I breathed in that mouth-watering hit of caffeine and watched the ripple of broad shoulder muscles encased in another immaculate suit, I wondered whether I would associate this particular brand of coffee with him for ever.

He turned just then, a small smile playing around his lips as his gaze tracked me from head to toe and back again. As he noted my attire his smile widened, what looked dangerously like triumph gleaming in his eyes.

I forced my gaze away, partly because I didn't want to confirm it and partly because in the morning light, with the sun streaming in, he looked far too delicious for my sanity. Reminded me far too vividly of how thoroughly I'd explored his body last night.

How I craved more?

'Can I get you anything? Coffee? I've had breakfast laid out for us if you're hungry.'

I shook my head. 'I'll take the coffee, but I don't want any breakfast. I've already eaten.' He didn't need to know it had only been a couple of bites of toast, hurriedly wolfed down because I'd got caught up in another woefully mismanaged Bingham file and almost missed leaving on time to get here for his eight o'clock deadline.

He nodded and poured a second cup, then added a dash of cream. When he reached me, he stared at me for a handful of seconds before holding out the cup. 'Good morning, Wren. You ready to begin?'

His voice was a low rumble that travelled through me, reminding me how his lips had felt trailing the sensitive skin of my neck. The sweet abrasion of his stubble against my breast. The filthy decadence of his tongue capturing and swirling around my nipple.

I accepted the cup without answering. Saying yes would be deemed surrender and I couldn't give in, not until I'd exhausted every avenue. Because while I could rightly claim that Perry had been the one to agree to this deal, it wouldn't stop another confrontation with my board, another round of questioning my decision and intentions. Another call from my mother under the guise of checking in on me but really to lament about the path I was taking.

Shaking my head, I approached where the papers were laid out.

'Wren?'

Refocusing on him as he joined me, I glanced at him. His expression was just as resolute as last night, but his eyes held the gentleness that conveyed understanding of my predicament. My guts tightened against the need to sink into that gentle look. It was the opposite of what I needed.

I set down my briefcase and coffee and pulled out a chair. 'I have a long day ahead. Shall we get on with it?' I said crisply.

His gentle expression evaporated, and his face hardened but he joined me at the table, pulling out the chair for himself before settling into it.

'I checked with the subcontractors this morning. Looks like this morning you withdrew your magnanimous offers?'

I wasn't going to give him the satisfaction of admitting my impetuous mistake. 'Is that a question?'

He smiled. 'Just an observation. And an offer of thanks for one less pain in my arse.'

I'd gripped that taut arse last night. Heat tunnelled through me and I moved my gaze to the papers in front of me. 'Sure. Shall we move on to the next item on the agenda?'

He nodded, then took a sip of coffee.

I tried not to let my gaze drop to his lips. I really did. But a mere eight hours ago those lips were devouring mine, and, as much as I hated to concede it, he was one hell of a kisser. Combined with the knowledge of how much sweet havoc he could wreak with those lips between my legs, surely I could forgive myself for five seconds of indulgence?

'Do you need a minute, Wren?' he asked, a thread of amusement in his voice.

My gaze shot up to meet his and he was smiling knowingly. Without breaking eye contact, he nudged the agenda sheet towards me. 'I went to the trouble of printing it out in case you didn't check your emails this morning. So we can be on the same page, as it were,' he added with a definite smirk.

I picked up the paper and quickly scrutinised it. There were twelve items on the list, mostly spelling out in black and white the tasks I was supposed to perform. I already knew the hours I was supposed to devote to the project but one item in particular made me glance up sharply.

'You expect me to go to dinner with you on Wednesday?'

He nodded briskly. 'A tequila producer I've had my eye on for a while is in town this week. He has a new specialised brand coming out around the time we open the first hotel. I want you with me because technically this should have been your job but I'm hoping you'll help me convince him to supply exclusively to us for at least three months before he rolls it out to the general market.'

I frowned. 'I already had a supplier lined up for you.'

'Did you?'

The tight edge to his question made me pause for a second before answering. 'Yes, I did.'

'That's curious. Because I'm sure there's an email in my inbox telling me we'd lost our potential liquor supplier due to non-communication with Bingham Industries.'

The throb of shame was more powerful this time. I tried to hide it by taking a sip of my own coffee. Slightly more composed, I set the cup down. 'I've had lot on my plate, as you know. This project with you isn't the only thing occupying my time.'

He stared at me for another stretch of time before he nodded. 'I'm not too fussed about losing that supplier, to be honest. His product was great but not spectacular. This new one promises to be rather exceptional. That's why I don't want to lose it. So, you'll come with me on Wednesday, yes?' he pressed.

A business dinner with him to secure a supplier wasn't a complete concession. I'd been in this business long enough to know contractors came and went for any number of reasons. Even if Bingham Industries managed to pull out of the contract, I could at least help Jasper secure this small part of his project.

I shrugged. 'Sure, I can do dinner. What time do you want me?'

His eyes darkened. 'I'll pick you up at seven at your place,' he said, his voice deep and raspy.

It would've been far more professional to arrange to meet him at the restaurant. And yet, I found myself answering, 'Okay.'

His smile grew warmer, his gaze several degrees hotter as it dragged over my face to rest on my mouth. Time stretched taut and charged with far too much sexual intensity, before he stared down at the paper. 'What's next?'

We worked through the next few items, and with each one I reassured myself that nothing was set in concrete. Sooner or later, once Jasper realised the futility of a Mortimer-Bingham deal, replacing me would be a simple matter of snapping his fingers.

And if he didn't?

I dismissed the question. Just as I attempted to

suppress the quiet excitement that was building inside me as we went down the list.

My head snapped up as Jasper abruptly rose. 'More coffee?'

A small bolt of surprise went through me as I realised I'd finished mine. I nodded as he walked over to the buffet cabinet, glancing at me over his shoulder. 'Are you sure I can't get you anything?'

I was about to refuse, but my gaze went to the clock and I noticed we'd been working for an hour. As if on cue, my stomach rumbled. It wasn't enough to get his attention but I knew it would eventually if I carried on working without eating.

Setting my pen down, I rose, rounded the conference table and joined him. Trays of warm, mouth-watering pastries were set out next to platters of fruit, juice carafes and assorted condiments.

Jasper grabbed two plates and handed me one.

Our fingers brushed as I took it from him. He heard my sharp intake of breath and stilled, staring down at me.

For several, electrifying seconds, we stayed frozen.

Then, as if pulled by invisible strings, I swayed towards him. At the very last moment, I caught myself, veering away towards the food.

Dear God, what is wrong with me?

He'd gone down on me in the maze and, somehow, I'd managed to work on and off with him for two weeks, but one little tumble on my sofa last night and my concentration was shot to hell?

A little bewildered, I randomly selected food while desperately attempting to downplay how badly Jasper affected me. How badly I wanted to lean into that strong column of his neck, breathe in the aftershave that had so tantalised me last night.

Of course he'd put the brakes on then, though. Which meant, like me, he probably didn't think it was a good idea—

My thoughts stumbled to a halt when he laughed. 'That's the spirit. I love a woman with a healthy appetite.'

I blinked, then glanced down at my plate. My very full, very heaped plate of food. I cringed, aware of the flush creeping up my cheeks.

Then his words registered. Who was the last woman with a good appetite who'd occupied his attention? Did he have a girlfriend? It suddenly struck me that we'd had two sexual encounters without knowing the basics about each other. An uneasy, wholly unwelcome sensation tightened my chest. Surely, he wouldn't do the things he'd done to me if was seeing another woman?

He's a Mortimer, isn't he?

The twisting sensation inside me intensified.

'I guess you were pretty hungry, after all?' Jasper continued.

I dragged my focus from his imaginary harem to the embarrassment of my heaped plate. 'God, there's enough to feed an army here. I don't need all of this. Not really. I was just…'

Just wondering who else you were going down on when you weren't turning me inside out with your tongue…

As I shook my head free of the thought, he stepped closer. 'Here, I'll take a couple of those off your hands if you want.'

I watched, a little annoyed for being so easily distracted by him as he transferred a bagel and croissant from my plate to his. He left far more than I needed on my plate but somehow I didn't protest as his free hand landed in the small of my back, scrambling my brain as he guided me back to the table. 'Come on, let's get back to it,' he said.

In between watching him take healthy bites out of his food and attacking the next item on the agenda, I demolished several pastries, mentally promising myself another twenty minutes on the treadmill at my next gym session.

I didn't object when he returned to the buffet table and brought back a bowl of fruit, only squirmed stealthily in my chair as I watched him toss a grape into his mouth.

God, what the hell was so fascinating about watching this man eat? Whatever it was, I couldn't stop myself from watching him swallow, the movement of his Adam's apple curiously erotic enough to shoot arrows of desire into my pelvis.

'Are we done?' I asked, more out of desperation than anything else.

'More or less,' he replied.

'What else is there?'

For the longest time, he didn't reply. When he reacted, it was to reach into the fruit bowl and pluck out a ripe, juicy strawberry. Then he rolled his chair around the table, breaching the gap between us. 'There's something else I want to talk about.'

Something dark and decadent in his voice made my thighs tingle, my breath rush out in a lustful little pant. 'Oh?'

'I feel the need to apologise for the way I left things last night.'

The reminder reduced the tingles but didn't demolish them altogether. 'You came to deliver a message and I received it loud and clear.'

'I'm not talking about business, and you know it.'

'Do I?'

He leaned forward, held the fruit against my bottom lip then trailed it lazily from side to side. 'I left you hanging,' he murmured throatily. 'I'm not in the habit of doing that.'

Curiously compelled, I licked the fruit before answering, 'I'm a big girl, Jasper. I can take it.'

His nostrils flared in arousal. 'Not if you don't have to.'

I sucked in a breath, the scent of the strawberry and his aftershave a potent mix that rendered me strangely breathless. 'You don't owe me anything…'

'Okay. But you still owe me one minute, possibly two.' He pressed the fruit harder against my mouth. 'Open,' he instructed gruffly.

My lips parted and I took the fruit. His gaze dropped to my mouth as I held it between my lips for a moment then bit into it. Sticky juice trickled down one corner of my mouth. His gaze latched on to it for one tight little second before, groaning, he lunged forward.

He devoured half of the fruit as he sealed his lips to mine.

As if a switch had been thrown, feverish electricity consumed us as we consumed each other. He rose, his urgent hands landing on my waist to yank my body into his. My hands flew up his broad shoulders, explored for mere seconds before spiking into his hair.

Jasper's tongue delved into my mouth, licking away the last of the juices before tangling with mine. Desire shot through me, lifted me onto my tiptoes as I strained against him. Wanting more.

My vibrator last night had come nowhere close to satisfying the need clamouring anew inside me. The thought that Jasper was equally ravenous for me thrilled my blood as he deepened the kiss.

The faint sound of a ringing phone momentarily reminded me of where we were, the possibility that someone could walk in on us at any moment.

With a monumental effort, I broke the kiss and

laid my hand on his chest as I fought to catch my breath. 'Jasper, I…the door…'

Without letting go of me, he walked us a few steps to the middle of the conference table and snatched up a small remote. Aiming it at the door, he clicked a button and I heard the distinct sound of it locking.

Burnished eyes pinned me where I stood. 'No one will disturb or hear us now. The room's sound-proofed.'

My breath shuddered out, my fingers tightening on his nape even as I questioned my sanity. 'Jasper…'

He dropped his lips to my jaw, trailing little erotic bites before he caught my earlobe between his teeth. 'I regret not making you come last night. I sure as hell regret missing the chance to be inside you, even if it was only for one minute.'

My laugh emerged shakily. 'You're assuming I would've let you.'

Just like last night, his lips explored the pulse in my neck. Shivering in delight, I angled my head, granting him access.

'My negotiating skills are exceptional, Wren. I'm sure we would've come to some agreement had I stayed. But no matter. I have a new proposition for you. One I'm sure will satisfy us both.'

My arsenal was depleted. I had very little to fight him with. But he didn't need to know that.

'What is this proposition?' I asked, my in-sides dipping alarmingly at how much I wanted to know. How much I hoped it was something I could agree to.

Yeah, my head definitely needed examining.

He held on to me but eased his torso away from mine. 'You're brilliant and sexy. You've driven me insane thus far but I don't think I've hidden the fact that I want you. Hell, at this point it goes beyond want.' His eyes burned into mine as he inhaled slowly.

My throat dried at the raw, potent need in his voice. A tremble commenced inside my belly as he continued.

'Don't think I haven't noticed you still haven't given me a clear-cut answer as to whether you intend to work with me or not. But I have a way I think we can co-exist for the immediate future. A way that might make working with me a little more bearable?'

I didn't think there was any way forward that wouldn't incite my family's disapproval but I held back from mentioning it. Somehow, discussing family feuds in this moment felt…wrong. 'I'm listening,' I said.

He dropped his forehead to mine. 'You know I'm dying to fuck you. And I know you're not completely immune to reciprocating.'

I couldn't deny it. 'I think you got your answer last night.'

He gave a lopsided smile. 'Even though you also invited me to leave several times?'

I raised an eyebrow. 'You annoyed me. And I'm complicated.'

'Well, maybe this is one thing we can agree on. I'm great at giving you orgasms, despite withholding one last night.'

A husky laugh left my throat. 'Are you seriously tooting your own horn?'

He shrugged, an arrogant gesture that was so completely natural I wouldn't have been surprised if he'd been born with it. One hand trailed up from my waist to rest beneath my chin. His thumb rubbed my lower lip and I felt his erection jerk against my belly. Heat arrowed between my legs, making my core wet and needy as I waited for him to elaborate.

'Okay, here's the deal. For every six hours you devote to this deal, you get an orgasm.'

My mouth sagged open. 'I…what?'

His head dropped and delivered a hard, quick kiss before drawing back. Hazel eyes stayed on mine, his easy manner belied by the fact that every word out of his mouth held fierce determination, a promise to deliver on what he was offering. 'I think it's a better way for us to relieve our frustrations, if you like. Why scream with anger when you can scream with pleasure?'

I refused to examine why I wasn't completely outraged, why, contrary to every scrap of common sense I possessed, I was held rapt and completely aroused by his proposition. 'Let me get this straight. You want to buy my cooperation with orgasms?'

That wicked little smile tilted one corner of his mouth again. 'I want us to make love, not war,' he offered.

I raised an eyebrow. 'Wow, are you sure you're not on some two-for-one deal on clichés?'

His fingers dug into my waist to pull me closer still, ensuring I felt his hard cock against my belly. I shuddered, unable to help but push back, revelling in the power and promise of him. I was racked with mounting need; my gaze darted to the shiny expanse of the conference table.

Jasper followed my gaze and laughed. 'We can christen our new agreement right there, if you want, sweetheart.'

I swallowed, unable to believe that I was contemplating this absurdity. The excuse was that I'd arrived here with very little option but to continue to work with Jasper for the time being. Loyalty to my family dictated that the prize of working with the Mortimer Group was forbidden to me as a personal career choice, but while I was contract-bound to work with him, was it wrong to help myself to the cherry on top when he was freely offering it?

Between the mess Perry had left the company in and pressure from my mother, I didn't plan on dating anyone soon. Jasper's proposition ensured that we could work relatively friction-free, while enjoying a side benefit we both wanted.

The promise of sex lit a fuse in my blood. Before I got completely carried away with it, the question that'd niggled at me for the last hour rose again. 'Is this suggestion of yours inconveniencing anyone else?'

His brow knotted. 'What?'

'Are you dating anyone, Jasper?'

His frown cleared but his eyes remained mildly accusing. 'I'm not sure how to interpret you believing I would give you orgasms while seeing another woman.'

I tried to stop the wild relief flowing through me. 'Is that a no, you're not seeing anyone else?'

'It's a no,' he confirmed with gritted teeth. 'You may not have a very high opinion of me, but I do have some standards, sweetheart.'

His censure shamed me a little, but I brushed it away.

'I'm waiting for an answer, Wren. You want me, I want you. Are we going to do this, or not?' he pressed.

He was still doing that thing with his hips that drove me insane. Just as it had last night. That knot of need I thought I'd dampened with my vibrator came roaring back, stronger than before. The thought of walking out of here nursing that ache suddenly became unthinkable. Unbearable.

Keeping my gaze on his, I reached between us and unbuttoned my jacket. Slowly, I shrugged out of it, then tossed it on the nearest chair.

Jasper followed the action with eyes ablaze.

Next, I reached for his tie, loosening it before snapping it free of his collar. He swallowed, and I smiled.

Leaning forward and trailing my lips up to his throat, I whispered in his ear, 'I accept your proposal, Jasper. And I'd very much like to christen your conference table. Now, please.'

He hoisted me up as if I weighed nothing, and between one frenzied heartbeat and the next I was laid out flat on his conference table and he was staring down at me with eyes that promised mind-altering passion.

CHAPTER SIX

I'D CHOSEN MY attire specially today because I'd needed the confidence boost; and because I'd accepted that the way I'd been handling things the past two weeks needed to change.

And perhaps—okay, extremely possibly—I'd also chosen my underwear because, deep down in a place I didn't want to examine too closely, I'd hoped *this* would happen.

Between frenzied kisses and the need to explore every inch of his sleekly muscled body, I wasn't certain which one of us undid my silk blouse. But I was certain which one stopped in their tracks, mouth hanging open at the sight of the sea-green lace bra I wore beneath it.

I hid a pleased smile as Jasper growled beneath his breath, his eyes rapt on my chest.

My lingerie was the indecently expensive kind, concocted of gossamer-thin scraps of lace, strings and silk, bought on a slightly tipsy whim while late-night online shopping, then shoved deep into the underwear drawer with much chagrin after the hangover wore off and the package arrived on my doorstep.

But in this moment, I patted myself on the back as Jasper's hands hovered reverently over my breasts, as if he wasn't sure whether to worship me or devour me.

'Jesus Christ, Wren. You're exquisite,' he breathed, his eyes darting from my chest to my face and back again.

'Not too exquisite to touch, I hope?'

He started to reach for me, then paused. 'Tell me you weren't wearing this underneath that damned trench coat when you came into my building two weeks ago?'

'Why would I want to stop torturing you by satisfying your curiosity?'

He raised an eyebrow, even while his frantic gaze dropped to latch onto my peaking nipples. 'Because we just agreed to call a truce?'

Trailing my finger down over the firm, tanned skin covering his clavicle, I decided to give a little. 'I wasn't wearing this exact same set, no. Now, are you going to unwrap me or make me wait?' I demanded softly.

With effortless ease, he divested me of my blouse. It landed on the floor, but I didn't care. Because my busy fingers had done some unwrapping of their own, exposing the most perfect set of abs I'd seen outside a magazine. I touched his skin, almost moaned at how warm and firm and utterly delicious he was. About to put my mouth where my hands had been, I whimpered in protest as Jasper pushed me back firmly.

Reading his intent, I relaxed, reclining on the table as he stepped back, took me in, then groaned. 'I'll never be able to take a meeting in this room without picturing you like this.'

'You'll get through it somehow, I'm sure.' I arched my back, the cool surface momentarily chilling my skin; making my nipples harder. He saw the reaction and charged forward with another animalistic snarl.

'I don't like being the only one without a shirt on, Jasper.'

Cracking a taut smile, he jerked off his jacket and tossed it away. A crook of my finger and he was leaning over me. Strong hands framed my hips, trailed up my ribcage as I attacked his remaining shirt buttons. The moment I bared his chiselled torso, I dragged my fingernails over his taut, smooth skin.

'Fuck, that feels good,' he groaned, his gaze latching on to the lace doing a very poor job of hiding my arousal from him. 'As much as I'm dying to get you naked, I don't want to risk ripping anything off… this time. We both need to walk out of here with as many of our clothes intact as possible.' He cupped my lace-clad breasts, squeezing with an urgency that telegraphed his need. 'Help me out?' he requested hoarsely.

I wanted to tell him to rip it off, if only for the

novelty of experiencing such raw passion for the first time in my life. But I bit my tongue. There were other ways to achieve the mindless state his eyes promised. Trailing my fingers back up his torso to his neck, I dropped my other hand to the first strap and slowly lowered it. 'Like this?'

His head jerked in a nod. 'More,' he commanded.

I tugged down the strap another fraction, bearing the top of my breast and exposing the smallest hint of a nipple.

'More, Wren. More. Show me those perfect breasts I tasted last night.'

'Hmm, how do I know you're not going to leave me hanging again?' I teased.

A dash of hectic colour highlighted his cheekbones. He nudged my hips to the edge of the table, until there was no mistaking his hard, potent ridge. 'I promise, this time I'm not stopping until every inch of my cock is buried inside you. Now, please take that damn bra off before I rip it off with my teeth.'

A shiver coursed through me, pooling heat between my thighs. I felt myself getting wetter and sucked in a deep breath to compose my erratic heartbeat. I was dying for him to take me, and, though I suspected this would be more memorable than my previous sexual encounters, I still wanted him to work for it. My instincts warned me that giving in too easily to Jasper Mortimer was the absolute wrong tactic to take.

With a saucy little smile, I abandoned the bra and

reached for the hem of my skirt. He watched me, his face tightening with every passing second as I nudged the material up my thighs until my panties were exposed. A projection in my mind's eyes of how I looked—semi-naked and sprawled out, open to his gaze—sent a hot rush through me, followed swiftly by a pulse of feminine power as I caught his expression. He liked this. Hell, he more than liked it. In a fight where it seemed I was losing at every turn, it felt good to reclaim some ground.

'Take my panties off, Jasper,' I instructed, my voice a husky mess. 'The bra stays on.'

He didn't need a second bidding.

He dragged my panties off with a smooth move that made my heart miss several beats. And in the flip of a switch, I sensed a shift in the power balance. Firm hands grasped my thighs, parted them boldly so he could stare down at my damp flesh. A deep breath expanded his chest as he passed his thumb over my engorged clit. My whole body jerked, a spasm of pleasure rippling through me at that smallest touch.

Lust-dark eyes darted to my face and then back to my core. 'I'm going to enjoy fucking you, Wren,' he declared with gruff anticipation.

His dirty words made me hotter; more impatient. I tried to grasp him with my thighs, nudge him closer, to get this show on the road. Jasper merely smiled, put his thumb to his lips and decadently sucked off my wetness as he looked into my eyes.

'You want it hard or slow?'

Again, I felt my face flaming, even as excitement fluttered in my belly. No other man had ever asked me that. And how pathetic was that? Or had I not been interested enough before to vocalise my own needs?

'Do I have to choose? Can't I have both?'

His smile widened, the confident stamp of a man who knew how to wield his sexual prowess. 'You can have whatever you want, sweetheart.'

I swallowed at his thick promise; watched him reach into his back pocket for his wallet. He plucked out a condom, tore it open and gifted me another erotic sight of watching him slowly lower his zip.

I already knew he was thick and long, but I wasn't quite prepared for the beautiful sculpture of Jasper's cock or the pleasure I took in watching him glide on the condom.

Then he was reaching for my thighs, dragging me even closer to the edge of the table. Breathing harshly, he teased his length over my hot, wet core without entering me, his eyes on my face as he tormented me.

Wrapping his hands around my waist, he tilted his hips in one smooth movement and thrust deep inside me. A curious little sound left my throat, a cross between a muted scream and sheer delight at how deeply, completely he filled me. Then for the longest time he held still, his eyes shut and jaw locked tight.

'Again, please,' I gasped.

Exhaling, he withdrew, slowly…and repeated

the penetration. Fiery desire shot up my spine, my hands scrambling for purchase on the table. 'Oh, God, again. Please,' I begged.

He gave a low, ragged laugh and started to thrust in earnest. My breath shortened, panted as he fell into a steady, mind-bending rhythm. My eyes drifted closed as pleasure collected deep in my pelvis but after a moment, I prised them open, the need to watch Jasper too overwhelming to deny.

And he was a glorious sight. His hooded gaze was rapt on my face, a lock of hair draped over his forehead as he shuttled in and out of me. Dear God, he was beautiful. An animal. One concentrated fully on me. The fierce light in his eyes said he would deliver on every single sexual promise he'd made.

'Tell me more, Wren,' he urged thickly. 'I want to hear everything you're feeling.'

I wasn't sure why that demand rattled something inside me. When was the last time anyone had asked me what I felt? All my life I'd been subjected to what everyone believed was good for me without considering my input. I knew this was just sex, that he'd set himself a goal he was determined to achieve, but something inside me still lurched as I scrambled around for adequate words to describe this unique experience. 'It feels good. So good.'

'What else?' he demanded, a touch harshly.

'The way you're holding me down. I like it.'

His fingers convulsed on my waist, tightening briefly as he pulled me into another thrust. A tiny scream left my throat, the sensation sharper, even more exquisite. 'Yes! More of that. Faster.'

'Fuck yes,' he breathed, as if I'd delivered the very thing he wanted. He dragged me lower until my bottom hung off the edge of the table. Arranging my legs up until they were curled around his neck, he leaned forward, plastered his lips over mine in a dirty, carnal kiss; a brief but frantic duelling of the tongues before he surged back up. His breath emerging in harsh pants, Jasper widened his stance and slammed even harder inside me. A louder scream left my throat, my back arching off the table as sublime sensation curled through me.

'Come for me, sweetheart. I need to feel you come all over my cock.'

Needing somewhere on his body to anchor myself, I wrapped my fingers around his forearms. Moments later, I smashed through the barrier of no return.

'Oh, God, I'm coming,' I whispered, a strange transcendental sensation washing over me as I was thrown headlong into my climax. It arrived as a forceful tsunami, threatening to rip me apart from the inside. My nails dug into his arms when bliss crashed over me, dragging me deep, deeper than I'd ever been before in my life. Longer than I'd ever experienced.

When the storm abated, when I could again prise open eyes I couldn't remember closing, it was to find Jasper propped on his elbows over me, his incisive eyes absorbing my every twitch and gasp.

A half minute passed before I realised he was still hard and solid inside me. Shock must have registered because he gave a tight smile, his face a mask of deep arousal, ruthlessly controlled.

'Did I leave you hanging?' I attempted to tease, although the shifting emotions inside me left me wildly unsettled in the aftermath.

'That one was for you. Watching you come was a pleasure I wasn't about to deny myself.'

'But?'

He didn't answer immediately. His head dropped a few inches, his mouth taking my nipple and sucking hard before, at the sensitive shiver coursing through me, he raised his head.

'But now I get to experience what it feels like to come inside you.' His voice was a raw throb of anticipation that tingled every nerve in my body.

Before I could draw breath, he snatched me off the table. He disengaged long enough to flip me around and repositioned my legs, until my feet met the floor, and then bent me over the conference table.

Then, as if he had all the time in the world, Jasper ran his fingers through my hair, over my neck and down my spine. He unclasped my bra, trailed kisses where his hands had been, and cupped my breasts. As if he knew how sensitive I was, he merely squeezed and fondled them for another minute without teasing my nipples. Then he nudged me upright; my back to his hot, muscled chest, he wrapped one arm around my waist. 'Raise your arms, Wren. Wrap them around my neck,' he whispered in my ear.

Wearing my heels and stockings with my skirt around my waist and my arms angled backwards around his neck, I felt dirty and decadent. Apparently, he thought so too because his breathing grew frantic and rapid. 'You have any idea how long I've imagined you like this?'

I smiled. 'Hmm, roughly about two weeks?'

He laughed. 'Try a whole lot longer, sweetheart.'

With that, he thrust upward inside me.

Every single thought dissolved from my brain as Jasper began to fuck me again.

With his free hand he explored me, from chest to thighs and in between, and when I began to lose my mind again, and his thrusts grew erratic and much deeper than I thought possible, his fingers delved between my folds, expertly strumming my clit in exquisite motions that sent me surging into the stratosphere once again.

His head aligned with mine, I heard his low growls as I started to come. 'Christ, Wren. You feel fucking amazing. So tight and hot and beautiful. *Yes, yes, yes,*' he hissed in sync with his thrusts as we drowned in our mutual orgasm.

Coming down from the second high was just as surreal, and when he pulled out of me and perched me on the table, a twinge of loss staggered me. Watching him stroll to the cabinet, I felt weirdly unmoored, turned inside out as I struggled to get my emotions under control.

None of my previous encounters had affected me this much. But this was still just sex. Great sex. It was the height of stupidity to get emotional or evangelical about it. I repeated those words feverishly to myself as he returned. Striving for composure, I lifted my head, meeting his gaze with a cool smile as he set down the stack of tissues on the table. 'May I?' he asked.

What little poise I'd scrambled together threatened to evaporate at his request.

Stop it. This didn't mean anything. So he cared about my comfort. Big deal. About to tell him I was a grown woman and he didn't need to attend to me, I found myself biting my lip and nodding.

The gleam in his eyes said my answer had pleased him but in the next moment the expression was gone. Surrealness engulfed me again as he cleaned me up, then, plucking my panties off the floor, he sank low and looked up at me. Our gazes connected, I stepped back into my underwear and he pulled it up my legs slowly, his gaze dropping once to rest on my pussy for a long, prolonged moment before sliding the underwear back into place.

Perturbed by how unnerving his aftercare was, how needy it made me feel, I jerked upright and cleared my throat. 'I need to get going.'

Jasper rose calmly, stepped forward and spiked

his fingers through my hair. Tilting my face up, he dropped a soft, brief kiss on my lips.

With every cell in my body, I wanted to prolong the kiss. I sucked in a breath when he stepped away, the loss echoing inside me.

God, what the hell is wrong with me?

A little desperately, I retrieved my bra, slipped it back on before reclaiming my blouse. I kept my back to him as I buttoned it up and slipped on my jacket. On slightly firmer ground, I passed my own fingers through my hair and then gathered my papers off the table.

And turned around to discover Jasper was fully dressed, too. Hell, he was so immaculately put back together, it was as if he'd had way too much experience at this.

Nope. I most definitely wasn't going to think about how often he'd done this. I'd never been possessive or jealous about sexual partners in my life. I wasn't about to start.

'Are we good?' he asked, walking towards me.

My head shot up. 'Of course.'

His gaze raked my face before, nodding, he reached for the control and unlocked the door. 'Good. I'll walk you out.'

I tightened my fingers around my briefcase. This was stupid. I should welcome the chance to escape this room, to regroup. Nevertheless, when his hand arrived in the small of my back, I couldn't help the shiver that coursed through me. I had a long hallway to traverse before I got into the lift; a long hallway where his employees would probably catch a glimpse of my dishevelled state.

'Are you sure everything's okay?' Jasper asked, a frown between his eyebrows.

I started to nod, but then paused.

He leaned down, trailing his lips over my cheek before kissing the corner of my mouth. 'There's a quicker way out of the building if you prefer?'

I looked up, hating myself for the relief bursting through me. Then a thought scythed through the feeling. I glared at him. 'Do you sneak all your lovers through the back door?'

His eyes narrowed. 'Believe it or not, this is the first time I've done it in here. I don't intend it to be the last time though. With you.'

I hated the spurt of excitement that sprang up in my belly. 'The front door will be just fine.'

He smiled, and again I got the funny feeling that I'd pleased him. Mentally, I shook my head. I really needed to get out of here.

Thankfully, the office floor was less busy. And Jasper in calm, professional mode as he walked me to the lift eased my nerves. About to utter a brisk, professional goodbye, I looked up in surprise when he walked into the lift with me. 'What are you doing?'

He didn't answer until the lift doors shut. Then he stepped into my space again, one hand cupping my nape.

'I need one last kiss,' he said gruffly. He sealed

his mouth to mine, tongue curling round mine in a kiss so possessive, so hot and sexy, my toes curled. All too soon, the lift reached the ground floor and the doors parted. With clear reluctance, Jasper released me. But not before he caressed his knuckles down my cheek.

'Have a good day, Wren.' And then, as I shakily stepped out of the lift, he added, 'I'll see you back here tonight at six.'

Before I could ask what he was talking about, the doors slid shut.

A little breathless and a whole lot flustered, I stumbled out of his building then paused on the pavement to check the email that had pinged into my inbox. Jasper.

Six hours until your next orgasm. We can use up three of those hours working tonight. Don't be late.

I tried to summon all the righteous indignation I could think of. But as I hurried to my office, all I could think of was how good he'd felt inside me. How the day was going to absolutely drag until I saw him again. How quickly I could make up the extra three hours I needed.

How much I feared—with addiction stamped into my family's DNA—that I was already way too obsessed with Jasper Mortimer's sexual prowess.

CHAPTER SEVEN

THAT BRACING, TERRIFYING thought turned out to be the impetus I needed to block Jasper from my mind for the better part of the morning, despite my phone pinging intermittently with text messages from him. Even the perfectly valid reasoning that answering his texts could be deemed work and therefore contribute towards my six-hour accumulation terrified me a little when my heart leapt at the idea.

Perhaps fate thought it prudent to deliver me from my increasingly frantic Jasper-induced withdrawal symptoms. Because just before midday, when the door to my office swung open, my heart lurched for one giddy moment at the thought that it was him, before plummeting at the sight of the woman framed in the doorway, dressed from head to toe in designer white, complete with radiant pearls.

I couldn't help but wonder if my mother's inability to feel affection for me was because she resented me for choosing to earn my living rather than marry into it, as she had.

Stifling the bruising thought, I looked past her to a visibly flustered Alana who mouthed *Sorry* before hurriedly closing the door. 'Mother. Did we have an appointment?'

'You're not senile, Wren, you know we don't. Just as you know the reason I don't have an appointment for this meeting is because you've been avoiding my calls. You've left me no choice but to chance this visit. And you know how I feel about impropriety.'

I gritted my teeth, wondered for a wild moment if one of Jasper's texts had included an invitation for a working lunch. And whether I should've accepted it.

No.

If my mother was the frying pan, Jasper was most definitely the fire. Regardless of how pleasurable it'd been to dance in the flames this morning, I needed to pace myself or risk being incinerated. Inhaling calm, I rose from the desk, approached where my mother was pulling off stylish winter gloves to drop them along with her designer handbag on the coffee table. My spirits sank lower at the sign that this wasn't going to be a quick visit.

'I'm sorry, I've been busy. What can I help you with?' I asked, keeping my voice even.

Eyes a shade lighter than mine studied me with cool assessment. 'There's something different about you.'

Oh, Christ.

I sucked in another calming breath and reminded myself I was a grown woman, not a child terrified of chastisement or one desperate for her mother's approval. Or, heaven forbid, her mother's love or whatever dregs remained after she'd already given the lion's share of it to her husband and son. 'I'm not sure I know what you mean, Mother.'

One well-plucked eyebrow rose. 'Don't you? Maybe not. But you were definitely more…flappable the last time I saw you.'

I wasn't going to admit, even to myself, that the skirmish with Jasper had helped me tap into confidence and determination reserves that had been in danger of dwindling recently. Perhaps it wasn't even the sex. Maybe it was accepting that negotiating a better deal with Jasper was better than opposing him and letting Bingham's go down in a fiery blaze. Whatever. For now, I was keeping the wolves away from the company door and I wasn't ashamed about it. 'Perhaps it was because you knew where Perry was and what he was up to but decided not to share it with me?'

My mother was too cultured to roll her eyes but not averse to pursing her lips and delivering a frostier stare. 'Your brother is in Arizona now, getting the help he needs. Let's be thankful for that and not drag him into this, shall we?'

'And what exactly is this?'

She took her time to sit, crossing her long, shapely legs. I thought about offering her tea, then suppressed the urge. Instinct warned me that the reason for her visit wouldn't go down well, tea or no tea. And I wasn't going to prolong it more than necessary. 'You've been seen colluding with that Mortimer boy again, Wren.'

Several protests rushed to the tip of my tongue. Firstly, that Jasper wasn't a boy but very much a man, in every sense of the word. Secondly, that I couldn't wait to *collude* with him again. In various positions I hadn't been able to stop myself from imagining all morning. 'Again?' I echoed, buying myself a little time.

'Anyone with decent eyesight saw you two at the party. And you've been seen at the Mortimer building, too.'

'Because we're partners in a business deal, Mother. A business deal Perry signed with him, which you already know about. Even if you didn't before, I know you have eyes and ears on the board now.'

'And you assured that same board that you would fix any tiny lapses your brother committed while he wasn't quite himself. Or did I get that wrong?'

My heart hammered against my ribs, this time with anger and pain. 'You may not want to hear it, Mother, but the problems Perry left behind are a lot more than *tiny lapses*. I'm just trying to make the best of the situation we now find ourselves in.'

Her face hardened. 'Is that your way of telling me you're about to let this family down? Need I remind you that it's exactly because of *that* family that we find ourselves in this situation in the first place?'

The vise tightened around my heart. 'I'm sorry you think I'm letting you down by doing everything I can to save our company. Would you prefer a complete stranger take over, one without the family's best interests at heart?'

She waved me away with a flick of her wrist. 'Now you're just being overdramatic. If your father or Perry were here—'

'But they're not!' The sharp rebuttal stopped us both in our tracks. A flash of pain crossed her face and I swallowed the sudden lump in my throat. 'They're not, Mother,' I repeated firmly. 'But I am. And I'm doing my best. I promise. Please trust me?'

The plea earned me nothing but a colder stare, which in turn hardened the edges of my pain. 'And I hate to say this, but regarding the feud—are we really blameless?' Was Jasper right? Maybe we needed to lance this boil once and for all, give the wound a chance to heal.

Or maybe not; judging by the paleness of her cheeks and the tightening of her jaw, my mother wasn't of the same mind. 'How dare you?'

I pressed a hand to my eyes. 'How dare I? Maybe I'm tired of fighting, Mother. Maybe I just want to use my energies to save this company rather than perpetuating a ridiculous fight that should've ended decades ago.' I dropped my hand.

She surged to her feet, her eyes flashing disappointment that shouldn't have eviscerated me, but did. 'Your father would be ashamed of you.'

Pain lacerated deeper, enough to drive my fingers into the back of the sofa opposite where she sat. 'Just as you are?'

Her delicate nostrils flared, the exquisite cheekbones standing out in relief as she stared at me. 'Excuse me?'

'Nothing I've ever done has been good enough for you, has it?'

Her mouth worked but no words emerged for several seconds. Then, 'You've known since you were a child what I expected of you—'

'What about what I wanted for myself? Did that count for anything at all?' I blurted, aware my emotions were in danger of running away with me.

'What counts, my dear, is that you seem determined to do the opposite of what's expected of you. I've never understood that about you.'

As usual I was getting nowhere. My mother was entrenched in her thinking where I was concerned. No amount of talking would sway her. So I shook my head. 'I don't want to do this now, Mother.'

'I should think not. I'm not sure what's got into you, but you need to remind yourself where your allegiances lie. Your brother most certainly did.'

For a moment I experienced a resurgence of that searing jealousy I'd tried to suppress for so long. My mother's blind love for my brother and father had made me wonder what I lacked that her love couldn't extend to me. For so long, I'd hated that I couldn't answer the question. In my weakest moments, I still did.

But I'd learned to survive without that emotion in my life, hadn't I? Surely in time I'd learn to do without altogether? The hollow inside me mocked that forlorn hope. If I could live without it, then why had Jasper's gentleness affected me so much? Why did I, even now, yearn for it when the probability of it being ephemeral—like my mother's regard—was the true reality?

Just sex. Given and taken. That was all I had to give Jasper. It was delusional to believe I *could* give anything more when my reservoirs had never been filled.

'Is that all? I have work to do, Mother.'

Her lips pursed, then she snatched her gloves and bag off the table. 'If my feelings and opinion are worth anything to you, Wren, then you'll think harder about distancing yourself from the Mortimer boy. His family have brought us nothing but grief and if they've done it once, they'll do it again. Nothing you say will convince me otherwise.'

She sailed out without deigning to deliver the air-kiss she normally dispensed when we were in public. I told myself I was glad, but the searing realisation that I craved even that small show of false affection made my gut twist in mild sorrow.

God, was I really that needy?

I was still mired in that maelstrom of anguish and anger when my phone rang minutes later. I reached for it without stopping to check the caller. And experienced a different emotion entirely when Jasper's deep, sexy voice flowed into my ear. 'Sushi or Greek food?'

I scrambled to focus. 'Umm…what?'

'Your choice for lunch.'

'Neither.' My appetite was non-existent after dealing with my mother. 'I wasn't planning on eating lunch. I had a very big breakfast,' I replied, then felt heat swelling through me at the double entendre.

The wickedly sexy man on the other end of the phone laughed, sending electrical currents along my nerve endings, making a mockery of my effort to keep him at arm's length. 'Hmm, so you did.'

'Wow, seriously?'

His laughter deepened, surprisingly numbing a layer of my pain. 'Your fault, sweetheart. You teed that up nicely for me.'

I felt a smile playing at my lips and immediately killed it. 'Thanks for the offer of lunch, but no, thanks.'

Jasper went silent for several moments. 'What's wrong?' he asked.

My fingers tightened on my phone. 'What makes you think anything is?'

'Don't play games with me, Wren. We're past that.'

That suggested a new level of relationship I wasn't sure I was ready for, even business-wise. And yet, I found myself answering, 'I had a disagreement with…someone.'

'A board member?' he pressed.

'No.'

'Your mother?'

A gasp left my throat before I could stop it. 'How do you know?'

'Wild guess. With Perry temporarily out of the picture, I'm thinking it could be one of three problems—board, family or lover. And since I'm your lover and I'm being on my best behaviour…'

The remainder of his deductive reasoning melted away, his words eliciting a fizzle of warmth.

Jasper Mortimer. *My lover.*

Lover. Love.

The smile evaporated.

No.

'Wren?'

I snapped back into focus. 'Yes?'

'Tell me what's wrong.'

God, why did that occasional gentleness from Jasper erode every ounce of my resistance? Why did I want to bask in it, roll around in it until I was covered head to toe in warmth?

Because you've never experienced a bona fide version of it. Surplus recycled affection has never been enough for you. Never will be.

But was it wise to accept it from Jasper? Was fate really that twisted as to show me a glimpse of what affection looked like from the very last person I could accept it from? Of course, it was. Because wasn't karma that cruel? I inhaled a settling breath, but he spoke again before I could will common sense into our interaction.

'Before you tell me it's none of my business, know that I've been in your shoes,' he said, again in that calm, even voice. 'More or less.'

Curiosity swallowed me whole. 'How?'

His laugh was a little sharp. A little edgy. 'What's worse than a parent who tells you how to live your life?'

I frowned at the puzzle. 'I'm...not sure how to answer that.'

'Try parents who don't care at all.'

My heart squeezed, this time for the hardened bite of pain he didn't hide. 'I... I'm...' For whatever reason, the *sorry* stuck in my throat. Probably because, freshly bruised from my run-in with my mother, a part of me felt as if it was a betrayal to my family. Or maybe I didn't want even a sliver of softer feelings to slither through my cracks in case the floodgates tore wide open? Either way, bewilderment kept me silent.

'It's cool, Wren. Loyalty is a big deal to me, too, even when the people we're loyal to don't deserve it,' he murmured and, absurdly, tears prickled my eyes.

Jesus, I was pathetic. Determined to wrestle my feelings under control, I cleared my throat. 'Well. This has been fun and all, but I really need to get back to work.'

Expecting him to convince me otherwise, or at the very least remind me I was beholden to him via our contract, I was a little stunned when he said, 'Okay. Bye, Wren.'

Disappointment seared deep as I ended the call and set the phone down. Then spent an absurd amount of time analysing our conversation. What had his parents done to him? As far as I knew, Jasper's parents lived overseas. According to the grapevine, they hardly involved themselves in Mortimer businesses any more. Had their reclusiveness extended to their own children? Did I have more in common with Jasper than I wanted to?

Realising I was spending way more time dwelling on Jasper's phone call than I had my mother's visit, I fought to put both out of my mind. Until a knock on my door revealed yet another surprise, this time a smiling Alana holding a white takeaway box bearing a well-known exclusive Greek restaurant logo.

'This just arrived for you. It smells amazing,' she said, placing the box on my desk before departing.

The giddiness in my heart bloomed as I reached for the note taped to the side of the box. Opening it, I read the bold scrawl.

They may take your good mood, but never let them take your appetite.
Jasper

The note was so absurd I burst out laughing. On wild impulse, I grabbed my phone and sent a two-word message.

Thank you.

The speech bubble started immediately. Breath held, I waited for his reply.

My pleasure. Oh, and just for clarity, not answering my earlier texts doesn't mean it didn't count as work. I make that sixty-five minutes so far. Call me when you're ready to make up some more time.

I knew I should resist, that I was straying far too close to liking our skirmish-banter-tiny-moments-of-emotional-synchronicity, but I couldn't help reaching for my phone again as I opened the box and groaned at the heavenly smelling moussaka, feta cheese salad and tiny bites of grilled lamb. Helping myself to small portions of each dish, I went through his earlier texts, answering each query between bites.

He didn't answer until the last text and email was sent and I was stuffed to the gills after a final sinful bite of baklava.

Mood improved?

Eyeing the half-empty boxes, I smiled and answered.

Much. Thank you.

Any time. See you tonight.

I sailed through the rest of the day, surprisingly focused after my turbulent emotions, and when I arrived at the Mortimer building to find Jasper caught up in another meeting, the idea that had been mushrooming at the back of my mind on my way over sent me wandering into the empty office next to his. He found me there twenty minutes later, with my copies of the Moroccan deal spread out on the desk while I pored over equipment-delivery schedules and personnel management.

'Would it be totally sexist to say you look good behind that desk?' he drawled, leaning casually against the doorjamb.

I bit my inside lip to stop myself from smiling. To stop my insides from melting at the sight of him, tie loosened, hair slightly dishevelled, his long legs and spectacular body framed in a bespoke suit that highlighted his masculine perfection. 'Yes, it totally would.'

Hazel eyes glinted as he rounded the desk I'd appropriated and perched on the edge, his muscled thighs a tantalising touch away. 'You should punish me for my heinous crime, then,' he said in a low purr.

I sat back in my chair, futilely willing my racing heartbeat to slow, while blatantly eyeing him from head to toe. 'Hmm, I think I will. Just give me a few seconds to devise an adequate torture.'

A sexy smile lifted the corners of his mouth and I tightened my gut against the punch of need that threatened to leave me breathless. His eyes left mine to cast a look around the room. 'I take it you've decided to make use of the office?'

I shrugged. 'Since the contract says I need to spend time here, I thought this was best.'

His smile widened. 'I agree,' he said, then those sinful eyes dropped to scrutinise my body just as I did his. He swallowed when his gaze reached the hem of my pencil skirt. Desire spiralling through my veins, I deliberately crossed my legs, allowing the hem to ride higher.

When his eyes met mine again, flames blazed high and dangerous. 'Two hours, forty minutes,' he murmured, reminding me of how much time we'd spent on work so far.

A rush of heated anticipation to my core almost made me groan. Correcting him to say he was off by a vital thirteen minutes felt a little too needy so I let it go. 'I have a bit more to catch up on, so I suggest you leave me alone.'

His gaze dropped to my lips, lingering for an indecently long time. 'Can I get a little bit of that punishment first?' he asked thickly.

No. Say no.

Of course I didn't. Because this morning already felt like a lifetime ago. And damn it, he'd fed me and made me feel better after that argument with my mother. What was wrong with a little give?

Relaxing even further in my chair despite wanting to jump him, I crooked my finger. Hunger deepening in his eyes, he gripped my arm rests, his face hovering over mine. Slowly, I wrapped my fingers around his loose tie and tugged him closer until he was a whisper away. Then I slowly licked my bottom lip.

With a deep groan, Jasper breached that last inch between us, yanked the chair close and fused his lips to mine. Decadent minutes of sliding tongues, playful nips and frantic groping later, I pushed him away.

'I really have work to do, Jasper. And you're wasting my time.' I cringed at the breathless mess of my voice.

He stayed where he was for another handful of seconds, his throat working, his eyes fixated on my kiss-bruised lips, savage hunger and a clear reluctance to end our entanglement pulsing from him.

And yes, it pleased a deeply needy part of me to see him fighting his own need for me. Battling to get himself under control. And when I spotted the thick bulge behind his fly, I fought a hard battle of my own. But ultimately, I knew this was for the best. That I needed this vital distance to control my needs. Before they escalated out of my control.

CHAPTER EIGHT

TWO HOURS, THIRTY-NINE MINUTES.

That time was emblazoned across my brain as I guided Wren into the exclusive restaurant in Fitzrovia on Wednesday evening to meet the tequila supplier.

The ambient lighting and tropical atmosphere of the Spanish fusion restaurant suited my mood and I watched the lights play on Wren's flawless skin as we approached our table. I'd been unable to take a complete breath since she stepped out of her front door wearing the sleeveless, thigh skimming, butthugging moss-green dress. The soft material clung to all the right places and I'd barely been able to keep my eyes on the road on the drive over.

I wasn't entirely sure whether to squander the entire time wining and dining this potential business partner and making her wait as payback for the way she'd tortured me for the last two days, or devote exactly two hours and thirty-eight minutes on Paolo Alonso and spend the last minute locating the nearest flat surface to rip Wren's panties off and drive myself into her snug pussy the way I'd been dying to do ever since the lift doors had shut between us on Monday.

Within fifteen minutes of us being seated, I sensed it would be the former, and not because of the need to torture Wren. Our guest seemed hell-bent on a different type of torturing of his own. Paolo was in no mood to discuss business. The Mexican businessman was only interested in regaling us with tall stories of his journey from simple farmer to multi-millionaire tequila manufacturer.

Every attempt to steer the discussion back to business was merrily lobbed away.

I was hiding gritted teeth behind a sip of wine halfway through the main course when Wren leaned her elbows on the table and smiled at Paolo.

'La Tromba, the name of your tequila brand. That means whirlwind, doesn't it?' she asked.

Paolo grinned. 'It does, *sí*. I named it after my wife,' he mused. 'From the moment I met her until now, she has never stopped making my life…interesting.' A faraway look entered his eyes, private enough that Wren looked away. Straight into my eyes. I stared right back, not bothering to hide the depths of my hunger for her.

Her eyes widened a fraction, but, sweet heaven bless her, she didn't shy away from what I was projecting. Which was that I wanted her more than I'd ever wanted another woman. That I intended to have her the second our six-hour deadline was up.

She matched me look for look, her nostrils flaring slightly as she brazenly acknowledged my intent.

A throat cleared. Paolo. Had he asked a question? Or merely narrated another anecdote? When I looked his way, he raised his glass in a silent salute, which I answered. 'To feisty women and all the exciting ways they keep us on our toes—eh, *amigo*?'

'Sure,' I responded, then grabbed the bull by the horns. 'So, are we doing business, Paolo?'

'It's probably prudent for me to take a day to think on it.'

'But come tomorrow you'll be saying yes, right?' Wren pressed. 'Because otherwise you'd be disappointing me greatly for misjudging you for an astute businessman.'

Shrewd admiration flickered in his eyes. 'Ah, the very fine art of complimenting and challenging that women seemed to have honed over the ages. How can I resist?'

Wren's gaze met mine and we both silently acknowledged that he still hadn't said yes. 'I've sent you all the paperwork. What will it take to convince you tonight?' she asked.

Another flicker of respect, then he set his shot glass down. 'For La Tromba to be the signature drink you serve on the opening night and for the next seven nights. You can throw your vintage champagne and whatever else you like at your guests, but I want my tequila to be the showpiece. Dare I say even base the whole event around it?'

'You aren't trying to hijack my launch by any chance, are you, Paolo?' I asked, my voice firm enough to reflect my seriousness.

He laughed. 'I'm striking a good business deal by getting myself as much of the action as I can. You would do the same, my friend.'

'Seven days is out of the question. But I think we can make something work, can't we, Wren?'

She nodded. 'I'll speak to the event organisers, come up with something to show you by Monday. Provided you give us your agreement tonight,' she said, her eyes steady on his, her smile replaced by steely determination.

Paolo smiled. 'I understand why you brought her along, *amigo*. She drives a hard bargain.'

Wren's challenging gaze slid to mine, and I fought the urge to squirm in my seat. 'You have no idea.'

Paolo grinned and smacked his hand on the table. '*Bueno*, we have a deal.'

Wren smiled in triumph. She looked so stunning in that moment, I wanted to climb over the table and taste the beauty of it. The urge intensified as she snuck a glance at her watch. We'd been here close to two hours but Paolo was only halfway through the extensive tapas he'd ordered. At the very least we were looking at another forty-five minutes until this ordeal was over.

I forced myself to finish my steak and salad, my

temperature skyrocketing with every sultry glance Wren slid my way.

I almost groaned in relief when the waiter arrived to clear away our plates. Only to glare at Wren when she smiled and asked, 'Would you like some coffee, Paolo?'

Before I could utter the strenuous objection firing up my throat, her left hand landed on my knee. Without glancing my way, she toyed with her small diamond pendant with her right hand as her left slowly caressed up my thigh.

Was she really about to stroke me into a frothing frenzy beneath the table? *Fuck yes*, my senses shrieked.

Paolo contemplated the tequila bottle with longing before he shook his head. '*Sí*, I'll take an espresso.'

I watched in frustration as the waiter hurried away to fetch the beverage, then I bit back a tight groan as Wren's clever fingers landed on my steel-hard cock. She stroked me through further small talk as we waited for the espresso, and then under cover of observing the waiter set out the coffee, her fingers slowly lowered my zip, reached inside the opening in my boxers and wrapped her hand around my hot length.

Sweet holy hell.

Stars burst across my vision as she stroked me harder, all the while smiling through another Paolo anecdote. When she toyed with the head of my dripping cock, smoothing the liquid over me in an expert pump, I gripped her wrist, terrified for a second that I would disgrace myself in the restaurant.

'Another nightcap, amigo?' Paolo asked, once he'd finally finished his drink.

'No!' I stopped, cleared my throat. 'I mean, I need to call it a night. I have an early morning meeting.'

He looked from my face to Wren's, a smile twitching at his lips before he nodded. 'You're right, I better get back to my hotel, too.'

As I reached for my wallet, I wrapped my fingers over Wren's, allowing her to stroke me one more soul-searing time before easing her away. And then she threatened to blow my head clean off when, under the guise of fixing her hair, she flicked her tongue over the fingers that were wrapped around me a moment ago.

The knowledge that she was tasting me, right there in front of our guest and restaurant patrons, was so shockingly arousing I knew I'd need five minutes to get myself under control before standing. As if she knew the havoc she'd created, she rose. 'I just need to dash off to the ladies. Shall I meet you at the front entrance, Jasper?'

'Sure,' I croaked.

She smiled, turned to Paolo. 'I'll be in touch in a few days, and I look forward to seeing you in Morocco at the launch.'

'If I didn't think you would do me bodily harm,

my friend, I'd think of poaching that one from you,' Paolo said as Wren walked away.

My grin was all teeth, no humour as I stared him down. 'Yes, I would. So don't even think about it.'

He laughed and rose from the table. Jaw clenched and thankful for the low lights in the restaurant, I joined him as we headed for the door.

Once he left, I eyed the ladies' room, every cell in my body straining to storm through the doors, find the nearest empty stall and fuck Wren into a stupor. And damn the consequences. Before I could give in to the urge, I saw her walking towards me.

Bloody hell, she was gorgeous. I wanted her so badly, everything inside me ached with it. The novelty of it all stunned me for a moment, made me wonder if there wasn't something...*more* to all of this.

Then her perfume was filtering through my senses and I was cheerfully stepping back from examining that peculiar feeling. This was about sex. And business. Nothing more.

Yeah, right... That's why you told her about your rubbish parents. That's why you've been thinking about her non-stop for weeks. That's why something inside you tightened with unfamiliar concern when you heard the pain in her voice on Monday.

I pushed the mocking voice away and held the door open for her. In lust-charged silence we headed for my car, our strides picking up speed. It was past eleven at night and the street was quiet and dim.

Enough for a torrid little quickie. But I didn't want that. Nor did I want to risk someone capturing us on camera. I wanted a feast. I wanted to gorge on Wren until this stark hunger inside me was assuaged. Then I wanted to feast some more.

Nevertheless, for a single moment when we reached my car, we stared at one another across the low hood, her eyes projecting everything we intended to do to each other.

The beeping of her phone wrenched us from the lust trance. When mine pinged five seconds later, the spark in my chest sent fireworks through my blood.

'You set your alarm for the six hours, too?' I asked, inordinately pleased that I wasn't caught in this madness alone.

She shrugged, although a bashful look crossed her face before she composed her expression. 'No need to work overtime if I don't have to.'

'Of course not. You're nothing if not super-efficient, right?' I teased.

The tiniest smile quirked her lips as she slid into the car. I gunned the engine, aiming the car towards the nearest main road when she asked in a low, raspy voice, 'Where are we going?'

My fingers tightened on the wheel. The moment I'd dismissed a quickie on the hood of my car, my mind had zeroed in on the next quickest option. Still, I forced myself to list them all. 'We have three choices. Your place. Mine. Or the penthouse suite at a hotel four minutes away.' My breath locked in my throat, praying she would choose the last option.

'Which hotel?' she asked, her gaze boring into me.

Mentally crossing my fingers, I answered, 'Mortimer Mayfair.'

Perhaps we weren't past the hurdles of our family history but surely she wasn't going to let that get in the way of what we both wanted?

We reached a traffic light and I turned my gaze on her. The look in her eyes was a cross between apprehension and rebellion. It was that same rebellion I'd seen during her interaction with her mother. Wren Bingham wasn't a woman who toed the line. I freely admitted it was partly what drew her to me. Was she going to throw caution to the—?

'Okay.'

Scarily heady sensations rushing through me, I caught her hand and pressed a kiss to her knuckles. 'Excellent choice.'

I shaved half a minute off our journey time. Using the allocated private parking reserved for my family in the underground car park would add at least five minutes to our trip so I pulled up to the front of the hotel, tossing the keys to the valet the moment I stepped out.

A minute later we were in the private lift. To preserve that little bit of my fraying control, I parked myself in the opposite corner from her, but I still couldn't keep my eyes off her.

'You're looking at me with those caveman eyes again, Jasper,' she mused, reaching up to free her bound hair in one sexy little move.

Far from being offended, I laughed, then gripped the railing as her hair tumbled down around her shoulders. 'I can't help it, sweetheart. I'm going insane pondering where to start with you.'

Alluring green eyes on me, she reached into her clutch. I wanted to tell her refreshing her make-up was unnecessary since I intended to besmirch it all in the next five minutes. But she chopped me off at the knees by extracting the tiniest, laciest thong I'd ever seen, dangling it right in front of my face. 'Maybe this will help.'

'Fucking hell, Wren,' I croaked, every drop of blood rushing south until I was terrified I was actually going to pass out. 'You left the ladies' room without panties on?'

She stepped forward, raising the scrap of lace higher. 'I was a little too wet to keep wearing them, you see.'

My jaw dropped as the lift doors parted. I stood frozen as she closed the gap between us and tucked the panties into my handkerchief pocket, then sauntered out of the lift, her mile-long legs making short work of the hallway that led to the suite's double doors. She tossed her clutch on a nearby console table, then, with a saucy look over her shoulder, grasped the handles and pushed the doors open. 'Are you coming, Jasper?'

Sweet Lord in heaven, was I ever? I stumbled after her as she crossed the vast living room to stop in front of the floor-to-ceiling glass window. Below us, London was spread out in a carpet of lights. In the darkened room, all I saw was Wren's stunning silhouette as she braced her hands on the glass.

Before I reached her, I'd wrenched off my jacket containing the panties I was definitely going to keep and unfastened the first few buttons of my shirt.

'I like this view,' she said, casting another wicked look over her shoulder.

'Then stay there. Take it all in,' I suggested, intending to do some sightseeing of my own. I reached her, curled one hand over her plump buttocks as I swept her hair aside and dragged my lips along her elegant neck.

Her shudder and soft moan went straight to my cock. My hand tightened on her soft, rounded arse. 'I should spank this naughty little bottom for walking around with no panties on.'

Her shiver said she liked that idea. Very much. 'Do it,' she muttered, her hands spreading wide on the glass, even as her hips rolled into my groin.

'Fuck, Wren,' I groaned, the indecent thought of reddening her behind punching a fresh bolt of lust through me. With fingers that weren't quite steady, I tugged up her dress as my tongue licked up the side of her neck. The moment she was exposed, I delivered a light slap to her derriere.

A hot little gasp left her lips. 'Oh!'

'You like that?' I growled.

'Yes. Again,' she commanded.

My fingers delved into her hair, gripped her lightly and turned her head to receive my kiss as I spanked her again. I swallowed her next gasp, devouring it the same way I wanted to devour her. Two spanks later and we were both so excited I was in fear of this getting out of hand. Releasing her, I undressed, then reached for the condom. Before me, Wren wriggled out of her dress and bra and tossed them aside, her eyes green flames of need as she watched me.

'Hurry up, Jasper.'

I tugged the condom on, then froze for a moment, arrested by the spectacular sight before me. 'Not yet, baby. I need to look at you.' Despite our previous dalliances, this was the first time I was seeing Wren completely naked. My mouth dried as I took in every inch of her silky smooth skin, the graceful arch of her spine, trailed my fingers from her nape to her tail bone. 'Fuck, you're so beautiful.'

Her head dipped a fraction, another bashful look fleeting across her face before the siren returned, her eyes commanding me to grant her wish. 'I need you inside me, Jasper. Right now.'

And since that was exactly what I wanted, I braced both hands on her hips. 'Open your legs wider for me,' I rasped.

The moment she did, I positioned myself at her heated entrance. Then, volcanic need threatening to rip me to pieces, I thrust inside her. Her scream echoed my gut-deep groan. I lost all sense of time and place, the only sensation the tightness of her sheath as she welcomed me in. 'Fuck, Wren. Fuck!'

'More, Jasper. Give me more.'

I kept thrusting until sweat coated both our bodies, until her final hoarse scream ended in convulsions that milked my own release from me. Bracing one hand on the glass to keep me upright, I planted kisses on her neck and shoulders as we caught our breaths.

Something inside me tightened when she reached back and trailed one hand over my thigh. The idea that she needed to touch me as much as I yearned to caress her kept me at the window far longer than I would've done if she weren't touching me.

I wasn't one for post-coital cuddling, and yet I couldn't find any reason to move away. When my kisses trailed to her jaw and she turned into my kiss, my insides continued to sing and twist and sizzle in a way I wasn't too keen on exploring. And when she gave another soft moan, I knew I was gone.

'We did leave it open-ended as to how many times we fucked once the six hours were up, right?'

Her sultry little laugh went straight to my balls, making me hard all over again. 'I believe we did.'

Bending low, I scooped her up in my arms and strode for the bedroom. 'Wonderful. Let me know when you've had enough.'

* * *

'Let me know when you've had enough.'

Jasper's words reverberated through my mind as I packed for the week-long trip to Morocco a week later. Far from experiencing the emotional apathy I had with my two previous relationships, I felt...alive. Quietly unfettered. As if something inside me were straining to break free.

Perhaps it was all the glorious sex.

Perhaps it was the inroads I'd made into renegotiating the terms Perry had initially tied Bingham's to.

Paolo had signed on the dotted line to be the exclusive tequila supplier for one year in not just the Moroccan resort but in all Mortimer hotels. And as of last night, I'd received a firm *maybe* from Jasper to shorten the one-year profit-margin projections to nine months, a term that I fully intended to reduce to six months before we touched down in Marrakesh.

Success on that front would mean, by summertime, Bingham's could well see a healthy profit from our association with the Mortimer Group. Not that my board was in the mood to heap accolades on my head. Nevertheless, the blatant grumblings had... lessened in the past week. At least from the board members.

My mother on the other hand...

As if summoned by thought, my phone rang. It took a moment to locate it beneath the mountain of clothes I was sorting through, on account of sudden nerves over which clothes Jasper would prefer to see me in.

The thought that I was even remotely interested in pleasing him made me pause for a shocked moment before answering the phone. 'Mother, I'm afraid I can't talk for long—'

'Why? Because you've decided to publicly draw a line in the sand, show me where your true loyalties lie?'

My breath caught at the acid in her voice. 'What are you talking about?'

'You were seen, Wren. Coming out of the hotel with the Mortimer boy last week. And don't bother to convince me it was business.'

My teeth gritted, the urge to demand she stop calling him a boy bubbling up in my throat until I swallowed it down. That insult was minor in the grand scheme of things. As, I was further stunned to realise, was the revelation that I'd been spotted leaving the Mortimer Mayfair. The sharp bite of remorse I expected to feel never arrived. And when I exhaled it was with a certain…pain-edged freedom that made my throat ache when I answered, 'Okay, then, I won't.'

It was her turn to gasp. 'You're not going to bother denying it?'

'Why should I, Mother? It's true. I was in the hotel with Jasper. And it wasn't business. Is that what you called to condemn me about?'

She went silent for a frozen moment. 'Of all

the men in this town, Wren,' she asked bitterly. 'Why him?'

I shut my eyes, a wince catching me hard inside because I'd asked myself the same question at least a half-dozen times since that moment in the maze. And every answer had only deepened my bewilderment. Because not even once had I considered simply…walking away, regardless of the fact that I'd demanded he release me from our business deal. 'No explanation I give is going to satisfy you, so why put ourselves through it?' My question emerged solemn and reserved, directly opposite to the churning in my belly. Something was happening with Jasper. Something I seemed powerless to stop.

'I guess there's nothing more to discuss, then, is there?'

The finality in her tone unnerved me. Enough to make my answer rushed. 'Mother, can you trust me for once? Please? I'm trying to salvage this for all of us.' The worrying thing was, I wasn't sure if the business was the only thing I was attempting to salvage.

'You want me to trust you when you've openly thrown yourself into the enemy's bed? Oh, sweet girl, don't you know this will only have one unfortunate ending for you? Don't you know that's what they live for?'

Jasper's face materialised before my eyes, the ruthless and dogged determination in getting his way. I couldn't deny that so far things had worked in his favour. Mostly. But I planned on changing that.

'It…won't,' I replied, then…stronger when my voice wobbled, 'It won't.'

My mother sighed. 'Your father deluded himself about getting into bed with vipers once upon a time, too.'

Before I could reply the line went dead.

I hung up, hurt and incensed. And when tears filmed my eyes, I dashed them away with an impatient hand. Wasn't there a saying that history repeated itself only if we didn't learn from it? Why was my mother so determined to write me off?

The answer shook through me, terrifying me into blindly throwing random items of clothing into the suitcase. Who the hell cared what Jasper preferred? I would dress for myself and no one else.

Still, my senses jumped into sizzling life when my phone pinged with a message from him.

Be there in ten.

I was waiting by my front door when he pulled up in his Aston Martin. When he started to get out, I waved him away, wheeling my suitcase towards the boot. 'I'm fine. Just pop the boot, please.'

A frown twitched across his face as he flicked the button. I stymied another flare of unease when I saw his suitcase—a top-of-the-range designer exclusive with his name monogrammed in neat letters.

Get a grip, Wren. You're now annoyed because the billionaire you're sleeping with has nice luggage?

'Whoa, did you wake up on the wrong side of the bed, sweetheart?' he enquired dryly when I got into the car.

I shut the door with a tiny slam and yanked on my seat belt. 'What if I did?'

He stared at me for a moment, then nodded. 'Right, you're itching to pick a fight with me. Fine. Go ahead. As long as we get to make up properly afterwards.'

That should've angered me more. Instead, part of me leapt in excitement while the painful knot in my belly expanded. I shook my head, my thoughts bewildered. 'Can we just go, please?'

He set the car in motion and stayed silent for the first few miles.

Far from the silence easing my churning emotions, I grew even more unsettled.

After another few minutes, he sighed. 'Can I take a wild guess at what's eating you up? You're raging at fate for matters that aren't in your control? That had nothing to do with you but in which you're fully embroiled somehow? And the more you think about it, the more it pisses you off, and the more ridiculous guilt eats you up?'

I shifted in my seat, a little riled and lot bewildered by his acuity. 'Don't shrink me, Jasper.'

A wry, cynical smile curved his lips. 'I'm not. But have you considered that I'm stuck in the same situation? My nightmare of a father did something to yours and now the sins of our fathers are being visited upon us.'

'Don't you mean the sins of *your* father?' I snapped.

He flinched. 'Since we're talking about Hugh Mortimer, renowned bastard and destroyer of lives, then yes, maybe I am willing to take full responsibility on his behalf.'

A touch mollified, if a little unjustly since I suspected my father also bore some of the responsibility, I breathed through the easing of the knots inside me. 'Careful there or I'll take you up on that *mea culpa* you're bandying about.'

He shrugged. 'Take it, sweetheart. It's all yours.'

The peculiar thickness in his voice made that curious little hook catch once more in my midriff. Only this time it was positioned higher, dangerously close to where my heart hammered an erratic tattoo. He switched lanes in a suave move, increasing our speed. He said nothing more after that and I gladly welcomed the silence, a chance to contemplate how best to deal with my mother.

When we pulled into the private-jet section of the airport just outside London forty minutes later, it was with the acceptance that it would be better to let things play out, show her the proof of my success when I accomplished what I meant to. Anything else would be akin to banging my head against a stone wall.

What if it's not enough?

That bleak little question echoed through me, threatening to dull my enjoyment of my surroundings long after I'd boarded the seriously opulent Mortimer jet.

But with the even bleaker thought that this was a cycle I'd found myself repeating with my mother, and that, like before, I needed to snap out of it, I forced myself to look around. To steep myself back into the present as the plane taxied down the runway and rose into the sky with a smooth take-off.

The inside of the 747 private jet was worthy of its own spread in a premium airline magazine. I'd flown in enough such jets in my modelling days to recall that the general layout meant the bedroom suites were located at the back.

Back then, I'd done nothing more than sleep to mitigate jet lag, but I grew hot and needy at the thought of changing that on this trip. The flight to Morocco would take a little over four hours. The possibility of stepping off the plane as a member of the mile-high club made me tingle.

On the tail of that thought, Jasper stepped out of the cockpit where he'd gone after take-off. And just like that, my breathing bottomed out.

In my unsettled mood, I'd failed to clock what he was wearing and as he strolled down the aisle to-wards me it struck me that I was seeing him in less formal clothes for the first time. Then came the more potent acceptance of how devastatingly handsome he looked in whatever attire he wore. Today's selec-tion of white polo shirt with raised collar, coupled with khaki chinos that hugged lean hips and hard, muscled thighs, lent him a charming swagger and assured sophistication that made my mouth dry and my chest palpitate like a hormonal schoolgirl the closer he got.

And when he was close enough to touch, those distinctive eyes piercing mine, it was all I could do not to launch myself at him. Because being in Jasper's arms was a guarantee that every other thought would be pushed out. That I would only be consumed by him. Which was a scary thought in itself...

Don't you know this will only have one unfortunate ending? Don't you know that's what they live for?

'You still have war and pain in your eyes,' Jasper murmured, a thoughtful observation forged with a little steel and a lot of contemplation. 'Will you permit me to find a way of combating that?' he asked.

The shiver that went through me was a warning against embracing that offer. It was strong enough to make me shake my head. 'I'll pass, thanks.'

If my answer displeased him, he hid it well. In a blink, the steel was gone from his eyes and he was taking the seat next to mine. 'Something else, then? Champagne? Or shall I order us something to eat?'

With my mother's warning still echoing through me, I lifted a leather briefcase from where I'd dropped it next to my seat.

'I'm not hungry. And the champagne can wait for a while.'

I pulled out the newest version of the contract and

placed it in front of him. We'd been dancing around with a parry and thrust that was frankly a little too thrilling. But the bottom line was that I had to secure Bingham's business interests regardless of whether I shared Jasper's bed or not.

'You said you'd consider a nine-month profit-sharing clause. I've changed my mind. I think a six-month contract is a more viable option.'

He remained silent for almost a minute. Then his shrewd gaze flicked over my face. 'Convince me.'

'Hobbling Bingham's into working with one hand behind our backs stymies your productivity, too. We need money to make more money. With an earlier profit-sharing contract, you make half a per cent more than you would in the next six months. I've done the figures.' I rose from the chair. 'I'll go and freshen up while you look it over.'

Instead of concentrating on the file I'd placed before him, his eyes travelled over my body. 'Or we can look it over together and I'll help you freshen up when I'm done?'

I smiled even while my pulse leapt wildly. 'No can do. I wouldn't want to ruin your concentration.'

'Too late for that,' he responded, his voice hoarse with arousal.

I leaned over and tapped a finger on the file. 'Deal with this, Jasper. It's important to me that we're on the same page by the time we land.'

While we'd been embroiled in enough sexual tension to break a few records, business had never been muddied by sex. This deal, for better or worse, meant too much to both of us to allow that so I was confident, once I left the room, he'd give it his full attention. Still, I basked in the sizzling heat of his regard as I headed for the rear of the plane. When the stewardess directed me to the bathroom, I thanked her, then, unable to resist, glanced over my shoulder.

As I suspected, Jasper was engrossed in the file, eyes slightly narrowed as he digested the facts and figures I'd painstakingly put together.

I took my time in the well-appointed bathroom, splashing cool water over my wrists and touching up the very light make-up I'd worn. My unbound hair didn't need much attention, but I ran a brush through it all the same. Then, with nothing more to do, I left the suite.

To discover Jasper had moved from the living area into the business area and spread out more papers on the desk. He looked up as I entered.

'I've read your contract. There are a couple of issues that need ironing out.'

'Oh?' It wasn't a flat refusal. I could work with that.

'I think you're underutilising manpower on the ground. At least three per cent of the staff members can double up on other tasks without affecting quality or productivity. Here, take a look.'

I joined him at the table and within ten minutes I was admitting the sheer genius of Jasper's input.

'Give me an hour and I'm sure I can find other areas to increase productivity,' I countered.

He gave an appreciative smile. 'Do that and we have a new deal.'

My breath caught. 'Really?'

'Really. And once we're done with that, we can get down to what's bothering you and the reason why you haven't kissed me since I picked you up.'

CHAPTER NINE

HER FEATURES TIGHTENED and I knew she was about to shut me down. 'I don't need you to fix my problems, Jasper.'

An expected response. One I fully intended to smash through. 'When that problem directly impacts me, I think I'm entitled to a basic understanding of what's going on.'

Her eyes flashed with annoyance. And I admitted quietly to myself that it was way better than the bitter, silent pain I'd seen there before. That kind of pain was acidic, had a tendency to eat away inside you until only a husk remained. The last thing I wanted to see was the woman I was growing increasingly attached to stripped of her vibrancy. Of the passion that blazed through everything she did.

'Impacts you in what way?' she challenged.

I raised my eyebrow and let her read the answer on my face.

'You mean sex?' There was a tight edge to the question that made me wonder if the surface answer wasn't what she wanted. And fuck if that didn't thrill me. I wasn't sure how much of myself I could give but if she wanted more, I would oblige. Up to a point. Because I was a Mortimer, after all. And we were renowned for the amount of dysfunctional baggage we tended to lug around.

'Not necessarily. But I expected the trip thus far to be a little more…stimulating.'

She stiffened, her back going ramrod straight. 'I didn't throw myself into your arms like an overeager teenager when you rocked up in your fancy car, so I must be defective somehow?'

'Stop. You're deflecting.' I hardened my voice.

She opened her mouth, about to snap my head off, but then swallowed and looked away. The weight of that action sat uncomfortably in my gut. Wren never shied away from confronting me. Added to that weight was the realisation that I would fix it, regardless of what it was. Regardless of my suspicion that this would hit close to my own parental issues. Issues I'd happily placed in a vault my whole life.

I cupped her chin and redirected her gaze towards me. 'Tell me what's bothering you, Wren. I may not have crystal-clear answers for you but, much like this contract here, we can figure our way through it, even if it requires several iterations before we're satisfied with it.'

Her eyes grew suspiciously filmy, then she blinked them clear. 'It'll take much longer than a few weeks of hard negotiations to unravel a lifelong conundrum.'

Her voice was solemn, much more subdued than I'd ever heard it, and that unnerving weight in my gut grew.

I rubbed my thumb over the smooth-as-silk skin of her jaw, felt her pulse leap beneath my touch. 'I get that. But conundrums remain that way if you leave them alone. Shove them into the light. Show them to me, Wren. I want to see.'

'Why?' she asked, her voice a little bewildered.

Why indeed? I could've given her the flippant answer, told her I was a ruthlessly determined Mortimer who despised secrets and wanted full disclosure for the sake of our business dealings. But since I hid fat, ugly secrets of my own...

I shrugged. 'I've seen you in business mode and I've seen you content with a well-put-together meal. I've watched you wow a room full of corporate sharks and had you aggravate me with a trench coat I'm still determined to burn the first chance I get. Your many facets fascinate me. This sad version of you irks me. If helping you work through your pain is the only way for you to free yourself of it, then it's a task I'm volunteering to undertake. No strings attached.' Yeah, that last bit was a white lie. I wanted a few strings. The kind of strings that made me want to feed her when she was hungry. Tear a few arseholes to shreds when they upset her. Bask in her smile when she was happy.

She swallowed, and I caught another sheen of tears in her eyes. Then, determinedly, she dragged her chin from my loose grip. 'I won't be deemed weak by divulging things that trouble me, Jasper,' she said, her voice low but stern, her warning clear.

'Believe me, Wren, you're the last person I'd consider weak.'

Green eyes locked on mine, probing for several moments before, satisfied by whatever she was looking for, she nodded. 'Let me get this business out of the way. Then I'll let you feed me champagne and whatever delights your chef has in store for us.' Her gaze flicked past me to the double doors that led to the master suite. 'I might even let you experience that other facet of me you enjoy so much. Then…maybe I might tell you a thing or two about…stuff. Agreed?'

The weight shrank in direct proportion to my expanding relief. 'Agreed, but with one tiny addendum.'

One perfect eyebrow rose. 'Yes?'

'Since you'll be working full-time on Mortimer business, shall we dispense with the six hours nonsense?'

Her smile slowly grew, banishing a few shadows in her eyes. And the reappearance of my vibrant, gorgeous Wren made something unnervingly vital shake loose and free inside me. Instinct warned me that it might be irretrievable. For the moment, I didn't scramble to chase after it. Because her smile was knocking me for six and I wanted to bask in it until I passed out.

'You have yourself another deal, Jasper Mortimer.'

It was a good and bad thing that Wren was a meticulous businesswoman. It meant that she came up with the goods eventually. But it also meant that we were left with only forty minutes to eat and fuck by the time she presented me with the promised solution. I happily signed on the dotted line of the new contract while the stewardess poured the celebratory champagne. The moment she left us alone, we wolfed down the succulent array of canapés and finger food the chef had prepared before we stumbled into the master suite.

'Bloody hell, we only have thirty minutes,' I grumbled against her lush lip as my fingers dived beneath the light pink cashmere sweater she'd worn to combat the cool English weather.

Her laughter was sultry and musical, her earlier mood finally evaporated as she tackled the zip to one ankle-high boot. 'I'm confident you can make me come at least…twice before we land.' She drew back, teasing in her eyes. 'I'm not overestimating your prowess, am I, Mr Mortimer?'

I chased after her cheeky mouth, playfully biting her lower lip before I growled against it. 'Challenge fucking accepted.'

We tumbled into bed in a tangle of half-undressed frenzy, laughing and growling our frustration until, gloriously, she was naked, her sinuous body warm and welcoming beneath my eager caress.

Knowing I had to wait a few hours more to discover what was bothering her threatened a return of that unease, but then she was rising above me, a siren with her willing captive, the look on her face ethereal and breathtaking as she sank down, taking me inside her tight, hot channel. Then she rolled her hips in a sensual claiming that had my breath hissing out.

'I love it when you do that.'

Hands on my chest, she smiled wider until I was certain I would get lost in it. I didn't give one little damn. Instead I focused on rising to her sensual challenge, my own smug smile appearing when she threw her head back and screamed her first orgasm. Then a second. And just for the hell of it—and probably irritating the hell out of my pilot for ignoring his announcement to return to our seats and fasten our seat belts—a third.

She was locked in my arms, light shudders wracking her beautiful body, as the wheels touched down in a smooth landing in Marrakesh.

From the many hours of work I'd poured into the project, I knew the resort was situated on the outskirts of Marrakesh, midpoint between Essaouira and Agadir. What I hadn't known was that we would be travelling there by helicopter after disembarking Jasper's plane.

A further surprise arrived when he slid behind the

controls of the sleek and powerful-looking aircraft with discreet lettering announcing it as a property of the Mortimer Marrakesh Resort.

'You're piloting this thing?' I asked when he donned the headgear and passed me a smaller set.

His teeth flashed in a boyish grin that tunnelled straight into my chest. 'Don't worry, sweetheart, I've had a pilot's licence since I was twenty-one. I think it'll come in handy when I have to step in to ferry VIP guests to the resort. And who knows? It might even knock a quarter per cent off your staffing streamlining.'

Two things struck me just then, the first being that Jasper would most likely spend a great deal of his time here to ensure the resort got off to the good start the projections predicted. And secondly that his absence would…devastate me.

Because…*because*…

My mind seized up, unable to grapple with the emotions mushrooming inside me.

'Wren?'

I heard the frown in his voice but couldn't summon the nerve to look him in the eye. In case he read the very thing I was unable to accept myself? Still feeling tasered by emotions I wasn't ready to deal with, I answered, 'Yeah, sure, I think we can manage that.' Aware that my answer was spacey at best, I forced myself to rally and smile his way as I slid on my head gear and buckled up.

Hazel eyes bored into mine for an extra few seconds before his large hand squeezed my bare thigh. 'You good?'

Perhaps because he was inside me less than twenty minutes ago, or because I was really losing my mind, I dropped my hand on top of his. 'Yes. I am.'

His answering smile hit me square in the solar plexus but even though I was braced for it, it still took my breath away. As did the arid but incredibly stunning landscape as we took off and headed west.

I basked in the beauty of Morocco, happy to play tourist as Jasper pointed out various landmarks. But the most breathtaking of all was the distant but majestic vista of the endless, snow-capped Atlas Mountains, a watchful range of giants dominating the horizon.

'The resort is coming up now, on your right,' Jasper said after fifteen minutes, his voice intimate through the headphones.

Sliding up sunglasses I'd worn to protect against the mid-afternoon sunlight as he went low enough for a close view, I was awed all over again at my first sight of the hillside resort.

Rather than one giant building, it was a sprawling collection of sand-coloured mini castles, joined together by long interconnecting walkways, which would offer spectacular views of landscaped gardens and the Atlas Mountains on either side through elegant Moorish archways.

After landing and an introduction to the general

manager in the cool, marble-floored interior of the staggering beautiful reception, I discovered on the tour that followed that those archways had been painstakingly hand-painted in swirls of gold and bronze and turquoise.

Each mini castle contained four luxury *riad* penthouses, complete with private pools, hammam suites and endless sources of pampering and relaxation facilities, a true desert oasis unlike any other.

While I'd seen it all laid out in one report or another in the past few weeks, experiencing it in person was a thrill that drew increasingly loud gasps from me as we toured the extensive grounds. At my latest one, Jasper turned to me, a wide grin splitting his exceedingly handsome face.

'Am I blowing your mind a little bit, sweetheart?' he drawled, assured in that fact even before I answered.

'You're blowing my mind a lot,' I replied. And not just with the architecture. More and more, it seemed as if getting on the plane and leaving England behind had lifted a layer of tension off us despite our little charged conversation.

His smile widened, then slowly morphed with sexual heat, increasing in temperature until that space between my heart and stomach tightened with a new kind of tension. The one that warned the addiction I'd feared I was succumbing to had probably passed the point of no return.

When he caught my hand in his and brushed

his lips across my knuckles, I experienced an even harder kick. And when he kept hold of my hand for the remainder of the tour that once again led us outside, I let him, that fiercely intimate connection of palms gliding together a sensation I suddenly didn't want to do without.

Outside, a long rectangular pool was banked by a palm grove, offering the perfect balance of sun and shade that meant guests could linger for hours, the inviting water sparkling in the sunlight.

A little further on, amongst fig and citrus trees that sweetly scented the air, giant awnings resembling the wings of a Bedouin tent offered more stations of shade, with plump cushions and beaten leather pouffes laid out on Persian carpets. It was a seductive and decadent invitation to lounge and indulge, to free up one's senses to the pleasures the resort provided.

I felt the last of the tension leave my body as we meandered back into the resort.

'Ready for the *pièce de résistance*?'

'There's more?'

His hand tightened around mine. 'The jewel in the crown. You'll like it, I think.' He stopped to order a tray of mint tea and refreshments at the concierge desk before ushering me into a discreetly tucked away lift that didn't jar with the blend of traditional and contemporary gold and turquoise decor. Pressing a button that only had a star next to it, he pulled me into his arms as the lift doors

shut, content to simply hold me as we were whisked
seven floors up.

We stepped into the foyer of what was clearly
the largest of the mini castles. A discreet plaque an-
nounced it as the Tower Suite and I soon discovered
why when, after a jaw-dropping tour of the decadent
master suite housing the largest four-poster bed I'd
ever seen, I stepped out onto an equally vast terrace.
No, to call it a terrace was a gross understatement.

The tennis-court-sized space came complete with
turrets, parapet and three-hundred-and-sixty-degree
views, the interior accommodations perfectly centred
and smaller versions of the whole resort repeated in
the vast space.

'Oh, my God, this is incredible! You can experience everything the resort has to offer without leaving the tower if you don't want to.'

He nodded. 'That was the general idea. Even the
desert sand can be brought to you if you wish it.'

Stopping at the rectangular bathing pool fash-
ioned from the same coloured turquoise tiles accent-
ing the decor, I trailed my fingers through the cool
water. 'I've never felt the need to be clean the way
I do right now.'

Strong arms wrapped around my waist, his voice
a husky rasp in my ear, 'Hmm, I can't wait to watch
you bathing under the stars, with just moonlight covering your skin. Well…moonlight and me.'

My laugh felt as unfettered as the contentment
seeping into my bones. Then, his words sinking in,

I turned within the confines of his arms. 'Wait, I don't get my own suite?'

He looked a little startled, then mutinous before he quirked one brow at me. 'Do you want your own suite? I'm sure I can organise one for you if that's what you want?' His tone said he would do so reluctantly.

But it was a moot point anyway because it wasn't what I wanted. I yearned to spend every spare moment with him. 'No. I'd love to share this suite with you.' Why not go all out and embrace this temporary insanity?

The shadows left his eyes, that almost conceited confidence drenching his smile. 'Brilliant answer.'

The wind-chime doorbell went and Jasper excused himself to answer it. A sharply dressed waiter wheeled out a silver trolley, positioning it under one of the four awnings where a traditional floor seating of rugs and cushions was laid out.

'Thank you, Azmir. I'll take care of the rest,' Jasper said.

The waiter left with a huge tip and a wide smile and when Jasper held out his hand, I joined him, happily kicking off my platform shoes that went with the orange and white polka-dot sundress I'd hurriedly changed into before disembarking the plane.

Reclining against one thick cushion, I accepted a plate of sandwiches, which I finished in record time. With my second cup of mint tea, I sighed my pleasure at my surroundings.

Everything I'd experienced so far impressed a bone-deep belief that I was doing the right thing by not walking away from this deal, regardless of what my mother wanted. It had every promise of becoming the kind of exclusive, six-star resort reserved for the elite. Even without the Mortimer name attached to it. And with Jasper fronting it, I wouldn't be surprised if there was already a mile-long waiting list.

No wonder Perry had bent over backwards to grab a piece of this.

Thoughts of my brother made my mind veer down a different path.

'Hey, why the frown?' Jasper asked.

About to give an evasive answer, I surprised myself by blurting out the truth. 'I was thinking about Perry. I'm wondering whether he'd think I've stolen this project from him. It was his baby, after all.'

It was a testament to the kind of family we both came from that he didn't think the question absurd considering Perry and I were siblings, supposedly working for the same team.

'Have you heard from him?'

I shook my head, a wave of concern and sadness washing over me. 'I don't expect to even if places like that allowed contact with family. Things weren't that great between us even before all of this.' I waved my hand at the resort.

Jasper nodded. 'You think he'll be angry because he'll believe he teed it up for you to hit the winning shot?'

I frowned, knowing he was making a point. 'You don't think he did.'

He snorted. 'Absolutely not. And I'll be happy to set him straight on that score. Sure, you and I have had a few ups and downs but think of the progress we've made in the last three weeks. It sure beat the months I was chasing him around to stop this project from suffering a catastrophic and costly setback.'

The praise was welcome but the hollow feeling inside remained. 'Telling him is one thing. Getting him to accept it might be something else.'

'And you believe it's that something else that might drive a deeper wedge between you?'

Feeling a mournful little lump climbing into my throat, I took a hasty sip of tea. 'I don't know. On the one hand it seems inevitable that he'll resent the progress I've made. On the other, I'm hoping I get lucky and he comes out of rehab, all goodness and mercy, champing at the bit to end our...estrangement.'

Jasper only frowned deeper. 'Were things really that bad?'

My lips twisted, my inner voice mocking the hope of my latter statement. 'You sound surprised. I got the impression your family wasn't sweetness and light, either.'

His lips twitched sardonically. 'We aren't but our dysfunction is curiously programmed to infect the parent-child bond rather than the sibling one. Don't get me wrong, Damian only recently emerged from some self-imposed secondment in New York and Gem is busy with her own family.' He shrugged. 'I don't see much of them, anyway.'

'And let me guess, you prefer it that way?'

The flash of disconcertion on his face told me I'd hit the nail on the head. For some reason, that deepened the chasm yawning inside me.

Before I could ask him more questions about his family—mainly to deflect from answering painful ones about my own—his eyes speared me again. 'Was that what was bothering you this morning? The friction between you and Perry?'

Staring into the leafy green depths of my tea, I answered, 'No, it was the parent-child part. I'm lucky enough to have it from both sides.'

'Tell me,' he encouraged, much as he had on the plane this morning.

'My mother saw me leaving your hotel last week. Amongst my many other failings, that apparently makes me an irredeemable traitor to my family.'

His jaw clenched tight, his face a gathering thunderstorm. 'Wren—'

'Which is rich, considering they barely acknowledge my existence ninety-nine per cent of the time. I've been barely a Bingham since before my father died.'

This time my voice did break the smallest fraction. He heard it. Abandoning his tea, he slid his fingers over my nape and pulled me into a tight embrace. Unfortunately, that only reminded me of every other embrace I'd been deprived of for as far back as I could remember. I dissolved into Jasper's arms, tears I seemed to have battled all day resurging, this time spilling down my cheeks as I buried my face in his chest.

I felt…cherished. Protected in a way I'd never done before in my life. As unwise as everything indicated, I wanted to hang on to it. Absorb it into myself until it became a part of my soul. Until I could look back on it some time in the dismal future and bask in its afterglow.

'I'd love to say fuck them all but it's not as simple as that, is it?' he rasped, a deep understanding in his voice that spoke of his own demons.

Tears welled faster. 'No, it's not.'

His chest heaved in a long sigh, then I felt his lips brush the top of my head. 'Our inability to kick them permanently out of our lives doesn't mean they get to control us, though, correct? Only you have the power over you. No one else.'

The depths of bitter conviction in his voice said this was as much about him as it was about me. I looked up and his jaw was set in iron, his gaze on a faraway point I suspected didn't involve me. And yet, I still felt…wanted.

The earlier need to probe his own family situation rose again but I was a little terrified and a lot selfish to lose the warmth and security of his arms. So I bit my tongue, closed my eyes and breathed him in.

After an eternity, I felt his gaze on my face. 'Are

you glad you came? And don't say yes because this is work,' he tagged on gruffly.

Raising my gaze, I met his. 'Yes, I'm glad I came,' I replied, my voice a husky mess. We were crossing an invisible but dangerous line and yet, I was…exhausted with resisting its magnetic pull.

Jasper dropped his head slowly, and I held my breath until his lips sealed over mine. We kissed with slow languor, allowing the heat to build between us until we were both breathless.

He raised his head in torturous increments and when he spoke, his lips still brushed mine. 'The sunsets here are quite spectacular. Want to experience the outdoor bath tonight?'

I shook my head. 'Too tired to appreciate it,' I replied, just as a yawn caught me unawares.

He stood and held out his hand. 'I think an early night is on the cards. We have a full day tomorrow.'

I frowned, trying to remember the itinerary and realising…there was none. 'What exactly is happening tomorrow?'

That boyish grin, totally lethal to my state of mind, flashed into life as I let him help me up. 'Everything.'

With that ominous declaration, he tugged me back into the *riad*, to the master suite. Then, catching my hem, he freed me of my dress and panties, and nudged me into the bathroom. Bypassing the Jacuzzi bath, he switched on the jets in the shower, then made short work of undressing himself. All the while watching me with an expression that made my breath catch and my heart squeeze.

To mitigate the erratic mess that was my pulse and my emotions, I reached for an apple-shaped bottle with an exquisitely carved stopper top in the shape of the M'Goun Valley rose, the national flower of Morocco.

Jasper stopped me with a soft grip. 'No, let me.' He took the bottle, uncapped it, poured a decent measure into his palm, then motioned for me to come closer. I watched him rub his hands together, that simple act so intensely erotic, my nipples beaded and my thighs clenched hard with desperate need. 'I've dreamed of at least two dozen ways to do this.'

Swaying towards him, I lifted eyelids that were curiously heavy to meet his gaze. 'We've showered together before.'

'Hmm, but always when one of us had to rush off somewhere. Or when one of us needed to fuck the other super urgently.'

Heat rose up my body. Yes, so I'd attacked him the last time we'd been in the shower together. 'No need to rub it in my face.'

'Oh, I intend to rub it in all right. All over your body.'

Laughter caught me completely unawares, a peculiar strain of joy fizzing through me. It died in a sigh as Jasper's hands proceeded to wreak exquisite magic on my body. I didn't bother to hold back my moans of pleasure because it felt disingenuous in this place. Instead, I closed my eyes and gave myself over to him. And by the time he swung me into his arms and carried me to the four-poster, I was a boneless, mindless creature, ready to receive everything he had to give.

Like the kiss before, the lovemaking was indulgent, decadent and slow, tapping into the rhythm of the land.

And just like before, I blinked back tears when it was over. Then gasped with a different sort of pleasure when, with a touch of a remote, the doors slid back to reveal the insanely gorgeous sunset he'd promised.

From the perfect vantage point of our bed, it felt as if we were being treated to the creation of an extraordinary oil painting. The world itself seemed ablaze, streaked with the richest scarlet, vibrant orange and saffron yellow.

'My God, that's beautiful,' I whispered.

Jasper pulled me tighter against him. 'Yes. And just in case I didn't mention it before, I'm glad you came, too.'

Later, when it all went wrong, I would remember this moment.

The moment that last sane string unmoored me from reality as I knew it and gaily wove its way through the air into the hands of the last man I should've trusted it to.

The next day, rested and sated from glorious early-morning sex, we set off on dune buggies to a desert encampment half a mile away that formed part of the resort. The objective of the visit was to judge the experience as a possible business retreat and relaxation exercise. The twelve Bedouin tents were each large enough to host up to thirty guests and, as evidenced by the signals from our laptops as we got down to work, the business facilities were more than adequate.

By lunchtime we'd pronounced it a success and moved on to the next item on the agenda. Thrilled at the rate we were checking things off our extensive to-do list, we didn't stop until after the sun had gone down.

Dinner was an exquisite lamb and vegetable couscous cooked in an authentic tagine, followed by a creamy locally made dessert of sugared almonds and crushed dates served over a baked yoghurt. Over rich, cream-laced coffee, Jasper regarded me with heavy-lidded eyes. 'I'm getting you in that bath tonight.'

Since the stars were shining bright and I'd had exactly the same idea, I smiled. 'You have my full cooperation.'

With a heart-stopping smile, he reached for the tablet next to his coffee cup. I'd discovered to my delight that most amenities within each suite could be operated digitally and when I heard the sudden rush of water hitting the cavernous bath, my temperature rose. I set my coffee down as Jasper reclined back in his seat, his eyes promising everything he intended to do to me. But I intended to flip the script on him tonight.

'How long do we have until it's ready?'

'About eight minutes.'

I smiled. 'Hmm, that's long enough.'

Telltale heat scored his cheekbones. 'For?'

'For me to drive you a lot crazy.' I crooked a finger at him. He rose, prowling over to me in a way that made every cell in my body sing. When I made space between my knees, he stepped into them, hands hanging loose at his sides.

Slowly, teasingly, I placed my hands on his calves, then dragged them up. Arousal darkened his eyes as I explored muscular thighs for several seconds before heading north. He hissed out a breath when I brushed my knuckles over his very prominent erection. Keeping my eyes glued on his, I unbuttoned his chinos and drew down the zip. Another slow but firm tug freed his beautiful, engorged cock.

I gripped him, revelling in the hot smoothness of him, while attempting to contain the wildfire hunger rushing through me.

Still keeping my gaze on him, I pumped my hand once…twice. 'Would you like me to taste you, Jasper?'

His fists clenched convulsively. 'Holy hell, yes,' he rasped.

Moaning in anticipation, I leaned in close and wrapped my mouth over his broad head. A thick groan left his throat and I felt a light tremor wash through him. Ravenous, I took more of him in my mouth, my tongue shamelessly circling and licking as pleasure swelled through me.

'Ah, that's so good, Wren.'

I explored his cock from root to tip, licked and sucked and teased until he was panting, one hand firmly lodged in my hair as he fucked my mouth. I was so absorbed by the filthy and beautiful act, I protested when he started to draw away.

'I'd love to come in that gorgeous mouth of yours, sweetheart, but the bath's waiting.'

The bath I'd forgotten about. A little drunk on him, I watched him tear off the rest of his clothes, then tackled mine. Together we stumbled to the immense rectangular bath that could easily have accommodated a dozen.

Jasper paused long enough to tug on a condom before stepping into the warm water and helping me in. Dropping down onto the last step, he stared up at me, his eyes blazing. 'Do it, Wren.'

With a needy moan, I braced my hands on his shoulders. Then slowly, my eyes locked on his, I sank down, taking him deep inside me. Shudders of bliss wracked us both as I fucked Jasper into a panting frenzy. Lips bruised, nails raking over flesh as our simultaneous orgasms swept us under.

And when it was all over, he carried me deeper into the water, making space for me between his thighs so I could recline against him. Soft lingering caresses followed, my dreamy gaze on the stars above our heads as minutes drifted by.

Perhaps it was that sense of being untouchable by life's cruelty in that special moment that made me speak up just then. 'Can I ask you a question?'

His answer was a contented rumble, his lips trailing kisses against my bare shoulder. 'Sure.'

'Your father. You called him a destroyer of lives. Why?'

Jasper stiffened behind me, the hand caressing my thigh freezing. 'Bloody hell, Wren,' he replied. 'I have the most beautiful woman in the world bathing under moonlight with me. The last thing I want to talk about is my father.'

I said nothing, leaving him with the option to answer or not.

Another minute drifted by. 'Fine. Yes, he was.'

'Why?'

Another long pause. 'He called me weak for trying to be the peacemaker of the family. For as long as I could remember, he butted heads with Damian. Even Gem, to some extent. But I was the boy who wouldn't fight the bullies in school; the one who happily gave away his pocket money to the poor kid I felt needed it more.' Bitterness coated the laughter that punctuated his words. 'He particularly hated that when my teachers mentioned it to him, thinking they were doing me a favour and praising me for it. What they didn't know was that Hugh Mortimer was all for anarchy in the name of dividing and conquering.'

It was my turn to stiffen, the evidence of his father's ruthlessness the very thing that had created our feud in the first place. But as I heard his clear opposition my soft heart felt for him.

'He would've been prouder of me if I'd thumped everyone who eyed me the wrong way. And he didn't pull his punches by keeping that shit to himself.'

I twisted in his arms, my shocked gaze searching his. 'He hit you?'

Relief poured through me when he shook his head. 'No. Weirdly enough, he had a line he wouldn't cross. Apparently. But he wasn't shy about delivering emotional bruises.' He laughed again.

I cupped one taut cheek. 'Jasper, I didn't mean to bring it all up—'

'It's fine. He's no longer in my life. And I may be many things now but weak I'm definitely not.' The harsh proclamation sent a cold shiver over me.

No, Jasper Mortimer wasn't weak. I knew that first-hand.

And when he dragged his lips over my jaw and unerringly claimed my mouth again in a ruthless kiss, I wondered whether there was a warning in there for me, too.

CHAPTER TEN

'MORNING, SLEEPYHEAD.'

The miniature roller coaster that had taken residence inside me over the last three days since our arrival in Marrakesh performed a deep spiral at the sound of the sexy voice in my ear. Despite the sensation, I grinned, rolling over to find Jasper perched on the side of the bed, completely naked and looking gloriously virile in the morning light.

'Sleep well?'

I nodded, sighing at the memory of what felt like the best three days and nights of my life. Days filled with work that didn't feel like work at all and nights of transcendental sex.

'Good.'

Hoping I'd get a good-morning kiss, I silently grumbled when he turned away and reached for something on the bedside table. 'Pick one.'

I glanced down at the two envelopes stamped with the Mortimer logo in one corner. The wicked gleam in his eyes made me glance suspiciously at the mysterious offering. 'I don't think...'

'Do you trust me?' he murmured.

The right answer was…no. Perhaps love and affection were conditional but I'd discovered that even after jumping through hoops the way I'd done for my family for most of my life, they'd still let me down. And while cloud nine felt like pure heaven, my instincts shrieked for me to beware. Or, at the very least, take it down a notch the way I'd been utterly unable to since we arrived.

'Don't overthink this, Wren,' he said, his voice a low rumble. 'It's all good, I promise.'

Stupid tears clogging my throat, I plucked the nearest envelope and tore it open to distract myself before I blubbered in front of this man. Again. The words blurred for a minute. When I blinked and they came into focus, my stomach dropped to my toes.

'No way. I want the other one.' I lunged for it.

He held it out of reach, his hazel eyes dancing with humour. 'No, you picked that one, so we're doing that. Unless you're afraid of heights?'

'I never agreed to abide by your rules. And no, I'm not.'

A glimpse of steely ruthlessness surfaced in his eyes. 'So are you going to back out or are you going to trust me?'

Like before, I felt as if he was testing me, weighing me up for something more profound than…sweet heaven…*paragliding* in the desert. Again, the urge to say no pummelled me. Again, I held it at bay. Then I responded with a compulsion pulled from deep within me. 'Okay, fine. I'm going to trust you. This once,' I added, drawn by a desperate need to protect myself, emotionally and otherwise, despite the growing suspicion that it might already be too late.

An hour later, after a succulent Moroccan breakfast of yoghurt, dates, rich coffee and muesli, we left the resort.

I was pleasantly surprised when we arrived at the adventure camp set several hundred metres high up in the High Atlas Mountains. The makeshift camp I'd expected turned out to be a first-class, well-run outfit, with different groups for different levels that put me slightly at ease. The safety lesson further eased my nerves, enough to spark excitement. But not enough to fly solo when given the option.

The smouldering looks Jasper sent me as we suited up said he was pleased I'd chosen to double up with him; the intimacy of being strapped in tight against him only underlined that fact.

Regardless of all of that, my nerves nearly gave out as we stepped closer to the cliff edge.

'Jasper…wait, I don't think I want to do this—'

'One small step, Wren. That's all it takes,' he whispered in my ear. 'One small step and the belief that you're not alone. That I won't let anything happen to you.'

Dear God, what was he doing to me? I glanced back at him, saw the unshakeable promise in his eyes, and just like last night I wanted to open myself up and fill my soul with it. For however long it lasted.

With that assurance cloaking me, I swallowed, stepped forward into nothingness and felt my belly drop away from my body.

For the first five seconds, sheer terror gripped me, my scream searing my throat. But over the strong rush of air, Jasper spoke again. 'Sweetheart, open your eyes. See what your bravery has earned you.'

Reluctantly obeying, my jaw dropped as the beauty of my surroundings slowly engulfed me.

Now that we were in the air, it was as if I were sitting on a soft, swaying cushion. And below us, the majesty of the mountains and trails gave a true bird's eye view. 'This is…incredible,' I murmured, delight replacing terror.

'Told you,' Jasper said smugly.

I glanced up, saw his smile and the easy confidence with which he operated the glider and ventured a smile of my own.

'Want to go higher?'

At my nod, he sent us soaring higher, then, before I could catch my breath, his lips pressed close to my ears. 'Look to your left.'

I looked and gasped out loud. 'Oh, my God.'

A flock of grey-winged geese on their migration path flew in perfect V-formation about fifty metres away. Caught on a warm thermal, their wings barely moved, the only movement the graceful undulation of their necks. Totally entranced, I stared until my eyes watered, until my smile threatened to split my face.

When Jasper alerted me that he was changing direction, I felt a moment's sadness, then intense joy that I'd experienced this once-in-a-lifetime moment. My heart slamming against my chest, I wondered if that was a harbinger of my relationship with Jasper. Was he destined to blaze through my life like a comet, then fade away once this trip was over? Because really, once the last few teething issues in our contract were ironed out, there would be no need for further day-to-day contact.

And as we glided towards our designated landing spot, the ground rushing up at us, my breath was snatched from my lungs. Because I knew the seventy-minute flight would've been right up there with the most intensely exhilarating thing I'd ever done had I not felt another thunderbolt of emotion the moment we stepped back onto *terra firma*.

Despite suspecting this was coming, I stood shell-shocked and completely willing for Jasper to believe, as he laughingly loosened my harness and pulled it off, that it was the flight that held me tongue-tied. While all the time, the sonic boom of revelation ripped my life apart.

I was in love with Jasper Mortimer.

I struggled to hold myself together as he trailed a finger down my cheek, his eyes caressing my face. 'You should feel this free every day, Wren. Let the baggage go. It suits you.'

I must have given a satisfactory response, because

his teeth flashed in another devastating smile before he took my hand and walked me back to our SUV.

In the car, I grabbed my laptop and attempted to make notes about the experience, even though my focus was shot to pieces. Thankfully, it kept Jasper from engaging me in conversation, gave me the reprieve to contain the uncontainable.

My heart had handed itself over to my family's worst enemy and I knew deep in my bones that it was irretrievable. Did I even want it back? In a different world, had there been a chance with Jasper, would I have taken it? While my soul wanted to scream *yes*, my head forced me to face reality.

We'd gone from regular sex sessions for the sake of peaceful contract negotiations to a week in a desert paradise already counting down to its conclusion.

None of it reeked of permanence or commitment. And even if it did, did either of us have the tools to sustain it in the long term?

Shaken by the glimpse of the desolate future that awaited me, I was relieved when, on arriving at the resort, Jasper was handed a note that made him frown.

'I need to make a call to London.'

The tightness in his voice temporarily prised me from my inner turmoil. 'Is everything all right?'

His lips firmed. 'It's Gemma. She's been trying to reach me. So has my aunt.' He anticipated my next question with a shake of his head. 'I can't tell you why because I have no idea.' When he raised his gaze from the note, I caught a glimpse of apprehension.

'Go deal with it. I'll be fine.'

He gave a brisk nod and strode away, tension vibrating off him.

As quickly as my relief arrived, it evaporated. I was in love with Jasper. And whatever permutation I came up with showed our liaison as heart-wrenchingly temporary. My mother's stark condemnation and Perry's possible reaction aside, Jasper had initiated this thing between us out of frustration over my reluctance to sign on to his deal. Would we even be together otherwise?

If you want to know, ask him.

For the first time in my life, I shied away from my rational inner voice. Every inch of my soul recoiled against receiving another rejection. And yet, when the voice retreated under the relentless force of the shower I took when I returned to the suite, I mourned its silence.

My senses were still in turmoil when Jasper stalked into the *riad* half an hour later. His hair stood in haphazard spikes, as if he'd repeatedly run his fingers through it.

'Is everything okay?'

'No,' he growled. 'I need to head back to London.'

My heart lurched. Was this over already?

Dear God, I'm not ready!

The need to stop the damning words from spilling out kept my lips firmly shut as he paced to the liquor cabinet. His jaw remained set as he splashed a finger of cognac into a glass, then glanced over at me, one eyebrow raised. When I refused the silent offer of a drink, he picked his up and swallowed it in one gulp. Setting it down with suppressed force, he faced me.

'There's a board meeting tomorrow morning that requires my presence.'

I frowned. 'You didn't know it was happening?'

Granite-jawed, he answered, 'Hell, no. But I have no intention of missing it.'

Questions crowded my brain but his forbidding demeanour dried them all up. And really, wasn't this short, sharp shock of a break exactly what I needed?

No, my senses screamed. *Take whatever you can get.*

And then what? My chest squeezed painfully as desolation took hold. When Jasper crossed over to me, slid his hands into my hair, it was all I could do not to melt against him as he fused his lips to mine. To do everything my instinct warned me would only intensify the impending anguish.

'I'm sorry, sweetheart, but this is unavoidable.'

I forced a nod. 'It's fine. But I think I'll stay, make sure everything is in place before I leave.'

He took a long moment to reply and when he did it was with a curt nod. 'Okay. I'll send the plane back for you in a couple of days. And I'll take you out to dinner when you get back to London.'

One small step, Wren. That's all it takes.

The words that fell from my lips seared my insides raw and bloody. 'No. I don't think that's a great idea.'

A frown clenched his forehead. 'Why not?' he growled.

'What are we doing, Jasper?' I blurted before I could stop myself.

To his credit he didn't give me a flippant answer. And even when his hands dropped, his gaze remained fixed on mine. 'Do we need to label it? As long as it feels good, why question it?'

'But that's the problem. How long would it feel good for?'

I was aware I was worsening the mood when his eyes shadowed. 'Wren—'

'That ride this morning? It felt exhilarating. But it ended.'

He shrugged. 'So we'll choose the next adventure. And the one after that.'

'That's all life is to you? A series of thrilling rides?' If so, how long before I was a stale experience he needed to replace with a more stimulating one?

He paced away from me. 'This is so not the time to be dealing with this, Wren.'

A part of me felt sympathy for him. Whatever reason had triggered the unscheduled board meeting, it'd rattled him. But the grounded part of me stressed this was exactly the moment to end this, before I lost even more of myself. 'Is there ever a right time?'

His eyes narrowed, my answer obviously incensing him. 'Nice try, sweetheart, attempting to slot me into some ordinary box you usually reserve for past lovers.' His phone beeped and his jaw gritted after a furious glance at it. 'I need to leave for the airport. But trust me on this…this isn't over.'

'Isn't it?'

With strides powered by frustration, he returned to me, dragged me against his body and stole another hard, tongue-stroking kiss. 'Fuck no, it isn't.'

Self-preservation insisted I didn't prolong this moment, so I pursed my lips, remained in the living room as he stalked to the bedroom. Five minutes later, his suitcase was at the door. Another kiss and he was gone.

And for the next twenty-four hours, I remained in suspended animation of heartache, anguish and mind-shredding debate as to whether I'd done the right thing.

Then it all ceased to matter as all hell broke loose.

'Let me get this straight. You called a board meeting to get us to vote for you to stage a hostile takeover of Bingham Industries?'

I stared at the man who'd had the audacity to claim a seat at the head of the conference table. The years had turned his hair white and his face weathered. But those piercing eyes and that cruel mouth were the same.

The roar in my ears was nothing compared to the tight vise around my chest. Wren would never forgive me for this. I'd left things in a precarious enough state in my rush to return to London. And taking her to Morocco would be seen by her as the perfect opportunity to get her out of the way in order for my family to stage this ambush. Hell, I'd feel the same in her shoes. Which was why I needed to end this debacle asap.

'You have balls of steel, I'll give you that,' Damian murmured from his place two seats over. Next to me, my cousin Gideon snorted and reclined deeper in his seat, his expression reeking of boredom. I knew it was deceptive because he wouldn't have attended this meeting at all if he were uninterested. But he knew what the instigator of this meeting had done to me. To my siblings. Just as I knew he was here to support me. Hell, maybe my family wasn't so dysfunctional after all.

'Big, fat ones. Trouble with big balls is, expose them like this and they're stupidly easy targets,' I tossed in.

Hugh Mortimer's gaze turned to ice, his gaze tracking his eldest son's, then Gideon's before meeting mine. With me, he lingered, as if trying to spot the weakness he'd condemned me for all those years ago.

I stared him down. *Look all you like, old man. I'm immune to you now.*

He blinked first, his gaze shifting to take in the other Mortimer board members. 'Have you all gone soft in my absence? Bingham is ripe for the plucking.'

'Along with a hundred or so other struggling companies. Why this one in particular?' I taunted.

'Because it's the lowest hanging fruit, that's why,' he answered, his voice booming across the room.

'So much hot temper, Hugh. Calm yourself before you suffer a stroke.' This from Aunt Flo, whose gaze threatened to turn my father into icicles.

To my left, my cousin Bryce sniggered. 'This is way more fun than the reality TV shows Savvie's addicted to,' he murmured.

I allowed searing jealousy to consume me for a moment before I shrugged it off. If I let my guard down, I'd walk away with nothing. Destroy for ever the possibility of having what Gideon, Damian and Bryce had with their new but thriving relationships. Hell, even my wild-child cousin, Graciela, had settled down and was insanely happy with her new man.

'I don't have time to sit around all day debating this. This company isn't in the habit of staging hostile takeovers. I, for one, don't intend to start now.' I glanced at Uncle Conrad, chairman of the board. 'Shall we put it to a vote?'

He glanced at my father, his expression apprehensive. 'Um…'

'I vote nay,' I snarled.

Gideon's hand barely left the armrest. 'It's a *fuck, nay* from me.'

'And from me,' Damian growled, his eyes shooting daggers at the man who'd sired us.

I lost interest after Aunt Flo, Bryce, Gem and Graciela also sided with me. Even if the remaining board members voted against me, I'd still win.

The second the votes were counted and confirmed as fourteen to six, I rose from the table.

All my calls to Wren so far had gone to voicemail. The moment I'd discovered what my father was up to, I'd tried reaching her in Marrakesh, only to discover she'd packed her bags and left without waiting for my plane. She was probably still in the air. Or blocking my calls.

Stomach hollow at the strong possibility it was the latter, I reached for my phone again. It would be easy to check which flights had left Marrakesh—

'Jasper, a word.'

I stiffened at my father's voice. Damian's eyes narrowed. But when his gaze flicked to me, I nodded. Ten seconds later, I was alone with my father for the first time in years.

He sauntered away from me, hands deep in his pockets as he looked out of the window for a full minute before turning to face me. 'I expected you to be the loudest dissenting voice and you didn't disappoint. Still grappling with that bleeding heart, son?' he sneered.

The bite of his condemnation was less…sharp than I'd expected. 'You say bleeding heart, I call it exercising good business sense. You still know what that is, don't you? Or are you so locked on this trifling obsession you can't see straight?'

He inhaled sharply. 'What did you say?'

'You heard me. When are you going to let this go?'

'Not for as long as I draw breath, that's for sure.'

I studied him for a handful of seconds. 'There's more to this than just business, isn't there? What really happened between you and Bingham?'

I didn't expect him to answer but, surprisingly, he responded. 'The upstart had the nerve to try to steal your mother from me.'

Shocked laughter barked from my throat. 'All of this because some guy made a pass at your wife?'

Volcanic rage built in his eyes. 'He disrespected me. No one disrespects me, boy. No one.'

My humour evaporated. 'I'm not a boy. And in case you haven't heard, George Bingham is dead. Don't you have better things to do than to wrestle with a ghost?'

His nostrils flared but the hard rejoinder I expected didn't arrive. Eyes eerily similar to mine considered me for several seconds, before a hard smile twisted his lips. 'I heard you were sleeping with her…the Bingham girl. I didn't think you would be so dense. Obviously, I was wrong.'

'I'd seriously watch it, old man.'

The flicker in his eyes said my warning had got through. 'Answer me this, son. Would you let it go if someone made advances on what you considered yours?'

He clearly knew which buttons to press because the answer was *hell, no.* Wren was mine. She'd been mine long before that first sizzling episode in her maze. But scent-marking her was one thing. Destroying countless lives over an overblown feud was another. 'No, I won't,' I answered my father. 'But neither would I use a bulldozer to squash a gnat.'

'Ah, ever the peacemaker, eh, son?'

A flash of pain and anger twisted inside me. Then curiously the ache eased, leaving in its place a feeling of…acceptance. Calm. Some things just weren't meant to be. 'You keep calling me son, and I really wish you'd stop.'

His eyes narrowed. 'Excuse me?'

'No, you're not excused. Stop calling me son because you haven't earned the right. You were simply a biological ingredient that helped form my existence. You made it clear your children were simply a means to an end. So do us all a favour, *Hugh*, and go back to wherever the hell you came from.'

I headed for the door, the urgency to get to Wren a nuclear force inside me.

'Come back here, Jasper. We're not done.'

I delivered the same corrosive smile his genes had helped me perfect and had the satisfaction of watching his eyes widen. 'Oh, yes, we are.' I turned away from him, then veered back to make the final, vital point. 'Stay away from Bingham's, too. Or so help me, I'll devote every single penny of my many billions to crushing you.'

Every second of my trip to Wren's house four harrowing days later felt like a light year. Unsurprisingly, Hugh hadn't heeded my warning. And even without the weight of the Mortimer board behind him, he managed to cause an uproar that gripped the city. Every photo I saw of Wren looking anguished as the tabloids hounded her intensified my fury. Staying away from her until I resolved this disaster had felt like death by a million cuts.

My mouth dried as I turned into her street. While my trusted spies had confirmed she was home, gaining entry was another matter.

But I couldn't give up now. Striding to her front door, I leaned on the doorbell. My heart leapt as I heard faint steps and her voice ending a phone call.

Then, 'Fuck off, Jasper.'

'No, sweetheart. I'm not leaving.'

The door burst open. 'Who the hell do you think you are, coming here like this?'

'Let me in, Wren. Please.'

'Are you deaf? I said fuck off.'

God, she looked glorious. Fierce pride elevated her chin even as pain clouded her beautiful eyes. Unable to heed her request, I simply shook my head. 'No.'

Her face twisted as she tried to hang on to her composure. 'You cut me off. Wouldn't even take my calls. Now, my lawyers tell me I'm all out of options and I have forty-eight hours to accept your terms. So, I guess you've come to gloat?'

'No, I haven't. And I'm not the one threatening you. It's my father.'

She paled, her hand dropping from the door. 'What?'

'Let me in and I'll explain.'

Numbly, she stepped back, then flinched from me as I turned to her.

Gritting my teeth, I went down the hallway into her living room, relieved when she followed. Since there was no point beating about the bush, I launched into explanation. 'I didn't answer you because I was dealing with my father. The board backed me against him, Wren. Our contract is airtight. As for that farce of a takeover, it'll happen over my dead body.'

Her jaw sagged open. 'What are you saying?'

'I'm saying that before end of business today, the threat to your company will be over. And before I'm finished with him, Hugh will know that his lastborn son isn't weak. That like I've always done, I'll fight for those who matter to me. To the death if I have to.'

Her eyes grew into alluring saucers and I wanted to grab her, wrap her tight in my arms and never let go. But we'd been through the mill the last few days. I knew it would take more than a few declarations to make things right. Plus I had a feeling that, while I might have won this skirmish with my father, he would continue to be a nuisance for a while.

As those thoughts flashed through my head, the light died from her eyes. 'It's too late, Jasper. The Bingham board are seriously thinking of selling—'

'Fuck that. You won't be selling Bingham's. Not to someone who'll break it into little pieces and sell it, and certainly not to my father.'

Her chin went higher. 'It's not up to you, though, is it?'

I tried a different tack. 'Did I tell you Damian is married now?'

She frowned. 'What?'

I shook my head, the very thought still bewildering in the extreme. 'My hard-hearted, closed-off brother, whose only friend in the world is my certifiably psychotic cousin Gideon, is in love. With an actual red-blooded woman. Who apparently loves him back.'

Her confusion grew. 'Why are you telling me this?'

'Because he's proof that the unthinkable can happen. And they're not just in love, they're also in business together.'

'That's great, but were they locked in a family feud before they got together?'

'No, but fuck that, too,' I snarled. 'Tell me you don't want this to end, once and for all, Wren. That we haven't paid enough for the wrong decisions our parents made?'

She swallowed and that small hesitation sparked hope in my chest. Her gaze flicked to the phone she'd tossed onto the coffee table, and my instinct latched on to it.

'Who were you talking to just now?'

Her lips pursed for a second. 'Perry. Apparently he's allowed phone calls after the first four weeks.'

'What did you talk about?' I pushed, that blind hope still building.

She slicked her tongue over her bottom lip. 'He said he didn't hate me for sealing the deal with you. Or…for going out with you.' The relief in her voice was palpable.

'Good. What else?'

'He said he would support me in whatever decision I make about the company. And…'

'And what?'

'He knows he was the favourite child, that I got a raw deal when it came to our parents' love. He wants me to forgive him for taking advantage of it.'

'As he should.' I paused for a heartbeat before speaking the words that blazed from my soul. 'While you're giving your brother a chance, would you consider giving me one, too?'

Panic flared over her face before her gaze swept away. 'I told you, I'm not some lost cause you need to save. You can go ahead and bid for Bingham's if you want but I—'

'I love you. Does that count?'

Her jaw dropped and a visible tremble shook her body. 'What?'

'I love you, Wren. And you're far, far from a lost cause. You're fit to command armies and your indomitable spirit makes me fall harder for you every passing second.'

She inhaled. Right before her eyes narrowed into accusing slits. 'You refused to take my calls. You left me floundering in the dark for days, Jasper!'

'Because I was scrambling to stop Hugh from getting his hands on Bingham's. Between Gideon, Damian and I, we've been up round the clock for days, blocking every conceivable avenue Hugh might exploit.'

Several layers of anger drained away. 'You... have?'

'If it was just a question of money, it would've been easy. Between the three of us, we have enough to stop Hugh financially. But before you got your lawyers to implement the freeze on the votes, he was busy trying to buy off your board members. And I was busy trying to put this together.'

Her gaze dropped to the document I held out. 'What is that?'

'A solution I'd love for you to consider when we're done taking care of what's more important. I love you, Wren,' I reiterated. Because I needed her to hear it. To know that the powerful emotion that had taken root inside me when I wasn't looking and fused itself to my very soul wasn't going away. 'I think I fell in love with you five years ago, at the intern's seminar.'

Green eyes grew shiny and I dared to go closer, to hope for an echo of what I felt. 'I don't... I can't...'

'Sweetheart, be brave. One last time. Let's defy the odds and shove our happiness in the faces of our doubters.'

A shocked gasp left her lips. 'Perry said something just like that.'

'And I'd kick his arse for stealing my thunder if I didn't wish with every fibre in my being that you would consider it.' Unable to bear being apart from her, I stepped closer, cupped her chin and nudged her gaze to mine. 'Please, Wren. You mean everything to me. I want to build a life with you. I want to see that smile every day, wait with bated breath for you to blow me away with your brilliant mind. And, sweet heaven, I want the privilege of fucking you every chance I get, even if some of those include you and a certain trench coat I've decided can stay. For now.'

Her laugh was music to my ears and manna to my soul. Too soon, it died away. 'Are you sure, Jasper? This upheaval…it feels like a lot.'

I nodded. 'I get it, and there will probably be a few more to come. But would you rather face it alone or with a seriously handsome dude who worships you?'

Again that smile threatened to make an appearance.

'Take the step,' I pleaded.

Her breath caught and her hand rose as if to touch me. I held my own breath until she did. Then I tugged her into my arms, groaning as my lips found hers. But far too soon, she pulled away.

'Wait. Tell me you didn't know what was happening when you left Morocco.'

I grimaced. 'All Gemma would tell me was that I was needed at the board meeting. I think she suspected I wouldn't attend if she told me Hugh was the one behind it. I didn't know, sweetheart. It killed me the way you found out. But hopefully, I can make it up to you.'

She glanced at the document, then her gaze returned to mine. 'I was terrified you'd betrayed me, Jasper.'

'Never. For as long as I live, I'll never let you down that way. Or in any other way. You're mine. I fight for what's mine. And you are right at the top of that list.'

Tears filled her eyes and neither of us cared when they drenched her cheeks. Because she was smiling through them, her arms encircling my neck. After another long, soul-stirring kiss, she whispered in my ear, 'Do you want to know when I fell in love with you?'

The electric shock that went through me held me rigid. Then, pure happiness blazing through me, I said, 'Yes, I do.'

'When you took me into the sky with the promise to be the wind beneath my wings and laid the world at my feet.'

A knot in my throat hoarsened my words. 'You have my promise that I will do that for you every day, Wren.'

Fresh tears filled her eyes but she looked more beautiful than ever. 'Only if you let me do the same for you.'

'Deal.'

We kissed, long and deep and soul-sealing. 'I love you, Jasper.'

'My heart and soul and trust and body are yours. And if you can squeeze in a wedding before the launch, I swear to you that I'll find another fraction of love for you.'

Her laughter branded my soul and I vowed to wear it with pride. Because I was Wren's and she was mine.

'Challenge accepted.'

EPILOGUE

THERE WERE MOMENTS in the past three months when I was a little bit ashamed of the precious time I'd wasted fighting this feeling even though I recognised things had played out the way they were supposed to.

That pain and desolation made this all-encompassing bliss suffusing me now even more precious.

'You're smiling again, Wren. I swear if you don't get your act together, you'll blow this for me.'

'Sorry.' I laughed at my almost sister-in-law's mournful voice. 'I can't help it.'

Gemma Mortimer approached, tweaking the veil she'd tweaked a dozen times already. 'I know, but maybe just…pretend for five seconds? I really want to see Jasper's face.'

'Why?'

Gemma shrugged. 'Just…a little payback for all the tricks he pulled on me when we were kids.'

The woman who was fast becoming as precious to me as her brother stared at me with pleading eyes.

Damn, those irresistible hazel Mortimer eyes. 'Three seconds, that's all I can give you.'

Gemma whooped. 'I knew you were awesome when you chose me as your maid of honour.'

My smile widened, my heart swelling at the closeness between the siblings these past few months. But my heart was even more grateful for the transformation within my own family.

As if summoned by my thoughts, my mother walked in as Gemma retreated.

Agnes wore a burnished orange lace dress that perfectly complemented the tan she'd cultivated in the pre-wedding week we'd been in Morocco. But her attire wasn't what interested me. The tentative smile that grew at my silent welcome was what touched my soul, the light kiss she dropped on my cheek before stepping back what drew tears to my eyes.

An open conversation with her on my return to London, and then with Perry after his successful stretch at rehab, had stopped the rot of our relationship. Full recovery was a long way off, but my mother's raw admission that she didn't want to lose her daughter, that she'd taken a wrong stance in order to please my father, had helped.

'You look beautiful, Wren.'

'Thank you, Mother.'

She stepped closer. 'I hope this doesn't make you cry and ruin your make-up, but thank you for healing our family.'

Swivelling to face her, I felt a small sob burst out of me. 'Oh, Mum!'

Her own eyes watered. 'You've never called me that before. I... I like it.'

I gripped her hand as she sniffed. Then after touching up my make-up, she looked into my eyes. 'Your brother is ready to walk you down the aisle. Are you ready, Wren?'

'The love of my life is waiting for me, Mum. I'm ready.'

I watched the woman twirling expertly on the dance floor, drawing smiles and laughter from family and guests alike. Silently I shook my head in wonder as she caught my gaze and blew me a kiss.

My wife. Wren Mortimer-Bingham was my wife.

'Jesus, don't let her catch you with that idiotic smile on your face, Jasper. She'll own you for life.'

'Don't listen to Gideon,' came the rejoinder from Damian. 'I catch him staring at Leonie like that at least a dozen times a minute.'

I mourned the disruption of my adoration and turned as Bryce joined us. 'Yeah, I say don't watch her like that because it creeps the rest of us out.'

I couldn't help the laughter that barked out of me or the now familiar warmth that infused me. I'd come to recognise it as a different kind of love. The sustaining kind that was always there but buried beneath the clutter of other emotions.

All it'd needed was the right woman to help us

all buff off the hardened edges to rediscover the diamond-strong connection beneath.

And, sweet heaven, the shine of their love was blinding. For a silent moment we watched the women in our lives—Wren, Leonie, Neve and Savvie— dance some more.

'Are you ready to talk business or shall we wait for this sappiness to pass?' Damian muttered.

My gaze flicked from my brother to his wife, Neve, who looked up just then and sent him a secret smile. Then I gazed at my own wife. 'Don't hold your breath, Damian. This is a lifelong thing,' I replied.

He turned and watched me for a second. Then slapped me on the back. 'I'm proud of you, brother.'

The lump was still in my throat when I wove through the guests to my wife's side. Wrapped my arms around her, held her tight and just breathed her in as she threw her arms around my neck.

'I missed you,' I confessed. 'And I love you like mad, even though I still owe you big time letting Gem pull that prank at the wedding.'

Gemma had suddenly frozen halfway down the aisle, stared at me and mouthed *Sorry*. A heartless trick that'd nearly killed me until Wren stepped into view on her brother's arm, her smile incandescent.

Wren threw back her head and laughed now, and I shamelessly buried my face in her neck, basked in her joy and beauty.

'And how are you going to punish the love of your life?'

I kissed her long and deep, uncaring of who saw us. 'I'll come up with something, I'm sure. Right now, I'm a little stumped since you've blown me away with the success of this launch and I'm scrambling to see past your genius.' All around us, A-listers enjoyed the buzz and celebration of the opening of Mortimer Marrakesh. And according to the data, we were fully booked for several months.

Wren's fingers brushed my cheek, her eyes shining with love. 'You're the genius. For urging me to take this wild ride with you. I love you, Jasper. So much.'

'Are you glad we joined forces?' The document I'd brought to her flat had been a merger proposal between Bingham and the Mortimer Group. Her agreement had stopped Hugh in his tracks. He'd left London soon after and I didn't miss him one little bit.

'Absolutely ecstatic. I couldn't be happier. With you. With our life. With our partnership.'

'Hmm, but I bet I could make you a tiny bit happier…'

Her eyes sparkled. 'Let me guess. Are you going to take me flying again?'

'Any time you want. But for now…' I looked over her shoulder, spotted a darkened doorway that led to a secret place '… I promise a different, way better type of flying. Come with me?'

Her smile threatened to burst my heart wide open. 'To the ends of for ever.'

* * * * *

EXPOSED

CATHRYN FOX

MILLS & BOON

Danita Montes, thank you for all you do!

You are the best!

CHAPTER ONE

Gemma

MY PHONE PINGS—finally—and I jump from my buttery-yellow sofa as excitement jolts through me. I slide my finger across the screen and ask, "You've landed?"

"We just cleared customs, actually," my best friend, Mia, says, but the barrage of airport noises and announcements coming through her cell makes it difficult to hear her.

I press my phone harder to my ear and place my palm over the other one as I step outside my Belize villa, straight into my backyard oasis. God, I love it here. With the scorching, late morning sun falling over me and a medley of floral scents drifting by on a breeze, I take a rejuvenating breath and say, "Your driver will be holding up an orange place card with your name on it. Let me know when you see him." I would have picked the girls up myself—I really wanted to—but our small Porche fits only four—

with me behind the wheel, that makes five. By sending a driver, no one is left to cab it alone.

"Looking, looking," Mia says, and I can almost visualize her scanning the arrival lounge as she pushes through the crowd. Mia is a born-and-bred New Yorker—fast-talking, fast moving and the best friend I've ever had. We both work at my mother's art gallery—Swerve—in Manhattan. I love her to pieces and would be lost without her management skills. I'm the right-brained artist; she's the left-brained problem solver. Talk about a team made in heaven. "Wait. Hang on. Yeah. I think I see him. Come on, girls, follow me," Mia says.

A thrill grips my stomach. I'm so happy four of my closest friends have flown in for the weekend, eager to throw me a bachelorette party. Although to me, having them here, it's less about the partying and more about us being together again—it's been far too long since we've hung out, chatted and spilled secrets over tequila. Not that I'd ever tell them my deepest, darkest secrets. No, I'm the good girl, a senator's daughter who's always under scrutiny. If my secret dirty cravings ever landed in the wrong hands—were ever exposed to the wrong people—it could destroy my father's good reputation and my mother's high-end art gallery.

"I found him," Mia yells, pulling my thoughts back. "Get ready to party, girlfriend," she says. "I plan to feed you so much tequila you won't be able to walk down the aisle."

I chuckle at that. My wedding isn't until August, so I'm sure I'll be walking just fine by then. We're having my bachelorette party mid-July simply because we all lead extremely busy lives and this weekend was the only one that worked for everyone—and who wouldn't want to let loose in the Caribbean, right?

Oh, just my fiancé, Bentley.

I sigh. Bentley and I have been here for a week, and I thought we were going to spend time together before the girls all arrived, but sadly, his phone has seen more lip-action than me. Yes, he's a hardworking lawyer with his eyes on the Senate—my father loves that my fiancé is following in his footsteps—but we were going to treat this vacation like a honeymoon. Yes, yes, I realize our wedding is weeks away, and we're putting the cart before the horse, so to speak, but I'd rather an early honeymoon than to postpone until God knows when—or forever.

I have a big case coming up, Gemma. At this stage in my career, work must come first.

As his words bounce around inside my head, my gaze drifts to a gorgeous multicolor butterfly that just landed on the passionflowers weaving their way in and out of the wrought-iron trellis. So pretty, yet it does little to soothe that incessant ache inside me, one that's been there since my college days.

"It's about a thirty-minute drive," I tell Mia. "I can't wait until you guys get here."

"Same," Mia says. "Hey, are you okay? You sound a bit funny."

"Fine," I quip, injecting a bit of enthusiasm into my voice, but that's like wrapping a gift with cellophane. Pointless. She knows me too well.

"Everything okay with you and Bentley?"

"Fine, fine." I wave my hand even though she can't see me. "He's just been rather busy this week."

She goes quiet for a second, and I brace myself. Mia has never been a Bentley fan. She's questioned his love for me in the past, and mine for him. When she says things like "I plan to feed you so much tequila you won't be able to walk down the aisle," she's only half teasing.

But I've made my choice, and she's here to support me. That's what best friends do. Besides, it's not like I'm ever going to hook back up with my college love, Josh Walker, from college. No, he took my virginity and then broke my heart back at Penn State. We met when I used the Penn Pal app to find a safe escort home from a party. He was a little wild, different from the men in my social circle, and I fell for him. Hard. When he pushed me out of his life, for reasons I still can't understand, it destroyed me. After college, I vowed one thing to myself: no more bad boys.

I almost snort. Bentley is what one would consider the complete opposite of a bad boy, which is why my father likes him. Sometimes I think he likes him better than his only daughter. My father introduced us, actually. Bentley Banks is the son of dad's colleague, and my father had made a list of his attributes, informing me he checked all the right boxes and would be great husband material.

Sadly, there is one box he'll never check. No one has. Not even Josh Walker from Penn State. The fault is not entirely theirs. My deepest, darkest bedroom secrets are mine and mine alone. Not that Bentley could even come close to giving me what I want behind closed doors, even if I told him about my salacious desires—and gave directions. Josh, however... But I'll never know, because he sent me packing and my secrets are tucked away safely, locked in my heart behind an impenetrable vault. Why, you ask? Oh, because I was brought up to be prim and proper, and it's wrong to want such dirty things between the sheets. I never even touched myself until I was in my early twenties. *Sinful.* My mother's word regarding masturbation or sex for only pleasure, not mine.

"Listen, Gemma, if you're having second thoughts—"

"I'm not," I say, knowing Bentley is a good fit for my life, outside the bedroom anyway, and I do truly care about him and his well-being. "Just hurry up and get here," I say. "I miss you guys. That's all that's going on," I say, driving the point home—this discussion is over.

"I'll pay the driver extra to speed," she says, and that pulls a laugh out of me.

I end the call and walk the long length of our

pool toward the villa as birds chirp in the trees overhead. Bentley told me he was going for a swim, but he's nowhere to be found. As moisture pools on my arms, I step back into our air-conditioned villa and pad quietly across the tiled floor. I search for my fiancé to let him know the girls are on their way, but my steps slow when I hear whispered words coming from the den.

I walk quietly as an uneasy sensation trickles through my blood. Why the heck is he whispering? Does he not want me to overhear something? Call it woman's intuition, call it prewedding jitters. Call it whatever you want, but every instinct I have warns that something isn't right.

I press my back to the wall outside the door and listen. My gaze catches a photo bursting with the vibrant colors of Belize's breathtaking foliage. With my breath stalled in my lungs, my heart beats a little faster, pounds against my ribs, as Bentley's hushed side of the conversation reaches my ears. I listen for a moment longer, and as my rattled brain pieces the heard—and unheard—fragments of conversation together, a small sound catches in my throat. My knees weaken, and I flatten my palms against the wall for balance.

"Wait, I think I hear something," he says. "Gemma, is that you?"

I move away from the door, hurry quietly down the hall and step into our bedroom. Unceremoniously, I plunk down on the bed, my world tilting on its axis as I sink into the soft mattress. I blink once, then twice, as Bentley's cruel words circle my brain. It would be so easy to tell myself I misunderstood, so easy to just plaster on a smile and continue on, status quo, but the thing is, there is a part of me that knows this engagement—wedding—is nothing but a big, stupid mistake. That I might have said yes because it's what any good daughter would do when a father was pushing her.

Is that really how you want to live the rest of your life, Gemma?

Don't we get only one shot at this?

My muscles tighten, a headache brewing in the back of my skull as that truth pierces like a hot poker. Honestly, I am so goddamn tired of being that yes girl, so tired of walking the line and suppressing a side of myself that is expanding, pushing against that impenetrable vault, demanding to be unleashed. I take a fast breath and then another to steady the pounding pulse at the base of my neck.

"Hey, there you are."

I glance up to find Bentley standing in the doorway. He frowns and angles his head to the side, a familiar gesture when he's puzzling something out. "Everything okay?"

Oh, everything is fine, other than the fact that I just heard my fiancé talking to God-knows-who and telling her I was nothing more than a stepping-stone for his career and that he'd be there to see her as soon as he could. Oh, yeah, things are just peachy.

But…

Why am I not throwing things at him, screaming at the top of my lungs, accusing him of being a cheating asshole who uses others to further his own agenda?

Why not indeed…?

"Gemma?" he asks and crosses the room, and I spot the worry in his eyes. "Are you okay?" What? Is he worried I overheard him? He damn well should be, since he obviously has a lot riding on our marriage. I believe those were the *exact* words I just overheard. He glances at the phone beside me. "Are your friends coming?"

As his gaze travels back to mine, a million thoughts go through my head, and I make the fast decision to pretend nothing is wrong—for now. My girlfriends are here to throw me a bachelorette party, and I'll be damned if I'm going to let the man with his own agenda, and a hot piece of ass on the side, rain on my parade. Yeah, I'll party with my friends this weekend, they spent a lot of money to come here and I don't want to put a damper on their weekend. I'll break the news to them Sunday, before they all head back home. Then I'll deal with the asshole staring at me like he hadn't just ruined my life.

Ruined my life?

Maybe I have that all wrong. Maybe I should be thanking him.

"Everything is fine," I say, a strange calmness coming over me along with a new kind of relief.

"They were just picked up by the driver and should be here shortly."

He nods and puts his hands into the pockets of his khaki pants. "I have some bad news."

This should be interesting. "Oh?"

"I was just on a business meeting." He jerks his thumb over his shoulder. "Not sure if you heard me or not."

He's testing me, and since I'm not ready to drop the bomb yet, I say, "No, I was in the backyard. I thought you were going for a swim."

"Phone rang. I'll be flying back to New York tonight. I have some business that needs my attention."

Business. Yeah, right. Then again, whatever girl needs his attention tonight, he could very well be using her for something other than sex. I almost snort. I kind of hope she is getting sex. As vanilla as that might be. But I guess one of us should at least be naked between the sheets. I honestly can't remember the last time he touched me.

"How long will you be gone?"

"A week, maybe more. Depending."

"Okay." I stand up, walk to my desk, and grab a pen and paper. That will give me time to gather my thoughts and figure out the best way to end this relationship. Maybe I'll write him a letter—although that's a cowardly way to end a relationship, and that's really not my style, not even to a guy who is using me. But maybe tonight, after I've had too much tequila, I'll be able to get my thoughts in order and put on paper what a slimeball he really is. If I had my paints, I'd put my brushes to canvas to express myself, but I don't, so a letter will have to do.

My father will be upset at this change of events—and not because he's spent a fortune giving me the perfect wedding. No, he'll be upset because my breakup will be a reflection on him, spotlighting our family in negative ways. If it's a slow-news week, the media will sink their teeth into the broken engagement of the senator's daughter. I shake my head. That's what I'm worried about the most? Sad, but yeah, it is. My parents spent their lives conditioning me to think and act a certain way. To put career and appearance before everyone. I am so tired of it all.

He clears his throat. "You're sure everything is okay?"

Honestly, I used to overlook the way he cleared his throat a million times a day, but right now, the mucus king is annoying the living hell out of me. In fact, everything about him is getting on my last nerve, from the way his beady eyes are narrowed, trying to figure me out, to the way he's rocking on his feet. I fist my hand around the pen and resist the urge to stab him with it.

I paste on a dazzling smile and catch my reflection in the mirror. The sadness beneath the upturned lips catches me off guard. What the hell is wrong with me? The guy I loved in college tossed me away like I was yesterday's newspaper, and my fiancé was just insulting me on the phone to a girl he's likely hooking up with. *He has to marry me.* Not because he loves me but because it's good for his career.

Am I that unlovable?

I've been the good girl my whole life, done everything I was supposed to. Look where that's gotten me. Maybe I ought to just say the hell with it, throw caution to the wind, and for once in my life, do something I want to do—regardless of the consequences.

Yeah, maybe that's exactly what I'll do this weekend.

CHAPTER TWO

Josh

A RAP SOUNDS on my penthouse-suite door, and after a long day of inspections and dealing with staffing issues, I loosen my tie and snarl. Did I forget to put out my Do Not Disturb sign? With plans to get rid of whoever it is on the other side, and quickly, I scowl and swing the door open with much more force than necessary. The second I come face-to-face with my little brother—although at six foot four, two inches taller than me, he's not so little—my head rears back. Warmth and love race through me as he grins at me, his arms spread wide, and a smile parts my lips as I wave my hand for him to enter.

"What are you doing here, Nate?"

"Hey, what kind of greeting is that for your favorite brother?"

I laugh. "My only brother, you mean," I say as I pull him in for a hug. "Seriously, what are you doing in Belize? Shouldn't you be out at some photo shoot or filming your next big flick?" I take his chin between my fingers and turn it from side to side to examine his pretty face. My baby brother, now twenty-seven, grew up to be one hell of a good-looking guy, coveted by magazines and Hollywood alike.

"Don't be jealous that I got all the looks in the family," he teases, and I laugh again.

"I've missed you, but seriously, what are you doing here?" I shut the door behind him, and he wanders into my suite as I pour us each a glass of brandy. I swirl it around in the crystal glass and hold one out to him.

"Nice place," he says, stalling as he steps up to the deck and looks at the private penthouse pool.

"Uh-huh. Still doesn't answer my question."

He opens his arms and looks around my room. "Isn't this weekend the soft opening of your newest hotel?"

"Yeah, but since when did you ever come to a soft opening? You can see why I'm surprised, right?"

"I like a soft opening as long as it allows for a hard entrance," he teases with that bad-boy grin that has all the ladies dreaming of getting it on with him.

"Jesus," I say and shake my head. "I wish Mom hadn't dropped you on your head when you were a baby."

He laughs at that, even though it's a high possibility. After Dad was hauled off to prison for armed robbery, Mother Dearest lost herself in the bottle.

I stepped in to take care of two-year-old baby bro at the young age of seven, after he'd rolled off the change table and damn near split his skull open.

"This is Belize, bro. Only my favorite place on the planet."

I eye him. I love Nate more than life itself, but he's a sly son of a bitch, always trying to get his own way about something or another. He's here for a reason, something that has nothing to do with my opening. I can feel it in every fiber of my being, plus he has that telltale tic of tugging on the back of his hair when he's up to no good.

"Yeah, I know you do. You were the one who convinced me to open a hotel here, but that still doesn't explain why you've suddenly shown up out of the blue."

"Consider it my gift to you," he teases, and I'm seconds from putting him in a headlock to drag the truth out of him when he continues with, "I thought it would be fun to surprise you and to help you celebrate."

"Okay, don't tell me, then." I hold my crystal tumbler out in salute and we both drink to that. "And you know I hate surprises."

His phone pings, and he pulls it from his back pocket. He frowns as he turns from me to read the text. I leave him to his business and get rid of my tie and jacket and start working the buttons on my shirt. After spending the last few days ensuring the hotel was up to my standards, each boutique room designed to my specification—guest satisfaction is my main concern—I'm ready to throw on a pair of sweats and fall asleep in front of the TV.

Nate tucks his phone away and looks at me standing there in nothing but my dress pants and open shirt. "That won't do."

"What are you talking about?"

"We're going out to celebrate." He spreads his arms and looks around. "What is this, your tenth hotel now?"

"Something like that," I say, even though it's my twelfth.

"Then you need a real gift." He holds his arms open. "I mean, I know it's going to be hard to top me, but I'll see what I can do."

What is my baby brother up to? "What do you have in mind?" I ask cautiously.

He wags his brows. "You want me to tell you and ruin the surprise."

"Yes. I don't like surprises, remember?" I cross my arms and square off against him.

"I think you're going to like this one."

"Doubtful."

"Trust me on this, and you need to change." He steps past me and I follow him into my bedroom. He opens my closet and pulls out a polo shirt and a pair of chinos.

I point to the sofa in the other room, "That cushion has my name on it, and in five minutes, my ass plans to join it."

"Change of plans, bro." He holds the clothes out to me, and I ignore him.

I walk to my window, watch the trees sway in the evening breeze, and out of nowhere, that old familiar ache spreads through my chest. "You go ahead. I'm going to call it an early night. Guests will be arriving tomorrow, and I have the masquerade party to prepare."

He makes a tsk-tsk sound, and I glance at him over my shoulder as he finishes off his brandy. "All work and no play." I follow him back into the main room, and his glass hits the mahogany bar with a thud.

"Oh, I get lots of play," I say and present him with my brightest smile, even though it probably doesn't reach my eyes. It hasn't for a long time. The truth is, my boutique hotels cater to, let's just say, clientele with certain kinds of desires, and I can play all I want. I just don't want to. Not anymore anyway.

He tosses the clothes at me, refusing to take no for an answer. "It's my first night in town, Josh. Come on. I want to go out." I'm about to cut him off, but he gives me that damn pouty face that reminds me how hard our life was and how I'd do just about anything for him.

I take a deep breath and exhale slowly. "Why are you such a pain in my ass?"

He grins, knowing he's got me right where he wants me.

"Because you, my big brother, look like you haven't been laid in a long time, and tonight, we're going to go out, have a few drinks and have a little fun. You're lucky I'm here."

"Luck? That's what we're calling it?"

Okay, so it's true. I haven't been laid in a long time. The opportunity is there. I just... I don't know. I can't explain it. Maybe I'm played out. Not great for a guy who opens boutique hotels for those looking to play. I'm supposed to lead by example yet find myself wanting to crawl into bed at 9:00 p.m. I don't know who the hell I am, or what I want, anymore.

Well, maybe that's not entirely true. I know what I want. I just can't have her, which is why I pushed Gemma from my life back in college.

"You okay, bro?" Nate asks, and I nod.

I shake my head to clear it and shrug my shoulders to remove my shirt. "Yeah, maybe you're right. Maybe I do need a night out."

"That's my man," he says and slaps me on the back. He checks his phone again as I dress, and once I'm done, we take the stairs to the first floor. Nate never uses the elevator. It's a claustrophobic thing from childhood, and I'm not about to try to change that now. We all have demons that aren't going anywhere, so why bother fighting them?

In the lobby, I call for my driver, and the next thing I know, Nate is giving him directions to an exclusive club called Euphoria.

I've heard of the place. It's pretty elite. "How are we getting in?" I ask, a part of me hoping we don't.

He points to his face, and I just shake my head. "That ego is going to get you in trouble one of these days."

"Until then, let's go party like it's 1988."

If there's one thing my brother knows how to do, it's make me laugh. Humor has always gotten him out of bad situations—a childhood reflex. Not that I'd ever let anything bad happen to him. No, when Mom brought home "uncles" for a visit and they drank too much, I jumped in to be the punching bag to save my mother and little brother. When I was old enough to fight back, fewer and fewer came around and my mother blamed me. Damned if I do, damned if I don't, right?

"What do you know about 1988?" I ask.

"Nothing. I'm not a dinosaur like you."

"Fuck off." I shove him and he laughs. "I'm hardly a dinosaur at thirty-two," I say as I glance out the window. The car slows and I spot a young family walking down the street, swinging their little boy between them every couple of steps. My entire body clenches. A pain—longing—presses down on me, heavy, suffocating, weaving its way around my heart and stealing the air from my lungs.

I fake a cough to cover the rumble in my throat as my mind trips back to college days, to Gemma Long, to be precise. The only woman I've ever loved. Sweet Gemma Long was a senator's daughter. A good girl with a bright future ahead of her—one that didn't include a guy like me. I angle my head to see my brother and find him staring at me, watching the internal struggle going on inside my brain. Shit, I always hide that from him, but in these moments of weakness, he can see through me, and I hate that. I square my shoulders and push the past down, where it belongs. The car comes to a complete stop, and I reach for the handle, needing an escape from Nate's all-knowing gaze.

Laughter reaches my ears and my head snaps up. I catch a glimpse of numerous people dressed to party entering the club, their arms entwined, their laughter free and musical. For a brief second, my heart stops beating, and need pierces my soul like a lethal arrow. I try to breathe past it, because I have to be mistaken. I have to be. No way would the woman I've never stopped loving and was just thinking about be here in Belize, entering the same club as me, no less. I don't believe in coincidences. I have to be hallucinating. Yeah, hallucinating. That's the answer.

"You okay, bro?" Nate asks, joining me on the sidewalk.

"Yeah," I say and quickly pull myself together. "Thought I saw someone I knew, but it was a mistake."

He glances around. "Who was it?"

"Not important," I say, convinced I'm seeing things, simply because I let my mind drift to the past, something I never allow. But for some reason, in some moment of weakness I usually never give into—hell, I have no idea where Nate and I would be today if I didn't lead with strength and control—

my mind conjured up the woman who is still friends with my brother but could never be mine.

Before I can stop it, my mind once again trips back to those days. I was doing my master's when Nate started college and became instant friends with the senator's daughter. I thought they were an item, until she used the Penn Pal app and I escorted her home from a frat party. From that night on, we were inseparable, and I still consider it a gift that she wanted me to be her first lover. The way she opened to me, the way she put herself in my hands, not really knowing what she was doing. I was so achingly gentle with her—giving her just what she needed—and I treasured what she was giving me. I was so fucking in love with her.

I swallow against the tightness in my throat. I'm sure Nate stays in touch with her, but I don't ask because I don't want to talk about her, don't want to hear about her engagement to some douchebag lawyer who is much better suited to her lifestyle. A guy like me would drag her good reputation through the mud, and I care too damn much about her to do that.

We're stopped at the entrance by a muscle-bound bodyguard. He holds his hands up and asks for our names. Nate gives him that Hollywood grin, and the guy's face relaxes. "Wait. You're Nate Walker, right?"

"The one and only," he says and gives me a wink.

"Can I get a picture?"

"My pleasure."

The bodyguard hands me his phone, and I snap a few pictures as they both play it up for the camera. "Go on in," he says but stops me. He glances at Nate. "Do you know this guy?"

Nate taps his chin like the smart-ass he is, and I just shake my head. "I'd be happy to go home," I say.

He laughs. "No, no. That's my big bro," he says to the bodyguard, who drops his hand and lets me pass.

Loud music reaches my ears and it occurs to me that I might be getting too old for this shit.

"There's seats at the bar," Nate says, and I follow him through the crowd, the sweet scent of perfume thick in the air. Bodies bang against mine. A laugh curls around me and I spin, once again expecting to see Gemma. Jesus, what the fuck is wrong with me? I guess ever since reading about her engagement in the papers, it's been ripping away at the Band-Aids covering old wounds. Maybe my little brother is right. Maybe I do need to get laid tonight.

Nate orders two shots and hands me one. We clink glasses and follow it with beer chasers. I begin to relax, the stress of the last few days falling away from my shoulders. A woman sidles up to my brother. I can hold my own in a crowd of women, but I'm pretty invisible when he's around. That's okay, though; he enjoys the attention much more than I do. He speaks to the woman for a moment, but then his cell phone pings again and he turns from her.

He punches away on his phone and ribbons of unease worm through my veins. What the hell is going

on with my happy-go-lucky brother? He never inter-
rupts a conversation to take a text. A few mintues
later, he ends the texting and plasters on a smile,
but I know him well enough to know something
isn't right.

"What's up, Nate?"

He scrubs the stubble on his chin. What is it the
magazines call those prickly hairs…deliciously sexy?
I almost laugh at the thought.

"Nothing. Just have to hit up the boys' room."
He glances out at the dance floor, almost like he's
searching for someone, and once again, I stiffen.

"Are you in some kind of trouble?"

"No, bro," he says and slaps my back.

He disappears and I turn toward the bar and order
another shot. I throw it back and slam the glass down
with more force than necessary. I glance around the
room and check my watch. Seconds slip into minutes, and before I know it, a half hour has gone by.
Where the fuck did Nate go? I push from my seat
and make my way to the men's room. Something isn't
right. I feel it in every fiber of my being. I push the
door open, find the stalls empty, and I'm about to
head back to the bar when my phone pings.

Nate: Sorry, got sidetracked.

Me: Where are you?

Nate: Hotel, and I'm not alone.

I snort at that. Of course he isn't, but why the hell did he drag me down to this club with him only to disappear within the first five minutes? Truthfully, it's not like him. Neither is showing up at one of my hotels unannounced. Something smells funny, and it isn't just the guy standing next to me. Another wave of unease hits me like a sucker punch, and my mind conjures up the worst possible scenarios—compliments of my upbringing. Nate is the only family I have and if... My phone pings again.

Nate: Just head back to the hotel.

Me: Tell me you're okay.

A picture of him with some girl comes through, and I relax. Although the girl does look vaguely familiar. Then again, all the women I've encountered lately have been blending into one. No one sticks out or can hold my attention for any length of time. Not since...

Stop thinking about her.

Nate: See, I'm better than okay.

Nate: Go home old man.

Me: Fuck off.

Nate: Love you.

Me: Love you too, bro.

Nate: Just remember that, okay.

The hairs on the back of my neck lift. What the hell?
Why would he say something like that?

Me: What the fuck is that supposed to mean?

My grip tightens on my phone as I wait for an answer. When none comes, I figure he's busy with
other things—mainly the hot blonde. I shove my
phone into my back pocket and push through the
crowd. Outside, I call for my driver and stifle a yawn
as the warm night air falls over me. Now that I'm
not with my brother, a few girls flirt with me, but
I'm not interested. I politely decline and hop into the
back of the car when it arrives.

When I finally arrive at my hotel, the hairs on the
back of my neck once again begin to tingle. I tug my
wallet from my pocket and search for my key card.
What the fuck? My brother perfected pickpocketing
when we were young. I didn't condone it, but sometimes that was the only way we could eat. There are
things in my past I'm not proud of, which is why I
try to give back as much as I can, now that I've made
a success of myself.

I stop at the main desk to get a new one. "Hey,
Bianca, I've misplaced my key card." She gives me
an odd look, and I glance around the lobby. I'm not

sure what it is I expect to see. I only know my gut is sending warning signals, and I never ignore my gut. "Everything okay?"

"Yes, sir." She slides a new key card across the marble counter. "I put your brother in the Captain's Suite. I hope that is satisfactory with you."

"Nate's here?" I just assumed Nate would be staying in my suite with me, and if he was hooking up, he'd go back to the woman's place, not get his own room here.

"Yes, sir. He said you wouldn't want to be disturbed when you returned, which is why he asked for his own room."

What the hell is my little brother up to? I take the elevator to my penthouse suite and slide my card through the slot. The second I open my door, my world spins on its axis, and Nate's strange behavior tonight suddenly makes complete sense. Oh, and yeah, I'm going to fucking kill him.

CHAPTER THREE

Gemma

"HELLO," I SAY when I hear the door open. A shiver of excitement goes down my spine and I shift in the chair I'm tied to. I giggle, wondering what the girls are up to. We were all on the dance floor, having fun and doing shots, when we ran into Nate Walker, the younger brother of the man who broke my heart. Nate and I are friends. We go way back, and while he knew the bachelorette party was this weekend, I was shocked that he showed up—and crashed it. Not that I cared. I love the guy like a brother.

We were all dancing, and the next thing I know, Nate and my friends were piling me into a party bus, blindfolding me and taking me God-knows-where. I shift in my chair and angle my head, trying to see through the blindfold, but they did too good of a job securing it.

"Are you going to dance for me?" I say and giggle some more when I hiccup. Maybe I shouldn't have had that last shot of tequila, or the five beforehand.

Footsteps cross the room, come closer, and I can feel a big male presence before me. Should I be scared? Nah. My friends would never put me in harm's way.

"If you're going to dance, you might want to remove my blindfold first. I'd like to watch."

He crosses behind me, and I shift, breathing in the enticing scent of man mixed with that of the beach and outdoors. A fine shiver goes through me when his fingers graze the back of my neck, and I exhale sharply. The last time a man's touch made me do that was back in college. Not even my fiancé, or rather ex-fiancé, could pull that kind of reaction from my body.

The knot behind my head loosens, and I blink my eyes into focus as the gorgeous suite comes into view.

"Should I turn around?" I ask, anxious to see the man my friends hired to perform for me.

Instead of answering, he circles me, and air rushes from my lungs in a whoosh when I come face-to-face, or rather face-to-crotch, with none other than Josh Walker. My gaze slides up, takes in the hardness on his face, the tightening of his jaw. My God, I don't think I've ever seen him so pissed off—well, except for the time he punched that paparazzi in the face. I open my mouth but can't seem to form a coherent thought. My mind races—images, memories, old hurts all crashing over me at once. Before

I even realize it, tears pool in my eyes, and he instantly goes soft.

"Hey," he says in a tender voice that pulls at my stupid heartstrings. I don't want him to be nice to me. It's easier to hate him that way. He drops to his knees, his big palm warm and comforting on the side of my face. "You okay, Gemma?"

"What's going on?" I ask as a tsunami of love and hurt tug me under until breathing becomes difficult. Why would my friends do this? They know the pain this man put me through. I struggle to fight tears, to stop myself from shattering before his eyes.

"I think your friends and my brother kidnapped you and brought you here to me."

His big hands work the ropes holding me to the chair, and as his fingers touch my body, it fires me up inside, reminds me that I'm a woman and that I have certain desires.

"Why?" I ask. "Why would they do this?"

He grips the rope and tugs, and, catching me completely by surprise, pleasure pushes back the pain and a low, needy moan catches in my throat. Josh goes still and glances at me with those dark, almost black, eyes of his. Is that arousal I see reflected in them? His gaze moves over my face, and as if testing me, he tugs on the ropes again. He gauges my reaction, but there is nothing, not a goddamn thing I can do to suppress the need rising in me. My nipples tighten beneath my thin, summery dress, and I squeeze my thighs together, aching for something long and hard to fill me. But good girls like me, a dutiful senator's daughter, should not want to be tied up and taken, right?

"Sorry, this is tighter than I thought. It's making it a bit difficult to loosen this one. Whoever tied these made sure you weren't going anywhere in a hurry."

"Nate tied them."

He frowns, like he's confused by that. "I have no idea why he tied them so tight, but I'll get you out of these ropes, so you can be on your way," he says, his voice an octave lower. I wince, but it's not because of pain. I love the way he's tugging on the ropes. "Am I hurting you?"

Please, hurt me...just a little.

Those words linger on the tip of my tongue, my body begging me to spill all my secrets, tell him all my deepest, dirtiest desires. Would it frighten him away or have him wanting to fulfill all my carnal needs? But I can't say anything. This man doesn't want me. He made that clear back in college when he kicked me to the curb.

"No," I say, my voice nothing but a breathless whisper. He works the knot, and I take his scent into my lungs, as I admire the athletic man on his knees beside me. "Why do you think they brought me here?" I ask.

"You tell me. They're your friends."

"Nate is *your* brother," I counter.

"I'll be having a talk with him, don't worry."

"I honestly had no idea you were even in town

or that they had this planned. I'm just as shocked as you."

And delighted.

For the first time since he took my blindfold off, a smile cracks his lips. "Disappointed that you're not getting your lap dance?" he asks, probably to lighten the mood. He never liked to see me cry.

I laugh to cover the emotions stabbing holes in the armor around my heart. "It's not too late."

His smile falls. "It's too late," he says, and I get that he's talking about us, not a lap dance. He's making it perfectly clear that tonight was a mistake. He lifts his head and my heart hurts as I gaze at him. "You really don't know why they brought you to me?"

I shake my head, but maybe there is a part of me that does know. Maybe they realize, like I have, that Bentley is all wrong for me, and they set this up to see if we could get back together. They all know I've never stopped loving Josh. He was the one who stopped loving me, so this little setup was a total waste of their time.

Or was it?

Josh and I were always good in bed. He might not have given me the dirty sex I crave, but we were still good together. Maybe tonight, judging by the heat I'd spotted in his eyes earlier, we could crawl into his bed, you know, for old times' sake. I'd make it clear it was his body I was after, not his heart. Yeah, I'd be sure to make that perfectly clear.

He backs up, goes to his bar and grabs me a bottle of water. He removes the cap and hands it to me.

"Thanks," I say, and his gaze moves to my wrists, a little chafed from the bindings.

He takes one hand into his and displays the utmost tenderness as he passes his thumb lightly over the reddened skin. "Does this hurt?" he asks.

"A bit."

"Sorry."

"It's okay. You weren't the one who tied me up," I say, and the muscles along his jaw ripple as he clenches his teeth, like he's in total agony. What the heck? Does he *want* to tie me up?

Without a word, he leaves, and I sip water until he comes back with some sort of salve. He sinks to his knees. His mouth right there, aligned with mine if I wanted to kiss him. Goddammit, I do. But I want to do more than kiss him. I want him to take my clothes off, tie me back up, spread my legs and have his way with me—all night long.

As if reading my mind, a tortured sound rises in his throat and he coughs to cover it. But it's too late. I heard it, and there is no way he can deny he wants me. Physically, that is. So why shouldn't we? I can't think of a damn reason why not. I mean, I no longer consider myself engaged, although I'm not ready to admit it to anyone. It's embarrassing that neither of the two men I was deeply involved with wanted me to the same degree in return.

"Let me," he says and dips his finger into the

ointment and lightly brushes it over my wrists. My God, this probably isn't supposed to be turning me on, right?

"Better?" he asks.

"Yes," I manage to croak out. He stands back up and puts a measure of distance between us, and I instantly miss his warmth. "What are you doing in Belize?" I ask.

"I'm here to make sure the soft opening of my hotel goes smoothly."

I take another glance around the luxurious room. I knew he was a businessman who owned properties, but I didn't know what kind of properties. "You own this hotel?"

He nods. "I open resorts around the globe. Belize is my brother's favorite destination, and he convinced me a boutique hotel would be a huge success. Did you know he was going to be here?"

"Yeah, we...talk. I told him about the engagement party, and I have a villa here," I say.

"You should be getting back to it. Back to your fiancé," he says, as he averts his gaze and moves to the bar to pour himself a stiff drink. "I'll have my driver take you."

"What if I'm not ready to go back?" I say. If all my friends brought me to Josh, they want me to be here. I'm not abandoning them if I stay, and with Bentley gone, they'll have the villa to themselves. They'll be just fine without me.

"You need to go back," he says, his words so thin

and sharp, they slice me like a sculpting knife. But beneath those words, simmering just below the surface, I can almost taste Josh's arousal. He's pushing me away, again, but what if he knew I wasn't asking for his heart this time. He picks up his phone and makes a call to his driver.

After he shoves the phone back into his pocket, he comes back to me and helps me from my chair. I wobble a bit, my muscles tight after being held in the same position for some time.

"I'll walk you out," he says.

Like the good girl my parents have trained me to be, I follow Josh as he takes me to the elevator. He's completely silent as we descend, but after we get off and make our way through the lobby, a painting on the wall catches my eye, and I nearly sink to the floor in shock.

"Josh?" I say.

"What?" he asks and turns back when he realizes I'm not following him.

I stare at the erotic art, take in the familiar fine lines of the model's naked body and the way her lover is tugging on the binds that tie her. "Where did you get this painting?" I croak out, my breath coming so fast now, I'm sure I'm going to hyperventilate.

"Why? What's wrong with it?" he asks.

"Nothing. It's just… Where did you get it?"

"I found it on an auction site, actually. I'd love to have more, but the artist didn't sign it. There's just a lily painted on the back, like it's the signature or something." He angles his head, his eyes assessing me. "Do you know the artist?"

I am the artist.

I don't say that, though. My erotic art is a secret. I can't imagine what the clientele at my mother's high-end gallery would think if they knew I created pieces like this in the privacy of my studio. If word got out, it could ruin the gallery's name.

"I...don't," I fib. I hate lying, I really do, but I can't tell him I did this. My gaze moves over the piece again. It was one of my favorites, and I took it home with me one night, hung it in my bedroom. I was devastated when my place was broken into and this piece went missing. I never knew what happened to it.

"Do you think you could find out, ask around at the galleries?"

I nod. "Sure. I can ask around."

He looks over the piece. "I'd love to find the artist. I'd deplete their supplies."

"You really like this?"

"Pieces like this are perfect for my hotels. I'd pay a hefty price to commission the artist."

I bite my lip to stop myself from smiling. A measure of pride wells up inside me, to know Josh loves my erotic art.

"I'll see what I can do," I say.

"I appreciate it." He gestures with a nod. "My driver is waiting."

As we move through the lobby, I glance around

and something niggles in the back of my mind as I admire the furniture, the erotic decorations of couples entwined. My gaze settles on a sign outside a ballroom. Masquerade Party.

"What's going on in there?" I ask.

"Nothing," he says briskly.

"It's not nothing. It says Masquerade Party," I challenge, a new kind of excitement racing through me. There is something more going on here, something he doesn't want me to know about, which makes me want to know all the more. I can be tenacious like that when I want to be.

"That's tomorrow night, for our soft opening."

"Identities are kept secret at masquerade parties. Why on earth would people want to hide behind masks at the soft opening?" He tugs on his hair, uncomfortable with my questions. I take a step toward the room. "Is it invitation only?" I ask, my interest piqued.

"It's for the guests staying here," he says.

As the tumblers all fall into place, my eyes widen. "This...this is a hedonistic hotel, isn't it?" Shocked and excited by this new revelation, my gaze flies to the man who can't seem to look at me. Holy God. My Josh—well, he's not *my* Josh—is into hedonistic sex and owns hedonistic hotels? How did I not know this? Why would he keep this side of himself from me?

Then again, I kept that side of myself from him. Even if I told him, spoke the words out loud, he still wouldn't believe I was not just pure vanilla, like I'd been in college.

"You're wrong. It's just a hotel. Nothing is going on," he answers gruffly, a clear indication that this conversation is over, as he takes my elbow to change my direction. Whatever is going on in that room or this hotel, he obviously doesn't want me to know.

"Josh—"

"You need to go, Gemma."

Could I be wrong? Is this just a hotel or is it a hotel that caters to those with special desires? If so, does Josh play? Damned if I don't want to hang around to find out. As I consider that, a fine shiver shimmers down my spine as equal amounts of hope and need well up inside me. With a firm grip on my arm, he leads me outside to the waiting vehicle. He opens the door for me, and I slide in.

I pull a tube of bright red lipstick from my purse, and swipe it over my lips. According to Peyton, who'd given it to me at my bachelorette party, it has aphrodisiacal powers. I guess we'll see about that. "It was nice seeing you again, Josh."

"Nice seeing you, too, Gemma. I hope you have a nice weekend with your friends."

I smile at him as he closes the door. Oh, I plan on having a nice weekend, only it's not going to be with my friends. No, it's going to be with him. He just doesn't know it yet.

CHAPTER FOUR

Josh

I CHECK MY phone again, but my little brother is not answering my messages. I pounded on his door last night after seeing Gemma safely to my car—and almost carried her right back to my suite when she put that fuck-me red lipstick on—but it's clear Nate's hiding from me. I knew he was up to something the second he showed up here. But I draw the line with meddling in my personal life, as well as Gemma's. She's as good as a married woman, for God's sake.

I take a calming breath. Getting worked up before the masquerade party isn't going to put my guests at ease. I strive to create a relaxed environment, where privacy is of the upmost importance. That security gives our guests the freedom to mingle and engage in different hedonistic activities without fear of exposure or judgment. Walking into that ballroom without total confidence in my security measures would not be conducive to the playful atmosphere I'm going for.

Once my tie is fixed, I pick up my mask and put it on. After giving myself a once-over in the mirror, I exit my suite and make my way to the elevator. Perhaps I'll find my brother in the ballroom and I can put this situation behind me once and for all.

Two women are wearing gorgeous form-hugging dresses, with masks covering their eyes. They're chatting and the excited energy in the air helps me relax even more. To know my guests are happy is my main goal.

The elevator arrives. "After you," I say, and one woman nibbles her lip before hopping on. That's when I realize she's Atlanta. She lives in New York, not far from my apartment, which I haven't been back to in ages, and she comes to all the soft openings. Oftentimes, we've played, and she's a sweetheart, mostly. That thought makes me laugh. When I say *mostly*, there are times she can be possessive of her flavor of the month, or week.

Her body brushes mine, a telltale sign that she's open for anything, and I give a nod, trying to muster the enthusiasm to flirt back. Goddammit, ever since setting eyes on Gemma, it's all I can do to maintain focus. I'm seriously going to kill my brother.

We reach the main level. I hold the doors open as the ladies exit, and I let my gaze drop to Atlanta's backside, hoping the curves of her ass will put me in the right frame of mind. But no. They don't. All that does is remind me of Gemma's sweet ass and how I'll never have my hands on it again. Leaving her once was the hardest fucking thing I've ever had to do. I can't go through that again.

I smooth my hand over my tie and glance around the lobby. Servers are walking around with trays of champagne while others offer hors d'oeuvres—I spare no costs for my guests. The guests help themselves, and the beat of the music in the ballroom seems to call out to them like a hypnotic lullaby. They slowly saunter in until I'm the last in the lobby. I hang back a bit and use that time to scan the room, to ensure everything is up to my high standards.

Matteo, the hotel manager, comes my way. "Mr. Walker," he says with a tip of his head. I grin. No matter how many times I've asked him to call me Josh, he prefers to keep it formal.

"Everything in order?" I ask.

"All nondisclosure contracts have been signed," he says with a smile. I brought Matteo here from our Milan hotel, and he's been working with the local staff to get them all up to speed. "Is there anything special you might need this evening, sir?"

"I have everything I need," I say, even though it's a lie. The one thing—or should I say the one person?—I need can never be mine, and finding her in my suite, looking so goddamn demure and innocent was a reminder of that.

Was she really innocent, Josh?

My dick twitches, unable to forget her breathy little moan when I tightened those ropes, the way she seemed to take pleasure in the chafes on her skin and the aftercare I provided. My brother should know better than to bind an innocent so tightly. What the hell was he thinking? Unless he knows something I don't. Like sweet Gemma Long might like it a bit rough.

I shake my head and quickly squash that thought. That's just wishful thinking on my part. Even if she wanted to play hard, she won't be playing with me. She's engaged to another man, which means she's hands-off.

I accept a glass of champagne and make my way into the ballroom. The soft murmuring falls over me, and I sip from my flute as I examine my guests. I walk slowly, nodding to those in disguise. A hand lands on my back, and I turn to find Atlanta.

"Dance with me, sir," she says. In the past, whenever she called me *sir*, my cock would rise to the occasion. But I'm not about to disappoint Atlanta. I'll dance with her and then find her a more suitable partner for this evening, one who isn't wallowing in his own self-pity. I seriously need to get over myself.

I pull Atlanta into my arms and she melts against me, her finger going to my jaw. She traces a path. "How are you enjoying the opening?" I ask.

She pouts. "When you said it was a soft opening, I didn't think you meant…soft," she says and pushes against my body.

Shit.

"Sorry, Atlanta. You know how opening nights

are. I have to be alert and make sure everyone is having a good time." A laugh trickles through the air, and I instantly stiffen—not my cock but my whole body. I have no doubt the second I set eyes on the person laughing, my dick will follow suit. A man I'd spoken to earlier walks by, and I tap his arm. He turns to me.

"Would you care to dance with this beautiful woman?" I ask. "I have some things to check on."

Atlanta appraises the man and gives a nod of approval. I leave them alone, and as I weave through the crowd, I catch her scent. *What the fuck is Gemma doing here?* Perfume clouds the air, but I can detect her scent anywhere, anytime. I follow my nose, and the second I see her in a tight black dress that showcases long legs and a curvy body, my dick stands at attention. It doesn't matter that she's wearing a mask; I know it's her. Only problem is, she's in the arms of another man. Is it her fiancé? Did she bring him here to torture me, pay me back for the fiasco of last night—even though I had nothing to do with tying her up?

I should leave. Head back to my room and put my fist through something. But I can't seem to budge. My legs won't allow me to make a run for it. The guy she's with trails his hands down her back, and I clench down on my jaw when his fingers linger over the sexy swell of her ass. If that's not her fiancé, I'm going to break his arm.

Cool it, Josh. She's not yours to protect.

Yeah, fuck that.

I cross the room, and the second she sees me, she inches away. "Josh," she says, instantly recognizing me, too, and my gaze zeroes in on the guy she's with. It's not her soon-to-be husband. He's a hotel guest looking to play, and he doesn't need to remove his mask for me to make the call. Blood boils in my veins, and I do my best to control it. Control is everything for me. It's how I raised my brother and myself. It's how I got us both through college. I can't ever lose it.

"Can I speak to you for a moment?" I say to Gemma.

"I'm dancing, Josh. Don't be rude."

I glance at the gentleman, and he knows who I am. "It's okay," he says. "I was just about to grab a drink." With a nod of his head he saunters off.

She eyes me. "That was rude."

"He had his hand on your ass, that's what was rude."

"How did you know it was me?" she asks.

I shake my head. "Did you think I wouldn't recognize you, even with a mask on? You recognized me, didn't you?"

"You stand out, Josh."

"You do, too," I say.

"So much for our masks." She removes her mask and laughs, a low musical sound that trickles through my blood and massages my balls. They tug tight, and

I put my hand in one pocket and adjust my pants to loosen the pressure.

"Are you okay?" she asks.

I rip off my own mask and drop it onto a nearby table. "No, I'm not okay. You shouldn't be here." I practically drag her into a corner, needing a moment of privacy with her.

"Why not?" she asks.

"This party is for guests," I inform her through clenched teeth as I try not to stare at her lush cleavage. My mouth waters. God, what I'd do to have those nipples in my mouth again, licking, tasting, sucking—just one last time. My traitorous cock thickens even more, strains against my restrictive zipper. I have no desire to have another woman in my bed tonight—outside of Gemma, of course, and that can't happen—which means I'm going to abuse the hell out of myself. I can't even remember the last time I was reduced to using my damn palm.

She reaches into her handbag and presents me with a room key. "I am a guest."

Shit.

"Gemma, you don't know what you're getting yourself into here."

She gives me a sweet smile. "That's the fun of it, though, isn't it?"

"You've not a clue what you're talking about," I say and continue to clench my teeth as she puts her hand on my chest. God, I love the way she touches me. With every ounce of strength I possess, I grip

her wrist with a little more force than necessary—
no, no, no, stop testing her responses—and remove
her hand from my body.

"Is this *not* a boutique hotel that caters to hedo-
nism?"

I take a fast breath. "Yes."

She places a hand on her hip, and her beautiful
tits jiggle. "You lied to me."

"It was for your own good." I resist the urge to
tug at my crotch. "You need to go."

She stares at me for a second, and I can almost
hear the internal battle going on inside her brain.
Her big blue eyes, full of vulnerability, blink up at
me, and my insides soften. Jesus, what is going on
here?

"You know what's best for me, now, do you?"

I try another tactic and soften my voice. "This
isn't who you are, Gemma."

She lifts her chin an inch. "Maybe you don't know
who I am, at all," she counters.

"I do know who you are, which is why..." I let my
words fall off. It's better not to dig up the past and
reopen old wounds by telling her I pushed her away
because I was the wrong man for her. She's judged
by the public every goddamn day of her life, and if
the tabloids exposed all my secrets, it would destroy
her image. They can say what they want about me. I
don't care, but I do care when it hurts her.

"Which is why...what?" she asks, her eyes blazing hot as she stares at me.

"Which is why you should go back to your fiancé. I can't imagine he'd be too happy to find you at this kind of hotel, with me."

"Am I here with you, Josh?" Her lips part slightly, and the vulnerability I hear in her voice is like a kick to the nuts.

"What do you want, Gemma?"

"My friends and your brother gave me to you for a reason. Maybe I want to live in this fantasy life you have here, just once. You say this isn't me, but maybe I want to pretend to be someone else for a while." She touches me again, her hand trailing down my chest, going lower and lower until she's touching my hard cock. "You don't seem to have too much trouble with that idea."

My mind practically shuts down, and I'm two seconds from scooping her up, taking her back to my room and having my way with her when one working brain cell kicks me in the groin to wake me the fuck up. "You're engaged, Gemma. I don't put my hands on another man's woman. I thought you knew that about me."

She looks down, the sadness in her eyes is like a fist to my gut. Unable to help myself, I put my hands on her arms. "What is it? Did he hurt you?" My protective instincts come out full force. The last time someone messed with a person I loved, they paid a hefty price.

A person I loved?

No, no, no. I can't go there with Gemma again.

Right now, judging from the way she touched my cock, I might be the man she wants, but I am not the guy she needs in the long run.

"Gemma, did Bentley hurt you?"

She shakes her head, and her curls tumble around her shoulders. "I'm breaking it off with him."

Fuck, she's getting prewedding jitters. She's been with Bentley for two years now. I've seen their smiling faces splashed all over the social pages in New York. Clearly, they're in love or she deserves an award for her stellar performance. What is really going on here?

"You're just getting nervous. It's natural." At least, I think it is. Then again, what do I know? I've never been close to engaged, never let myself get close to anyone. Not emotionally anyway. Not since Gemma.

"Josh," she says firmly. "It's over with him. He just doesn't know it yet."

I put my arm around her back and lead her from the ballroom. "Maybe you two should talk. Work things out."

"No," she says, firmly. "I don't want to go. Please don't make me."

The fear in her words, the worry and something else, something that sounds like she's been deeply hurt by her fiancé wraps itself around my heart and squeezes. I'm not sure what is going on, but when she looks at me with pleading eyes, how the hell could

I call for a car and send her on her way? I might be a lot of things, but I'm not a prick.

"Let me stay, Josh. Let me be someone else for a while."

I grip my hair and tug, about to say no, until the word "Please" spills from her beautiful lips. Fuck me. Maybe I should let her stay. She's clearly going through something painful, and I care too much about her to send her back to a situation she's running from.

"Who do you want to be, Gemma?" I ask quietly.

"I want to be like those women in the ballroom." She goes quiet as she takes in the women mingling, laughing and dancing. "I want to be carefree, just once. Able to do whatever I want in the privacy of this hotel. No cameras, no paparazzi."

I snort and her eyes narrow. "The paparazzi had better not show up, if they know what's good for them."

She frowns. "I'm so sorry that happened to you, Josh."

Her apology is a bit too late. Back when it happened, she let them crucify me. She never tried to stop the story, never used her position to get a retraction. On some level, I think she knows I'm not the guy she needs. I never held that against her, though. There was no point.

"The past is the past, where it should stay."

She hesitates for a brief second. "You're right, and this is the present and time to move forward."

She goes up on her toes, her mouth close to mine. "That's exactly what I'm doing. I signed the privacy agreement and I want all the experiences," she murmurs, the heat in her eyes a surefire sign that she's telling the truth.

I swallow hard. Jesus, how many nights have I thought about tying her up and having my way with her.

"I want those things…with you," she adds.

My heart thunders in my chest, crashes so hard against my ribs I worry they might break. But that's when I get what's going on here. I'm her last fling—someone she wants to play with, in a place where privacy is ensured—her last hurrah, before she settles into her prim-and-proper socialite life. Regardless, this isn't her and she has no idea what she's requesting or getting herself into.

"What you're asking for might ruin you, Gemma."

"Do your best."

"You have no idea what you're saying."

"You're right. But as long as I'm with you, I know I'm in good hands." She sidles closer. "Teach me, Josh… Teach me everything."

I shake my head, hardly able to believe what I'm hearing, until my mind drifts back to her heated gasp when I tugged on the rope binding her. Could I be wrong about her? Never in the past had she given any indication that she liked anything other than vanilla. She was a virgin when she met me. I took care of her, made sure the sex was soft and easy, the way any virgin would want, right? Is it possible that I missed all the signs, that she wanted more?

I'm not sure, but what I do know is I can't send her home, and I can't stop her from indulging in a little hedonistic fun for a little while—until she comes to her senses and goes back to the life she's built for herself, a life that does not involve me. One thing I'm sure about, however, is no man, and I mean *no* man but me, is going to touch her this weekend.

CHAPTER FIVE

Gemma

MY HEART JUMPS into my throat the instant he makes up his mind to let me stay here. He might not be vocalizing the words, but he doesn't have to. The answer is right there in the darkening of his already near-black eyes. He wants this every bit as much as I do. He might have tossed me away all those years ago when I offered up my heart, but this time, I know better than to put that on the line.

"Sex, Josh. Nothing more," I say, just to make sure my cards are on the table faceup. No confusion. No misunderstanding. No future.

He brushes the back of his knuckles over my cheek and I lean into his touch. "It's what you want, Gemma?"

"It's what I want," I say, and he puts an arm around my waist, his fingers biting into my hot skin in a tight hold, to keep me anchored to his hard body. What? Does he think I'm going to change my mind and run? For a while there, that seemed to be what he wanted. But the second I made it clear that this was just sex, he'd done a complete 180 and I plan to take full advantage of that.

He guides me toward the elevator, and I hesitate. Earlier, after checking in, the concierge gave me a tour of the place, including all the playrooms.

"Where are we going?" I ask.

"To my room."

I blink up at him, take in the muscles rippling along his jaw. My God, this man is intense, more now than when we were younger. But I like his intensity. He's a hard, type A personality, always in control, and when he puts his mind to something, he sees it to completion. I shiver, wanting him to turn that intensity on me—in the bedroom. In the past, he was soft and gentle, and I went along with it, because that's what good girls do. But this weekend, under the cover of a privacy agreement, I plan to let another side of me free. Will it ruin me? Will it be something I can't come back from?

I guess we're going to see.

In the empty lobby, he takes my hands, secures them behind my back, and I almost climax then and there. His gaze is like a rough caress as he scans my face and breathes me in. He dips his head and ever so lightly, brushes his lips over mine. A cry lodges in my throat as he takes my bottom lip between his and bites down, a teasing promise of things to come.

I'm so breathless, talking is difficult. "There are

other rooms, you know, much closer," I murmur, so damn anxious to get my hands all over his naked body, to have his on me in return. I think the long ride to the top floor might just kill me.

He drags me onto the elevator when it arrives. With his strong hands still touching me, he uses his elbow to jab the penthouse-suite button. "You're not ready for those other rooms," he announces, his voice a harsh whisper, and I go quiet to give that consideration. Maybe he's right, and I need to trust him and his decisions. Even though we have a past, and I'd been hurt, a part of me knows this man will do what's best for me.

I look at him with hopeful eyes. "When I am, will you take me to them?"

"Yes," he says, and I can't help but grin. Ever since I've known him, Josh has kept his control close and in check. Right now, however, he looks like he's strung so tight, he's about to snap. I'm not going to lie. I kind of like seeing him like this. Kind of like knowing I'm the girl who's turning him inside out.

The elevator takes us to the top floor. He quickly ushers me off, keeping me close to his body at all times, like his life might depend on the connection. I get it; I totally do. The sparks flying between us could burn down this hotel and every villa in a ten-mile radius. His grip on my hips is firm as he opens his door and unceremoniously pulls me in with him.

The door shuts with a thud, locking the real world out and us in. A thrill goes through my body and settles deep between my quivering legs. Once inside, he goes still and turns to me. His gaze rakes the length of me, like an animal about to devour its prey, and a hard quake, from the top of my head to the tip of my toes, racks my body.

"Cold?" he asks, his head angled, those intense eyes locked on mine.

"No."

He scrubs his face, tortured dark eyes momentarily sliding shut.

His eyes open, and big hands span my hips. He turns me to face the door. A second later my hands are enclosed in his, and he puts them above my head, braced against the surface. He murmurs into my ear, "Stay just like this."

I suck in a fast breath, loving the way he's taking control of me. But it's a control I'm giving him because I know he'll treasure it and care for me properly. It's hard to believe, after everything we've been through, that I still trust him like this. I just know better than to put my heart in his hands.

"Okay," I say breathlessly as I flatten my palms on the door, following his instructions.

His voice sounds a bit distant, like he's backed away, when he says, "You won't move, Gemma?"

I want to look over my shoulder, want to see what he's doing, but staying perfectly still like this comes with its own pleasure. Rustling reaches my ears, and I briefly close my eyes, visualizing him removing his tie and suit jacket. I always loved watching him undress. I could climax just from the masculine way he unleashes his tie.

"Answer me."

"I won't move," I finally manage to get out.

"Good girl." He's back again, his body close, his presence and scent overwhelming all my senses. "But you don't want to be a good girl, do you?"

"No, I don't."

"What do you want from me?"

"I want… I don't know, Josh. I just want everything. I mean I don't want *everything*," I say quickly, not wanting him to think I'm asking for more than his body. "I want new experiences. I want it rough…" I take a breath and admit, "I want it dirty."

He goes completely quiet and I remain still—well, except for my chest. It's rising and falling rapidly as he slides his big hands up my body, shaping my curves and brushing my outer breasts. A second later, he pulls his hands away, leaving cold where there was once warmth, and a measure of panic grips me. Has he changed his mind? I swear to God, if he shuts me out now, I'll melt right here, leaving nothing but a puddle of my former self on his penthouse-suite floor.

"Gemma." His mouth is near my ear, his breath hot on my flesh. My nipples ache in response. "Tell me now. Tell me you really want that. Once I get started, I just… I might… I might damage you." He exhales harshly, and a warmth trickles down my spine as his low tortured murmur wraps around my shattered heart, a soothing balm to the pain he'd once inflicted on me.

"Damage me," I say, conviction in my voice. I've always wanted him. Neither time nor distance has changed that fact. I almost laugh at that, considering my engagement to another man has never stopped me from wanting this one.

None too gently, he wraps my hair around his fist and tugs until my head is pulled back. I groan as pleasure forks through me, and his lips find the sensitive spot on the side of my neck. He kisses me and reintroduces his hands to my body as he pushes his hard cock into the small of my back.

I move against him, massaging his thick cock, as a whimper of need crawls out of my throat. One hand slips under my dress as he kicks my legs apart to widen them for him. I spread, and he groans against my throat. At the juncture of my legs, he tugs my panties to the side, and my whole body shakes with excitement.

"Yes," I cry out.

"Shh," he whispers. "Nice and quiet for me."

I clamp my mouth shut with an audible click, and his chuckle rumbles along my spine and strokes me deep inside. He breathes out heavily as he runs his finger along my seam, parting my lips.

"So, so wet, Gemma."

I swallow a cry, and want to buck against his hand, want to force him to touch me harder, put a finger inside me. His other hand goes to my mouth, and he pushes his thumb between my lips.

"Suck on me," he says, and I do as he asks.

Years ago, I never took this man into my mouth. I didn't think it was something he'd like. That almost makes me laugh. What man doesn't like oral sex? Now I realize he must have thought it was something the good girl wouldn't like to do. My sex clenches, excited that he's treating me differently this time, treating me the way I *need* to be treated. I want to cry out my gratitude. But I keep my mouth shut, like he instructed.

I suck harder, and he rewards me by brushing the rough pad of his other thumb over my aching clit. A whimper I have no control over catches in my throat, and he takes his thumb from my mouth. With one hand still between my legs, he unzips my dress, and unhooks my bra. They fall and snag on his hand as he pushes a thick finger into me. My fingers curl against the door, and my damn legs nearly give.

"Shh," he says again. "Just relax, and don't think about anything other than my finger inside you." He pumps in and out of me and presses his palm to my clit, grinding his hand against me. My entire body tightens, and pleasure centers between my legs. My God, I am going to come harder than I ever have before. It builds inside me, grows, expands, threatens to shut down my ability to breathe. I want to come, but I don't want this to stop. Ever.

"You like this, Gemma?" he says in my ear. "You

like fucking like this, up against the wall, your dress around your hips?"

"Yes," I cry out, and just like that I come. I try to think, to breathe, but all I can do is concentrate on the intense pleasure tearing through me. I come, and come and come some more, each clench harder than the last.

He growls and keeps his hand between my legs as I spasm around him while gasping for breath. I claw at the door, pound against it, as the world shuts down around me. Josh puts his other arm around me to hold me upright, supporting me as I give in to the most powerful orgasm of my entire life. My God, what I've been doing before could hardly be classified as sex. Now that I've had a taste of this, a bare lick of the icing, I want more.

I try to talk, but can't seem to form a full sentence. "That... That..."

"That was just the beginning," he says, and I press my face to the door and try to capture my breath. Once my orgasm subsides, he removes his hands and drops to his knees to pull my dress down. He touches one ankle and I lift it, repeating with the other. I tip my ass up, just to tease him and bite back a smile when he growls.

"You don't know what you're doing to me, tempting me like that."

I gulp at the raw hunger in his voice as he tugs my panties up high on my waist, the lacy material sliding between my ass cheeks. Do I want that? Do I like the

idea of him taking me where I've never been taken?
Yes, I do. I want to experience everything with this
man. I might not be going back to Bentley, but I'll
be going back to being the proper socialite once this
weekend is over, so I plan to take full advantage of
all he's willing to give me.

"Maybe I do know," I say.

CHAPTER SIX

Josh

FUCK ME SIDEWAYS.

I look at the gorgeous woman in front of me, and take in the way her hot, lush body is calling out to me, begging for more…begging for me to do *everything.* I should walk away. No, I should run away. I should put as much distance between myself and this woman as possible. But this is Gemma, and she needs something from me tonight—even though I'm sure she doesn't know exactly what that might be—and I plan to give it to her.

Tonight, my actions are reckless, and tomorrow, there might be consequences. *Might?* Yeah, there will be hell to pay and emotions to rein in. But there is no way I'm letting any man, other than me, touch this woman. Do I think she'll get her head on right and go back to Bentley? Yeah, I do. Do I think it's the right thing for her to do? Same answer. Right now, however, the night is ours.

"You think you might like it from behind, Gemma?" I scoop her up and her arms go around my neck as her lust-filled eyes meet mine.

"I might," she says, and I shake my head, amazed by the things she's saying. I walk into the bedroom and set her on the edge of the bed. I stand back and look my fill. My mouth waters as I admire her full, lush breasts, the way her pretty pink nipples are hardening under my close inspection.

"Open your legs," I say, and she puts her hands on her thighs and spreads for me. She pulls the lacy material to the side to expose herself, and I reach into my pants. Her eyes grow wide and her gaze drops as I take my cock into my hand and pump. I fist myself, from base to crown, and groan as pleasure rips through me.

"Do you have any idea how you look right now?" I ask.

Her gaze leaves my pumping hand and flies back to mine. "Like I want to suck on your cock?"

My entire body goes tight. What is going on with her? I shake my head, astonished by her actions, her dirty words. The Gemma I know wouldn't say *cock*, let alone put one in her mouth. She really does want to be someone else tonight, someone bold, wild… free. But this isn't who she really is, right? Something has just gotten under her skin.

"Am I right?" she asks.

"You're right," I murmur under my breath.

"Come here." She opens her mouth and holds her

tongue out to me, and I almost shoot a load right there. Does she have any idea what she's doing to me? She's the one saying she wants new experiences, but this, right here, is new and exciting and everything to me.

I take my cock and trace the curve of her lips. I let it settle on the nook in her upper lip. "Do you like to suck cock, Gemma?"

"I've done it," she says, with a shrug. "But it's not something I've ever loved doing."

"Then why do you want to do it now?"

She smiles. "Because I think I'm going to love having *you* in my mouth."

"I like your honesty."

"There is no reason for us not to be honest with each other, Josh." She takes my cock in her hand and gives it a little squeeze. "Do you think you're going to like having your cock in my mouth as much as I'm going to like having it there?" she asks, a teasing edge to her voice.

Before I can answer, she says, "Do you think if I suck you really good, you'll put this fat cock inside me?" She leans forward, taking me all the way to the back of her throat and I let loose a ragged moan, full of want and need, and lust and love. Wait, no, not love. I can't love her. Not again.

Have you ever really stopped, Josh?

I tuck those thoughts away as she sucks me, and runs one hand up and down my long length.

"You're killing me," I whisper. I grip her hair

and tug hard, giving her what she wants as my hand follows the motion of her tongue. She glances up at me, the lusty gleam in her eyes turning me on even more. She takes me deeper, choking a little, and I try to pull back. I don't want to come. Not yet. There are so many things I need to do to this woman first, but I don't want to stop her, either. She's enjoying this as much as I am, and that's a total mind fuck.

My cock thickens, and I'm so damn close I need to stop her. I extricate myself from her mouth and she looks up at me, concern in her eyes. I brush my finger over her lips and reach for my tie.

I wrap the material around my fist and her chest rises and falls quickly. "Take off those panties and get on the bed."

She stands and slides her panties down her legs. My cock jumps, and I take it into my hand and stroke myself. Once she's naked, she turns and, on all fours, crawls to the center of the bed.

"On your back, arms and legs spread." As she does what I order, I strip off my clothes and walk to the foot of the bed as she positions herself and exposes her hot-pink sex to me.

"You want this?" I ask and rub my cock a bit faster.

Heat colors her cheeks as she says, "Uh-huh."

"Show me how much you want it," I say, and she cups her breast with one hand and slides the other between her legs. As she touches herself, I gather more ties from the closet, and take one of her ankles in my hands. Her finger works faster between her legs as I wrap a tie around her ankle. "Are you sure about this, Gemma?" I ask. Even though her body is telling me everything, I need to hear the consent on her lips.

"Yes," she murmurs. "Please…"

Hearing her plea makes me impossibly harder, and my cock twitches, eager to be inside her, but I don't want to rush tonight. No, there will be no tomorrows, and I want this moment to last so I can savor every second of our time together. Yes, I told her I'd take her to one of the playrooms, but come tomorrow, I suspect she'll gather herself and run back home, where she belongs.

I secure one leg and then the other. The mattress dips as I climb on it, and wedge my body between her thighs. She whimpers, and tosses her head from side to side as I brush her fingers away from her sex. It's my turn to touch and taste. I climb up her body, taking her wrists and securing them to the headboard.

I move back between her legs and stroke her there. Her hips lift from the bed, and I widen her lips to get a better look at her. "So pretty," I say and lightly tease her clit by circling it with my thumb, coming close but never touching.

"Josh…please…"

I go down on my stomach and slide my hands under her thighs, lifting her to my mouth. I inhale her arousal, and she tries to move, to buck against my face. I exhale, and she quakes as my heated breath washes over her quivering sex.

I bury my mouth between her legs and lose my mind to reality as her taste explodes on my tongue. "Gemma, Jesus. I've missed the taste of you," I say, and slide my tongue all over her, licking and sucking.

She moves against me shamelessly, giving herself over to me completely. Lifting my head, I glance at her as she wraps her fingers around my ties and tugs.

"Please, Josh…"

I fuck her with my tongue for another minute, then reach into my nightstand and grab a condom from the complimentary box found in all the rooms. Safety first at my hotels. Her head lifts as I bite into the foil and roll it on.

"You like being tied up like this?" I ask her and run my knuckles over her thighs. "You like being at my mercy?"

"I do," she says, looking up at me.

I'm ready to lose it before we even begin. I want to please her. I want to get her off more than I want my next goddamn breath. Her fingers wiggle, and I reach up to make sure the binding isn't too tight. I give them a pull and her excited gasp squeezes my cock.

"I want you, Gemma. I want you so fucking much. I want to bury my balls in you and stay until morning."

"Then, take me. Put your cock into me and take me hard. Please…"

I fall over her, my hungry mouth finds hers for a bruising kiss as I jerk my hips forward and enter her with one hard thrust.

Her head falls back, and her cries fill the room. "Just like that," she says. Her hard nipples score my skin as I pound into her soft flesh, her hot, tight channel making it near impossible to hang on. She moans and writhes and lifts to meet each blunt stroke that takes us both higher and higher, until I'm soaring without a parachute. I gasp for breath, but the air is thin where I am. But breathing doesn't matter. No, all that matters is giving this woman the pleasure her body is begging for.

"Josh," she cries out, and I bend, take her lip between mine and bite her. Tomorrow, she'll be bruised, marked by this night in more ways than one. She's not the only one who will be marred. I can't think about regrets, though, not now, when I'm so close to having the orgasm of my life.

I curl into her, my ass taut as I give her more, everything, and let go of her lip to press hot, open-mouthed kisses to the hollow of her neck. I breathe in the scent of her skin, kiss the moisture from her flesh as I thrust into her.

The second she breaks, her ecstatic cries filling the room, I throw my head back and let go, joining her in release as her hot, tight channel grips me.

"Gemma," I murmur. Her breaths are fast and labored, and I collapse over her once her body stops spasming.

I find her mouth again, and we kiss as we breathe together, riding the high and reveling in post-orgasm bliss. She exhales as I pull free, and I reach up to unleash both of her hands. I bring her wrists to my mouth, one at a time, and kiss the chafe marks.

"Josh," she says, her voice raw and soft and so damn vulnerable my heart misses a beat. She rakes one hand through my hair and brings my mouth back to hers. I kiss her deeply, softly, but not with less hunger. I'll never, not in a million years, be able to sate my need for her. I break the kiss and release her ankles, treating them to the same kisses.

"Don't move," I say to her. I slide from the bed, remove the condom and come back with salve and a warm cloth for her. I gently rub the cloth over her sex, to ease the sting of my rough lovemaking, before applying lotion to her wrists and ankles. By the time I finish, she's sleepy, her lids barely open, but she still has that vulnerable look on her face when she gazes at me. I can't tell what's going through her mind, and while the sex was good—fantastic, really—now that it's over and the lust has cleared, is she worried she made a mistake? Is she regretting handing herself over to me, letting me go at her like a caveman? Is she worried that I really did damage her? I'm not sure, but one thing I do know is I should have been stronger. I should have never let the good girl play bad.

Christ, what have I done?

CHAPTER SEVEN

Gemma

I ROLL OVER on the bed, and even before I open my eyes, a huge smile curves my lips and a thrill goes through me. Last night with Josh was the best night of my life. I take a moment to reminisce, revel in the way he tied me up and owned my body, which is currently aching in all the right places. Thinking about the way he buried his face between my legs and brought me to orgasm has me warming all over.

Stretching, I reach for him, but when I find the other side of the bed empty, I jackknife up, a measure of panic moving through me. "Josh," I call out and glance around. The suite is big, and he could simply be in the other room. My gaze lands on the clock, and when I see that it's late morning, my nerves settle. He's a busy man, opening a new hotel. Sleeping in is probably not something he can easily do. But oh, how I wish he was beside me. I'd do just about anything to feel his touch, his kisses.

I slide from the covers and pad into the main room. "Ooh, breakfast," I say to myself when I see the tray with metal domes covering the food. Having no idea how long it has been here, I place my hand on a dome to find it cold. I frown, wishing I'd been awake to share the meal with Josh. I pour a cup of coffee and remove the lids to find blueberry pancakes, waffles and bacon. All cold. Oh, well. I toss a piece of bacon into my mouth and saunter around the room.

A ding comes from my purse, and I hurry to it. Plopping down onto the sofa, I read the message from Bentley, informing me he might be away longer than intended. The letter I'd written to Bentley after Josh sent me home the other night, still under the influence of tequila, catches my eye, and I ignore it. I don't intend to give it to him. In my mind, we're already broken up, and he's likely off with the woman he was talking to on the phone. I scroll through my text messages and find one from Mia. Instead of texting back, I call her. She picks up on the fourth ring, and I'm sure I've roused her.

"Hey, Mia. Did I wake you?"

"What time is it?" she asks and then groans. "Oh, God, my head."

"I guess you guys had a good time this weekend." A niggling of guilt starts in my stomach until I realize they were the ones who sent me to Josh two nights ago.

"Yeah, we've been having a great time. How about you?" she asks, her voice a bit more serious.

"Well—" I begin.

"Tell me," she blurts out. "Did you and Josh hook up?"

"You could say that," I say and smile as I hug myself. "Please don't tell anyone."

"It's over between you and Bentley?" she asks, and I don't miss the hope in her voice. Like I said, she never was a Bentley fan.

I exhale. "It's been over for a while, Mia. I just didn't have the nerve to finally break things off until…" I let my words fall off, still embarrassed to admit that he was using me.

"Honey, I'm sorry," she says. "Tell me what you need."

What I need is Josh, and not just in the bedroom. But he made it clear a long time ago that we were not going to have a future.

"Why did you send me to Josh? Whose idea was it?"

She goes quiet for a long time and then in a lower voice says, "We all think you two belong together, Gemma. We always have. I mean, we'll support you in whatever you decide, but when Nate suggested we kidnap you, so to speak, we all jumped on it. The funny thing is, Peyton had said something about kidnapping you before we even arrived." She goes quiet once again as my heart pounds against my ribs. "Are you okay?"

"I am," I lie. I'm not sure I'll ever be okay again. I desired last night. There is no denying that, but it was a reminder of the things I want but can never have. "You just need to know that Josh and I are not a couple. We never will be."

"Gemma—"

"We had sex last night, Mia. Amazing sex," I say, my bruised body a beautiful reminder of the things he did. "But that's all. That's all there ever will be between us. I'm not going to pretend otherwise. I'm glad it happened, though."

"Have you talked to Bentley?"

"No. He texted and said he's going to be away for a while. I'll talk to him when he gets back. I want to see you guys before you head home, though, but I don't want anyone to know about Bentley or that anything happened between Josh and me." I know I was going to tell them all about Bentley before they left, but with the way my head is spinning, I'm not ready to deal with their questions. When I return to New York, hopefully my head will be clearer, and we'll have a serious sit-down.

I hear a rustling sound. "We don't have to head to the airport for a few hours. Are you coming back here?"

I glance around the suite. "Actually, I have a room here. I think I'm going to stay. I don't want to go back to the villa."

"I can understand that."

"Let's all meet up for a bit of shopping down-town," I suggest.

"I'll wake the girls. I'll text you when we get

there." I'm about to end the call when she says, "Gem?"

"Yeah."

"We really only had your best interests at heart."

"I know, and I love you for it, but let's keep this all between us for now, okay?"

"Of course, and just for the record, Josh is a fool if he can't see how awesome you are."

I laugh, but the laugh holds no humor. I'm the fool for thinking he once loved me, or even that Bentley loved me. "See you soon," I say and end the call. I toss my phone into my purse, and the bag tumbles off the sofa. I hastily fish for the contents that spilled underneath, and toss it all back into my purse. I reach for another piece of cold bacon and make my way to the washroom.

Water droplets bead on the shower's glass door, an indication that Josh had been in the shower not too long ago. I breathe in the scent of his soap and trace my finger over the condensation as I work to tamp down the emptiness inside me. I can't let myself get upset. I knew full well what I was getting into last night, and today, instead of wallowing in the things Josh can't or won't give me, I should be enjoying all the things Josh did give me.

With that last thought in mind, I climb into last night's dress and make my way back to my room, two floors down. Once there, I lounge around a bit before I shower and dress in a light summery dress that falls to midthigh. A little fun, a little flirty and definitely chosen with a purpose. I want more of what I had last night, and this dress shows I'm having no qualms about it.

I walk out onto the deck, and the warm sunshine falls over me as I take in the nudity on the beach. My fingers itch to paint. I make a mental note to pick up a couple of sketch pads along with a few other, more intimate things when I'm out with the girls. I head to the main lobby in search of the man who holds my heart in his palm.

I'm instantly greeted by Matteo, who informs me Josh's driver will take me back to my villa. A little surprised at that, I explain that I'll be staying for the week. The strange, nervous look on his face fills me with dread.

Josh wants me gone.

Just then, I hear his voice, and I turn to find him talking to some gorgeous blonde who can't seem to keep her hands off him. I study the fit of his suit, the way it highlights broad shoulders and a muscular body. My gaze lands on his tie, and I close my hand over my wrist, rubbing the spot that he so gently soothed last night after tying me to his bed.

His head lifts, like he can feel my gaze, and he removes the woman's hand from his chest as his eyes drop to take in my dress. He tears his gaze away, says something to the woman and steps around her to head my way.

I watch him walk, mesmerized by his confident movements, and will my body not to melt to the floor as he closes the distance, the fresh scent of his showered skin filling all my senses. He nods to the manager, who returns the gesture and steps away.

"Gemma," he says, his gaze moving over my face, and as much as I'm trying, I don't think I can keep everything I'm feeling from showing. "Were you leaving?" he asks, and for a second, I think I hear disappointment in his voice.

I catch the eye of the woman who was touching him. "I didn't mean to disturb you."

"You weren't," he says and touches my elbow to lead me to one of the lobby chairs. I sit, and he takes the seat across from me and puts his elbows on his knees as he leans my way. "Last night probably shouldn't have—"

I shake my head to cut him off. I do not want to hear his remorse. "It did happen, and I don't regret a thing," I say, and the hard lines of his face soften.

"I just thought, under the stark reality of morning, you might see things differently."

"I'm not leaving," I state. "I'm going to stay for a while. I have no reason to rush back to my villa. My friends are leaving today and—" I stop, not wanting to say Bentley's name out loud.

"Are you sure that's a good idea? If anyone ever spotted you here, recognized you…"

"I don't care," I say and lift my head an inch. That's not entirely true, I do care but wish to God I didn't. I wish I could be who I want to be. Wish I didn't feel guilty for my wants and needs. Josh made me feel good last night, secure in my desires. There was no judgment on his part, and for that, I'm grateful.

He scrubs his face, and my heart pounds, wanting to touch him again, to feel his lips on mine. "Gemma, this place…"

"I know what this place is, Josh. I want to stay. I want to be someone else for a while, remember?" That someone else I want to be is *me*. The true me.

He shakes his head, and I'm about to tell him he can't stop me from staying when he says, "I can't, Gemma."

I angle my head, and blink. "You can't what?"

"I can't watch you with someone else. You know what this place is. You know what goes on here. I'm not sure I could handle seeing another man's hands on your body."

I lean toward him, so damn confused. "Why would that bother you?" I ask. This is the man who said we had no future, yet now he's saying he can't handle another man's hands on me. How does that make any kind of sense? Wait, have his feelings for me changed? Can I even allow myself to consider that? My heart has never been the same since he broke it. I almost laugh. At least he can't break it again, right?

"I don't think you know what you're doing, Gemma. I don't think you know what you want," he says, not really answering my question. "I don't trust your body in any other man's hands. I don't want to see you hurt."

"You're right. I don't know what I'm doing," I say. This is my first glimpse into a hedonistic lifestyle, and I'm a little lost. "But no man here can hurt me, Josh. My heart isn't on the table."

His dark eyes move over my face, the muscles in his jaw clenching as he chews on that.

I glance around, and when I spot the man I was dancing with last night enter the lobby, I give him a little finger wave. A low growl crawls out of Josh's throat. If I didn't know better, I'd think he was jealous.

"Maybe that guy will help me figure out what it is I'm doing. What it is I want."

"No," he says so firmly, so loudly, all eyes turn his way, including mine.

"No?" I ask.

"I'll help you."

A thrill goes through me, but I keep the excitement from my face. "You'll take me into a playroom?"

"I'll take you wherever you want to go," he says. He captures my hand in his. "What did Bentley do to you?"

I glance down, not wanting to talk about him.

"Gemma, if he hurt you—"

"No, he didn't hurt me," I tell him. Truthfully, I'm not sad that it's over, and if I hadn't overheard him, I never would have slept with Josh. I'm not a cheater. I guess I should be thanking Bentley. If I had married him, it would have been a mistake. But I can't tell Josh any of that. I'm embarrassed that Bentley was using me. "Even if he did, he wouldn't have been the first," I blurt out, and Josh goes completely stiff, his shoulders squaring as he squeezes my hand tighter, an apology of sorts.

"Gemma..."

Dammit, I didn't mean to bring up past hurts. "The past is the past, Josh," I say quickly. "Let's leave it there, okay? Let's start new." I glance around the hotel. "Let's start right here. A new beginning."

"Same rules as last night," he states, letting me know in no uncertain terms it's my body he wants.

"Same rules."

He gives a curt nod. "One week of being someone else. Then you go back to being you, Gemma."

I nod in agreement, even though deep inside I know that after one week with him, living out my every fantasy and being the woman I really want to be, going back to the Gemma I present to the world will be impossible. I'll have to find a way, though. This man doesn't want me, and I have a career as an artist to consider.

CHAPTER EIGHT

Josh

I CAN'T FUCKING believe I agreed to this. Then again, it's better that she's in my hands than someone else's. At least I'll take good care of her body, see to her properly. Not that I think any of the men here would do anything to hurt her. I don't. It's just that she's so innocent.

Christ, is that what I'm telling myself? That she has to be with *me* because this is all new to her?

Fuck, I guess I can spin this any way I want. Tell myself this is all about her, but there is a part of me, a big part, that wants her in my arms and in my bed. We might not be able to do long-term, but I can give her this week. Once she comes to her senses, she'll go back to Bentley.

Honestly, I'm not sure what's going on with them and can only assume it's cold feet since she straight up told me he hadn't hurt her. If he had, I'd have hunted him down and beat the shit out of him. But at the end of the day, Gemma and I live in different worlds, and I can't forget that. Losing her a second time will be harder than the first. What's that saying? It's better to have loved and lost than never to have loved at all? That's total bullshit and was probably said by someone who'd never loved and lost before.

I walk up to my window and glance at the private beach. I scan it, take in all the naked and near-naked bodies. My dick twitches. Not because of the nudity but because I've been thinking of Gemma. Hell, ever since I found her tied to my chair, I haven't been able to think of anything else. Not good when I have a hotel opening to oversee. I can only hope a week of hedonistic sex with her will help me move on—emotionally.

I'm about to step away when a movement catches my eyes and I spot Gemma sitting in the shade, a sketch pad in her hands. At least I think it's a sketch pad. From this distance, it's hard to make it out, but I'd know Gemma anywhere, anytime, and back in college, she was always sketching something or other. My cell pings and I pull it from my pocket to see a text from Nate. While I should be angry, I'm not. I can't stay mad at him.

Nate: How was the soft opening?

I shake my head and can picture his smirk.

Me: You're a sick bastard, you know that.

Nate: That's why you love me.

Me: Seriously bro, where are you?

Nate: Hiding out.

Nate: In case you didn't like the gift I delivered to celebrate your opening.

Me: You really shouldn't have done that.

Me: You know she's engaged right?

Nate: Yeah, but you two needed one last shot before she went through with it.

Me: What's going on with her and Bentley?

Nate: Not sure.

Nate: Let me try to find out.

I'm not sure why but I get the sense he knows something I don't.

Me: Come on back to the hotel.

Me: I promise not to kill you for all this.

Me: Slowly, anyway.

Nate: LOL, I'll come back if you promise me one thing.

Me: No.

Nate: Promise me you'll try, bro.

Nate: You two belong together.

Me: Just get back here.

I finish texting and shove the phone back into my pocket. He might think we're good together, and we *are* good together, but I don't belong in her world, as much as she doesn't belong in this one. I'm not going to do anything to jeopardize her career or her reputation. Yes, I'll give her this week, but that's it. I can only imagine what she's going to discover in this hotel will frighten her off anyway and send her packing sooner rather than later.

I head down to the lobby and take the back door out onto the beach. The warm sun shines down on me as I go in search of Gemma. I find her sitting cross-legged under a palm tree, so engrossed in her sketches, she doesn't even know I'm standing there.

"Hey," I say in a soft voice, not wanting to startle her.

She drops her pencil, her hand flying to her chest. "God, Josh. When did you get so stealthy?"

I squat down next to her, reach out and lightly brush a strand of hair from her face. "I didn't mean to scare you." She flips her notepad over, hiding it from my view. I laugh. She always used to do that. She doesn't like anyone to see her work in progress. "What are you drawing?" I ask anyway.

"Nothing," she says quickly. "Well, just some sketches of the beach." I look out, follow her gaze to the naked couple not too far away, who are lying on their sides, facing one another. Gemma has a wistful look on her face as she watches them.

"Do you know them?" I ask.

"No, they just seem like they're in love."

"Right," I say. "Does the nudity bother you?"

She looks at me like I might be dense. "Human bodies are beautiful, Josh. A work of art. Something to be painted and admired."

"Your body is a work of art, but I'm not so sure mine is," I tease, and wanting to put a smile on her face, I point to my crotch. "Men have, what you might call, all the farm parts. Not that attractive."

She stares at me for a second, and then she bursts out laughing, "Oh my god, Josh. For the record—" she leans into me "—I love all your farm parts, and when it comes right down to it, women are the farm. We carry the babies." Another wistful look comes over her heat-flushed face.

"You used to talk about having kids," I say and settle cross-legged beside her.

"I know."

I touch her hair, twirl it around my finger. "Is that something you still want?"

She shrugs. "I don't know. I don't know what I want anymore," she says and looks past my shoulder. She frowns and turns back to me. "What about you, Josh? Do you want the wife, kids, minivan?"

"No," I say quickly. "I wouldn't be a very good husband, or father."

"Why do you say that?"

A sound crawls out of my throat. "Oh, because I'm on the road all the time, opening hotels, and what do I know about kids?" I say, but that's not the whole truth, and from the way she's studying my face, I sense she gets it.

"Just because you never had a dad doesn't mean you won't be a good one. Look at Nate. You raised him."

"Nate's an egomaniac asshole," I say, smiling out of the corner of my mouth.

"He's not really, though, you know. He's actually one of the good guys. Like you."

"I'm not who you think I am, Gemma."

"Maybe I'm not who you think I am, either."

"You're a good girl."

She doesn't disagree. Instead she says. "I'll be good until you want me to be bad."

"That's the thing, though," I say softly. "It has to be what you want, not what I want."

She nods like she understands that. "If you're asking me what I want," she begins, then leans across to brush her lips over mine and finishes with, "it's you, without all these clothes on."

I laugh. "I'm not really into public nudity. Not that there is anything wrong with it, but if it's something you want to do—"

"Not really, but don't you have that private pool in the penthouse suite?"

"You want to go swimming?"

She nods, and I stand and run my hand through my hair. I wipe the sand from my pants and hold my hand out to her. "Did you have fun shopping with your friends?" I ask as I pull her to her feet.

"Yeah, I feel bad because they came to Belize to hang out with me, and I didn't spend any time with them."

"They tied you to my chair, Gemma," I say as we head toward the doors. "Don't feel too bad."

Her body visibly quakes at the reminder, and her eyes go big. "Oh, I forgot to tell you. I located the artist, the one who did the erotic art in your lobby."

"You've got to be kidding me!"

Her smile is wide, so pleased with herself. "Nope."

"I spent so much time looking, only to come up empty. Can I get the number?"

She puckers up her face. "Actually, no, she prefers to remain anonymous, but she'd be willing to send you a portfolio of the paintings."

"You're amazing, Gemma. You know that, right?"

"I don't know if I'd say *amazing*. I'd probably go with *phenomenal*."

I laugh at that. "Right. Phenomenal," I say.

"I'm in the industry, and I have connections," she

says with a wink. "But those paintings are going to cost you."

"I'll pay."

"I'll have her send me the portfolio."

"Will you go over it with me? I'd like to hear your thoughts."

She smiles, obviously liking that I respect and appreciate her opinion. "It'd be my pleasure." I open the door to the hotel, and she glances over her shoulder. "I wish I had my paints here." She frowns and walks inside.

I nod as an idea forms. "I really appreciate you looking into the artist for me. I don't even know how to thank you."

She gives me a sexy grin. "I'm pretty sure you'll find a way."

"Fuck, Gemma," I say as my cock twitches.

I hurry her to the elevator, but she has other things in mind. "I was thinking maybe the swim could wait." She takes my hand and leads me down the long stretch of hall where the playrooms can be found. My dick thickens as I think about getting her naked and playing with her.

She stands outside one of the rooms and toys with the doorknob. "I wonder what's in here."

"You know what's in there. All guests are given a tour after arrival. But we can't go in. We didn't book it."

Her grin is wild and mischievous as she reaches into her purse and pulls out a key card. "Maybe someone thought ahead." She slides the key over the lock, and the door buzzes open. I put my hand on her waist and guide her in. The room feels cool after being outside, and a shiver goes through her, although I'm not so sure it's from the temperature. She walks farther into the room, examines the vibrators and floggers neatly laid out in glass cabinets.

"These are interesting," she says as she trails her hand along the glass. She stops when she comes to a long black flogger with leather tails. "What does this one do?" she asks, her cheeks flushed from excitement. I study her for a second, and I'm beginning to second-guess who she really is and what she really wants and needs.

"How about I show you?"

CHAPTER NINE

Gemma

I BACK UP until the backs of my knees hit a square cube that looks like some type of ottoman. I sink down onto the cushiony material, my heart pounding against my chest as he opens the cabinet and removes the flogger. My entire body tingles with excitement as he gently swings the toy and hits his palm with the leather tails.

"Oh, my," I say, and he grins.

He steps up to me, his eyes a darker shade as he says, "Stand up."

I do as he says, and he takes a seat, his legs parted. "Take your clothes off," he says.

I step back even more and work the buttons on my blouse. His groan of excitement emboldens me, and I have to say I love the way he wants my body. I am not going to lament that he doesn't want my heart. No, this week, I just plan to enjoy all he's willing to offer.

Once my blouse is off, I wiggle my hips to pull

my shorts down. While shopping today, I stopped at the lingerie shop and picked out black lace panties and a matching demi bra. Black used to be his favorite color, and judging by the heat in his eyes, it still is.

"You are so damn sexy," he murmurs and slaps his hand with the flogger again. He stands up and puts his arm around my waist, tugging me to him. His hard cock presses against my stomach, and a moan rises in my throat. "Did you buy this for me?" he asks and puts his finger into the barely there band on my panties.

"Yes," I say breathlessly, and his knuckle feathers back and forth over my skin.

"So, these are mine, then?"

Not sure what he's getting at, I nod my head, and a gasp rips from my lungs when rough, none-too-gentle fingers rip the lacy material from my hips.

"Josh," I say as my nerve endings jump and a thrill courses through me. God, I love seeing him like this, too eager to get at my body to take my clothes off properly. I want more.

He takes the panties and tucks them into his pocket. "I'll be keeping these."

The next thing I know he's put the leather toy between my legs, tapping my thighs to part me. I widen my thighs and he looks down. "This is mine," he says and closes his hand over my sex. "Say it."

"It's yours," I answer, and he slides one thick finger into me. He doesn't move it, doesn't do anything. It's pure torture.

"Please," I murmur.

"These are mine, too." He grips one cup of my bra and pulls on it until my breast is exposed. Bending, he takes my nipple into his mouth and clamps down hard.

I groan and throw my head back, jutting my chest forward so he can take all of me. He nibbles on me, and the pleasure zings through my blood and floods my nether regions. I move my hips as I ride his hand, surprisingly unashamed of my needs. He goes still as he watches me. I'm so close to coming, when he pulls his finger out and backs up.

"No," I groan, ready to slide a hand between my legs and finish myself off until he gives a slow shake of his head to stop me. He steps up to the ruby-red cube and flips it open, until it's high on one end and curved to go low on the other. I stand there wide-eyed, shocked. I had no idea it was some sort of sexual positioning toy.

"Come here," he says, and I step up to him. He puts his hand on the back of my neck and bends me forward over the cushion, until my ass is in the air fully exposed. The cushions are soft, the position most comfortable...and dirty. I love it.

I whimper as he runs the soft leather tails over my back, and down my thighs. I shake my ass and squirm for more. When it finally comes, when he finally smacks my backside with the leather flogger, my mouth opens but no sound comes.

He doesn't hit me hard, just enough to send a jolt of pleasure through me, but the second he runs his palms over my flesh to soothe the sting behind, I exhale quickly…to cover the hot tears pressing against my eyes. As my stupid emotions get the best of me, simply from the way he's rubbing me gently, a tender, caring touch, I swallow and work to hide the storm rising up inside me. I'd rather he think the tears were the result of pain and pleasure, not the shattering of my already-scarred heart.

Keep it together, Gemma.

He hits me again, and as I cry out in bliss, he touches me in ways I've never been touched before, his deep, penetrating strokes hitting my G-spot with precision. Who knew this cube, or ottoman, or whatever it's called could make such a difference? I'm hooked. I whimper and wiggle and go perfectly still when he slides a small finger into my backside, just to the first knuckle.

"Are you okay with this, Gemma?"

"Yes," I murmur. "That feels…different."

"This is all you get for now," he says, and brushes his thumb over my aching clit.

I push against his finger, moving my hips up and down, grinding my clit into him and trying to get his pinkie deeper into my backside.

"Are you sure this is something you want?" he says casually, like we might be ordering off a menu, but beneath his words, I hear the tremor. He's as hot for this as I am and losing control by the second.

"Yes, I want your cock inside me. I want you to fuck me. Everywhere."

He exhales and the soft curses under his breath bring a smile to my face. He's coming unhinged, whether he wants to admit it or not.

He steps away from me and I cry out with need. But it turns into a whimper of delight when he steps in front of me, and tears his cock from his pants. He sinks to his knees in front of me, and catching me by surprise, he presses his lips to mine so gently, his kiss so tender, my heart jumps into my throat.

"I'm going to fuck you now, Gemma," he says, his voice deep and hoarse as his warm breath falls over my face. "Is that what you want, too?"

"Yes," I cry out without hesitation. I need this man more than he would ever know, in ways he could never know. If he did, if he thought my stupid heart was getting involved— he'd likely pack my bags and send me on my way.

He steps away from me and moves around the sex chair. A hard quiver racks my body when his callused hand lands on my back and he slowly drags it across my ass.

"You are so beautiful," he says. His cock taps my ass, and I wiggle trying to get him inside. He sinks to his knees, and the second he swipes his tongue over my clit, I lose it.

"Please, put it inside me," I say. He lightly touches my opening, probes me with his finger, and I whimper.

"Has it been a long time since you've been touched?"

"Yes," I admit.

"I'm sorry," he says. I glance over my shoulder to see a mixture of sadness and delight on his face. "Is that what's going on with you and Bentley?" he asks and pushes his finger into me.

"Yes…no… I don't want to talk about him," I say.

"Me, neither." A frown forms on his face, and his finger stills inside me.

"Josh?" *What the hell is going through his mind?*

"Yeah," he says, his eyes meeting mine.

"Do you…do this a lot?" I ask, and glance around the room.

"Not for a while." He shoves another finger inside me, and I moan. "I haven't played in a while. I sort of lost interest."

My heart seizes, and I'm seconds from scurrying away. "Do you not want—?"

"Gemma," he says firmly, holding me in place. I swallow at the seriousness in his voice. "I want. Let me show you how much I want."

My throat tightens at the intensity on his face. I shake my head, try to wrap my brain around the fact that this man had lost interest in playing—until I came along. I can't help but wonder if he's doing this to see if this is the real me, or to prove it's not.

Either way, we're both consenting adults, both enjoying each other's bodies to the fullest.

Speaking of fullest…

He grabs a condom before tearing the rest of his clothes off and quickly sheaths himself. In one fast thrust, he enters me, the position allowing him to fill me in a way I've never been filled. My body opens to his, my muscles relaxing against the chair as he drives impossibly deeper, hitting erogenous spots I didn't even know existed.

"Josh…" I cry and claw at the chair.

"I know, Gemma. I know," he says, his voice barely recognizable.

He pounds and plunges, his fingers gripping my hips for leverage, and he moves my body to get deeper. Our cries merge, the only thing existing is us, in this very moment. It's definitely something I could get used to.

One strong hand leaves my hips, slowly traces my spine and goes around my body to massage an achy breast. I love everything about this position, the way he's touching me, but I want to see his face, want to look into his eyes when he lets go.

He tweaks my nipple and angles my body—I thrill to the way he twists and manipulates me to increase my pleasure—so he can slide his hand down to touch my clit. The pleasure is so sharp, so intense, my body completely lets go. I pinch my eyes shut as I give myself over and climax so hard, I swear I'm about to black out.

My sex squeezes him and he curses silently behind me as he plunges, each hard stroke, each precise pound now for him—all for him, and I love that—as he chases his own release. I squeeze around him harder, and his growl of pleasure thrills me. I'm elated that I can do this to him. He pushes deep and lets loose a loud, coarse grunt, so steeped in pleasure my entire body quakes. God, I delight in the sounds he makes.

He lets go inside me, and I close my eyes to concentrate on each sweet pulse of pleasure as he depletes himself, and for a brief second, I wish there wasn't a condom separating us.

He falls over my back, his hot breath washing over my flesh. I revel in his body weight, the way his heart is pounding against my spine.

"Gemma," he murmurs when he can finally talk. "How does it just get better and better with you?"

"I think it has something to do with this chair, because I was thinking the exact same thing."

"Yeah, maybe," he says, sounding unsure and unconvinced as he pulls my hair from my shoulder and presses soft kisses to my neck.

"Let's get you back to my room and cleaned up."

"I'm not sure I can move my legs."

He laughs, and helps me to my feet. Instead of dressing, he scoops up our clothes, and removes two robes from a cabinet. His gentleness as he helps me into mine is astounding. He smiles and cups my chin, settling his lips on mine. It's a kiss of long-time lovers, not the kiss one gives someone when they're just fucking. Or perhaps that's just wishful thinking on my part. Then again, we do go back a long way, and while we don't have a future, nothing can convince me that this man doesn't have my best interests at heart. Honestly, this is all so confusing.

I gasp when he scoops me up. "What are you doing?"

"You said your legs weren't working, and if you're in my hotel—under my care, nonetheless—then it's my duty to take care of you."

My heart aches a little, wishing it was so much more. "You're doing this out of duty?" I ask as we exit the playroom.

"No, Gemma, I'm not," he says and looks away from me, putting an end to the conversation. My throat tightens, and I want to ask what he means by that almost as much as I don't. If he's not doing it because of obligation, does it mean he has deeper feelings? If he does, why can't we have more? Sometimes I really don't understand him. He presses a bell to call for the cleaners who come in and sterilize the rooms between guests.

With so many questions on the tip of my tongue, where they'll stay because I'm too afraid of voicing them for fear of rejection, I wrap my arms around his shoulders as he takes us to the elevator. A few minutes later, we're in his suite and he carries me to his gigantic bathroom. He sets me on the sink, and I stifle a yawn.

"Am I boring you?" he teases, his hair a ruffled mess from our sex. He looks so young—like the boy I met in college—so adorable, it hurts my heart. "Do I have to take things up a notch?"

I chuckle, and while I'd like that—I want to experience everything—I say, "I just haven't been getting enough sleep."

"We're going to rectify that," he states, and while I need sleep, I don't want to miss a minute of our time together. He turns on the shower and drops his robe. I stare at his gorgeous nakedness like I'm hypnotized.

"Like what you see?" he teases.

"I'm not sure *like* is a strong enough word."

"That's honest."

"Like I said, there's no reason for us not to be honest with each other." Who am I kidding? I'm not being straight with him, and from the darkness moving over his face as he scrubs his chin, it's clear he has secrets, too.

"Come here." Strong arms pick me up like I weigh nothing, and I slide down his body until I'm standing on shaky legs. I breathe in the scent of his skin as he slides my robe from my shoulders with exquisite gentleness and puts his hand on my back to lead me into the big shower.

I whimper, the warm water glorious against my skin. I stand under the rain shower, my limbs too weak to work, but they don't need to. Josh is right there, filling his hands with soap and washing me all over. I just remain there, immobilized, as he cares for me, lathering every hill and valley with unhurried hands. Sleep pulls at me, and I can no longer fight a yawn. Once I'm clean, he washes quickly, and I linger under the spray and watch him run big hands over his rock-hard body. I begin to heat up all over again, and a soft moan escapes my lips.

His head lifts, his gaze going to mine. "While I'd like to fuck you again, you need rest and then food." I'm about to protest, but he's not having any of that. "Let's just say I think I know better than you do what you need."

If he knew what I needed, what I honestly and truly needed, he'd know it was him. But I don't say any of that. Those words would scare him off.

"You put your body in my hands, so trust that I know what to do with it."

That is something I can agree with. He does know how to care for my body, just not my heart. He scoops me up again and takes me to his big bed. He sets me down and covers me. Cold moves through me when he backs up, but then he climbs into the other side and snuggles me, his big spoon to my little.

A wave of contentment washes over me. "I can't remember the last time I slept in the day," I murmur. "Wait, maybe I do."

"That summer where we made love on the boat all morning and slept all afternoon," he says, and my lids fly open. The fact that he remembers takes me back in time, and more importantly, takes me by surprise.

"Yeah," I say softly around the lump in my throat as his hand settles on my hip. One thing he's mis-remembering, though. We had sex; we didn't make love. Just like we're doing now, and I'm never, ever going to mix the two up again.

CHAPTER TEN

Josh

HER BODY SETTLES beside me and when her breathing changes, and she falls into a deeper sleep, I slowly inch away, not wanting to wake her. She stirs and makes a soft noise and it's all I can do to leave the bed. I'd like nothing more than to stay here with her today, tomorrow, forever. But forever is impossible, and right now I have some things to take care of, not to mention a newly opened hotel to oversee.

I tug on a pair of dress pants, button-down shirt and tie, and leave her a note to let her know I'll be downstairs checking in with management. I take one last longing look at her and quietly slip from the room. After an uneventful ride to the lobby, I exit the elevator and spot my brother sauntering in through the front doors, a group of women swarming him, and I just shake my head. I have no idea when he's going to settle down, but from the looks of things, he's in no hurry.

My mind goes back to my conversation with Gemma, and I appreciate her saying I did a great job with Nate. That's not the same thing as being a father, however. I probably didn't discipline him as much as I should have, and I'm not sure I'm made of the right stuff for a family of my own. Underneath it all, Gemma can pretend to be whoever she wants this week, but she's still a girl who wants the white picket fence and children. I don't think that's something I can give her, and I don't know why the hell I'm even thinking about it. She's engaged, for Christ's sake. Well, maybe they're on a break, but he's the guy she needs. If not him, then someone like him, someone who fits in her world.

"What the hell are you doing?" I ask and pull my brother from the swarm of women.

"Keeping my fans happy," he says and pushes his hair from his face, looking like an easygoing surfer boy. "Something you wouldn't know about."

"And that's how I plan to keep it. I'm not a spotlight hog like you."

"Hog?" he says, all indignant-like, as I pull him in for a hug.

"I mean that in the nicest possible way," I assure him with a laugh.

"How could I have taken it any other way?" he teases in return, but then he goes serious. It's such a rare sighting my stomach clenches up.

"What?" I ask.

"Is Gemma still here?" He glances around and frowns when his search comes up empty.

I nod, and his shoulders relax. "I don't know why that makes you happy, little brother."

"Because you two need to work things out."

"There is nothing to work out. What was between us is in the past, where it's going to stay."

He ignores me and says, "I still haven't found out what's going on with her ex. As far as everyone knows, the wedding is still on."

His words leave a sour taste on my tongue and a knot in my stomach. She told me it was over. Why the hell am I the only one privy to the situation? Uneasy thoughts from earlier today, when we were in the playroom, come back to haunt me. Is it possible that she's here for lessons, to mix up her repertoire in the bedroom? She was always vanilla between the sheets, and while there is nothing wrong with that, her actions are so different from the college girl I once knew. Can a leopard really change its spots? Was I wrong in second-guessing who she really is and what she wants and needs? One thing I do know is: I don't know anything.

"She told me that she was breaking it off."

"She hasn't said a thing to me," Nate says, and once again, I sense he knows more but isn't saying. I'm not sure what he's keeping from me or why he wants to.

"This just doesn't add up," I say and shake my head. She asked me for a week; I'm giving it to her.

Delving deeper is not in my best interest. "Doesn't matter anyway, I guess."

He eyes me like I might have just grown a tooth out of my forehead. "You sure about that?"

"Positive," I say. "Gemma and I are just friends."

"Friends who are fucking."

I shake my head. Why did I ever think I could get anything by him? Since there is no sense in denying it, I say, "Right, friends who are fucking, and that's all this is. She's going through something, and I can't say no to her or send her back. Not right away anyway."

"You're helping her with something?"

"She asked me for something, and I'm giving it to her."

"Because you still love her."

It's a statement, not a question, but I'm not answering either way. It's a road I don't want to go down, feelings I don't want to examine too closely. "Did anyone ever tell you that you ask too many questions?"

He holds his hand out and starts putting his fingers up one by one. "My agent, my directors, my cast mates, my annoying big brother—"

"Okay, okay, I get it."

"I do have a question for you, though." Once again, he's serious, and I just can't wait to hear what's going to come out of his mouth next.

"What?"

"If you and Gemma have no plan to ever get back

together, maybe I could ask her out? I always thought she was beautiful, and we get along really well."

He's fucking with me—he always thought of her as a sister. But he's trying to get a reaction from me. Sadly, I don't disappoint. My body hardens, every muscle clenching tightly. Blood boils in my veins to imagine her with anyone else, and that's crazy because she has a fiancé waiting for her. Nate puts his hands on my shoulders, that playful smirk back on his face.

"Yeah, that's what I thought," he says.

"Want to know what I think?" I question in response.

He laughs. "That I should fuck off."

"Pretty much. Now go, before I kill you for kidnapping Gemma."

"Kill me? You should be thanking me."

I reach for him and he steps back, palms up. Laughing, he says, "Okay, bro. I need sleep anyway. Catch up with you later?"

"Uh-huh," I say as he saunters toward the staircase.

I turn my attention to the guests in the lobby, and after mingling and chatting to hear people's reactions to the new hotel, I make my way to Matteo's office and wake up the computer. After a quick search, I pull my phone from my pocket and make a call. I spin in my chair and look out the window as the guests soak up the last of today's sun, and place my order. A noise at my door draws my attention and

I turn to find Gemma there. My heart leaps at the sight of her in a summery blue dress that looks easy to remove.

I cover my mouth and lower my voice, not wanting her to know what I'm doing, and she frowns and begins to back up. I quickly hang up and jump from my chair.

"Where do you think you're going?" I ask and drag her to me.

"Sorry to interrupt," she says. "I didn't realize you were on the phone."

"You weren't interrupting." I brush a strand of hair from her face. "Did you sleep okay?" She nods. "You found my note?"

"Yes, and yes." She smiles. "Although I would have preferred to find you next to me when I woke up." Her smile falters. "But I know you're busy, and if I'm taking you away…"

"You're not." I back up, bringing her with me, until I'm sitting on the edge of my desk. "You look like you have something on your mind."

Her phone buzzes and she ignores it.

"Still just waking up." She glances at her buzzing purse, and her smile wobbles as my gaze moves over her face. "My brain isn't quite functioning. I need about a gallon of coffee."

I nod. "I remember how no one could talk to you back in college until you had at least two cups. Such a bear," I tease.

"You remember that?" Her goddamn phone is getting on my last nerve. Whoever is on the other end is refusing to give up. "Are you going to get that?" I ask, ready to answer it myself.

She gives a fast shake of her head and the fresh scent of her shampoo reaches my nostrils. "I don't really want to talk to anyone right now."

"Trying to be someone else for a while. I remember," I say. "Is real life that tough for you, Gemma?"

She goes quiet for a long time, and her phone finally stops screaming. "My life isn't hard, Josh," she says. She was always a little embarrassed about her wealth, given I held down numerous jobs just to get through school. "It's just that my every move is scrutinized."

"There's nothing easy about that, Gemma. You don't have to pretend it isn't hard." I jab my thumb into my chest. "I was there back in college when the paparazzi showed up and took pictures of us together. I was there, Gemma. I know what it did to you. I also see what my brother goes through. I see the show he puts on for the world—pretending to be something he isn't. He doesn't have to do that for me, and he knows it. Neither do you. Okay?"

She nods. "Okay." She sniffs, and adds, "I hated what they did to you, Josh." Her hand closes over her stomach like she's in physical pain. "Hated it."

"Hey," I say softly. I flex my biceps to get a re-action out of her. "I'm a tough guy." She offers me a shaky smile at that, and I go serious again. "Lis-ten, I could handle it, Gemma. I dragged myself up from the gutter, and they could throw whatever they wanted at me. They couldn't hurt me, but they could hurt you and your reputation by what they said about me, and I just couldn't have that."

She puts her hands over her face like she's trying to block the image and mumbles through her fingers, "I can't believe you punched that guy out."

"Why not? He deserved it, didn't he?" I shake my head and think back to the charges pressed against me at the time. Christ, I was lucky my ass didn't land in jail, but I'd do it again, no hesitation.

"Yeah, but you got in trouble for it."

"He was up in your face," I take her hands and put them at her sides. "What was I supposed to do?" My heart squeezes as water pools in her eyes. Fuck, I hate seeing her sad, which is why I could no longer be in her life. The damn paparazzi would never stop hounding her if she'd stayed with a guy like me. Sure, I might be a success now, but to them, I'll always be a nobody who doesn't deserve to be in Gemma's life. They can all go fuck themselves, as far as I'm concerned, and write whatever they want about me, but I will not stand for them hurting Gemma.

She takes a big, fueling breath. "That's what I like about this place. No one cares who you are or what you do. It's an easy environment to be in."

Is that why she's not told anyone about the breakup? She just wants to live in peace a bit longer? Or is it that she still plans to go back?

"I know you just said you liked the anonymity

of this place, but want to get out of here for a little while? Get some air?" She sure looks like she could use a fresh breath or two.

Her eyes go big. "I can't, Josh." She points to nowhere in particular. "Out there..."

Out there, she can't be seen with a guy like me. I get it and I'll never forget it. Obviously, she knows it, too. Lessons learned and all.

"I thought we could take the boat out, have dinner under the stars." I chuckle and shake my head. "Wait, that sounds kind of corny. Am I going to have to cash in my man card for saying something so mushy?"

"Mushy? Okay, for that you might have to cash in the man card." She laughs, and the joyous sound fills me with happiness and I laugh with her, feeling a new lightness about—not to mention a new closeness to—Gemma. She's easy to talk to, easy to be around. "But the dinner under the stars, I think it sounds romantic."

"That's because you read all those romance books." I brush my knuckles over her cheek. "Seriously, though. You want to? You always loved being out on the water."

She glances down like her mind is a million miles away. In a low, almost surprised voice, she says, "You remember that."

"Of course I remember that," I tell her. I'm not sure why that surprises her. Outside of my brother, she was the only other person I ever loved. I tip her chin up. "We never did get that swim in, so we can jump in the ocean."

Her face lights up. "Let me go grab my bathing suit."

I hold her to me and slide my hands down her back until I'm cupping her ass. "You don't need it."

Heat moves into her cheeks, turning them pink. "I like the way you think," she says.

I give her ass a squeeze and drop a kiss on her mouth before I stand up straighter. "By the way, Nate's back," I say. "He was asking about you." I'm not sure why I'm suddenly bringing up my brother. Maybe I want her to come clean and tell me what she's really up to, why she didn't tell her friends the wedding was off.

"I haven't talked to him since the night they all kidnapped me," she says. "I think he's been avoiding me." She bites her bottom lip, a worry line creasing her forehead. "Maybe he thinks I'm going to be mad or something?"

"Are you?"

"Not even a little bit," she tells me, her voice filled with conviction.

I like that more than I should. "You've reached out to him?"

She nods. "No response."

"He has a room here."

She goes thoughtful for a moment. "Does he, you know, use the rooms in your hotels?"

A sudden, piercing jolt of jealousy hits like a bolt

of lightning. "Why, did you want to use one with him?" I ask, like a total asshole. But Nate had gotten under my skin earlier, more than I would have liked.

She smirks. "You sound like you're jealous."

I stare at her. "What if I told you I was," I say, almost in challenge. Why am I doing that? Do I really want her to say she wants me to be jealous, because she wants a future? Christ, even if she did, I'd have to kibosh the idea.

"Then I'd say you were lying. I've never known you to be the jealous type, Josh."

Then I guess she doesn't know me well at all. And maybe she was right, maybe I don't know her, either.

"Come on, let's get dinner to go and get out on the water." I capture her hand, and I'm about to lead her to the lobby when her phone starts ringing again. I glance at her to find her worrying her bottom lip. "Maybe you should get that."

"Yeah, maybe."

"I'll get changed and go round up dinner. Meet you in the lobby in thirty?" I leave her to answer her call, and while I don't want it to matter, I am curious. Who keeps calling, and why does she not want to answer? I hurry to my room to change into a T-shirt and shorts, then make my way to the kitchen and order up pasta, bread and salad to go, and after it's ready, I head back to the lobby to find Gemma backed into a corner, chatting with Atlanta. Well, this can't be good.

"Atlanta," I say as I approach. "How are you enjoying the hotel?"

She makes an odd little purring sound. "It would be better if you weren't making yourself scarce," she says, humor with a hint of venom in her voice. "Gemma here has been keeping you all to herself." She eyes Gemma, her gaze traveling the length of her to size her up.

"Gemma is an old friend from college," I say. "We're catching up."

I shift the paper bags in my arms as Atlanta puts her hand on my chest, her manicured nails circling the logo on my T-shirt. "I'd like to catch up, too," she says, and turns back to Gemma. "Are you sure I don't know you? You seem so familiar."

"We should go," I say, not giving her the chance to figure it out. "We don't want dinner to get cold." I put my hand on Gemma's back and lead her outside. The warm, late-day sun shines down on us as we head to the wharf, and I don't need to turn her way to know her eyes are on me. "What?" I ask and step onto the pier, holding my hand out to her as it wobbles.

"She's like a barracuda."

I laugh as we walk the long length to my pleasure yacht tied up at the end. "She's not so bad once you get to know her."

"You two know each other well?" she asks.

"Now who's jealous?" I say.

"It was just a question."

"I'm with you this week, Gemma. Just you and me, no one else, right?" I ask.

"Right," she says.

We reach the boat and I help her on. "Why don't you get the food out, and I'll untie us and get us out onto the water?" She takes the bags from me, and I go through the process of getting the vessel underway. Once we're untied, I start the motor, take us offshore and drop anchor in a private cove. The warm wind washes over my face and the sun sits low on the horizon as I make my way to Gemma at the back of the boat. She's in the middle of uncorking the bottle of wine I brought.

"My favorite," she says with a gorgeous smile as she pours two glasses.

"I know."

"You seem to remember a lot," she says as she hands me a glass and takes a sip of her own.

Gemma opens the containers, and I grab a spoon and divvy up the ravioli.

"I remember that your favorite pasta was spinach-and-cheese ravioli. The chef made these special for you."

"That was sweet of him."

"Hey," I say. "I was the one who asked him to do it."

She chuckles. "Still need your ego stroked, I see," she teases. "See? I remember things, too."

"It's not my ego I need stroked," I say, wanting to see her cheeks turn that pretty shade of pink, and she doesn't disappoint.

She takes a piece of still-warm bread, bites into it and follows it with a sip of wine. "Yes, well, there are other things I remember."

"What do you remember, Gemma?"

She lets loose a contented sigh, the wine working on her body fast. She probably hasn't eaten much today.

"I remember back in college when I first met you. Nate was supposed to walk me home from that party, but in typical Nate fashion, he couldn't get away from all the cheerleaders who wanted to show off their twisty skills to him."

I laugh at that. "Twisty skills?"

She grins. "It was that night I used the Penn Pal app and met you. You strolled up like a knight in shining armor, ready to protect me on my walk back to the dorm, except you were wearing a football hoodie and jeans, of course, not real armor."

"Would you have preferred me in shining armor, on a horse or something? Donkey, maybe?" She laughs and I shake my head. "Where do you even find something like that anyway?"

"The dark web," she says, all conspiratorial, and we both laugh out loud. "Or probably any sex shop. Hey, maybe you could get something like that for one of your rooms." She holds her arms out and walks Frankenstein-like.

"It's armor, not the zombie apocalypse," I tease. "I'm pretty sure I wouldn't have to walk like that."

Chuckling, she takes another contented breath as

I brush her leg with mine under the table—playing footsies, like I did that first time I asked her out in college. She grins, knowing exactly what I'm doing.

"What else do you remember?" I ask.

"You were so smart, Josh. You worked so hard in all your courses. I admired the hell out of you and the way you cared for Nate. Kept him on the straight and narrow by leading with solid moral behavior."

I nod as the compliment has me remembering all those tough years trying to keep us both out of foster homes. I covered for my mother until we were old enough to make it on our own. No way did I want to risk them separating us.

"You've worked hard, too, Gemma. Now you're running your mother's studio and selling your own artwork, all with the hopes of one day opening your own studio." I smile at her. "One day, you'll get everything you need, I promise."

She frowns like she doesn't believe me, but she says, "You can't promise that."

"I just did."

She shrugs. "I guess a girl can wish, right?"

"Forget about wishing and forget about good things coming to those who wait. That is total bullshit. Good things come to those who get their asses out there and work for it."

She nods, and her eyes sparkle in the setting sun as day turns to night.

"I believe that, too."

"I know."

"What else do you know?" she asks and takes a bite of her ravioli. She lets loose a breathy sigh, and my dick thickens at the sweet, seductive sound.

"I know that after we eat, we're going to get naked and go for a swim."

"Aren't we supposed to wait twenty minutes?" She taps her chin. "I wonder how we can waste twenty minutes."

I pick up the bottle of wine and refill her glass. She eyes me. "Are you trying to get me drunk?" she teases.

"No, babe. I want you wide awake and aware of everything I'm doing to you," I say, and she clamps down on her bottom lip, clearly liking that idea.

"I was wondering something, Josh." She glances around, to the lights twinkling in the hotel. "Why a hedonistic resort? I had no idea you liked things like that."

"It's a niche market, something that was missing from the industry."

She shifts, like she's a bit uncomfortable. "Do you ever get embarrassed, or judged?"

"Embarrassed, no. No one should ever be embarrassed by their wants, Gemma. A person needs to own who they are, and when it comes right down to it, what happens between consenting adults is no one's business but their own. As far as judged, I'm sure I'm judged by some. Those people, though, if they can't accept me for who I am, they're not my friends and can shove their judgment right up their asses," I say, and that brings a smile to her face.

"I like that. I wish I had that attitude." She shrugs. "My upbringing was so strict. I had to act, talk and even eat a certain way. If I had moaned when eating ravioli, there would have been consequences."

I poke my fork into a ravioli and guide it to her mouth. "Open." She does and I slide it in. "Now moan." She does as I say. "Tell me what's wrong with that."

"Not a damn thing," she says, "and look at that, I just said damn."

We both laugh, and I can't believe how much fun I'm having with her, talking, getting reacquainted after all these years apart. I like this. A lot. Judging by the look on her face, she's enjoying it, too.

She takes another sip of wine, and I ask, "The phone call from earlier… It's not my business but I'm just wondering if everything is okay. Whoever wanted you was pretty insistent."

"Yeah, it was just my mother. Asking about some paintings."

"When you have your own gallery, you'll never be tracked down on vacation and will answer to no one but yourself."

"That would be lovely," she says, but there's a sadness in her voice. "It's expensive to open a gallery, and I wouldn't have enough of my art to fill the walls."

"Are you still painting landscapes and people?"

"I am," she says.

"Hey, maybe you could show me some of your work. Maybe I could display it in my hotels."

"If you only knew," she says, so low under her breath I almost don't hear her.

"What don't I know?"

She looks at me like she wants to tell me something but shakes her head. "How much I love this ravioli."

I let it go, for now. "Are you not painting anymore, Gemma?"

"I haven't for a while, actually. It's just… I don't know. I don't think I've had much inspiration lately."

"You seemed inspired earlier, on the beach."

"Yeah, I think the new setting has moved me. It's gorgeous here." She glances around, but then her gaze settles back on me. "Or maybe the new enthusiasm I'm feeling has something to do with you?"

I stand and reach for her hand. "Be prepared to be inspired."

CHAPTER ELEVEN

Gemma

I STAND AS he pulls me to him, and his scent, the warmth of his skin envelops me like a soft blanket. He cups my cheeks and places the softest kiss on my mouth. I melt into him and kiss him back, my emotions on a damn roller coaster ride on repeat. The boat rocks gently, and his cock thickens against my stomach.

I like that this man knows who he is. He doesn't hide the fact that he opens hedonistic hotels that cater to those with special desires. I spent my whole life disguising and suppressing my needs. Here, I don't have to. But this is a fantasy and when I go back to the real world, it's a return to the way things were. I almost told Josh the erotic art was mine. I opened my mouth and tried, but the words wouldn't come. I've hidden that side of myself for so long, spent a lifetime being prim and proper and being told that anything outside the norm—in bed and in my art—was sinful. My parents obviously don't see the beauty in the human body the way I do. Josh does, and I still can't bring myself to tell him.

Probably because he doesn't believe that any of this is me, thinks I'm pretending to be someone else. I could tell him, but he remembers that girl from college, and I'm not sure there is anything I could do or say to prove otherwise. Really, what's the point anyway? I'll be leaving here at the end of the week, whether he knows or doesn't know that this is who I am—a girl who craves the kind of sex he's giving me.

His hands move down my body, and he captures the hem of my light dress and lifts it. Just as he's about to remove my clothing and expose me, I realize there are other boats in the water. I go completely still and peer into the night. I can't see them, but can they see us?

"You with me, Gemma?" he asks, and I love the way he always checks in with me. His knuckles brush my outer thighs as he fists my dress in his big hands.

"I'm with you. I was just… Well, there are boats out here. I know what goes on here, and I was wondering if anyone might be watching us." He frowns and his eyes narrow as he glances around the vast ocean, like he's fighting an internal war. What the heck did I say to upset him?

"Here's the thing, Gems," he says softly, his mouth

twisted. "I get that you want to be someone else this week, but I worry you'll have regrets later—"

"I won't," I say quickly, and his head jerks back to me, his eyes locked on mine.

"Okay," he answers, even though he doesn't look like he believes me. He takes a deep breath and expels it like air slowly being released from a balloon. "In some of the playrooms, there are more than one couple. I think you know that."

"I do."

He takes a rough swallow. "If you want to dabble in voyeurism, we can. If you want those people on the boats to see you, I can arrange that."

"But…" I say, sensing his unease with all this.

"I'll do that for you if you want, but it's not what I want."

He'd do that…for me? My heart jumps into my throat as emotions flood me. "Josh—" I begin.

"I don't want to share you, Gemma." He swallows. "Christ, I don't even want anyone looking at your body. Not just because I think you might regret it, but because, well, fuck, I don't want to share you. I want you all to myself. I'm a selfish prick like that, but if you want to be seen, then—"

I put my finger to his lip to quiet him. "It's not what I want."

He frowns, his gaze moving over my face, assessing me. "You're going to have to clarify, Gems. You want me to share or not to share?"

"I want you all to myself. I don't want to, either. Especially not with Atlanta."

He grins. "So you were jealous?" he teases.

"I'm just not much into sharing, is all," I say, not really wanting him to think things are evolving past the sex-only relationship we agreed on. "Even when I was little, I'd lick the whole chocolate bar so I wouldn't have to divide it with friends."

He laughs. "You did not."

"Oh, yeah, I did." I poke my thumb into my chest and bring this whole conversation back to sex. "If I want something all to myself, I lick it."

He growls and grabs a fistful of my hair. "Jesus Christ, Gemma. When you say things like that…"

"You like it?"

"Yeah, I like it."

Grinning and loving how fast he's coming unhinged, I rip into his shorts and shove them to his knees. I drop down onto the deck and admire his cock as it stands at full attention. I stick my tongue out, and, starting at the base, I lick all the way to his crown. He fists my hair and wobbles, unable to move too much with his shorts bound around his legs. For a man who always has to be in control, I'm sure this is throwing him off, but he tied me up. Now it's my turn. Honestly, I had no idea how fun it would be to repay the favor and have him at my mercy. Will he beg me like I begged him? I guess it's time to find out.

"Mmm," I say, and lick him some more. "Look

at that. I can't share with anyone now. I guess this
is all mine."

"I like your rules," he says, his voice rough and
heavy with arousal.

I put my hand between his legs to cup his balls,
and he groans. I'm sure the sound will carry on the
water, although from the look on his face, 100 percent need living there, I'm guessing he doesn't care.

I lick him lightly, tease his shaft and crown until
he's pulsing and groaning and moving his hips, trying to get inside. I don't let him, though. No, I'm enjoying the way this man is fraying around the edges,
like an old pair of cutoff jeans. I exhale, and my hot
breath falls over him. He trembles from the top of
his head to the tip of his toes, and I take full pleasure in having the upper hand here.

"Mmm." I trace a vein with my tongue and lean
back as his cock pulses, eager for more of my attention. "You like that, Josh? You like me licking you
like this, getting you all hard and wet, making you
nice and slippery before you fuck me?"

"You're killing me, Gemma," he grumbles.

Playing with him, I inch back. "Oh, if you don't…"

"I do," he practically yells and guides my head
to his cock. "Please, Gemma. I'll lose my goddamn
mind or blow an artery if you don't take me in your
mouth, right fucking now."

Pleased with myself, I do as he asks, swirling
my tongue around him as I pump him with my fist.
He rocks into me, his hips curling forward like he

wants me to take all of him. It's impossible. That's not going to stop me from trying, though.

"Gemma," he growls. I steal a glance upward, and he throws his head back, so lost in what I'm doing to him, pride fills my chest. "You keep that up and I'm going to come."

I say, "Uh-huh," letting him know he's not going anywhere in a hurry. I want him to come. I've never swallowed before, never wanted to, but with him everything is different. Everything is perfect. His tortured sounds as he tries to hang on wrap around me and take me so high, I swear I'm going to climax just from getting him off.

"You are so good at that," he growls, his hand following the motion of my head as I move it up and down. He thickens, his veins filling with heated blood, and I hold him tight with my lips. He grunts and lets go, filling my mouth and throat.

"Gemma," he cries out as I stay completely still to let him enjoy each and every pulse. He's breathing so hard, I begin to worry he's going to pass out. I angle my head to see him and catch the heat and something so tender in his eyes that my heart misses a beat. My Lord, when he looks at me like that, like I'm the most amazing woman in the world, it messes with my head and my heart.

Keep it together, Gemma.

He gulps air to catch his breath—not an easy task, judging by how winded he is—and his gaze is predatory as he kicks his shorts off and tugs me to my feet.

My God, the way he is looking at me… I don't think
I've ever been more aroused in my life.

"My turn," he says through clenched teeth.

In a fast, greedy move, he spins me around and
presses my back to his chest. His soft lips, a contrast
to the hurried roughness he's displaying, find my
neck for a hot, wet kiss, steeped in need and starva-
tion. I angle my head to give myself to him, and he
reaches under my dress and almost brutally shoves
his hands into my panties.

Holy hot and dirty.

He slides one finger in and circles my clit. I quake
and nearly sink to my knees. He slides into me, giving me just an inch, and I moan at the delicious
ways this man teases me. "I'm going to slide in so
nicely." His head lifts. "After I lick and devour you,
of course."

"Of course," I blurt out, not even caring that I
sound like a raccoon who has gotten into a dumpster
full of Red Bull. He chuckles at my anxiousness and
lifts my dress to expose my panties. "More pretty
panties for me?"

"Yes." My stomach jumps in anticipation and
hope. "Are you going to rip them off and keep these
ones, too?"

"If I want." He toys with the barely there lace
band, a smirk on his face, but beneath it all, he's a
hot mess, just like I am. He's not even a little bit in
control of himself, and, try to hide it all he wants, I
can see through him.

As I take pleasure in that knowledge, he slides his hand inside the lacy band, and I widen my legs to give him access. He inhales, like he's breathing me in, something to draw on when this is all over. I do the same and as I exhale, the sound of my panties shredding reaches my ears.

I take a fast breath, loving this sexy, impatient side of him. "You're awfully hard on my clothes," I murmur.

"I'm going to be hard inside you in a minute." He drops my panties onto the floor, next to his shorts. He grips my dress and I lift my arms to let him tug it off. My bra follows, until I'm completely naked, his to do with as he pleases.

"Lie back," he commands in a soft voice. The table is cool against my hot skin, refreshing. I grip the sides of the table as he drops down, aligning his face with my sex. That first sweet touch of his hot tongue, soft against my lips, nearly does me in.

"God, yes," I cry out. He pushes his tongue into me, tasting me deeply. I am so in love with what he's doing to me right now I could stay in this position for the rest of my life, or at least the rest of the night. But I want more. God, what has this man done to me?

He slips a finger inside me, his mouth all over my sex, licking and drinking and sucking, and the moans he's making turn me on even more. As he gets a little more frenzied, his mouth rough and his teeth sharp, pain and pleasure mingle until I'm done.

Lost. Gone to everyone and everything but this man and this moment.

"Christ," he growls when my body begins to quake, and he pulls his finger out quickly and shoves his hard cock into me. I gasp and clench harder around him as he fills me so nicely. The sight of him sliding in and out brings on another orgasm in seconds flat. He looks shocked, and I can't even believe it myself.

"So good," he says and grips my hips, pulling me closer to the edge so he can get in deeper. Our flesh pounds, and I let my head fall back to take in the stars dancing in the dark night as well as the stars dancing behind my eyelids when I close them.

Heaven.

It's the only way to describe what Josh is doing to me. He digs his fingers into me harder, and I reach up and cup my breasts.

"Pinch your nipples," he orders in a voice I don't even recognize.

He leans over me, his dick high inside me and takes my nipple between his teeth. A sharp tug centers between my legs as he bites down. "Yes, yes," I murmur and roll my head from side to side.

As he pumps into me, and gives my breasts the attention they're craving, heat once again builds inside me. "Josh, oh, Josh, I'm… I'm…" My words die on my lips as he swells inside me, his own orgasm approaching as my hard climax massages his long, hard shaft.

"Yeah, baby, that's it," he says and lays his head between my breasts as he comes with me.

I put my hands on his head and stroke his hair. He cuddles closer and I chuckle. He always used to love when I did that years ago. I know all his little sensitive spots and how to pleasure him with the lightest of touches. As he tingles in ecstasy, goose bumps break out on his arm. In some ways, being with him like this is just like old times. In some ways, it's not. I'm experiencing more, allowing myself to take what I want, to show a side of myself I've never shown any other. It's very freeing and I'm not sure I could be like this with any other man. As I revel in my post-orgasm bliss, one working brain cell kicks in and panic jumps in my stomach.

"Oh my God," I blurt out.

He stiffens and goes ramrod straight. "What?" Dark, worried eyes move over my face.

I jackknife up and put my hand on his hard chest, right over his pounding heart. "Josh, we...we didn't use protection."

"Fuck," he says and grabs a fistful of hair. "I'm so sorry, Gemma. This is my fault. I was so damn anxious to be inside you I never stopped to think."

"The fault isn't entirely yours, Josh. I was just as anxious. God, we're like two teenagers! You'd think after all the sex we've been having, we wouldn't still be so crazed."

"Yeah, you'd think," he says, as dumbfounded by our actions as I am. He backs up, picks up his

T-shirt and drapes it over my shoulders to keep me warm. His thoughtfulness wraps around me more than his shirt. "Let me get you cleaned up, and then we need to talk."

I nod and tug his big shirt around me. A second later, he's back with tissues. He wipes between my legs and pulls on his shorts. "Here," he says, handing me my clothes. I pass him his shirt, and after we dress, he sits on a chair and taps his leg. "Come here."

I sit on his lap, and he adjusts me until I'm facing him and my legs are wrapped around his back. Trying to make light of this, even though the results could be catastrophic, I say, "Isn't this what got us into trouble in the first place?"

He puts one arm around me and brushes my hair back. "I'm clean, Gemma. I promise you that. I know you're clean, too. You don't even have to tell me that. But there are other things we have to think about, obviously."

"Pregnancy, I know."

He glances at me—little boy lost—and tears press against my eyes and my throat squeezes tight. There is no one in the world more deserving—more in need—of a family than Josh Walker, and everything about it terrifies the hell out of him. I wish he could see what others see. He is the nicest, kindest man I know, and he'd be a terrific father. Nate is a testament to that.

"I'm on the pill," I say. He's about to exhale, but

I put my fingers to his lips, and he holds his breath. "At least I was until I was kidnapped. I forgot them at the villa when I went back to get some clothes. I was just so overwhelmed with everything that was happening, and you had condoms, so I just didn't worry about it."

He shakes his head, real worry emanating off his tight body. "What are we going to do?"

"I think we're okay, I'm really close to the end of my cycle." I touch my belly. "I can already feel the cramps."

Relief moves over his face. "Thank God." He holds his hands up. "Wait, no, I don't mean about cramps. That's awful, actually."

"I knew what you meant." I touch his face and he leans into my hand to absorb the warmth. "I'm pretty sure you didn't just impregnate me," I say, and an odd sense of disappointment barrels through me, catching me by surprise. What. The. Hell?

"That would have been a huge mistake. I'll be careful next time. I promise," he says and kisses me softly.

"Right," I say, even though I'm suddenly not sure I 100 percent agree with him. Would having his child be so bad? I can't think of any reason why I wouldn't want his baby growing inside me. Other than the fact that a husband doesn't come with the pregnancy.

Josh was right. This was a mistake. Too bad it doesn't feel like one.

CHAPTER TWELVE

Josh

JESUS, I CAN'T stop smiling. I must look like the village idiot to the guests and staff as Gemma and I saunter into the hotel, our hair still wet from our late-night swim. After the most incredible sex, our bodies warm and sated, we jumped in the water and I laughed like I haven't laughed in years. Everything about her fascinates me, intrigues me, makes me want to give her the world. And I will. Once this week is over, I'll give her back to the world she belongs in. Until then...

I check my phone to see if my plans are in place, and Gemma glances at me. "Everything okay?" she asks, having caught me on the phone a few times tonight. I could tell her what I'm doing, but I prefer to surprise her. Unlike me, she likes surprises.

"Everything is fine."

"I'm not exactly sure it is," she says, her voice wavering.

CATHRYN FOX 131

I turn to her, note the unease on her face. My stomach clenches and she says, "Everyone is looking at us." She shifts closer to me. "I'm used to that but not here."

"Don't worry about it." I check my watch, then glance around to see the staff serving champagne, taking the attention off us. "No one is looking now, and your privacy is protected here, and they were looking because the starlit catamaran tour starts in twenty minutes, and I'm totally not dressed for it."

She goes still, her eyes wide. "Josh, I'm so sorry. I shouldn't be taking you from your duties."

"It's fine. I don't have to go."

"Yes, you do," she says, and with a stern look on her face, she points to the elevators. "Go get changed, and get your sweet ass back down here and engage with your guests."

"What about you? Aren't you coming?"

"If it's okay, I think I'm going to go to bed early. Maybe do a bit of reading. I'm spent."

I hesitate, not wanting to be away from her for any length of time when we have so little of it. But she's been up late, and if she wants to call it an early night, I'm not going to stop her. "Okay, go get some sleep."

"I never said I was going to sleep. I said I was going to read, and I plan to wait up for you."

I shake my head and exhale loudly.

"What, you don't want that?" she asks, genuine worry on her face. My heart leaps.

"No," I say quickly to reassure her. "It's just that

I'm getting hard again, and these shorts are unforgiving."

She laughs. "I don't know what you're worried about. Most of these people were on the beach today, and many of them were…well, you know." She frowns as soon as she says that.

"What?" I ask.

"Atlanta is giving me the evil eye. When you go out, do you have to…?"

"I don't have to do anything I don't want to do," I tell her. "And the only one I want to do is you. You licked it, so it's yours, remember?" I say, wanting to pull a laugh from her. It works, and she relaxes. I hold my hand out. "Give me your phone."

"Why?" She crinkles her nose and pulls it from her purse.

"I'm putting my contact information in here so you can text me if you want." I hand it back and she runs her finger over the screen, like she's savoring my number in her phone. "Or, you know, if you want to do a little video call naked, I'm okay with that, too."

Her eyes light up. "Oh, I've never done that before."

I touch her face and drop a kiss on her forehead. "That's because you're a good girl, Gemma. Now go on up and get settled in bed. I'll come find you when this is all over. I have a surprise for you."

She heads to the elevator and I check in with Matteo, letting him know I'll be right back down to get the party started. I hurry to my room and change into casual dress clothes more suitable for the nighttime tour. The whole time, my thoughts are with Gemma and how I'd much rather be snuggled in her bed, holding her while she reads.

Fuck, that is not good. Not good at all.

This is just sex, dude.

With that reminder, I head back downstairs and lead the guests to the dock where the catamaran and the crew are waiting. The whole time I can feel Atlanta's eyes on me, and I play nice, not wanting to offend her. It's not her fault she's expecting something different from me. A person isn't just supposed to change, transform into someone else before your eyes. No wonder she's confused.

Gemma, however—she's transformed before my eyes. While she's still that kind, sweet, artistic girl from college, she's turned into a salacious woman who takes what she wants. Is she pretending to be someone else, or could that be the real her? Even if it is the real her, she clearly wants to keep that side behind closed doors. Christ, when I mentioned getting out of the hotel, going somewhere, she flinched at the idea. A girl like her can't be seen in public with a guy like me, even if that's something we both want—although I can't speak for her.

I take a drink from the tray as the server comes by, and the champagne feels good on my parched throat. My phone pings, and I instantly smile when I pull it from my pocket and see Gemma's name. I grin at the image of her lacy panties displayed on her bed, ones I've yet to tear.

Gemma: My one last good pair.

Me: Not for long.

Gemma: :-(

Me: Missing me?

Gemma: Just giving you incentive to hurry back.

Me: I'll be there as soon as I can.

I put my phone away and marshal my dick into submission.

With a drink in hand, I mingle, and even though I'm making small talk, my mind is on Gemma. Sweet, sexy Gemma, whose desires can be fulfilled by only me. Dammit, she'd better not be using this hotel, and all it has to offer, including me, to enhance her performance in the bedroom for Bentley. I can't even bring myself to think about that. It fucks me over in ways that cut deep. Really, it shouldn't upset me. What she does when she leaves here is not my business—even though it feels like it should be.

I push that thought from my mind and move to the back of the party boat. Soon enough, Atlanta finds me. "Hey," I say and put on a smile. "I hope you're enjoying Belize."

"Having so much fun," she says. She sighs and glances at the stars. "You really like her, huh?" she says, and the thoughts of Gemma make me smile. She laughs lightly and puts her hand on my chest. "You don't even have to say anything. It's written all over your face."

I shrug and make light of it. "I like her."

"No kidding." She takes a sip of her champagne and taps the flute against her chin. "I can't help but think she looks familiar."

"Maybe you met her at one of my hotels," I fib. It doesn't matter if she places her, we all have a confidentiality agreement, but I just want to be extra cautious, because confidentiality is of the utmost importance to Gemma.

"Yeah, maybe," she says. "So is she the one who's going to turn the most eligible bachelor into a married man?"

I laugh it off. "No," I say firmly, and she eyes me like she can see beneath the façade. Even if I wanted that, the answer is still no. I knew it when I was in college and I know it now. But that doesn't stop my mind from wondering. What would it be like to come home every day to Gemma? To talk over dinner, to fall into bed every night and wake up together every morning? What would it be like to have a little one running around calling out for Mommy and Daddy?

My entire body goes stiff at that last thought. Holy

shit, her pregnancy scare must have hit me harder than I realized, although suddenly and for no apparent reason, I'm not as frightened by being a father—if Gemma was by my side. Would I make a good dad? I honestly have no idea, but I was a big influence over my brother, and other than his ego, he's one hell of a great kid.

The ego, though, that's only for show. Underneath it all, I know exactly who he is just as much as he knows who I am. Whoa. What does that say about him kidnapping Gemma? Sure, he thinks we belong together, but does he know something I don't? If he did, he'd come right out and tell me, wouldn't he? Then again, I guess there are some things a guy has to learn on his own.

I blink and realize Atlanta has been waving her hand in front of my face. "Josh, where did you disappear to?" she asks.

I blink again and shake my head to clear it. "Sorry, was just thinking about some work things."

She frowns. "Yes, I just bet you were." Someone calls her name and she turns and waves. Her gaze goes back to me. "I'll let you get back to thinking about your work things." She wiggles her fingers at me and adds, "But I'll be looking forward to your *work* being behind you." With that she disappears into the crowd.

A strange, uneasy feeling erupts inside me. Once Gemma and I are done, I'm not sure I can go back to my playing days. I think I'm all played out, actually. My phone pings again, and my thoughts shift as I pull it from my pocket. A sexy image of Gemma in bed pops up, and I glance out to see how far we are from shore and how long it might take me to swim back.

It's ridiculous, I know, but I can't wait to see her again. I wish to fuck I wasn't this excited, but there is little I can do about it. I text back and ask her to send more and wish I hadn't. Getting a hard-on out here on the boat, where anything goes, isn't a great idea. I don't want to give anyone the wrong notion. I lift my head, and my smile fades when I catch Atlanta looking at me, a strange, unidentifiable expression on her face.

Unease ribbons through me as a smile touches her mouth and she quickly turns away. Dammit, are my feelings for Gemma that transparent? If others can see it—hell when we're together we give off enough electricity to light every one of my hotels for a month—can Gemma see it, too? If she can, is she expecting more from me? But she's a good girl, right? Wanting to escape her real world for a while. She doesn't belong with me.

Or does she?

CHAPTER THIRTEEN

Gemma

I WAKE WITH a pressure low in my stomach, and my eyes slowly open. I reach across the bed and touch the man who came in late and crawled in next to me, holding me to him as we both fell asleep. There was no hurried sex, no rush for climax. No, last night was so sweet and tender, just the two of us holding each other, basking in our warmth and touch as slumber pulled us under.

I turn and watch him sleep, and as much as I've been trying to keep this casual, keep it about sex, it's a losing battle. I was half in love with the man before I found myself tied to his chair. Okay, maybe that's not entirely true. I was totally in love with him before any of this ever happened. He might have gutted me back in college and I might be the world's biggest fool, but I never stopped loving him.

I tried to move on, and I did, with Bentley. I cared for him, I still do, but there was no way I could love him when my heart was in another man's hands. I sigh heavily and push the blankets off. In the bathroom, I find a robe, slip it on and quietly step outside. The warm morning sun falls over me, and I walk to the pool, sit on the edge and dip my feet in. I sit there for a long time, gazing at the beach below and all the early morning sun worshippers, some in clothes, some completely naked. My fingers itch for a paintbrush.

The door clicks behind me, and I turn. My heart wobbles as a very sexy, very sleepy and rumpled Josh comes my way. Dressed in only his boxers, I'm gifted with a view of his hard body.

"You're up early," he murmurs as he drops down behind me, putting his legs around me.

"I slept well," I say. Likely a result of his body next to mine, cradling and comforting me. "How about you?"

"Same." He pulls my hair from my neck, and I lean against his shoulder. We both stay like that for a long time, just being together, breathing, relaxing, enjoying the comfortable silence falling over us.

"Hmm," I say, giving a contented sigh. I glance around, and for the first time in a long time, I have a full day with nothing to do but hang out with Josh. Although I'm sure he has work to do, and I understand that. Thinking about work has me tensing up a bit. Before I return to the real world, I'll have to talk to Bentley. I'm definitely not going to give him the letter I wrote in the heat of the moment. That was just a way to get my feelings down. I'll talk to him in person when the time is right, and while the conversation is necessary, I'm not one for confrontation, so it won't be easy for me.

"Something on your mind?" Josh asks, clearly picking up on the changes in my mood.

"Just thinking about Bentley," I say. Shoot. "I mean…" I begin, scrambling to explain, but he stops me.

"How about some breakfast?"

"Josh, I—"

"Blueberry pancakes?" He moves away from me and stands. I block the sun from my eyes to see him. "They always were your favorite."

"I wasn't thinking about Bentley," I blurt out.

His gaze moves over my face. "Gemma, you either were or you weren't."

"I was, but it's not like it seems."

He nods, his lips forming a straight line as he pinches them. "Do me a favor."

"Anything."

"Just don't think about him when you're with me."

My stomach coils. "You don't understand."

"What I understand is we have until the end of the week, and if you're with me, I want you to be *with me*." His gaze moves over my body, hungrily, possessively, and if I didn't know better, I would definitely say he was jealous. Could I be right? Could Josh be jealous of Bentley? I have to be wrong. Nothing has changed between us since college. Nothing to make him change his mind on a future together. We've been having sex. That is all.

"I want that, too," I manage to push out past a tight throat.

His shoulders relax, and he holds his hand out to help me up. "Okay. Come on. Let's get something to eat, and then I have a surprise for you."

"A surprise? What did I do to deserve a surprise?"

"You don't have to do anything to earn a surprise, Gemma. You should be given surprises every day. Doesn't Ben—" He lets his words fall off. "Sorry, we're not talking about him."

I stand and say, "I don't need surprises every day, Josh." What I don't tell him is I need him every day. "And no, the guy we're not talking about never gave me surprises." That's not entirely true. It was a big surprise when I overheard him on the phone, but I'm not about to say that. It's so damn embarrassing.

"A girl like you should be treasured and worshipped, Gemma." My heart lurches. My God, if he thinks that, then why did he push me away, why did he just remind me of our timeline? I want to ask, but I'm too afraid he'll think I want more and send me packing this morning. Instead, I close my mouth and avoid confrontation.

He pushes my hair back from my face and stares at me for a long time. I stare back, having no idea what's going through his head, but from the frown lines creasing his forehead, it must be one hell of an internal battle.

He places a soft kiss on my mouth as he leads me inside, his hand on my hip like he needs the constant connection, and my head spins. I wasn't thinking of Bentley like he assumed and probably shouldn't be thinking of him at all when I'm with Josh. I could try to explain, but when all's said and done, does it really matter? He's sending me packing at the end of the week.

My stomach takes that moment to grumble and he chuckles, easing the tension inside me. "Do you want to do room service, or head to the dining room?"

"How about we head down and eat on the back deck."

He nods in agreement, but there's a hint of mischief in his eyes when he says, "Let's grab a fast shower."

He pulls my robe from my shoulders and drops a soft kiss on my tingling flesh. We head to the shower and he turns it on and adjusts the spray. Reaching for me, he takes my hand and he leads me in. The temperature is cool. And it's glorious against my warm flesh. He soaps his hands and runs them all over me, leaving me aching and needy everywhere he touches.

He washes me in silence, touching me with tender care. His hips bump me, pushing me forward until I'm close to the tiled wall. Without words, he takes my hands and presses them to the wall and slides his own around me to cup my breasts. A small sound of pleasure escapes my lips and I close my eyes, give in to the sensations pulling me under.

"Would it be risky to have sex without a condom again?" he asks. "They're in the other room, and I don't want to be away from you for one second."

My heart jumps, and my brain races to catch up to the rush of blood. If he knew he was going to have sex with me in here, why didn't he bring a condom with him? Is he really willing to take that risk, especially after he nearly stroked out when we forgot last time? On some level, does he want to get me pregnant, or is this really just about how good it felt without a barrier? I have no idea anymore, and when he slides a hand down, my body goes on hyperdrive. My brain is too aroused to even puzzle things out.

"I'm sure it will be okay," I say, offering myself up to him. His hard length presses against my backside, and my sex clenches, searching for something hard to squeeze around.

He slips a finger in me, but he doesn't need to prepare me. When it comes to him, I'm always ready.

He grips his cock and in one slick, smooth motion he slides all the way inside. "Gemma."

I glance over my shoulder, take in the pure ecstasy on his face and grip the wall as he moves his hips, easily moving in and out, until I'm soaring.

"Yes, just like that," I say, and then my heart is overflowing with all the things I wish I didn't feel for this man.

"Feel good, babe?" he asks, even though the sounds I'm making are a dead giveaway.

"Yes, more please."

"You like this position for making love?" he asks, and he pulls out and plunges all the way back in, stealing the air from my lungs, but it's not the sex that's making me breathless, it's the words he used.

Making love?

Is that what we're doing here?

"Yes," I answer. "I love it, but I want to see you and touch you."

"You will. I promise."

"Does it have something to do with my surprise?" I ask.

He slides his hands up and massages my breasts. "Maybe," he says with that undignified grunt that I love.

"I can't… Oh, God…wait…to see…" My clenches begin in my core and build as he moves in and out, one hand gliding between my legs to stimulate my clit. I pound one fist against the shower wall as my body lets go, a storm of need crashing over me as I break like a dam.

"I love when you come like that," he growls into my ear, his cock thickening inside me, announcing his own orgasm. I gasp as he pumps and pumps until we're both struggling for breath.

He stops spasming, and lifts me until my back is pressed against his hard chest. With his cock still inside me, he backs me up until we're under the spray, and I just stand there in total contentment, unwilling to think about the real world and what lies beyond this resort as he adjusts the spray.

When I can finally speak again, I say, "I have a surprise for you, too."

He pulls out of me, and I instantly miss his warmth. "I don't like surprises, remember?"

"Everyone likes surprises, Josh."

"I don't," he says so firmly I turn in his arms. "I thought you knew that." I glance at his face, take in the darkening of his eyes. As I once again absorb that little-boy-lost look, my heart goes out to him.

"Josh," I say and put my hands on his face. Growing up with a father in jail and an absent mother wasn't easy. Presenting a happy family to child protective services so he and his brother wouldn't be separated had taken its toll on him. All of that was horrible, but it made him into the man he is today. A man who is strong yet tender. Kind and giving. A man who is afraid of commitment. Is that why he pushed me away? Is he afraid that I'll leave him before he can leave me? Tears press against my eyes, but I blink them back. He's not a man who wants pity. He's a man who wants—no, needs—love. He's just too afraid of it. "I'm sorry."

He closes his hands over mine. "You don't have anything to be sorry for."

"The portfolio with the paintings came in this morning," I tell him. "That's what I meant by a surprise."

His mood changes, and his face lights up. "Fantastic. How about we look them over at breakfast?"

"You mean after my surprise."

He laughs, and it lightens me inside, melts a bit of the tension. "Before. I'm starving." He slaps my ass and turns the spray off. We dry off, dress and, keeping close to one another, we head to the dining room, taking a seat outside under an umbrella.

"I love it here," I say as I pull my tablet from my bag.

"Me, too. This place is going to hold fond memories," he says with a grin.

A sense of emptiness swirls around my stomach as I think about leaving, and I work to ignore it. "Where do you go from here?"

"I'm going to hang out for a bit, make sure the grand opening goes smoothly, then honestly, I don't know. I've opened twelve hotels all over the world."

"But…?" I say, sensing something is off.

"I think this might be the last one."

"Really?" I ask as I pull up the portfolio.

"I've been on the road a lot. I think I'm just getting tired of it." He laughs, but beneath the sound, I can sense his loneliness. "I can't even remember what my Manhattan apartment looks like."

"I remember what mine looks like," I say, and my stomach tightens. It's full of Bentley's things, which I'll have to box up and ship to his place. "I'll be moving out of it." Honestly, I don't want to go back to an apartment that reminds me of my ex and his betrayal, even if our breakup is for the best.

Josh looks at me long and hard, and instead of asking why I'll be leaving my apartment, he says, "How about those paintings?"

I turn the tablet his way as the server takes our order. I sip on my coffee and glance at the paintings from the other side of the table. "Come on over here so we can look at them together," he says.

I shift to the chair next to him, and our legs touch under the table. It's so strange. It's like we both need the contact. He flips through the pages, a smile on his face.

"These are gorgeous, so sensual. Why is this artist not famous?" He leans closer to the tablet. "Has she even signed them?"

"I think she wants to be anonymous."

"Why on earth would someone with this kind of talent not want to show it off?"

I shrug, but he's right. It is insane that I can't show off my work, be who I really am.

He sets the tablet down. "I want them all. Every last one of them."

My head rears back. "You can't be serious."

"Why can't I be?" he asks as he picks his coffee cup up and takes a drink.

"Do you have any idea how much that will cost?"

"Doesn't matter." He gives a dismissive wave of his hand. "One thing, though. I really want them signed."

I frown. "I'm not sure she'll be willing to do that."

"I'd love for them to be signed," he says, then moves the tablet to the center of the table when the server comes with our breakfast. "Either way, I want them, but can you try to persuade her?"

"I'll see what I can do. Where do you want them shipped?"

"I'll be here for a while, so let's have them sent here, to the hotel."

I write an email to Mia and ask her to set it all up. I have him type the hotel's address, then hit Send.

He smiles and nods like he has full faith in me, and I like that. I also like how much he adores my paintings, appreciates the naked body as a work of art and not something…sinful. We dig into our food, both of us quiet, lost in our own thoughts. I can't stop thinking about my work and how I'd love to open my own gallery. I played the dutiful daughter and fiancée for years. Would "coming out" really have that big of an effect on my parents? Would they disown me?

Yeah, probably.

But am I going to spend the rest of my life ignoring and suppressing my needs, hiding who I really am? I mean, we get only one shot at this thing called life, right? Shouldn't I be doing what I want, pursuing the things that make me happy and bring me pleasure—like Josh does? God, I'm so tired of pretending. Even after everything Josh and I have been through this week, I can't bring myself to tell him what really happened with me and Bentley or that I'm the artist who created those gorgeous nudes. All the shaming has played a huge role in the person I am today.

Maybe it's time to change that. Maybe it's time

to step out and say "This is me. Take it or leave it."
Maybe I *will* sign those paintings for Josh, when they
arrive, and let him know exactly who I am. Then
again, what am I hoping to achieve? That he'll realize the good girl isn't so good and we can have a
future together?

Could that be the real reason he sent me packing
all those years ago?

CHAPTER FOURTEEN

Josh

SHE SWALLOWS HER last bite of pancake and sets her fork down. My heart aches as I think about her leaving at the end of the week, and I cough to hide the hurt rising up from its darkest corners, crawling over the barrier I erected years ago. This time around, there isn't much I can do to keep the love I have for this woman from spilling over. But feelings and actions are two different things, and no matter what, I'll always act with her best interests at heart.

"Are you ready for your surprise?" I ask.

She wipes her mouth with the napkin and glances at me like Nate used to on Christmas morning. No matter how old he was, I made sure there was a present under that tree for him. I loved seeing him happy, just like I love making Gemma happy. In fact, I'd love to make her happy for the rest of her life and—

I instantly abort that thought. For her own good, we can't have a future. Although if she ended up pregnant from all the sex… My thoughts come to a screeching halt. Holy hell. Is that why I wanted to do it without a condom? On some level, am I hoping she gets pregnant so she doesn't have to leave—because I'm not sure I have it in me to send her away a second time? Wow, I'm far more fucked up than I ever realized.

"I thought you'd never ask," she says, dragging my thoughts back.

"I take that as a yes." I stand and pull her to her feet. "Come with me, then." We head inside and I take her down the long hallway, and swipe my key over the lock. I turn to her, take in the quizzical look on her face. "What?" I ask.

"I wasn't shown this room on the tour," she says and scans the door, like she's trying to find the name of the room.

"That's because it wasn't a playroom before, and it still isn't. Not for any of the other guests, anyway. This one I had designed just for you."

Her eyes go wide. "For me?"

"Yes," I say, and press my lips to hers for a deep kiss, loving the look of pleasure on her face. Has no one ever done anything special for this woman? What the hell is wrong with Bentley? Maybe I'll have to have a talk with him—with my fists. Gemma deserves to feel special; any guy with her should know that. Maybe he really doesn't deserve her. If he's not treating her right, he sure as hell doesn't.

You'd treat her right, Josh.

As that little voice in the back of my brain taunts me, promising a future with her, I push open the door and wave my hand for her to enter. That little voice, however—selfish as it is—is not thinking about what's best for Gemma. But, going back to a guy who doesn't worship her... Is that really what's best for her? That would be a big fat no in my book.

She walks past me, her scent lingering in my nostrils as a little gasp catches in her throat when she sees all the tubes of paints lined up along a table. "Josh, what is all this?" I follow her to the table and pick up a tube of paint.

"You're an artist and don't know what a tube of paint is when you see it?"

She laughs. "I know. But what is all this for?" She looks around the empty room, nothing but a crisp white sheet folded beside the paints. "What do I paint on? Is there canvas or do I use the sheet?"

I poke my thumb into my chest. "You paint on me. I'm your canvas and you're mine, and these are edible paints."

She laughs out loud. "No way." Her eyes glisten, and my heart thumps as it overflows with love. "This is about painting each other?"

"Yes, and when we're done, we're going to make art on that sheet." I grin. "Sound fun?" Her eyes go impossibly wider, and I revel at her childlike enthusiasm.

"It sounds like the most fun ever," she answers. "Body-sheet art, I love it."

"Good, that's the reaction I wanted."

"I can't believe this." She glances around again, completely dumbfounded. "I've never done anything like this. It's so…"

"Juvenile," I say with a laugh.

"Yes, exactly, and everything I want to do…with you." She turns to me and puts her arms around my neck. "I would never have been allowed to do something like this growing up." Her pretty eyes widen. "My God, if I accidently got ink on myself, my mother would lose her mind. I always had to act and dress a certain way." I smile at her and she gives me a hug so steeped in love and emotions I could fucking break down and sob for her lost childhood, and for my own. "Is it any wonder I rebelled?" she says, almost to herself.

"Is that what this week is all about, Gemma? Rebellion?"

"It's about freedom," she says and looks down.

"It's about being someone else," I say, and that little voice nudges me again, suggesting there is more going on here than I realize. "You can be free here with me all you like. No judgment, no fear of reprimand."

"I wish it could be like this all the time. I wish I could be more like you. You don't care what anyone thinks of you."

I nod, but it's not entirely true. I care what she thinks of me, but generally, I live my life the way I want to live it. That's not to say I haven't been judged over the years. I have. Big-time. So have the people who've hung out with me, and it's not always fared well for them. Gemma is a prime example. The papers did a number on me, which reflected badly on her.

"No matter what I do," she begins, a new kind of sadness in her tone, "I have my mother on one shoulder, my father on the other constantly reminding me that my actions reflect the family name."

"That's brutal, Gemma. Deep inside, though, you must know they want what's best for you, too."

"I'm not even really sure they do, and that's a horrible thought to have."

"They want you to be happy, right?"

"As long as it fits in with their plans for me."

"What if you veered from those plans because something outside of what they deemed acceptable made you happy?"

Ah, why the hell am I asking that? Oh, probably because I'm outside those plans and trying to find a way to keep us together.

"They'd probably disown me," she says and frowns, like she has something very important on her mind.

"Maybe not. Maybe they would support you in whatever you did."

I would never want her to lose the love of her parents. That's the last thing I want, but Gemma has to live her own life—for her. I know firsthand what it's like to have absent parents, emotionally and physically, and I'd never want her to experience that kind of pain.

"Maybe," she says, but her voice lacks conviction.

"I think it's really important to follow your own dreams, not those of someone else."

I brush her left shoulder and then her right.

She narrows her eyes. "What are you doing?"

"I just tossed your parents away. Now that they're gone, what is it you want to do?"

She opens her mouth and hesitates. I angle my head and wait as she looks around the room, but her shoulders slump. Whatever it was she was about to tell me is now buried.

"I want to paint," she says. "I want to open my own gallery. I want to sell all my paintings, not just some of them."

I nod, not really sure what she means by that. "If you had your own gallery, where would you want it to be?"

"Manhattan. I love Belize, and love visiting, but my heart is in Manhattan. I just can't imagine how that would go over, especially if I showcased all my paintings—even the ones that are closest to my heart."

"What's wrong with selling all your paintings?"

She goes quiet for a moment, thoughtful. What is going through that creative mind of hers? She lifts her head like she just had a revelation, and I can almost feel the lightness about her. "Not a thing, really," she says, as she gives a light laugh. "Not a thing at all, and I'm sure my work would make a big splash and shake up the stuffy art world."

I laugh with her. "I think it could use a good shaking, don't you?" I'm not sure what other paintings she's talking about—the ones that are close to her heart. She's obviously not ready to talk about them or show me, and I'm not going to pressure her.

I pull my pinging phone from my pocket and see that it's from Matteo. There's some paperwork that needs my attention. "This will have to wait for just a little bit. I have some work to do, but in the meantime, why don't you go ahead and paint without me?"

She gives me a quizzical look. "Isn't the point of this to paint each other?"

"Come on. I have another surprise for you."

I take her hand and lead her into the hall, pulling the door shut behind us. This room is completely off-limits to anyone else. It's something special, just for the two of us.

She nudges me with her hip. "Aren't you full of surprises today?"

"I'm full of something," I say, and she laughs.

She goes up on her tiptoes and kisses me. "I like what you're full of."

My heart crashes, because I like everything about this woman. Like? Fuck, no. I love everything about this woman.

"I like you, too," I say. I take her hand and lead her down the hall and out the back door toward the beach. Right under the tree where she sat sketching yesterday, I have an easel, sketch pad, and all the pens, brushes and paints she could ever want.

"Josh," she says with a little squeal. "Is this for me?"

"I thought you might like it. You seemed to like this spot, so I thought—"

Before I can finish, she throws her arms around me. "I love it. I can't believe you did this. I mean, I can. You're so considerate and thoughtful, and I was thinking yesterday how I wish I had my paints with me, but I didn't want to go back to town, and this is so perfect, and oh my God, I'm rambling. I do that sometimes when—"

I kiss her, hard, to stop her rambling, so she can gather her thoughts. I love seeing her this happy, but she always used to rattle on when she was over-whelmed. Her arms go around my neck, and our lips linger. Her eyes slide shut, and we just stay like that; no words need to be said for how we're feeling.

I can't deny my feelings for her. I can't even try, and she's feeling this every bit as much as I am. I'm sure of it. We're going to have to talk before this week is over. Really talk. I need to know where she stands. At first, I thought she should go back to Bent-ley. Now I'm not so certain. I also thought keeping her out of my life was what was best for her. I'm not sure of that anymore, either. But the biggest thing I'm not clear about… Is she pretending to be someone else, or am I looking at the real Gemma—a woman who has been hiding wants and desires that match my own?

If so, what am I going to do about that?

CHAPTER FIFTEEN

Gemma

THE WARM SUN shines down on me, my heart full of love and lightness as I paint the naked couple on the sand, who I'd spent the other day sketching on my pad. Bodies entwined on the beach, legs and arms twisted as the lovers worshipped each other's hills and valleys. The scene is absolutely gorgeous and breathtaking. I still can't believe Josh set this all up for me, and I have been anxious all day to try out the paint room designed just for us.

I stand back and examine the lines of my work, pleased with how it's turning out. When this is done, I'll show Josh. Then he'll know who really painted the one hanging in his lobby and those he admired and purchased in the portfolio. I can't wait for him to put it together. Once he does, he'll come to realize I'm not pretending to be someone else. This is the real me. If that was the reason he sent me packing—and it would be just like Josh to try to protect me—this could change everything, right?

Honestly, the more time I spend with him, the more I think that's why he broke it off with me. He goes beyond to protect those he cares about, and back in college, it was clear he cared about me. Which made the breakup especially confusing. I shake with excitement, anxious to see if this changes things for us, because the longer I think about it, the more that makes sense.

Until that moment of revelation happens, and I show him, instead of telling him, I'm going to keep on painting. As I pick up my brush, I actually allow myself to consider opening my own gallery, selling my own erotic works. It will no doubt shake up the art world, shake up my parents. Josh is right, though. I need to be living the life I want to live—following my own dreams. My parents will simply have to accept me for who I am. If they don't... Well, I guess I'll cross that bridge when I get to it. I also can't forget I'll have to cross that bridge with Bentley sooner rather than later.

I just hope my parents, their friends and the art community can see that my explicit designs are beautiful, something to be admired, not hidden in the back room of the studio because they're scandalous. The human body is not something to be ashamed of. Heck, why is everyone so afraid of nudity? Especially when there are so many other horrible things going on in the world. Truthfully, I'm tired of feeling ashamed of my work, my wants and desires. Being here with Josh has taught me acceptance of myself and my needs. There really is *nothing* wrong with me. I'm completely normal.

I continue to paint, missing Josh's presence but knowing he has work to do. I'm beginning to believe when this week is over, we might be able to have a future together. We've grown even closer, and he talked about moving back to Manhattan permanently. What happens in Belize doesn't have to stay in Belize, right? Hope fills my soul and I can't help but smile. We clearly need to talk, and I sense he wants a deeper conversation, too. I just hope it's about a future, that this time around he wants what I want.

"Something funny?" I glance up and spot Nate coming my way. I jump from my stool and throw my arms around him.

"What's funny is that you've been in hiding, and I know how hard it is for you not to grace the world on a daily basis with that pretty face of yours."

He grins that sweet playful grin that has girls shedding their panties. Not this girl, though. I love Nate like a brother, but Josh, I love like a man, a partner, the guy I want to father my kids. I can't be wrong about him this time. I just can't.

"It's almost like you know me." He rocks on his feet. "Seriously, though, I was worried you might be mad at me, and I wanted to give both you and Josh some time together."

"When you kidnapped me, I thought you were taking me to some strip joint."

His mouth drops like he's astounded. "Don't tell me my brother didn't strip for you."

I laugh. "What he did or didn't do is none of your business."

"It is my business," he says casually and glances over my shoulder. "Hey, what are you working on?"

I grab a sheet and drape the canvas to hide my work. I don't share my work until it's finished, but I'm even more protective of this work. I want to unveil it to Josh first. "Nothing I'm ready for anyone to see."

"Is it dirty?" he teases, but underneath, I sense he's not teasing at all. Is it possible Nate has always been able to see the real me, no matter how hard I try to hide it, and that's the reason he brought me to this hotel—to Josh?

"It's not dirty. It's beautiful," I tell him and he nods.

"Yeah, I know." He blinks innocently, and my heart melts a little. "You're not mad at me?"

"I could never be mad at you," I say.

He glances around, then zeroes back in on me. "I have a question and you don't have to answer."

I put one hand on my hip and brace myself. It's so rare I see him serious like this. "Ask."

He narrows his eyes and takes a breath. "Are you and Bentley finished? The papers are still talking about your wedding. Is it still on?"

I let loose a low, slow whistle. "That's more than one question, and the answer is this. Bentley and I have to talk." I'm not about to tell Nate that it's over before I tell Bentley. Yes, I told my best friend Mia, and the man I love, but it's only fair that Bentley is the next to know. He probably should have been the first to know, actually, but under the circumstances…

"I wouldn't have kidnapped you if I thought you two were right for each other. I know it's not my business, but I knew you weren't happy."

My shoulders tighten. "What makes you say that?"

He shoves his hands into his pocket and kicks a pebble, looking like a child caught with his hand in the cookie jar.

"Nate?" I ask, unease zipping through my veins.

"I didn't want to tell you this."

"Tell me what?"

"I don't want to hurt your feelings."

"Just tell me, please."

"I saw him. About a month ago. In Manhattan. He wasn't alone. They were trying to be discreet, but I caught them."

My stomach tightens and I simply nod my head. "I haven't said anything to anyone other than Mia. It's embarrassing, you know."

"He's the one who should be embarrassed."

"I overheard him on the phone," I confess. "I was sure he was seeing someone."

"He's a fucking asshole and I'm sorry he hurt you."

"I'm surprisingly okay, Nate. I just…don't want

anyone pitying me or saying I can't keep a man." I cover my face. "It's mortifying. I'm embarrassed for anyone to know."

"You can trust me, Gemma. It's not my place to say anything to anyone. We've been friends a long time and I would never betray your trust. I also never would have interfered during your bachelorette party. I just couldn't stand by... And I hoped that by spending time with my brother, you two would finally come to your senses and get back together." He grins. "From the smile on your face, I'd say something is happening."

"It's complicated, Nate."

"Un-complicate it."

I laugh and put my hands on his shoulders, appreciating him coming clean with me. He cares about me; that's why he kidnapped me. "I love your easygoing attitude, and I love how you care about my well-being. You're a good friend, Nate."

He opens his mouth and shuts it again as his gaze lifts, looks past my shoulders. He grins and gives me a hug. When he lets me go, I turn and spot Josh coming our way. My heart jumps at the mere sight of him, only to stall when I spot the hard clench of his jaw. He's pissed about something.

My hands fall from Nate's shoulders, and, loving brother that Josh is, he walks past me and puts Nate in a headlock. Nate laughs and starts poking Josh in the chest as Josh runs his knuckles over Nate's hair, messing it up. I stand back and laugh at their antics. Typical brothers, although they are anything but. Josh's whole life was about taking care of Nate, but I think this last week the tables have turned and Nate is the one looking out for his brother's best interests, and mine.

"What's your problem? You said you weren't going to kill me."

"What I said was I wouldn't kill you *slowly*, and this isn't about that."

"Oh, it's about me hugging Gemma."

I have no idea what they're talking about or why Josh wouldn't want Nate hugging me, but I pass it off as a brother thing as the two rough it out.

Josh finally lets his little—although bigger—brother go. Nate stands back and smirks as his gaze goes back and forth between the two of us, and I know my secret is safe with him. He won't tell Josh that Bentley had been cheating—that I wasn't enough for him. That I'm unlovable.

But I've felt anything but unlovable in Josh's arms this week. He always made me feel special, even back in college—right up until the moment he dumped me. It's different this time. It has to be.

"What are you smirking at?" Josh asks and folds his arms.

"Nothing. Just waiting for a thank-you," Nate says, and Josh reaches for him again. Nate ducks and taunts his brother with his middle finger. Josh turns to me.

"See what I have to put up with," he says, the love

for his brother shining in his eyes and warming my heart. All those years ago, when the paparazzi dug into his past and wrote horrible things about him, they had no idea what they were talking about. They looked for only the worst and refused to see the man I see, even when I sent a letter to the editor asking for them to apologize. Josh is the best man I know. He's not just the man I want, he's the man I need. He makes me a better person and has given me confidence in myself.

"Thanks, Nate," I say, my voice a breathless whisper.

"Now that's what I'm talking about," Nate says, but neither Josh nor I are looking at him. No, we're looking at each other. Need and lust and want and love shimmering between us. "I think I'm going to go," Nate says. He holds his hands out. "The gravitational pull between you two is a little off the charts. Unless, of course, you want me to stay," he jokes. "This is a hedonistic hotel. I mean what goes on—"

"Go," Josh says, and Nate laughs as he saunters away. "Love you, big brother."

"Love you, too," Josh says as he gathers me into his arms, and I wish he was saying those words to me. Ignoring the stares, and I swear I can feel Atlanta's eyes drilling into the back of my head, Josh kisses me, deeply, firmly, with passion. I'm breathless by the time he inches back.

"I've missed you," he says.

I chuckle. "I can tell."

But he's not in a teasing mood. He's gone serious, much like his brother had gone serious earlier. He looks at my easel, his face sincere. "Did you have a nice afternoon painting?"

"I did. Thank you for all this."

He now stares at me, his eyes dark, full of questions that don't come. "How about we do some painting of our own?"

My skin tingles all over, eager to feel his hands on me again. It's not just my body involved. My heart is beating double time. "I would love that," I say, my voice a low, soft murmur.

He puts his mouth close to my ear and grumbles, "Let's go make our own art." He raises his hand and calls for a staffer to put everything away in a secure space.

With my work taken care of, his hand captures mine. His legs move quickly, with determination, and I laugh, loving how he can't get me alone fast enough. I hurry, practically run, to keep up with his fast pace, and I'm breathing a whole lot faster as we come to an abrupt stop outside the playroom. Although I think it's more from excitement than anything else.

He opens the door and ushers me in, and I smile as I breeze into the room, never having felt so free to create and have fun doing it. I turn and go still. "What is that?" I ask. I examine the big wooden wheel with nylon spokes.

"It's a spider's web," he tells me.

I step up to it, run my fingers over the thick wood and note the handcuffs. "How exactly do you plan to use this?" I ask, shivers of excitement racing up my spine.

"I plan to cuff you to it and paint you," he says, "until you're screaming my name and begging for more."

I grin. "While I like that idea, maybe I'll handcuff you."

His eyes narrow. "Is that something you want to do?"

"Maybe," I say. Oh, but it is. It totally is. My mind races, visualizing him strung tight as I tease him with the brushes until he sheds the last of his control. He's always held that control close, it's how he survived in a world that wasn't fair to him, but he's safe with me.

I open the paints and pour them into the trays as Josh stands back and watches me, everything about the man completely overwhelming me. I glance up to see his small smile as he unbuttons his shirt.

Heat zings through me as he shrugs out of it, and it slides to the floor. "Anything in particular you'd like painted on your body?"

"You're the artist, you decide, and you're overdressed." He takes his pants off, his boxers following.

"I'm getting all kinds of ideas," I say as I take in the thickening of his cock. He steps up to me and takes over, putting the paint into trays so I can undress. I make a show of removing my clothes, slowly peeling my dress from my body, and he groans when no bra and underwear follow—because I'm not wearing any.

"You've been walking around all day like that?" he growls.

"All day."

His face tightens, like he's in total agony. "It's a good thing I didn't know that."

"Why?" I arch a brow and lightly run my fingers around the outer edges of my breast, as I brush my tightening nipples with my thumbs. His body goes tense. "What would you have done?"

"I would have ravished you."

"Josh," I tease, standing before him completely bare, completely confident in myself and my wants. "You know it now."

"Right, and I plan on ravishing you."

He dips a brush into the pink paint and swirls it around. He turns to me and lightly brushes my nipple. I quiver as the bristles tickle me in the most delicious ways. As much as I want him to continue, I take the brush. "Me, first," I say and glance at the spider's web.

He growls. "This is what you want?"

"Have you ever been tied to one before, Josh?"

"No," he says, his voice a deep, thick rumble.

I angle my head, take in his stance. "This week is about being someone else and trying new things." His chest rises as he takes a big breath. His tendons are so tight, I'm sure they're going to snap. I'm about to tell him we don't have to when he speaks first.

"Only for you, Gemma. Because it's what you want, and I'm not going to say no to you. Never for anyone else, though. Never."

My pulse jumps, and I swallow against a tight throat. "I'd never do anything to hurt you, you know."

He nods and steps up to the wheel and puts his arms in the cuffs. They're Velcro, and he can escape anytime he wants, but it's what they represent—the lack of control—that seems to frighten him a little. Honestly, the fact that he's giving himself over to me like this… It's a gift, and I don't take it lightly. Even when we were younger, he always held a little of himself back from the world—from me. This time, it's different. This time, we're older, and wiser and holding nothing back.

I secure his wrists and go up on my toes to kiss him. He kisses me back, and I run my hands over his hard body. He quivers beneath my touch, and I step back and reach for a tray of silver paint.

I brush it over his chest, and his eyes shut as he takes in a big breath. "Tickle?" I ask.

"Yes." I continue to mark his body, making crisscrosses. I walk behind him and paint his back. "What are you painting?" he asks, and he glances down and tries to figure it out.

I grin. "You'll see."

I go to the table, grab a darker shade to shadow the crisscrosses, and he trembles beneath me. I swirl the brush on his inner thighs, and his growl cuts through me. I love seeing him like this. Down on my knees with his cock inches from my face, I can't seem to help myself. I lean in and take him into my mouth and his curses reach my ears.

I give a contented sigh. "This gives a whole new meaning to erotic art," I say, and my hot breath on his tight skin causes his cock to jump and hit me under the chin. I chuckle. "It's all fun and games until someone puts an eye out."

"Gemma," he growls as I pick the brush up and continue a slow exploration of his body, teasing and tormenting him until he's squirming, his fingers curled into fists. I honestly can't wait until it's my turn, but I'm not done with him yet.

I dip into the blue paint and brush it over his face. He shivers. "Cold?" I ask.

"No," he says. I test it on my skin, and his head dips as I paint myself. He tugs on the bindings like he's eager to get his hands on me. I sink back to my knees and take his thick length into my mouth, sucking until he's growling like a leashed animal seconds from breaking free.

He swells impossibly more beneath my tongue's ministration, and I inch back, refusing to let him come no matter how much I'd love to taste him. I want him inside me when he lets go. I want to feel each hard pulse in my body. The ripping Velcro reaches my ears and I grin. I guess he's reached his boiling point.

"My turn," he growls. He pulls me to my feet and turns me until I'm pressed against the wheel. "You don't get to have all the fun."

"Weren't you having fun?"

"Fuck, yeah, I was. I just need…" His words fall off as he secures my hands and feet. I stand before him, exposed, free, safe in his care. Catching me by surprise, he leans in and places the sweetest, softest kiss on my lips. His hand cups my cheek with the utmost tender care. "You're beautiful, Gemma. When you give yourself to me like this…" Once again, his words trail away, and he shakes his head like he's either mystified or in total agony. Either way, I love the way he's looking at me, like I'm a treasure to be worshipped. "But payback's a bitch," he says, a mischievous grin splitting his lips. "Wait, what did you paint on me?" His face twists as he tries to figure it out.

"Later, when we lay the sheet out and make love on it, you'll see."

"Well I'm not as creative as you, so don't have high expectations," he says as he dips the brush into the pink paint and circles my nipples. A hard shiver racks my body.

"That tickles."

"Told you."

He sinks to the floor and settles between my spread legs. Taking his good old time, he dips into the paint, and using long slow strokes, he runs the brush up my inner thighs. My sex clenches as he comes close but never touches.

"Josh," I murmur.

"Is there a problem, Gemma?" he asks, teasing me with each luxurious stroke.

"That feels so good."

He makes a show of dipping the brush into the paint again, and soft humming noises rise in his throat as he shifts closer, his breath hot on my sex.

"What are you painting?"

"Flowers. Lilies. They're still your favorite, right?"

"You remember that?" I ask, my brain cells barely working.

With the bristles, he spreads me, and begins painting petals around my sex. All thoughts evaporate when he says, "So pretty."

I whimper as he brushes my clit—slow, even strokes, back and forth, back and forth. My head drops back and I move my hips, eager for more. He moves away from me, and my eyes jerk open. "Please," I say.

He circles me, and I go perfectly still. The only audible sound in the room is his heavy breathing. A brush touches my back, and he runs it down my spine. A hard quiver racks my body, and my panting changes, becomes rougher as he paints my backside.

"You're a work of art, Gemma," he murmurs, then blows on my body like he's trying to dry the paint. He puts his hands through the web and cups my breasts, his cock against my back. I move against him and massage his erection. He groans into my ear and bites down on my shoulder.

"Yes," I cry as pain and pleasure mingle.

"I want to touch every inch of you." He pulls my cheeks apart. "I want to be inside your body, everywhere."

"I want that, too," I cry.

He squeezes my ass and presses hot, open-mouthed kisses to my neck and back, going lower and lower until I'm a quivering mess. "Josh, please…"

His hand goes between my legs and he inserts a finger into my sex, and I ripple around him, so turned on, I'm at the breaking point.

"Does this feel good?" he asks.

"Yes."

He fingers me a little longer, and I gasp when he pulls out. My gaze is latched on his hard, gorgeous body as he walks to the table, grabs the sheet and lays it out on the floor.

"Let's mess this up," he says.

I nod, and he comes back and frees my hands and feet. He takes my wrists to his mouth, and his lips are soft and warm as he presses them against the chafe marks. "On the sheet, on your back," he says.

I do as he says, and widen my legs for him. He crawls in between my spread legs and falls over me. Even though we're in the missionary position, nothing about this feels vanilla. He pushes into me in one fast stroke and I gasp as he fills me. Our bodies are slick from the paint, and we smudge each other as we rock together as one.

His eyes never leave my gaze as we make love,

and his lips find mine as he takes me over the edge in seconds. He growls as my come sears his flesh and my muscles ripple around him, gripping him hard.

"So good," I cry out.

He rolls, positioning me on top of him as my orgasm settles, and he sits up, takes one breast into his mouth and reaches around my body, sliding a small finger into my backside. "You want me in here?" he asks.

"Yes," I say. "I want that with you. I want everything with you."

"My pants, I have lubrication."

I laugh lightly as I slide off him and reach for his pants. "Something tells me you had this all planned."

I pull out the tube, and equal amounts of excitement and nervousness race through me as I examine it.

"I won't hurt you," he says, and my heart pinches tight when he puts his big palm on my face, touching ever so gently.

"I know," I say, forgetting all past wounds as I completely lose myself in him.

He cups the back of my head and brings me in for a kiss. Our tongues tangle, and I melt into him. He pulls my body until I'm on top of him, and he rolls me until I'm on my stomach. Warm hands cup my cheeks and he pulls them apart, his growl of longing in my ear.

He tucks his shirt and pants under my stomach, lifting my ass. Gentle fingers slowly explore me, widen me, prepare me for his girth. I writhe against the floor, and he slides a hand under me to play with my aching clit.

I move against his hand, pushing back and forward as new sensations rocket through me, and I'm crying out for more, but I know he won't take me until I'm fully prepared. He spends a long time playing with me, until I'm begging.

"You sure, Gemma?" he asks.

"God, yes," I say, more than ready for him to take me everywhere, claim every last inch of me.

He pours a generous amount of lubricant between my cheeks, and slowly enters me, giving me one glorious inch after another. Pain and pleasure mingle, and my eyes slide shut to revel in the new sensation and how my body is opening for him. He falls over me as he gives me his last inches, and kisses the back of my neck.

"You with me?"

"I'm with you," I say, as he owns my body, and my heart.

"You feel so good. I love taking all of you." He moves inside me and presses his palm to my clit as he inserts a thick finger into my sex. "I am so close," he says.

As he fucks me everywhere, I move my upper body, rub my breasts on the sheet, making beautiful art as we make beautiful love. Before I even realize what's happening, I'm exploding all over his fingers, my tightening body pulling an orgasm from him.

"Gemma," he cries out, and I love hearing my name on his tongue as he lets go. A growl crawls out of his throat, and he bites into my shoulder, leaving his mark on me in so many ways. He depletes himself and slowly inches out, caressing my flesh softly with caring, loving hands.

My heart pounds with the love I have for him. He puts his mouth close to my ear and whispers, "Let me take you back to my room so I can give you a bath and take care of you." I make a sound, too spent to speak. "Would you like that, Gemma?"

"Yes," I manage to get out. He lifts me with his strong arms, and the second my eyes meet his, I know in my heart, my life will never be the same again.

CHAPTER SIXTEEN

Josh

I WALK THROUGH the hotel, my heart light and happy as I greet all the smiling guests, some checking out, and even more checking in, now that the soft opening is over and the staff are all up to speed—all the kinks worked out, so to speak. I'm pleased with how things turned out, even more pleased that I spent the week with Gemma.

Gemma.

That woman has gotten under my skin and clawed her way right back into my heart. Again. Although, had she ever left? After our fun body-painting session—and I still can't believe I let her tie me up, gave up control for the first time in my life—we've been together nearly every waking moment. The last couple of days, however, she's been disappearing to finish her painting and acting a bit secretive. I'm not sure why but guess it has something to do with the unveiling of her work. I can't wait to see the finished product. She promised it would be soon.

Tomorrow is the end of our week together, and I hope the beginning of something more. She's awakened under my touch, given herself to me in so many ways, I still can't quite wrap my brain around the fact that this is the same girl from college.

When I first found her in my suite, I never thought she belonged with me, but after this week, after seeing this other side of her, it's clear the sexual goddess who isn't afraid of trying new things is the woman she was meant to be. She'd been suppressing all her needs and desires, and going back to the life she was living will only stifle her. I can't let that happen. I won't.

I head outside to her favorite painting spot, but my heart sits heavy, her absence felt all the way to my gut, when she's nowhere to be found. Her easel, canvas and paints are gone. I glance around the beach, catch Atlanta staring at me but don't spot Gemma. Maybe she's in the suite, waiting for me. I head to the elevator, and my cock thickens just thinking about that. The more time I spend with her, the more I want her. I almost laugh at that. She's an addiction I can't—don't want to—quit. This time around, after she exposed her body and desires to me, it's clear there is more to this girl who presents prim and proper to the world.

She doesn't belong in circles where she has to hide, and it's well past time we had a talk. Everything in her touch tells me she wants the same things as I do. I have to make sure, though. Her life is under a microscope, and maybe there is a part of her that won't show the real world another side of herself. Perhaps being seen with me—a guy from the wrong side of the tracks—isn't something she's ready for or even wants. I mean, there are certain expectations placed on her.

Fuck, this could be the end of us. Maybe I'm crazy hoping she'll live the life she wants to live—not what is expected of her. What if she doesn't, though? What if she wanted only a week of freedom and nothing more?

I can't go there. I can't love and lose her again. It might just kill me.

I step from the elevator and open the door to my suite. "Gemma, are you here?" I ask. My voice is met with silence, and I plop down onto my sofa and pull my phone from my back pocket. I shoot off a text to her and wait. A strange, uncomfortable feeling grows in my gut as I stare at my phone, wait for the answer that never comes.

Where the hell could she be?

I stand, ready to go searching for her, when my phone falls from my fingers. I bend to pick it up, and that's when I spot a piece of paper peeking out from under the sofa. Had it fallen off the coffee table? I pick it up, and I'm about to toss it back on the table, figuring it must be something Gemma dropped, when curiosity gets the better of me.

I unfold it and sit back down, and my heart jumps into my throat as I read the hastily scribbled words— in Gemma's handwriting. My lungs suddenly grow heavy and inflating them becomes a whole lot more difficult as the world slows and the meaning of the words on the paper settle in my brain. What the ever-loving fuck is going on? Is this a Dear John letter, meant for me?

Not the man I thought you were.
We don't belong together.
I never want to see you again.

There's more, but these three phrases continue to jump out at me. I read the note in its entirety a couple more times, trying to make sense of it. I somehow can't quite wrap my brain around the idea that this is meant for me. But what if it is? What if she *was* pretending to be someone else, was experimenting in my world, only to discover I'm not what she expected. Maybe the good girl really is...good.

I stand and pace to my window. I glance out at the pool and unlock the door to step outside. The warm afternoon sun shines on me as my rattled brain bangs around inside my skull. I scan the beach, still trying to put the pieces together. Nah, this can't be for me. Unless, of course, the good girl really was pretending to be someone else. I snort, because if she was pretending, she's one hell of an actress. The way she touched me and kissed me and made love to me said so much—I wasn't just the man she wanted, I was the man she needed.

Something niggles in the back of my brain, and I reach for it, pull the pictures of her smiling face splashed across the social pages back in New York to the forefront of my brain. They looked lost in love, and I thought she was, either that or she deserves a trophy for her stellar performance. Was she acting with me or acting with him? What is really going on here?

Unless all of this week was about something else. Payback, maybe, for pushing her from my life all those years ago, and she didn't have the guts to say what she really thought about me—to my face. I shake my head because that's not her style at all. At least, I didn't think it was, but this is her writing, and she was acting secretive, and of course my brother has yet to hear that she's broken things off with Bentley. Maybe she's never had any intentions of ending things.

Anger, fear, love and loss mingle in my heart. All those years ago, everything I ever did was to protect her. *But did she protect you, Josh?* No, she did nothing when the article about me came out. Other than say she was sorry. Maybe she never really cared about me—because actions speak louder than words. Except for the words on this paper. They're loud and clear. I shove the paper into my pocket and stalk to the door, tug it open with more force than necessary and stab the elevator button. The doors ping open and I find Atlanta standing there, her body tanned and slick, barely hidden behind a tiny bikini.

"Atlanta," I say and stand back, giving her room to exit.

"Actually, I forgot something downstairs. I'll ride back down with you," she says.

I climb on and press the button for the lobby. Inching back, I lean against the rear wall and stare straight ahead.

"You look tense," Atlanta says and puts one hand on my shoulder. I flinch at her touch, and her brow narrows. "Something the matter?"

"Just some things on my mind," I say.

"I can help you with that," she purrs and presses up against me.

"It's not a good time," I say and try to remove her, but she coils her hands around my neck and holds on.

"Here I thought now would be a good time," she says with a smirk, like she knows something I don't.

"What do you mean?"

"Now that Gemma is back with her fiancé and out of our hair, I thought you were free to play with whoever you wanted."

My stomach tightens, and my throat goes dry. "What are you talking about?"

"Bentley. He's here." Her eyes go wide. "You mean you don't know anything about it?" I stare at her. "She's with him now, in the lobby. I finally figured out the other day who she was when I saw the article on her and Bentley. They looked like they were having a lovely reunion downstairs, judging by all the touching and kissing going on. I guess she's done here now, headed back to her circle, where she belongs."

I shake my head and try to make sense of what she's saying.

She gives a humorless laugh. "I wonder if she was here to learn a few things. You know, to spice up her honeymoon."

I must be hearing her wrong. Yeah, that has to be the answer. But even as I tell myself that, the letter I found burns a hole in my pocket.

Am I not the man she thought I was? Did I take things too far with the good girl and scare her off? No, that can't be right. Then, what is right? I don't know, but I need to talk to her and I need to do it now.

"Wait, how did Bentley know she's here?" I ask.

She gives a casual shrug. "He is her fiancé, Josh. I assume she called him to come pick her up?"

"She wouldn't have wanted him to know," I say, mostly to myself. Although she was acting secretive. Could she have called him to come for her?

"Unless she was here, learning things for him." She gives me a playful wink, then continues with, "That makes sense doesn't it?" She blinks at me with hopeful eyes. Who the heck is she trying to convince, me or herself?

I grip her hands, about to tug them from my neck. "Atlanta, what did you do?"

"Me?" she asks innocently. "Nothing." I open my

mouth to speak and she cuts me off. "They're engaged, Josh. Nothing has changed that. Not even her
being here with you. The wedding is still on. Just
today, I read an online article about the extravagant
guest list. I have my phone. You can read it if you
don't believe me."

The elevator doors ping open, and I look over
Atlanta's head, my gaze colliding with Gemma's. Her
eyes go wide, but I don't think it's because Atlanta
is wrapped around me, it's because Bentley has his
arms wrapped around her in a loving embrace that
she isn't trying to fight—like I am.

Atlanta turns when my eyes harden. "See? I told
you she was with him." She uncoils herself from my
body and follows me off the elevator. Gemma's gaze
goes from me to Bentley, back to me. "She's where
she belongs, Josh," Atlanta says, and in that instant,
I'm 100 percent certain she was behind it. She'll be
banned from the hotels for this, but it doesn't change
the fact that she's right. Gemma is where she belongs, and it took me seeing her with Bentley to get
my head back on straight.

"You're right," I say, clenching down so hard I'm
sure my teeth are going to crack. I take Atlanta's
hand, drag her back into the elevator with me, letting Gemma know in no uncertain terms that I read
her loud and clear. The doors bang shut, and I lean
forward like I was just sucker punched three million times and brace my hands on my thighs. How
could I have been so wrong about her? How could

I have thought she wasn't a good girl at heart? That she was simply repressing that side of herself in front of those in her circle? How could I have thought we belonged together? My heart thumps so hard, I'm sure I'm going to crack a rib. I swallow against a dry throat, the crackling sound reminding me of the note in my pocket.

Well, fuck me.

I guess the Dear John, or rather Dear Josh, really was for me. Just then my phone rings and I don't want to answer it. There isn't anyone I want to talk to. It continues to ring, getting on my very last nerve.

"You should probably get that," Atlanta suggests, keeping a bit of distance from me this time. I guess she can sense that I'm ready to snap, and that she's aware there will be consequences for overstepping and breaking code.

"Fuck," I say and tug it from my pocket, ready to turn it off, until I see the call is from Matteo. "Shit."

The elevator stops on my floor, and I slide my finger across the screen as I step off. Atlanta follows me off the elevator, and I give her a nod before I walk away and head straight to my suite and let myself in. "Josh here."

"Josh, it's Matteo," he says, his voice soft and hesitant, and I get whatever it is he has to tell me, he doesn't want to.

"What's up?" I ask, hoping there isn't a problem with any of the guests or rooms.

"Miss Gemma asked if I'd box up the painting she left in your art room and send it to her."

"Did she now."

"She left the key to the room up in your suite, and I didn't want to allow her in without your permission." I don't miss the worry in his voice.

"Of course. You're just following my orders not to let anyone in."

"I don't know how she had a key in the first place."

"I gave it to her. It's fine, Matteo."

"Thank you, sir," he says, his voice full of relief. "Should I box it up?"

"I'll take care of it," I say. I should just let him. The stuff in that room is going to remind me of what I loved and lost, but I guess I must be some sort of masochist, because I'm going to go see this painting that she's been anxious to unveil—for reasons I can't quite figure out. Heck, maybe it's something she plans to put in her home with Bentley after they marry. I laugh. It's either that or sob like a fucking baby.

I grab the paint-room key and open my door to find my brother standing there, his hand raised, ready to knock. I go completely still at the worried look on his face.

"Are you okay?" I ask.

"I think I'm the one who should be asking you that, bro."

"I'm fine," I say, as I close my door and step around him.

"Could have fooled me."

"Just have some things to take care of." The elevator doors open as soon as I hit the button, and my brother follows me on.

"Things like going and getting Gemma and bringing her back here?" Nate asks.

My gaze jerks to his.

"I saw her leave with that asshole," he explains.

"It's where she belongs, Nate." He opens his mouth to say something, and I shake my head. "I don't want to talk about this. There are things you don't understand."

He folds his arms as the elevator descends. "Let's see if I do understand. Years ago, after you two were photographed and hounded, you broke up with her. You don't think you're good enough or belong in her world."

My heart pounds as I stare at my brother.

"Okay, since you're not correcting me, let me go on. You pushed her away for her own good, because you thought that was what was best for her."

"It was."

"No, it wasn't. No one deserves to be in the world she lives in." He shivers like the idea repulses him. "One where she has to hide, pretend, be something she isn't, all for the sake of her parents and their friends." He shakes his head. "Fuck them. Gemma is missing out on life and missing out on what she really wants to do."

"And you know what that is, do you?" I ask, doubtful.

We step off the elevator, and he follows me down the hall. I guess it doesn't matter if he enters the room with me. It's of no use now.

"Yeah, I do," he says. "Why do you think I brought her to you here, at the hotel?"

"You tell me."

"Because you two belong together."

I laugh as I swipe my key over the reader. "She left with Bentley. You said so yourself that she never broke it off with him."

"Maybe that's because we kidnapped her before she could do it."

"That doesn't make sense," I say and walk into the room. I glance at the sheet we made love on, study the pattern. That's when it occurs to me: she was painting chain mail on my body, although I'm definitely not her knight in shining armor. I'm nobody's knight.

"I don't know all the answers, Josh. I don't. But I've seen you two together. I've also seen her with Bentley, and they weren't happy. He was cheating on her," he says.

My gaze flies to his. "How do you know that?"

"I saw him, and I told her. I also told her I wouldn't say anything. I don't like to betray her trust but think it's important right now. You need to know."

"What a fucking asshole. She can't marry a guy like that."

"At least we agree on something."

I scrub my face and stare at the cloth covering her painting and shove my other hand into my pocket. I pull out the note and hand it to Nate.

"What's this?" he asks.

"Read it."

He smooths out the paper and frowns as he scans the scribbled writing. "What is this?"

"I found it in my room. I guess she must have dropped it."

Nate smacks his head with his palm. "Now it all makes sense."

"At least one of us is clueing in."

He shakes the paper. "This isn't for you. It's for Bentley."

"You don't know that."

"You're right. I don't, just like you don't know if it's for you. Did you ask her?"

"No, I saw her in Bentley's arms and left with Atlanta."

He shakes his head, incredulous. "God, sometimes you are so dense."

"Listen, Nate. I probably should have asked her, but in the end, I don't belong in her world, just like she doesn't belong in mine."

"The hell she doesn't," he says and tugs the cloth from the painting to reveal a gorgeous piece of erotic art. I instantly recognize the strokes, the composition, the textures and colors. The artist who did this is the artist who did the painting that hangs in the lobby.

My rattled brain slows as that sinks in. "Holy shit," I say and swallow. Hard. "Gemma is Lily, the artist of...the painting I have in the hall...the paintings I just purchased."

"The one and only."

He picks the picture up, turns it over, and in the corner, there's a painted lily and her signature. Gemma Long.

I touch it. "She signed it."

"I guess maybe that was her way of coming out, you know." He sets the painting back onto the easel.

"Why didn't she tell me?" I shake my head, the tumblers still not falling into place.

"Maybe she thought you wouldn't believe her. Maybe she thinks showing is better than telling. She sure was making a statement here."

"Why didn't you say so? Actually, how did you even know this?"

"I stopped by her studio one day to see if she wanted to go to lunch. She was painting and so engrossed she didn't see me, and I snuck a peek before she knew I was there. She never realized I saw anything, and she's private and obviously didn't want anyone to know, so I never said a word. I instantly recognized that painting on your wall. The only logical thing to do after that was kidnap her, steal her away from her douchebag fiancé and get her into your arms, literally."

I tug my hair. "Yeah, that's logical, Nate."

"This is who she is, Josh. If you think you were protecting her from you or thinking she belongs in a world where she's nothing more than a robot who answers to everyone and has to act like she's a goddamn Goody Two-shoes, you're wrong. If you ask me, I think the fact that she signed this is an indication that she is ready to break free. With you."

My stomach clenches tight, and the room spins a little as I back up and lean against the table. "Fuck."

"Yeah, you are kind of fucked, but do you remember what you used to say when we found ourselves in bad situations over the years?"

"Yeah, life is ten percent what happens to you and ninety percent how you respond."

"What did we do, Josh? What did we do to get ourselves out of bad situations?"

"Whatever we had to."

He grins at me and folds his arms. "So why are you still standing here?"

CHAPTER SEVENTEEN

Gemma

I PUTTER AROUND my apartment and haphazardly toss things into boxes, not really caring if I miss or not. I've already broken one of my favorite figurines, but whatever. Honestly, I'm tired. I haven't had much sleep since Bentley showed up at the resort last week, claiming he received an anonymous call about me being there. At first, he didn't believe it, until he saw me with his own eyes. Apparently, he was devastated, or maybe the word is *disgusted*. In the shock of it all, I can't remember what he said, only that it started with *d*. Can you imagine? What nerve. Calling me names after spending the entire week with another woman, with no intentions of breaking it off with me. That gave me a good laugh. Or not.

I scratch my skin, which feels like a million angry ants are crawling over my flesh, as I recall the way Bentley dragged me into his arms and forced kisses on me, catching me completely off guard when I told him we were over. He wouldn't take no for an answer, and he was causing such a scene, drawing so much attention—which I'm so damn tired of—I just let him hold me while I tried to talk some sense into him. Isn't that like me though, going along, not making a fuss? Forever being the good girl.

I am so done with that.

I think Mom and Dad have called about three thousand times each. I stopped answering after the first thousand. I am so done with their lectures—apparently, I'm done with a lot of things. Do they really think I'm making a huge mistake? I mean, even after I told them Bentley was cheating, that I was a stepping-stone for his career, my mother stuck a Band-Aid on it and said, "men will be men."

I certainly don't expect any man of mine to be unfaithful. I laugh hysterically at that. I don't have a man and don't see that in my future. What the hell is wrong with me? I'm damned if I'm a good girl, damned if I'm not. Josh didn't want me either way. I was wrong when I thought he'd broken my heart once and couldn't do it again.

Seriously, though, how could my parents care more about image than my well-being? My stupid heart sits heavy in my chest to think they care so little that they'd be happy to see me marry an ass-hole, just so I didn't ripple the water, or rather, ruffle the feathers on the hats of those in their social circle. What was it Josh said about those who judge him—they aren't his friends at all and can shove their judgment right up their ass? Yeah, I'm in total agreement now.

I head to the bathroom and grab all the things Bentley left behind and drop them into a box. I probably won't ship it to him. No, I'll probably put the carton and all his belongings on the doorstep and let the current downpour soak his things. That's the least he deserves after threatening me, telling me if I didn't go through with the wedding, he'd go to the papers, tell them where I was and who I was with, dragging both my and Josh's names through the mud—and my family's, I suppose.

I told him to go ahead. Josh doesn't much care about those things, and he wouldn't be ruining him, he'd be ruining me. But I'm already ruined, so what's the big deal, right? I snort, and it's really a half laugh, half cry. You'd think I'd be all cried out, my eyes all dried up after the tears I shed this week. But in the end, he didn't do it. No, that would ruin his chances of following in my dearest dad's footsteps.

I'm so tired, dead on my feet, I briefly close my eyes and quickly peel them open again. Every frigging time I shut my lids, even for a second, I see Josh's face. See the goodbye in his eyes as he reached for Atlanta and dragged her into the elevator with him.

I thought things were changed between us, I thought he wanted what I wanted, but no, he planned to set me free after the agreed-upon week. If there was more, wouldn't he have questioned what I was doing with Bentley, wouldn't he have fought for me? Does he really think I belong with a guy like that after the things I told him? Then again, what did I really tell him? How much did he know, other than Bentley hadn't touched me in a long time? Heck, the morning after we had sex, before he filled me with blueberry pancakes, I straight-out told him I was thinking of Bentley and he asked me not to do that when I was with him. He also knew I hadn't broken it off yet.

Oh, God, all that time we were together, did he think I'd eventually go running back? Outside of amazing sex, did I give him any reason to think otherwise? Was he just acting upon the information he had when he saw my ex's arms around me? Did I run off and hide because fears and insecurities of being unlovable got the better of me?

Should I have gone after him, dragged him from that elevator and told him everything? Oh, Lord, I think I should have. Is it too late? Is there any way to fix this?

A knock sounds on my door, and my stupid heart leaps. Could it be Josh? I hurry to the door, and frown when I open it to find Nate standing there, a big umbrella shielding him from the rain.

"Oh, it's you."

"Nice to see you, too. Were you expecting someone else?"

Not expecting, just hoping.

"No." I force a smile. "Sorry, I didn't mean to

sound disappointed. It *is* nice to see you." I wave my arm. "Come on in."

He closes his umbrella, leaves it outdoors and comes in. "About time. This dampness is messing with my perfect hair," he teases to lighten my mood.

That does pull a laugh from me as he shuts the door. "What are you doing here?" I ask.

"Can't a guy check on his friend?"

I sigh. "I guess you heard the news that things are over between Bentley and me."

He exhales, and eyes as dark as his brother's move over my face, "You made the right choice."

"Tell that to my parents."

"I'm sorry. I can't even imagine."

"They're saying I'm making a bad decision. They're not wrong."

His head rears back. "Whoa. You think breaking it off with Bentley is wrong?"

I give a fast shake of my head. "No, it just would have been a better choice to tell him before I went to Josh's hotel." Just saying Josh's name out loud brings fresh tears to my eyes. I turn so Nate can't see them.

"You didn't exactly go to the hotel," he says. "I kind of kidnapped you."

I give a humorless laugh and dab my eyes. I must look like hell to him. "I went back on my own, though. Still, I made some poor decisions. I guess I had it in my head that we were over because I'd written Bentley that note, and as you know, he was with another woman."

"So, the note was for Bentley." I spin back to face Nate, and he's nodding. "I knew it."

"Knew what?"

"Nothing. It doesn't matter." He jerks his thumb over his shoulder. "Come on. We're going out."

"I'm not going anywhere looking like this, and it's pouring."

He laughs. "Come on, Gemma." He smooths his hands down his shirt and gives me a playful smile. "Do you really think anyone is looking at you when you're with me?"

I laugh and put my hand on his chest. "Oh, Lord. You're right. What was I thinking?" Maybe I should go out? Nate always has a way of cheering me up with his easygoing attitude. I have no idea how he's so laid-back, especially after the rough childhood he's had. Although, Josh sheltered him from most things, always protecting and caring for those he loves. Always willing to take the brunt of everything for those who put themselves in his hands.

I put myself in his hands—in college and in Belize. Both times, he let me go. Which really doesn't seem like him unless he truly believes we don't belong in each other's worlds. If he saw the painting and put things together, would that have made a difference? God, I am just so confused.

"Are you okay?" Nate asks and waves his hand in front of my face.

"I, yeah…just thinking." I blink up at him. "Have you been talking to Josh?"

He nods, opens his mouth like he wants to say something and gestures with a nod. "Grab your bag. We're going out. You look like you need a drink or ten."

"I think too much tequila at the bar that night is what got me into this whole mess."

"No, I did," he says, his voice low and almost apologetic. "Now I'm going to get you out of it."

I narrow my eyes, take in the unusual seriousness on his handsome face. "What does that mean?"

He tugs on the lapels of his suit. He's awfully dressed up for a Thursday, just to hang out with me. "It means tonight, you're going to have the night of your life, one you'll never forget and one you'll thank me for—again."

"Again?"

"Well, you did thank me for giving you that week with Josh, didn't you?"

My stomach tightens, and tears once again press against my eyes. "Maybe we should stop saying his name?"

"Sure, but you brought him up. Now, hurry up, I have a car waiting."

I hurry to my room and call out, "What should I wear?"

"Put on a nice dress," he says.

"Where are we going?"

"It's a surprise."

"I don't like surprises," I say as I tug a little black number from my closet, comb my hair and reach for my lipstick.

"Yes, you do. It's my brother who doesn't like surprises, not you. See how I didn't use his name there?"

"Clever. Will it just be the two of us?" I ask. I've been avoiding all my friends since arriving home and haven't even had the energy to go to the gallery. I plan to leave my position there. No way can I work for my mother after she dismissed all my feelings and put what was best for her ahead of her daughter. Of course it's no different than it ever was. I guess I'm just a new person after that week with Josh. He taught me so much about myself and life and others. I need to start living how I was meant to. I honestly don't know what's next or where I'll work. But I'll face that later.

"That's better," Nate says as I exit the room. "Is that the red lipstick Peyton gave you at the bachelorette party?"

I crinkle my nose. "Yeah, you remember that?"

"I remember her telling you it had aphrodisiacal powers."

I laugh. "Maybe it does, maybe it doesn't."

He grabs my raincoat from the closet and helps me into it. His gentlemanly ways remind me so much of Josh. He did such a good job raising his brother. Outside, he opens the back door to the limo and I climb in. I have no idea why we're in a limo, and I honestly don't have the energy to ask. Combing my hair took the last of my vigor.

The swish of the wipers pulls me under, mesmerizes me, and I sit quietly as the driver takes us to God knows where. We eventually stop on a dark street, Midtown East, and Nate comes around to greet me, holding his umbrella over my head.

I glance at the buildings lining the street. "Where are we?"

"If I asked you to close your eyes, would you?"

"No," I say, and he laughs.

"Fine."

He holds his arm out, and I loop mine through it as he leads me inside a dark building. "What is going on?"

The lights flick on, and I glance around to see Peyton and Roman, Rylee and Sebastian, and Cason and Londyn standing there, staring at me, a mixture of wobbly smiles and hopefulness on their faces.

"Mia?" I say as I zero in on her. She waves her hand, and that's when I see the paintings on the walls.

My paintings!

I stumble backward. "Did you…did you do this?" I ask her.

"Yes and no," she answers.

I shake my head, trying to make sense of it all, when something that sounds like metal scraping metal reaches my ears. I glance past my friends to see Josh emerge from the back room, and tears pound behind my eyes.

"Nate?" I say and glance at him, hardly able to believe what Josh is wearing.

"We're going to leave you two alone to talk," he says and then winks. "You can thank me later."

"You can't go out there. It's pouring."

"Then you'd better hurry up and fix things with Josh before the dampness in the air makes his suit rust and prevents him from ever removing it."

I turn and take in Josh as he walks toward me in a knight-in-shining-armor costume, and my insides nearly burst with all the love I feel for him.

"Josh," I say, my mind racing, completely overwhelmed with everything going on here. Josh actually set up an art gallery for me—showcasing all my erotic art, which he actually owns.

His eyes are soft, dim, full of pain, regret and worry when he says, "I don't have a horse or a donkey. Clearly, I'm not a very good knight in shining armor. I'm a little too dense to be anyone's hero, but if you'll just hear me out…"

"Josh—" I begin, but he cuts me off.

He shakes his head to stop me, and metal rubs metal as he comes closer, and I can't help but grin.

"You think this is funny?" he asks, closing the distance between us.

My body instantly reacts to his nearness, and it's all I can do not to remove his armor and jump into his arms. "Yeah, a little."

"Maybe you're right." He takes a deep breath and lets it out slowly. One big hand captures mine and squeezes gently. "Giving you up all those years ago nearly killed me. This time…this time, I'm sure it did. I'm broken without you, Gemma. I can't go on. I don't want to go on without you in my life. You and my brother are the most important people in the world to me. You're my family."

"Why did you do it?" I ask quietly.

He swallows. "Finding you tied to my chair and then at the masquerade party... As hard as I tried, as much as I knew it was the wrong thing, I couldn't keep my hands off you."

"I wanted you to touch me."

"I know. I know I'm the guy you wanted. But I never thought I was the guy you needed."

Tears fall and my throat squeezes, pain making it hard to swallow.

"The stuff they wrote about me—"

"I tried to stop them," I say quickly. "I wrote letters asking for a retraction, and they wouldn't. I tried so hard, Josh."

He shakes his head. "Of course you did. I was a fool for thinking you wouldn't. You're a letter writer. I found the letter. The one you wrote to Bentley. I thought it was for me, and right afterward, I found you in his arms. I thought you ran back to your old life. I only wanted what was best for you."

"You thought that was what was best for me?"

"Remember the part about me being dense?"

I chuckle at that.

"For years, I told myself I was the guy you wanted, not the guy you needed. You once told me I was your knight in shining armor." He looks at himself. "Hence this ridiculous suit," he says. "But in all seriousness, in my heart I never believed I was

anyone's hero, but I want to be yours. Maybe it's because of my messed-up childhood. I don't know. All
I know is I screwed up. I always wanted you to be
the best version of yourself, always acted in a way
that I thought was best for you, but I missed a lot
of things. Like I said, *dense*." He touches my hair,
pushes it behind my ear.

"You did this all for me?" I ask, glancing around
the room when he stops talking.

"I saw how you signed the painting. I took it as
an omen, as weird as that sounds. But I took it as
indication that you were ready to be who you really
want to be. The thing is, though, family is important. I don't want you to lose them. I never wanted
that. I wouldn't want to do anything to jeopardize
your relationship with your parents."

"I did that all on my own, Josh."

He frowns. "I want to be your knight in shining
armor, but if you don't want any of this, if you want
to fix things with your family…" He pauses to snap
his fingers. "I can put these up in my hotels and shut
this place down, but if you do—"

"Josh, you were wrong. You're wrong about a lot
of things."

He goes stiff, not that he already wasn't, in his
armor. Which looks completely frigging adorable
on him, and I still can't quite believe the extremes
he went to.

"You *are* my knight in shining armor. You rescued me from myself. The most important person I needed rescuing from."

His face relaxes, and he looks up at me with so much hope in his eyes. "I am?"

"You always were, and you're wrong about a couple more things."

He exhales, sounding defeated. "That doesn't really surprise me."

"You've always been the man I need. Always."

He pulls me closer.

"And the third thing you were wrong about..." I wave toward the window. "My family is right here. Someday, maybe I'll make amends with my parents, but a lot of it is on them right now."

"I love you, Gemma. I love you so goddamn much." My heart lurches when his eyes water, showing me his warm, vulnerable side, the side that doesn't need to be in control when he's with me because I would never hurt him. "I was so afraid I'd lost you."

"I love you, too, Josh. I've never stopped." Tears fall from my face and I glance toward the big window, and that's when I see our friends—our family— peering in the window, completely drenched. "Oh, my God," I say. "We need to let them in." I make a move to go, but he holds me.

"First this, Gemma."

He struggles, like, really struggles to go down on one knee and reaches inside the costume to pull out a ring. "I love you, my fair maiden. Will you marry me and make me the happiest knight in all the land?"

I laugh. Hard. "Yes, I'll marry you, my dearest knight in shining armor."

He puts the ring on my finger. "I want to kiss you now, but I'm afraid I can't get up."

Happiness fills me as I laugh. I bend to kiss him, and we both topple over. He tries to help me, but somehow I end up pinned beneath my knight. There is nowhere else I'd rather be.

"Is this what the rest of our lives is going to be like?" I ask as our friends come rushing in to help us up.

"Pretty much," he says.

"I'm so glad," I say as I pull his mouth to mine.

Nate clears his throat. "Um, I believe a thank-you is in order."

* * * * *

LET'S TALK

Romance

For exclusive extracts, competitions
and special offers, find us online:

- facebook.com/millsandboon
- @MillsandBoon
- @MillsandBoonUK

Get in touch on 01413 063232

MILLS & BOON

MODERN

Power and Passion

Prepare to be swept off your feet by sophisticated, sexy and seductive heroes, in some of the world's most glamourous and romantic locations, where power and passion collide.